CRAZY
HOT

There was no sound, no warning, but in that instant she knew she wasn't alone.

The fact no sooner registered than a steely arm wrapped around her waist; at the same time, a powerful hand clamped over her mouth. Before she could kick or scream, he pressed her up against the shack's wall—pressed hard, his whole body flat against her back, immobilizing her.

"I'm not going to hurt you, but I can't vouch for the guys in the four-by-four." His voice was soft and gravelly, and very close to her ear, his breath blowing across her skin as he spoke. "We're going to stay just like this for now. Real quiet, until they leave. Got it?"

She managed a sharp, terrified nod.

"Are you lost? Is that why you stopped?"

She debated her answer for a second, but then shook her head no.

"Then I guess that leads us to the obvious question." He spoke so quietly, she had to strain to hear him. She had to focus on him, focus on his breathing and slow down her own. "Did you come here looking for me?"

CRAZY HOT

Tara
Janzen

A DELL BOOK

CRAZY HOT
A Dell Book

Published by
Bantam Dell
A Division of Random House, Inc.
New York, New York

Dell is a registered trademark of Random House, Inc., and
the colophon is a trademark of Random House, Inc.

ISBN 0-7394-5954-6

Printed in the United States of America

To the lovely and generous
Loralee for creating CHM
and for sharing her
enthusiasm for all things
MP with dignity, grace,
and humor. Nothing is forgotten.

AUTHOR'S NOTE

Anyone familiar with the beautiful city of Denver, Colorado, will notice that I changed a few parts of downtown to suit the story. Most notably, I took Steele Street and turned it into an alley in lower downtown, a restored historic neighborhood in the heart of Denver known as LoDo.

CRAZY HOT

PROLOGUE

WASHINGTON, D.C.

DROPPING A SEALED MANILA ENVELOPE on the desk, General Buck Grant eased himself into his chair and stretched out his bad leg. If he'd been a horse, they would have shot him two years ago. Instead they'd stuck him in a windowless office in a nondescript annex about a thousand light-years from the Pentagon and a good three thousand miles from the nearest action. Some days, he thought the horses had the better of it.

But maybe not today. He tapped his fingers on the envelope, took a breath, then bit the bullet and broke the seal.

UNITED STATES DEPARTMENT OF DEFENSE

Office of the Honorable William J. Davies,

Assistant Secretary of Defense for Special Operations and Low-Intensity Conflict

To: General Richard "Buck" Grant
Re: Special Defense Force, SDF
Mission: Classified/Official Orders to Follow

Buck,

You wanted them. You've got them, though God only knows what you can do with them. The only thing the first two are good for is larceny. The only thing they've proved good at is saving their own butts.

- Dylan Hart—your wild card. There is no record of his existence before the age of sixteen, when an arrest warrant was filed by the Denver, Colorado, police for grand theft auto. The next time he shows up is in Leavenworth, compliments of the CIA. He was there less than twenty-four hours before someone high up at the State Department intervened and secured his conditional release—the condition apparently being that he sign his life over to us. All I can say is, it must have been someone damn high up. All I can guess is that this "damn high-up someone" is the same person who got this thing thrown on my desk and picked you as this guy's new jailer.

- **Christian Hawkins**—an ex-con who spent two of his formative years in the Colorado State Penitentiary in Canon City for murder. His conviction was overturned when another man confessed to the crime. Prior to the murder charge, he had one arrest for grand theft auto. Both his and Hart's arrests were related to a chop shop at 738 Steele Street in Denver, Colorado.

- **Staff Sgt. J.T. Chronopolous USMC**—exemplary soldier.

- **Sgt. Creed Rivera USMC**—exemplary soldier.

The reassignment of the two Marines to your team will depend entirely upon the success of your first mission. Should Hart and Hawkins obtain their objective without getting themselves killed, or worse, getting caught, due consideration will be given to your request. Though both Rivera's and Chronopolous's juvenile files were sealed, I did note that both men grew up in Denver, and both, at various times, listed 738 Steele Street as their address. I don't know how you found these guys, Buck, or why, but I hope to hell you know what you're doing. Which brings us to your last request.

- **Captain Quinn Younger USAF**—Are you out of your ever-loving mind? The man is a national hero, a legend, the standard by which all other fighter pilots will be judged for the next forty years. Do you really think he'd be willing to sacrifice a brilliant

career to get involved with a couple of misfits
like Hart and Hawkins on a black ops, special
reconnaissance team whose chances of surviving
their first mission are zip and none? No way in hell.
His record is as pure as the driven snow. A lot of
people worked damn hard to get it that way, and
they don't want you digging up dirt. So don't.

A word to the wise, Buck—there's a reason
your office is next to the boiler room in a
hell-and-gone annex. Don't let these guys be the
excuse the brass needs to finally force you out,
and, yes, that includes me. I know you got a rough
deal over that Iraqi "mishap," but you know the old
saying, if you can't save your ass, at least save your
pension.

Remember, don't call us. We'll call you. And
good luck—you're going to need it. The betting
pool is running a hundred to one against your SDF
team obtaining their objective.

Buck set the papers back on the desk and found himself grinning. He'd take that bet. He knew Dylan Hart. He'd met Christian Hawkins and he'd been to 738 Steele Street.

His grin broadened. Larceny? Hell, the Honorable William J. Davies didn't know the half of it. The two Marines, Chronopolous and Rivera, were as good as his, and Younger? Hell, Younger would be begging to get on the team. Hart and Hawkins would "obtain their objective" all right. He didn't have a doubt about it. The only doubt he had was whether they could do it and get back out alive—but that was why the "damn high-up" man at the State Department had chosen him. He'd made mistakes, chain of command mistakes that had cost him his third star and landed him in the hell-and-gone annex, but he'd never made mistakes with the lives of the soldiers under his command. He knew how to train men to win, how to train them to survive no matter the situation, the conditions, or the odds.

Misfits, soldiers, or heroes, it didn't matter. By the time he got finished with them, they'd all be shooters and looters. They'd all be warriors. They'd be the heart and soul of an elite team of special forces operators code-named SDF. *Hell, yeah.*

CHAPTER

1

EIGHT YEARS LATER

NOTHING MOVED in the shimmering heat.

Good God, Regan McKinney thought, staring over the top of her steering wheel at the most desolate, dust-blown, fly-bit excuse for a town she'd ever seen. The place looked deserted. She hadn't seen another car since she'd left the interstate near the Utah/Colorado border, and that had been a long, hot hour ago.

CISCO, the sign at the side of the road said, confirming her worst fear: She'd found the place she'd been looking for, and there wasn't a damn thing in it. Unless a person was willing to count a broken-down gas station with ancient, dried-out pumps, five run-down shacks with their windows blown out, and one dilapidated barn as "something."

She wasn't sure if she should or not. Neither was she sure she wanted to meet anybody who might be living in such a place, but that was exactly what she'd come to do: to find a man named Quinn Younger and drag him back to Boulder, Colorado.

Quinn Younger was the only lead she had left in her grandfather's disappearance, and if he knew anything, she was going to make damn sure he told the Boulder Police. The police never had believed that Dr. Wilson McKinney had disappeared. Since his retirement from the University of Colorado in Boulder, he'd made a habit of spending his summers moseying around the badlands of the western United States, and according to the results of their investigation, this year was no different.

But it was different. This year Wilson hadn't checked in with her from Vernal or Grand Junction, the way he always did, and he hadn't arrived in Casper, Wyoming, on schedule. She'd checked. It was true he was a bit absentminded, but he'd never gone two weeks without calling home, and he would never, ever have missed his speaking engagement at the Tate Museum in Casper.

Never.

He loved nothing better than to rattle on about dinosaur fossil beds to a captive audience and get paid for doing it. At seventy-two, nothing could have kept Wilson from his moment of glory—nothing except some kind of trouble.

Quinn Younger, she mused, looking over the collection of broken-down buildings. Sheets of tar paper flapped on every outside wall, loosened by the wind. Half the shingles on the roofs had been blown off. The two vehicles parked in front of the gas station were ancient. Over fifty years old, she'd bet—a pickup truck with four flat tires, and some kind of rusted-out black sedan up on blocks.

If Quinn Younger did live in Cisco, he was stuck there, and nothing could have made less sense. He was a former Air Force pilot, for God's sake, a national hero. He'd been shot down over northern Iraq enforcing a no-fly zone and made the covers of *Time* magazine and *Newsweek*, and the front page of every major newspaper in America. His survival behind enemy lines and daring rescue by the Marines had become the stuff of contemporary legend. He was a one-man recruitment poster for the United States military.

Not a bad turnabout for someone who at sixteen had been on a fast track to juvenile hall and probably the state penitentiary, until a judge had put him in her grandfather's field crew for a summer of hard labor digging up dinosaur bones. Wilson had been damn proud of the young man, one of the first to be pulled off the streets and out of the courts of Denver and given a second chance with him. Outlaws all, Wilson had called that first crew of boys, but over that long, hot summer, he'd begun the process of turning outlaws into men—and at least in Quinn Younger's instance, he'd felt he'd succeeded.

Regan wasn't so sure. Not anymore. She'd met Quinn Younger once that summer, if one awkward encounter constituted a meeting, and despite his subsequent rise to fame and glory, the image of him as a shaggy-haired sixteen-year-old car thief with coolly assessing eyes and a slyly artful grin was the image lodged in her brain. Looking at Cisco did little to change the impression. Neither did the cryptic entry she'd found written on her grandfather's desk calendar, the entry with Quinn Younger's name in it that had brought her to this nowhere spot in the road in Utah.

With an exasperated sigh, she returned her attention to the buildings. The town was eerie, damned eerie, but she'd come a long way, and the least she had to do was check the place out. If Wilson or Quinn Younger was there, or had been there, she was going to know it before she left.

Ignoring her unease and a good portion of her common sense, she put the car in gear and pulled back onto the road, heading for the gas station.

SHE'S stopped in front of Burt's old place," Peter "Kid" Chronopolous said, looking through his scope.

Quinn glanced up from under the hood of the '69 Camaro parked in the barn and wiped the back of his hand across his mouth. "Stopped?"

All kinds of people drove by Cisco. Every now and then somebody pulled over to the side of the road and got out their map to figure out where in the hell they'd gone wrong. Damn few people pulled into town and stopped—with good reason. Out of the seven buildings still standing, not a one of them looked anything less than forbiddingly deserted. Other than the shop and living space the SDF team had built into the barn to use as a safe house, the buildings were deserted.

"Yep." Kid's gaze was still trained on the gas station through the scope. "And now she's getting out and going in." The younger man's voice stayed calm and steady, but Quinn sensed his heightened sense of readiness. Most lost tourists, especially lost *women* tourists, would not go wandering into Burt's place. Most, however, wasn't all, and Quinn wasn't inclined to jump to conclusions. Not one damn thing had happened in Cisco in the two weeks he and Kid had been stuck there. A woman in Burt's didn't mean their luck was changing or that the action was picking up, not by his standards.

"Take her picture and send it through the computer," he said, returning his attention to the Camaro's engine. The car was barely street legal as it was. Changing out the pulleys to work with the boost had pushed it right to the edge. Kid could have his fancy Porsche. Quinn was putting his quarter-mile money on the Chevy.

"I'm on it, but I think you better take a look," Kid warned.

Quinn lifted his head again, looking over the engine at the twenty-three-year-old ex-Marine. Kid—who for numerous reasons was also known as "Kid Chaos"—was the newest member of SDF and he was definitely jazzed. His eye was glued to the scope; his body was tense and alert. Of course, the boy had been roughing it with Quinn since the middle of June. Possibly it was merely the sight of a woman, any woman, that had gotten his juices going.

Or maybe Roper Jones, the man currently at the top of General Grant's Most Wanted list, had tracked them down.

Setting aside his wrench, Quinn straightened up from under the hood, testing his left leg before trusting it to completely hold his weight. He limped across the shop floor and turned on the laptop Kid had rigged up to half a dozen cameras around Cisco.

Despite a serious addiction to fast cars, extreme sports, and general mayhem, Kid was a certifiable electronics wizard—an electronics wizard with way too much time on his hands since they'd been holed up in the desert, waiting for the heat to die down in Denver. Kid had wired the ghost town to within an inch of its life for twenty-four/seven surveillance. Getting hurt in their line of work came with a few interesting consequences, the least of which was Kid watching over him like a mother hen, and if lately Quinn had been feeling like he'd washed up on the wrong side of thirty with not much to show for it but a friggin' barn to live in and a busted leg, well, he had no one but himself to blame. He'd made some bad choices—especially that last damn choice he'd made in the rail yards on the west side of Denver when he'd gone up against Roper and his goons.

Quinn typed in a couple of commands, activating the cameras in the buildings. When the camera in Burt's came on, the image of a woman filled the screen.

His brow furrowed. The only female assassin he'd ever

seen had been sleekly fit and buffed on steroids. She'd also moved with the prowling gait of a hungry panther. Not this woman. She was randomly picking her way through the dust and the tumbleweeds inside the gas station, peering over countertops and around half-fallen beams. A broken chair caught her unawares in the shin, and she swore under her breath.

Colorful, Quinn thought, his lips twitching in a brief grin. *Definitely lost tourist material.* No trained hunter would swear because of a measly shin hit. No truly trained hunter would have run into the chair in the first place. After rubbing her leg, she continued on, looking around with curiosity and caution, but not with deadly focus—and not with a weapon in her hand or visible anywhere on her body.

In short, she did not look like a killing machine. What she looked like was a schoolteacher—the luxury model. And oddly, to someone who didn't know many school-teacher types, she looked faintly familiar.

Her honey blond hair was piled into a ponytail on the top of her head, but a lot of silky swaths had tumbled back down, giving her a mussed-up, just-out-of-bed look. She wore a soft-looking lavender shirt and a pair of jeans, both of which appeared to be standard mall issue, and both of which revealed a perfectly average, if decid-edly nice, and very nicely endowed, female form.

Plenty there for Kid to get excited about, Quinn thought. Maybe even something there for he himself to get ex-cited about, if he'd been in the market for that kind of excitement, which he wasn't. The only female in Cisco that Quinn was interested in fooling around with was the one he'd named Jeanette, she with the supercharged 383 LT1 stroker under her hood. The smartest move the woman in Burt's could make would be to get back in her car and get out of town.

"Have you got that picture yet?" he asked Kid, who had moved to the computer in the back of the shop.

"Running it through now, Captain."

Quinn let the rank slide, though he hadn't been a captain since a surface-to-air missile had taken him and his F-16 out over northern Iraq. Still, he had been a captain in the U.S. Air Force for a hell of a lot longer than he'd been a cripple holed up in Cisco.

Two weeks. *Shit*.

Dylan Hart, his boss at SDF, couldn't expect him to lay low forever. Quinn could only take so much sitting around listening to the wind blow through this nowhere town—Roper Jones was still out there, and Quinn needed to be out there, too. He needed to be back in the game.

He rolled his shoulder. It was healing. His leg half-worked. And he had a fucking vendetta with Roper Jones's name written all over it.

On the screen, the woman picked up a dusty pile of papers and looked them over, giving him a better view of her face. She was fine featured, with a dusting of freckles across her nose. She was pretty in a quirky way, not elegant, but cute, her eyebrows surprisingly dark in contrast with her hair. Her chin was delicately angled, but definitely set with determination. Her eyes were light, the color indiscernible on the screen. At odds with her all-American looks, her mouth was lush, exotically full, and covered with a smooth layer of plum-colored lipstick.

Okay. She was nice. Very nice.

The whole package was nice.

"Not a known felon," Kid said from the back of the shop.

Quinn absently nodded. He would have been damned surprised if the woman's picture had matched that of a known criminal, especially given the kind of wiseguys in Kid's current files.

"Try the official database," he said, knowing it was another long shot. Despite his niggling sense of familiarity, the chances of the woman in Burt's being part of an officially sanctioned U.S. government service were exceedingly damn low. And she sure as hell didn't belong to SDF, the very *unofficially* sanctioned group of Special Forces operators that he and Kid were part of. General Grant, the two-star who deployed them, would never hire a woman for fieldwork.

"Already on it," Kid confirmed.

Quinn kept his gaze glued to the woman. Where in the hell, he wondered, had he seen her? He didn't forget faces. He didn't dare, and he knew hers.

Or had known her.

"*Son of a bitch*," Kid swore behind him, showing more emotion in the one small phrase than he had in the whole two weeks they'd been camped out in the desert.

"You've got a match?"

"No, but it looks like we've got more company," Kid said, striding back toward the scope.

Quinn looked through the far window and saw what Kid had seen, a blue SUV coming off the top of a rise in the highway—and slowing down, way down.

"Two men, no visible weapons, but they don't look happy," Kid said from his position at the scope. Quinn watched him quickly scan the rest of the horizon and come back to the SUV. "They're checking out the woman's Ford . . . and . . . they're . . . well, hell. They're heading out of Cisco. What do you make of that?"

"A coincidence? Or maybe Cisco has just gotten real friggin' popular." Quinn limped back to the Camaro and picked up the Beretta 9mm he always kept close by.

"Maybe" was all Kid conceded as he checked the load on his rifle, a highly "accurized" sniper's M40.

Quinn and Kid weren't getting paid to take chances. Not today. *Keep your heads down and don't get your asses shot off* had been Dylan's orders. A couple of weeks ago, when his body had still been pretty messed up, Quinn had been willing to follow orders. But he was mobile now. His stitches were out, and he was ready to get back to the job of taking Roper Jones down. If the unhappy guys in the four-wheel drive were part of that job, great. He just had to get Little Miss Tourist out of the way.

Damn. In about five minutes, if she was an innocent civilian looking for ghost town junk, she was going to wish she'd driven right on by Burt's old place and Cisco. What he didn't like to think about was that niggling sense of familiarity and the possibility that what she was looking for was him—though God knew how a woman could have tracked him down in Cisco. Or why.

"Call Denver," he said to Kid. "Tell them we've got company. I'll get the woman."

"No," Kid insisted, quickly coming around the desk at the back of the shop. "I'll get her. You . . . uh, should be the one to call."

Quinn narrowed his gaze at the younger man and was gratified to see him falter just a bit. It took a lot to make Kid Chaos falter.

"What I mean is, Dylan would rather hear the . . . uh, details of the operation from you . . . I'm sure." Kid didn't sound too damn sure to Quinn.

"Dylan's in Washington, D.C., and we don't have an operation yet," Quinn explained. "Skeeter's holding down the fort back at headquarters."

"Well, see, there you have it." Kid kept moving toward the door, each step slower than the last, until he finally came to a complete stop under Quinn's unwavering gaze.

Quinn knew the distance between the barn and the gas station. A hundred yards. "I can handle it."

Kid didn't look convinced. "Maybe she's a decoy. Roper Jones is not going to give up, Quinn. Not until you're dead or Hawkins gets him."

"Roper Jones is not stumbling around in Burt's Gas Emporium. A woman is, and I'm pretty damn sure we better find out why."

With a reluctant nod, Kid finally agreed.

Quinn turned toward the door, slipping the Beretta

under his shirt and into the waistband of his jeans. Hell. He wasn't making it easy for Kid to play bodyguard.

Bodyguard. Christ. He'd always been his own damn bodyguard, and done a damn good job of it—up until two weeks ago in those West Side rail yards.

The memory gave him an instant's pause.

Okay, he admitted. The Roper Jones heist had gone down bad, real bad, and Hawkins had literally had to scrape him off that friggin' back alley, but they'd gotten what they'd been after that night and he was healed now. He was ready to get back in the game. More than ready.

He slanted the computer screen a quick glance as he passed by. Plum lipstick. Lavender shirt. Golden ponytail.

Hell. She didn't look like she was ready to get in the game. She didn't look like she'd ever even heard of the game. Ready or not, though, she was about to get her first taste of it.

Chapter 2

SHE'D MADE A MISTAKE coming here, Regan decided, and she'd wasted a whole lot of time doing it. There was no sign that Wilson had ever been to Cisco. If Quinn Younger had been here, well, it looked like he was long gone now, too.

Inside the gas station she'd found nothing but dust and spiders, greasy old oilcans, and tanker receipts.

Dragging her hair out of her eyes, she glanced through the nearest broken window at the other buildings and sighed. She'd come this far. She was going to have to search them, too. She'd never rest easy if she didn't.

Not that she was resting particularly easy, sifting through Burt's dust. Up until last night, when she'd found the mysterious entry on Wilson's desk calendar, she'd lived her life in a manner that had all but guaranteed she would never find herself in a situation like this—alone, in a deserted town, looking for a man she might need and didn't know. Her job in the paleontology lab at the Denver Museum of Nature and Science was everything Regan McKinney wanted. Her career was intellectually stimulating and yet fit within well-defined parameters of quietness and security. Haring around the world on wild adventures had been her parents' idea of living. It had also put them in an early grave. Regan wasn't having a thing to do with it.

At least she wouldn't have, if Wilson hadn't disappeared—or wandered off. More than once over the last two weeks, she'd wondered if that wasn't really the case. He'd aged in the last few years, truly aged, his body taking on a fragility she wouldn't have thought possible in the robust dinosaur hunter and flashy orator who had always been her grandfather. What had once been an endearing absentmindedness was possibly becoming something more, something she didn't want to think about too much.

She'd found the charger for his cell phone in his bedroom, which explained why she hadn't been able to reach him that way. All her calls to the places where he was supposed to have spent the night had only confirmed the worst: He was lost.

She had to find him. He'd raised her and her little sister, Nikki, after their parents had died. The three of them were a family, and she was terrified that if she couldn't find him, nobody would.

The sound of an approaching car brought her head around. A blue SUV passed by Burt's big front window heading west. According to her map, the road through Cisco turned into a scenic byway once it hooked up with the Colorado River. With the thermometer hovering over the hundred-degree mark, she figured the river was the only smart place to be going in Utah in June.

Admonishing herself to get back to business, she left the gas station through a half-hung back door and made her way across a stretch of barren ground toward the nearest shack. A quick look around inside only confirmed her suspicion: Quinn Younger wasn't living in a two-room hovel in Cisco.

Wild-goose chase, she thought, turning around to leave. That's what she was on, a lousy wild-goose chase. Five more buildings to go and not so much as a crow or a dust devil stirred in the whole damn town.

Correction, she told herself, coming to a stop just inside the hovel's doorway. The blue SUV was back, and it was pulling up in front of the gas station. Before it disappeared around the corner of the building, she saw two men inside. Suddenly she wished she'd parked her car someplace else—like Arizona. Slamming car doors revved up her heartbeat and made her doubly aware of how precarious her position might be.

She backed deeper into the shadows of the broken-down room. And froze.

There was no sound, no warning, but in that instant she knew she wasn't alone.

The fact no sooner registered than a steely arm wrapped around her waist; at the same time, a powerful hand clamped over her mouth. Before she could kick or scream or even register the depth of her alarm, he pressed her up against the shack's wall—pressed hard, his whole body flat against her back, immobilizing her.

Adrenaline washed into her veins on a river of stark, icy fear.

"I'm not going to hurt you, but I can't vouch for the guys in the four-by-four." His voice was soft and gravelly, and very close to her ear, his breath blowing across her skin as he spoke. "We're going to stay just like this for now. Real quiet, until they leave. Got it?"

She managed a sharp, terrified nod.

"Good. Now take a breath, then tell me if you locked your car before you went into the gas station."

She had to think for a second before she nodded. Yes, she'd locked her car. It was a careful city-girl's habit.

"Are you lost? Is that why you stopped?"

She debated her answer for a second, but then shook her head no, telling the truth. She wasn't lost. Scared senseless, but not lost.

"Then I guess that leads us to the obvious question." He spoke so quietly, she had to strain to hear him. She had to focus on him, focus on his breathing and slow down her own.

It wasn't going to happen. Not as long as her heart was racing, totally at odds with the slow, steady beat of his.

She could feel it against her back. She was frightened, but he wasn't. He was calm, breathing normally, holding her, but—she realized—not crushing her, not hurting her. It was very effective, what he was doing, and made all her diligently attended self-defense classes moot. He had immobilized her in one second flat. She felt shrink-wrapped between his body and the wall. She could feel the splinters in the boards and the old nails where they protruded. A cobweb was draped across her face, and she had to blink to keep the dust and spider silk out of her eyes.

Finally, after what seemed like an eternity, he asked his obvious question.

"Did you come here looking for me?"

The slight loosening of his hand over her mouth gave her just enough leeway to turn her head. He was close, and she was so scared, it took a couple of seconds for his face to register. When it did, she slowly nodded. Yes, she'd come all the way hell out to Cisco, Utah, and had the holy crap scared out of her just so she could find him. He was unmistakable, his eyes dark green and deep set beneath black lashes and the straight dark lines of his eyebrows. His hair was longer than on the framed *Newsweek* cover Wilson kept at home, the lines of his face more defined by the intervening years, but it was him, Quinn Younger. And if Wilson had thought him an outlaw at sixteen, her grandfather should see him now.

"What's your name?" he asked, slowly removing his hand from her mouth. A small, thin scar slanted across his cheek, showing pink against his deeply tanned skin, telling her he hadn't had it long. Flecks of pale, fine-grained sand dusted the ends of his midnight black hair. His body was warm, very hard against hers, and if she wasn't mistaken, the cool, steely ridge she felt at the base of her spine was a gun. The imprint of it had slowly registered over the last few seconds, and now she was sure: Quinn Younger was armed.

"Regan McKinney," she said hoarsely. Her mouth had gone painfully dry. "Wilson McKinney is my grandfather."

The slight lift of his eyebrows told her he recognized the name. The slow slide of his gaze over her face and the brief moment it spent focused on her mouth made her wonder if he recognized her. She wouldn't have thought it possible after so many years. It had been such a brief encounter, a few agonizing seconds of absolute mortification for a fifteen-year-old girl, and it most definitely hadn't been her face he'd been staring at.

A brief smile curved his mouth and he eased up on her body a bare degree.

"Don't move."

She nodded her head once. She wasn't going anywhere. He had a gun and was either slightly deranged, sneaking up on her like that, or he knew something about the guys in the blue SUV that she didn't. Either explanation was enough to freeze every muscle in her body.

But, by God, she'd found him. She'd found Quinn Younger. She hadn't expected to, not really.

He shifted his gaze to the open doorway, but she kept hers on him. He'd changed plenty from the clean-cut Air Force poster boy she'd seen on all the news magazines and national papers, but the classic structure of the face that had landed him on *People* magazine's Fifty Most Beautiful People list the year he'd been rescued out of Iraq hadn't changed. He was still drop-dead gorgeous, but in a wilder way, especially with the scar on his cheek. She'd be the first to admit that it was page 72 of the entertainment magazine she'd shown all her friends and tacked to her wall, not the *Newsweek* cover so proudly displayed by her grandfather. But she also had to admit that, even with his face basically unchanged, it was hard to reconcile the sexy guy in the *People* photograph—his mouth curved in a teasing grin, his uniform shirt unbuttoned, and his pants dangerously unzipped—with the deadly calm man pressed up against her and watching the back of Burt's like a hawk.

A juvenile delinquent teetering on the edge of a felony conviction—that's what Quinn Younger had been before he'd been given over to Wilson that long-ago summer for three months of fulfilling his societal obligations. An underage car thief with a knack for a sixty-second hot-wiring, before the ink had even dried on his driver's license.

Something crashed outside, bringing her head around. A man swore, and Quinn Younger stiffened and he pulled the gun out of his waistband.

"If this doesn't go down right, head for the barn." He

leaned in close to whisper in her ear. "Take the Camaro. My keys are in it. Just be damn careful when you put it into gear. First is tricky, and stay away from sixth. Sixth can get away from you."

Her already racing heart didn't slow down one iota at his words, or the drawing of his weapon. Sixth gear? She'd never heard of a sixth gear.

"If *what* doesn't go down right?" she asked in a forceful whisper verging on panic, looking from his face to his drawn gun and back to his face again. *Good God.*

He slanted her a questioning glance. "I thought you were going to tell me. You're the one those guys followed."

Followed?

"Me?" She hadn't been followed. "Why would anybody follow me?"

"Maybe they're looking for the same thing you are." His tone matched his gaze, very cool, very assessing.

Regan swallowed. He was trouble. She'd come looking for it and found it.

Damn.

The intense look on his face had her slowly turning her head back around. Through a sliver of an opening between the shack's wallboards, she saw enough to make her heart slam back up into overdrive.

The two men had entered the gas station, coming their way, moving silently through the shadows inside the abandoned building.

Every muscle in Quinn's body was taut, ready. He leveled his weapon and aimed at the first man. Regan got a sick feeling in her stomach.

Dear God, the last thing she wanted to see was someone murdered. A sob lodged in her throat. The soft, strangled sound was enough to make the two men stop. She froze, too, and behind her, Quinn leaned in closer, his free hand gently sliding over her mouth again. He was totally focused on the men. One had white-blond hair, his body athletically fit. The other man was dark-haired, much older and heavier. He looked used up and mean. Both were carrying guns.

Regan felt a bead of sweat trickling down the side of her face, and her knees started to tremble. Something terrible was about to happen, something violent she didn't want any part of—and yet, if those men had followed her, Wilson had to be in a kind of danger she hadn't even imagined.

The men slowly scanned the inside of Burt's, their expressions flat and serious. When the blond spotted something in the corner near the ceiling, a very brief, very curt conversation ensued. The only word she caught was "camera."

They started forward again. The blond man pointed to something on the floor. Directing the older man's attention, he traced an invisible line through the air, following something Regan couldn't see around the inside perimeter of the building. Burt's was full of junk, but Regan didn't remember seeing anything significant—until the blond-haired man said, "The whole place is wired to blow."

Quinn's hand tightened over her mouth to muffle her gasp, while the two men carefully backed up a step, turned, and very slowly started walking out of Burt's.

Regan would have slumped to the floor if Quinn hadn't been holding her against the wall.

He didn't move until the men were back in their car and were heading back down the road. They didn't go far, only about two hundred yards from Burt's, before they pulled off into the dirt and stopped.

"Let's go," Quinn told her, taking just enough of a step back to give her some breathing room. She started to slide down the wall. He quickly caught her around the waist with one hand while he slipped his gun back into the waistband of his jeans with the other. "Can you walk?"

"No. I don't know," she said, too frightened to lie. Her legs were trembling. "You . . . you were going to shoot those men."

"Me? No. I was just the backup. If they'd needed shooting, Kid would have done it. Now come on. If we stay close to the buildings, they won't be able to see us." He pulled her with him out the door into the bright sunshine and took off at a fast walk, his hand like a vise around her upper arm.

"Is th-there a bomb in Burt's?" The thought made her sick. She'd been wandering around in the old building like a complete idiot.

One corner of his mouth tipped up in what, under

other circumstances, could have passed for a grin. "No, but there are a hell of a lot of wires."

She was struggling to keep up, though Quinn Younger moved with a pronounced limp. Her gaze dropped down the length of his legs. His left knee seemed a little stiff.

He stopped at the corner of Burt's, keeping her behind him, and checked around the corner. Her gaze went to his left leg. He didn't keep his weight on it, but held it gingerly, the knee partially bent, the heel of his snakeskin cowboy boot lifted. His jeans were fraying at the seams, softly worn, revealing the lean musculature of the body beneath. His T-shirt was new, navy blue cotton with a red and white logo and the word WEATHERPROOF streaking across his back.

"Who's Kid?" she asked belatedly, remembering what he'd said.

"Kid Chaos." He glanced back at her over his shoulder. "My guardian angel."

THE blank look she gave him at that explanation was enough to bring a brief, disbelieving grin to Quinn's mouth. Regan McKinney. Sweet Jesus. He couldn't believe it. Who would have ever thought she'd show up in Cisco, Utah?

Not him.

Not in a million years.

He'd seen her naked once, or practically naked. Though truth be told, she'd filled out a bit since then.

Quite a bit, from all the curves he'd been pressed up against, but at the time she'd been an adolescent's wet dream come true.

Which was all so far beside the point, he couldn't believe he was even thinking about it.

Whoever those guys were, they were looking for her, and they'd been carrying guns. *Shit.*

"Come on. We've got to get to the barn." He took off again, pulling her along with him and taking a path that kept the other shacks between them and the road.

Regan McKinney with her amazingly lush, plum-colored mouth had ferreted him out in Cisco with a couple of mean-looking, .357-Magnum-toting mothers on her tail. He didn't believe in coincidence. Something was going down, and he was damn well going to find out what.

"KID? DID YOU GET head shots?" Quinn yelled when they entered the barn.

"Running them through the computer, Captain."

The voice came from the loft. Regan looked up, wondering what kind of man had a name like Kid Chaos and hung out in haymows, ready to shoot someone.

A young man wearing a tight black T-shirt and camouflage pants walked out to the edge of the upper platform and stared down at them.

My God. He *was* a kid.

Kid Chaos, boy wonder, the thought went through Regan's mind. He looked like one of the high school students who sometimes interned at the museum's lab. He was tall and well built, with short dark hair, and he barely looked old enough to shave—let alone carry the lethal-looking rifle slung over his shoulder and the black handgun shoved into a holster under his arm.

"They were packing some serious hardware," Quinn called out as they walked farther inside the barn, where two cars—one nice, one not so nice—were parked.

"And the woman?"

"Regan McKinney. Clean, I think." Quinn slanted her a glance, and Regan felt her cheeks grow warm in an angry blush.

Whatever these two were up to in Cisco, she doubted she was the one they needed to worry about. Quite the contrary, she was the one with reason to worry. She was in the middle of nowhere with a lot of armed men running around, and she hadn't been able to decide yet which ones—if any—were the good guys.

"Regan McKinney." Quinn gestured toward the haymow. "Meet Kid Chaos."

"Ma'am." The boy wonder didn't smile, but he nodded, and Regan automatically did the same.

Sniper, she thought, the word finally coming to her. That's what they called what he did. The realization unnerved her, and she wondered a little queasily if he'd had her in his sights before the two men had shown up.

Somehow, looking at him, she didn't have a doubt.

"Did you get through to Denver?" Quinn asked the younger man.

"Not yet. The guys in the blue SUV started back just before you entered the shack."

A double beep coming from the back of the barn had both men moving toward a computer set up on a desk. Kid sprinted down the stairs; Quinn limped between the two cars parked in the middle of the barn. He'd been hurt bad, from the looks of it, and she wondered if it was recent or an old wound.

She did a quick scan of the barn. The rickety exterior hadn't prepared her for the inside. It was spacious and orderly, despite the dirt floor and barnwood walls. It was also stifling.

Besides the cars and a slew of tools scattered on a bench, there was a refrigerator and another laptop set up on a table to her right, and that was about it. As the men huddled over the computer, it crossed her mind to bolt. She just as quickly discarded the idea. She'd come to Cisco on a mission, and by a stroke of luck—good or bad, she didn't know which yet—she'd succeeded. She'd found Quinn Younger. She wasn't leaving without asking him a few questions.

"This sucks," Kid said, glaring down at the computer screen.

Quinn went up behind him and looked over Kid's shoulder, then swore. "Vince Branson? I thought he was still in Chicago."

"Yeah, well, looks like he followed Roper to the new neighborhood."

Quinn swore again. "What's with the white-haired guy?"

"Nothing yet. I get a No Access message."

"I thought we had access to all the feds' files, good guys and bad guys."

"Yeah, well, up until last Christmas, I thought there was a Santa Claus, too." Kid kept tapping keys, his attention on the screen.

"What happened?"

"Superman sat me down and explained the facts of life." Kid flashed Quinn a grin, but it quickly faded when he returned his attention to the computer. "Look, I can hack through it, but that's going to take time, which we ain't got." He turned, his dark-eyed gaze locking onto Regan's across the length of the barn. "Whatever the hell those guys are up to, they followed her right to our front door. Which means we've probably been made."

In an instant Regan understood where he came by his nickname. The boy wonder definitely looked like he could do some seriously chaotic damage to anyone not on his side. From the accusatory glare in his eyes, she'd clearly just fallen into that category.

For a second, she reconsidered bolting out the door. Then she realized just exactly how far she would get, about half a step before Kid Chaos was all over her. Besides, she wasn't sure she had the strength to run very far in Cisco's heat. She needed to get back to her car, back to some air-conditioning.

"I don't *think* she's the enemy, Kid," Quinn said, leaning back on the computer desk and crossing his arms over his chest.

Regan felt herself flush again. What came off as a threat

from Kid Chaos was pure insult from Quinn Younger. He knew who she was, knew her grandfather.

"I came here looking for Wilson," she said. "That's the only reason I'm here. I don't know any Vince Branson."

"But he seems to know you," Quinn replied, pushing away from the desk. "What makes you think Wilson is here in Cisco?"

Before she could answer, Kid interrupted. "If you want me to get up there and take them out, I should do it before they have a chance to move."

Take them out? Alarmed, Regan shifted her gaze to the younger man. She knew exactly what he meant, and the words sent a chill down her spine. If ordered, Kid Chaos could become a one-man angel-faced death squad. What in the hell had she walked into?

"No. We'll let them have Cisco, if they can work up the balls to take it."

"What about her car? Dump it?" the boy wonder asked, and Regan's eyes got even wider.

"Whoa, wait a minute." She moved toward the two men and the desk, working to control the tremor in her voice. "No car dumping. No way. Not my car. If you want to dump a car, dump this one." She gestured at the car on her left, the ugliest piece of junk she'd ever seen. It had no paint, just four or five shades of black and gray primer. It had only half a dashboard. The rest was a snake pit of wires, gauges, and gizmos. It had no backseat, just a hold full of junk. What it did have was an engine sitting

under the open hood, a lot of engine even to her un-
trained eye.

On her right was a sleek Porsche, which according to
her grandfather had been Quinn's specialty as a juvenile,
before he'd gotten busted for stealing one too many.
With her next step, another memory clicked into place:
Quinn had told her to take his car, the Camaro, if things
didn't go down right.

She slowed to a stop and gave the ugly piece of junk a
closer look.

Yes, she thought. Beneath all the ugly was the classic
styling of a Chevy muscle car. It was definitely before
her time, but not before Wilson's—and the muscle car
Wilson had dragged home two weeks ago, a candy-
apple-red 1967 Dodge Coronet, for the love of God, had
been the start of her worrying that the old man was
actually losing his mind. Seventy-two-year-old men
did not drive supercharged Dodges. When three days
later he'd traded the Coronet in for a late-model silver
Porsche, she'd thought it was a dubious improvement.

Then he and the Porsche had disappeared.

She still wouldn't have thought of Quinn Younger if it
hadn't been for the entry in Wilson's calendar, but the
damning evidence was piling up all around her: muscle
cars and Porsches, Cisco and bad guys and guns.

He'd asked what made her think Wilson was in Cisco,
but she had a feeling he knew the answer to the question
a hell of a lot better than she did.

Her hands tightening into fists at her sides, she turned
to face Younger.

"I don't know what's going on here, and I don't want to know. Just tell me what's happened to Wilson." Her words were a demand, devoid of the fear she'd been feeling since Quinn had grabbed her in the shack. "Where's my grandfather?"

Quinn's eyes narrowed.

"Who's Wilson?" the boy asked, turning to Quinn.

"My mentor." Quinn said it thoughtfully.

"From the chop shop?"

A brief smile curved Quinn's mouth, and he shifted his gaze to Kid. "No. Wilson was way before Steele Street. Before the Air Force."

Oh, God, Regan thought, staring at him in disbelief. It was true. After all his glory, Quinn Younger had reverted to stealing cars for a chop shop—which proved the worst of what the note had suggested. She hadn't wanted to believe it. Air Force pilots didn't turn to lives of crime and end up living in ghost towns in Utah.

"You sold him those cars, didn't you?" Her demanding tone was gone, replaced by dreadful certainty. "And whoever you stole them from wants them back and has gone after my grandfather."

"Okay, you're losing me. I sold him *what* cars?" Quinn asked, cocking his head to one side, his gaze narrowing again. "And what do you mean someone has gone after Wilson? Who? Vince Branson?"

"I don't know, but he's disappeared. Just disappeared." She heard the tremor in her voice and hated it, but she couldn't control it, not anymore. "Just gone. Two weeks now. Right after he came home with the Porsche." What had Wilson been thinking, she wondered, to have dealt with the likes of Quinn Younger? Then she remembered: Wilson believed the man was a national hero. He hadn't known he was dealing with a thief.

"Have you told the police?" the thief in question asked, pushing off the desk and starting toward her.

"Yes." She took a step back, almost stumbled, and he stopped. "They don't believe me. They say this year is no different from any other time when Wilson's dropped out of sight for a while."

"But it is different," Quinn said. His inflection encouraged her to explain.

"Yes." It was so hot in the barn, she could barely breathe. "He always calls home, and this time ... this time ..." Her voice trailed off, and she wiped a trickle of perspiration from her brow with the back of her hand. It was just too hot to move. Too hot almost to think.

She squinted at Quinn Younger. He didn't look like he was buying her explanation. In fact, he looked incredibly skeptical—or terribly concerned. It was hard to read a man you'd only met once under awkward circumstances.

Very awkward, she remembered. She and Nikki had visited the Rabbit Valley dig on and off that first summer Wilson had worked with juvenile offenders. They'd had their own tent. Wilson had been so glad to have them with him, but the boys ... the boys had been a wild bunch. When one of them had walked in on her while she was undressing, she'd been shocked, and horrified, and embarrassingly mesmerized by his frankly appraising green-eyed gaze.

The same dark green gaze holding hers now.

"Kid, get some ice," he said, walking toward her. The younger man immediately turned toward the refrigerator against the back wall.

Regan didn't move. She wasn't sure she could without falling over. It was so hot. And so hard to breathe.

Don't panic, she told herself. She didn't have anything to prove to either one of them. But she would have their cooperation, by God—or she would have them in jail.

Unless they dumped her car and she never got out of Cisco alive.

Unless they killed her. They both had guns. Kid Chaos had two and apparently no qualms about "taking someone out."

Oh, great, she thought, feeling a breathless, dizzying panic flutter back to life in her veins despite herself. *Just . . . great . . .*

A*ND there she goes*. Quinn caught her as her knees buckled and she swooned in a dead faint. He swung her up into his arms.

"Now, isn't this just the *exact* complication we need," Kid said, returning with a bag of ice from the freezer, clearly disgusted with the new turn of events.

"I'll take care of her. Just help me with the car. We've got to get out of here."

"No shit." Kid rounded the Camaro and swung open the passenger door just in time for Quinn to lift Regan inside.

"Branson probably has a tracker on her Ford," Quinn said, buckling her in and setting the bag of ice next to her. "Find it, then dump her car at Wild Bill's. I'll see you back here in five minutes." He fished her car keys out of her pocket and tossed them to Kid.

"And if they move before then?"

"Then make sure they wish they hadn't."

Kid nodded and took off. No one could figure lines of sight better than a sniper, and given the angle of Burt's on the highway and where Regan had parked, Quinn figured Kid had a small but significant no-fire zone within which to maneuver. It would be skill, not luck, that eased Regan's car down the road without Branson and his buddy being able to see that it was gone or where it was going.

Quinn touched his fingers to the side of her neck and checked her pulse. She turned toward him with a soft moan, her eyes fluttering open and meeting his—and for a moment, he was lost.

Geezus, she was pretty. *And married*, he reminded himself, if his memory served—and it damn well did. The circumstances of Regan McKinney's wedding weren't something he was likely to forget. It wasn't something he'd bothered to think about for years, but it wasn't something he would forget.

Still, he couldn't help but look. She *was* pretty, really pretty. The video camera hadn't done her justice. Besides a golden, silky ponytail, she had the kind of bangs that fell across her eyebrows and down the sides of her face, accentuating her cheekbones.

And that mouth. How long had it been since he'd kissed a woman? Months, at least, but when he looked at Regan McKinney, it seemed like forever.

"You . . . you shouldn't have stared at me like that," she said, her voice breathless, her eyes darkly glazed.

He knew what she was talking about, and the memory came back in vivid detail: her standing in a pool of lantern light inside the canvas tent, a flowered shirt and a bra in her hands, clutched to her chest, but not covering her breasts. Her nipples had been pink, soft pink like her panties. Her mouth had been in an "O" of surprise, for the first few seconds anyway, and he'd gotten hard so fast it had hurt. God, he'd thought he was going to die right there on the spot.

It had been one of the most intensely sexual moments of his life, and he hadn't even touched her.

The only other thing she'd been wearing was a pair of white socks, and to this day he had a sincere appreciation for the whole bobby-socks sex fantasy. Yeah, he could dig it—especially if his fantasy lover was wearing pink panties and had blond hair and was completely stacked and had a mouth that was begging to be kissed—which of course they always were.

"I couldn't not stare," he admitted, lifting his hand and sliding a silken strand of hair behind her ear. "You were perfect."

"Oh."

Oh was right, as in *oh, shit*. He had to move away from

her before he did something he was guaranteed to re-gret—like kiss her. He'd gone to see Professor McKinney four years after that summer, after he'd started college and joined ROTC, after he'd set his life on a path that wasn't going to include lockdown in the state peniten-tiary. The old man had been pleased to see him, more than pleased, and eager to hear his plans, and a little less eager to explain why the house was in such a state. Quinn remembered there had been dresses tossed all over the dining room in the big old house up on the Hill in Boulder, fancy dresses. His granddaughter was getting married, Wilson had said, not the baby, not Nikki, but Regan, his oldest. Too young at nineteen, the old man had complained, but there wasn't a damn thing he could do about it.

Quinn hadn't seen the professor since, and he'd refused to admit, even to himself, that he'd gone to Boulder that day hoping to talk with the girl he'd seen practically naked all those summers ago.

His gaze drifted over the woman looking up at him from the contoured depths of the Camaro's bucket seat. That girl had grown into a beautiful woman. *Beautiful married woman*, he reminded himself.

Her nose was too broad across the bridge for her to be conventionally pretty, her eyebrows too dark of a con-trast with all that blond hair and her light gray eyes, but Quinn was no less intrigued than he'd been when he'd first seen her as a teenager. The lavender shirt that had looked so soft and fresh when she'd first stepped into Burt's had long since wilted in the heat. Dampened by her sweat, it clung to her body in a thousand fascinating ways.

In his tried-and-true fantasies, that night in the tent had continued with her dropping her shirt. An event as unlikely to occur now as it had been back then.

Right.

Taking a breath, he broke eye contact with her and tore open the top of the bag of ice.

"Here," he said, slipping a small cube between her lips. "Suck on this, and when you're done, I'll give you some Gatorade to get your electrolytes back up to speed."

"This . . . this was a bad idea, my coming here," she said around the ice, reaching for the seat belt clip. "And I . . . I think it's time I left."

"No." He shook his head, and she paused for a second. Then she rushed ahead, her fingers scrambling for the clip.

"I'll . . . uh, just take my own car, thank you."

He put his hand over hers, stilling her frantic movements, and her gaze slammed back into his.

"You don't have a car anymore," he told her, lying just enough to get his way—because he was going to get his way.

Thinking faster than he'd expected, she immediately swung her gaze around to the Porsche.

He did grin at that. "Nope. That's Kid's car, and I don't think he trusts you. He thinks you're with the bad guys."

"The bad guys?"

"Vince—"

"Branson and his friend," she filled in, surprising him again. "Are those the men you stole from?"

That little deduction startled a laugh out of him. Even only halfway with the program, she was quick, damn quick.

"Maybe," he admitted. Branson worked for Roper Jones, and SDF had definitely lifted merchandise from Roper Jones, the unusual shipment of crates Quinn had nearly gotten himself killed intercepting in the Burlington Northern's Denver rail yards.

Crates full of plaster casts, the old dinosaur doc missing, and Regan McKinney in Cisco—the connection had been forming in his mind since the moment he'd recognized her. He wasn't the only car thief and lower-downtown hustler who'd been handed over by the courts to Wilson McKinney that summer. Dylan Hart, Christian Hawkins a.k.a. Superman, J. T. Chronopolous, Zachary Prade, and Creed Rivera had sweated out three months in the professor's dinosaur bone beds with him, too.

Something was telling him that while he'd been laying low in Cisco, Dylan had gone looking for help with those crates in the wrong place—the worst place, if it had put Roper Jones and his goons on Regan McKinney's tail.

CHAPTER

4

JEANETTE.

That's what he called his ugly car. Jeanette.

Regan popped another ice cube into her mouth and stuck one more in her cleavage. Without the heat eating her brain, she'd decided she wasn't going to die.

Quinn Younger, Air Force ace and national hero, may have fallen on bad times, but he wasn't a cold-blooded murderer. By his own admission, he'd had no intention of shooting those men. The boy wonder did his dirty work for him, and the boy wonder was headed to Denver, in his own car. God knew there wasn't room for him in the Camaro, not even if there had been another seat, not with the equipment Quinn had been throwing in the back.

She was still sucking on the ice cube he'd given her when Kid Chaos burst back into the barn.

"They've backed off another hundred yards, parked behind the bluff, the idiots," he reported. "They can't see shit...uh, anything from back there." He cast her a quick, almost guilty glance. He was carrying the stuff out of her car, all of the stuff, including her purse—which he began looking through.

Great, she thought. The boy wonder was too chivalrous to swear in front of a woman, but didn't give a whoopty damn about rifling through her purse. Lucky her, she'd fallen in with gentlemen thieves.

"I saw them," Quinn said. "Didn't Branson lose three of his fingers in an explosion?"

Kid looked up from her purse, a sudden grin on his face. "Yeah," he said. "A block of C4 blew up part of a meatpacking plant in Chicago where Roper was holding a load of Colombian cocaine. Branson was there. No wonder he's so damn nervous."

Regan listened, silent, a lump forming in her throat that didn't have a thing to do with her ice cube. Her Ford Taurus had been a good car, a great car. It had never had a name before, but for the last five minutes, she'd been calling it Quinn Younger's Big Mistake. He couldn't just order Kid to dump her car somewhere and get away with it.

Her car. Gone. Just like that. Nobody stole Ford Tauruses. Her insurance agent had told her the Ford Taurus had a theft quotient of damn near zero, which had been a big selling point in its favor—for all the good it was doing her now.

She would get her car back. She swore she would.

Boulder was only half an hour from Denver. She could easily get home and go to the police and tell them about her stolen car and everything she'd learned in Cisco about Vince Branson and the guns and the cars and the two men in the middle of it all—and if they hadn't thought she was crazy before, that ought to clinch it for them.

Damn. She groaned. This sort of thing was not supposed to happen to her. It was light-years worse than anything her globe-trotting parents had ever been involved in—except her parents had died in some godforsaken South American country, buried under a pile of pre-Columbian earthquake rubble, and she wasn't going to die, not here, not today, so help her God.

"Who is Nikki McKinney?" Kid asked, and Regan's head jerked up.

"Her younger sister," Quinn answered, before Regan could think of a lie. "Why? What's up?"

Kid showed him a letter he'd pulled out of her purse. "Nikki McKinney's address matches the one on Regan McKinney's driver's license."

Quinn ducked down to look in the Camaro's window, his expression grim. "Does Nikki live with you?"

"It's no business of yours who lives—" Regan started defensively.

"Listen to me, Regan." He cut her off, his voice low and deadly serious. "Vince Branson is not someone to mess with. If he and his buddy picked up your tail at home this morning, then everyone in that house is a target."

Regan felt the blood drain from her face. She'd been so concerned for Wilson these last few weeks, it hadn't occurred to her that she or Nikki might be in danger—and yet look where she'd ended up.

"Yes," she admitted, praying she was doing the right thing. "We live with Wilson, the same house where you visited him that time."

Something changed in his face. She couldn't tell what. "He told you I was there?"

"He *was* very proud of you," she said, not bothering to hide the past-tense implications.

Quinn straightened up to look over the top of the car, speaking to Kid. "Call in a nine-one-one to SDF, and get Skeeter over there to do a little recon and stick until you get there. Regan will call and let her sister know you're coming. Now go."

Kid had shoved the letter in his pants pocket and had been moving the whole time Quinn was talking. When Quinn gave the final order, he was halfway inside the Porsche.

Then he stopped, and with a muttered curse, he stood back up.

"Don't even think it, Kid," Quinn said before the younger man could get a word out.

"Damn it, Quinn. You know my orders. I'm not supposed to let you out of my sight."

"Do you want *Skeeter* to do the intercept?" Quinn's voice rose incredulously, making Regan wonder what was wrong with Skeeter.

Kid obviously knew, because after swearing a small blue

streak, he got back into the Porsche and fired up the engine. The car instantly came to life with a low, purring rumble.

Quinn ran toward the barn doors, moving faster than Regan would have thought possible for a man with a limp. When the doors began rolling open, the Porsche was there, nosing out. Three seconds later, it was gone in a cloud of dust.

Regan didn't know whether to be relieved or not.

Probably not, she decided, going with her gut instinct.

Retrieving her purse from the driver's seat where Kid had tossed it, she opened it up and looked inside. As she'd suspected, he'd gone through everything, right down to her tampon holder and her cough drops—and he'd confiscated her cell phone.

Damn it.

She dragged her hand back through her hair, looking around for Quinn. She found him by the stairs, zipping up a duffel bag. He would have to give her a phone. He had to if he wanted her to call Nikki.

When he was finished zipping the duffel, he headed back to the Camaro and dropped the bag in the trunk. The last thing he put in the car was one of the laptops. The other computer had gone with Kid.

He leaned in through the passenger window, taking up *all* of her space, and slid the thin computer into the main slot on a metal box bolted to the car's frame between the gearshift and the engine firewall. A screen on the box blinked to life.

"I'll get a couple of cold drinks, and we're out of here," he said, slipping back out the window.

She released an unsteady breath and stuck another ice cube in her mouth. So far, things weren't going very well. Not only were Wilson and her car missing, now she and Nikki were in trouble up to their necks, and she still didn't have a clue as to why.

It was possible Branson and his buddy didn't have anything to do with her—but they definitely had something to do with Quinn Younger. And from what she'd seen, Quinn Younger definitely had something to do with her grandfather's disappearance.

Six hours, that's what it had taken her to drive from Boulder to Cisco. Six hours to make the biggest mistake of her life.

Okay, maybe the second biggest, she reconsidered. Marrying Scott Hanson had been a huge mistake.

Quinn dropped the hood on the Camaro, getting it to catch with a final solid push, before he slid in behind the wheel and handed her a bottled drink.

He gave her a quick once-over, and a familiar grin curved his mouth—familiar, she realized, because of the *People* magazine photo still taped to the inside of her closet door.

The reminder made her blush. She really should have taken his picture down years ago.

"Feeling better?" he asked. "You're looking a little flushed again."

"I'm fine," she said curtly, and his grin broadened.

"Great."

Something in his smile made her glance down at herself. One look was all it took for her to close her eyes and groan. Her lavender silk shirt was sodden, plastered to her breasts and nearly transparent in its delicacy. Between the sweat and the melting ice cubes and the time spent cozying up to her bag of ice, she looked like the first runner-up in a wet T-shirt contest.

She automatically crossed her arms over her breasts, hoping the action wasn't too obvious. Then he turned the key in the ignition, and all thoughts of modesty were drowned out in the rumbling roar of the Camaro's engine.

Her eyes flew open, and her arms shot out to either side, her hands clinging to whatever she could find to hold on to—the door panel on her right, and the gear console on the left. The whole freaking car was shaking and grumbling and growling. He pressed down on the gas, revving the engine, and the growling turned into an out-and-out roar.

Holy Mother of God. Wilson's Dodge hadn't sounded or felt anything like this.

Eyes wide, knuckles white, she looked at Quinn and wasn't the least bit reassured to find him frowning at a gauge. Something was wrong. He revved the engine again, and the resulting surge of power poured through her from the tips of her toes up the length of her spine.

She felt like she was riding a rocket. Jeanette was a beast—all ugly on the outside and pure animal from the rims up.

He gave the gauge a tap, and when it didn't budge,

bent his head down to peer into the maze of wires snaking around where the other half of the dashboard should have been. A few seconds of fiddling and a startling shower of sparks later, the needle on the gauge swung into action, responding with a smooth swinging arc to every ounce of pressure he put on the gas pedal.

Satisfied with the working of the gauge, he began inching the car out of the barn. Like a prowling tiger, the Camaro crawled across the dusty floor. A whole new fear took hold of her.

"W-wait...Kid said those guys are still out there. What if they're just waiting for us?"

"Oh, they're waiting for us all right," he assured her, "but they'll never catch us. We're going to outrun them."

Regan braced herself, remembering how Kid had taken off in his Porsche. But Quinn held them to a crawl, making the mighty Jeanette shoulder her way through every rut and over every ridge in the dirt road. Ahead of them, the highway out of Cisco stretched to the horizon with no Kid in sight. She twisted around in her seat. The road behind them was clear, except for the blue nose of the SUV peeking out from behind a low hill and a flash of sunlight glinting off something in the window.

"They've got binoculars." Her heart was racing, her palms sweating. "They've seen us and...and they're heading this way."

"And they're too late."

Or so he said, but even once they made it onto the asphalt, he kept the car in first, growling and rumbling and crawling along. Regan's stomach started tying itself into knots, and she quickly revised her estimate of their travel time. At the rate they were going, they'd be lucky to make Denver by next week, if ever.

She looked behind them again and felt sick. The SUV was on the road, accelerating.

Then Quinn shifted into second gear. Third, fourth, fifth, and sixth came in smooth, rapid succession, each gear change forcing a quantum leap in their acceleration. Her heart jamming in her throat, she watched the speedometer with growing alarm.

Sixty miles an hour had been a mere heartbeat from first gear. She missed seventy, the number went by so fast.

Eighty was smooth.

Ninety, and she started digging her fingers into Jeanette's hide.

One hundred.

She glanced up, and he flashed her a grin, the wind whipping at his hair, one hand easy on the steering wheel, the other on the shifter.

One hundred and ten.

One hundred and twenty and oh, shit... they were flying, Jeanette low to the road, roaring, the beast unleashed.

CHAPTER

LACE BRA.

Quinn kept his eyes on the road, mostly, but he couldn't help but glance over to the passenger seat every now and then.

She was wearing a lace bra beneath her wet shirt. The delicate tracery outlined against the lavender silk was unmistakable.

Lace.

God, it had been a long time since he'd kissed a woman. Since he'd undressed a woman.

He hadn't thought about it much lately, which probably said something about him he didn't want to know. He sure as hell hadn't thought about it since the rail yard rumble. At first, he'd been too busted up. Then Dylan had shipped him to Cisco and buried him in the desert to keep him out of the way. He knew Roper Jones wanted him dead. News of the hit had traveled fast, fifty thousand dollars fast, but, hell, it wasn't the first time Quinn had been on somebody's hit list.

It was just the first time Dylan had thought he might actually get hit.

Quinn didn't blame him. The disaster in the BN&SF rail yards had been the first time he'd needed somebody to scrape him off the street. Bullets had been flying; he'd been beaten and bleeding like a stuck pig from a head wound and an ugly gunshot that had torn open his shoulder. His knee had been wrenched damn near backward, and Hawkins had come out of nowhere, straight through the middle of the fucking melee, and gotten him out alive, if half dead counted as alive. Quinn hadn't been too sure at the time. Neither had Hawkins—but he hadn't admitted it until a few days later, when he'd dropped by the hospital.

"'Keep breathing, you son of a bitch'?" Quinn had asked, repeating Hawkins's words to him in that frickin' alley. "Is that the new SDF triage directive?"

Hawkins had just grinned. "I didn't haul my ass back down there and put it on the line to drag out a corpse." Tall and dark-haired, dressed in suede pants and a chocolate brown silk shirt, Hawkins—"Superman"—had draped himself with typical long-limbed elegance into one of the hospital's utilitarian armchairs. For being such a badass knuckle-dragger, he had a disconcerting habit of occasionally showing up looking like a GQ poster boy.

Quinn had tried to grin back, and failed. He'd hurt

everywhere. His leg was in a brace, his face tight with the stitches below his eye, and his shoulder even tighter.

God, what a way to make a living.

Wait for the drop, and when it comes, steal Roper blind. That had been the Defense Department's directive to SDF. No rules, take everything you can get, any way you can get it. Quinn and Hawkins had been working together for four months, working as far inside Roper's criminal empire and as far outside the law as their pasts could take them—and Hawkins's past was good for five to ten on any given day of the week. Superman was so connected with Denver's underworld, the government guys they worked with sometimes wondered what side he was really on.

Christian Hawkins had made his reputation years ago with the high-profile murder of a senator's son in lower downtown. Hawkins hadn't offed the kid, but he'd gone to prison for it. That gave him more chops than most on the street and made him invaluable as an undercover asset for SDF when they were on home turf. When it came to Christian Hawkins, only a few very select friends knew he wasn't bad.

"How's your cover?" Quinn had asked, biting back a grimace of pain when he tried to turn his head. That had been his biggest concern after the rail yard fiasco, that Hawkins had finally blown his cover by coming to his rescue.

"It'll hold. It always holds." Hawkins had shrugged. *No problem.*

Quinn hoped to hell it wasn't a problem. Roper Jones

was the scum of the earth, but up until last year, he'd been strictly Chicago scum. Now he was moving out of drugs, bookies, extortion, and prostitution into international arms deals—or so government intelligence had reported.

General Grant, SDF's commanding officer at the Department of Defense, wanted to nail Jones's ass, preferably before the CIA got him, but all Quinn and Hawkins had found so far was a lot of dirty money, a little stolen jewelry, and a few kilos of Colombian cartel cocaine. It was enough to put Roper away, yeah, but not what Uncle Sam wanted. If there were exotic guns running through Denver, so far they hadn't been Roper Jones's guns.

There hadn't been any guns in the rail yard crates either, not unless they'd been packed inside plaster casts. The only other time Quinn had seen so much plaster had been the summer he'd spent jacketing dinosaur bones for Doc McKinney at Rabbit Valley. He could see right now that he was going to have to ask Dylan again what in the hell had been in those crates that was important enough to have almost gotten him killed. Dylan's original answer of "Nothing we're looking for" was starting to look bogus.

He glanced at the woman in the seat beside him. Dealing in hot dinosaur bones was hardly up Roper Jones's alley. In fact, it didn't make any sense at all, but Regan McKinney had ended up on his doorstep, looking for Wilson. Hell, something was going on.

He slanted Regan another glance. He'd been thinking

about lace bras and sex before he'd gotten sidetracked by hit lists and guns, his body reminded him. Reminded him also of what a pleasant diversion it all could be. Of course, actually having sex with the grown-up version of a man's most treasured adolescent fantasy shot things way past diversion.

God, she was pretty, and soft, and still wondrously wet.

He shifted uneasily in his seat and forced his eyes back to the road.

"So, are you still married?" he asked. He was beginning to think not, but he had to ask. He had to know. Married women normally didn't live with their sister and their grandfather, and usually they took their husband's name, and just about all the time, they wore a ring. Regan was looking good on all counts.

Her silence gave him another excuse to glance over at her, and he had to wonder if she had the strength to white-knuckle-grip the door and the gear console all the way to Denver. Even at one hundred and twenty miles per hour, it was going to take a while to get there.

"How . . . how did you know I was married?"

Breathless, wrung-out, tense, and defensive—it was nice to know he hadn't lost his touch with the fairer sex.

"Wilson told me you were getting married the day I was at the house. There were dresses everywhere." Small mountains of baby blue dresses and one big white one with pearl buttons running all the way down the back. He'd never been so tight-jawed in his life as he'd been standing there saying good-bye to Wilson and looking at that dress.

He'd wanted it, by God, he'd wanted it and the woman who went in it. He'd wanted them for himself. Isn't that what he'd been working his ass off for—so he could have a chance with the granddaughter of a friggin' college professor, a Boulder-bred, pink-pantied virgin who was so clean it made him ache? That summer at the dinosaur camp, he'd watched her on and off as she'd come and gone, and fallen more in love and lust every day. He never had gotten up the nerve to talk with her, but he'd listened when she'd talked to Wilson and his grad students. With every word she'd proved herself to be way out of his league. She'd intimidated the hell out of him, which had only made him want her all that much more.

He'd been such a cross-eyed romantic sap at sixteen— and at twenty, when he'd been standing there looking at her wedding dress. He'd been so fucking galled by the situation, and it had only gotten worse in the following weeks, a whole helluva lot worse.

"Yes, well, the dresses. That was . . . uh . . . sort of a high point, the dresses," she said, a small catch in her voice, her gaze glued to the road.

"So marriage is a rough go, huh?" Considering who she'd married, he wasn't surprised to hear it. Fate had definitely been fucking with him when it came to Regan McKinney.

"Rough?" she repeated, and gave a short laugh, which broke her single-minded concentration on the road—

and that's when he got her attention, all of it. Her head came around, and her eyes narrowed in an offended glare. "My marriage isn't any of your—"

"Business. Right," he said, cutting her off. "I'm just trying to figure out what's going on here, trying to figure out why a man would send his wife to Cisco alone, and—"

"I'm not a wife," she interrupted him. "I don't have a husband. I make all my own decisions, including the very bad one to come to Cisco so I could get my car 'dumped' somewhere and be practically kidnapped by a couple of—"

She cut herself off, obviously thinking better of what she'd been about to call him and Kid. He didn't care. He'd gotten the answer he'd wanted. It was all he could do not to grin.

Things were looking up.

THINGS were going downhill fast, Regan thought, sitting back into her seat, her arms coming up and crossing over her chest. In truth, they could hardly look worse. She'd lost her car and was at the mercy of a . . . a speed freak in a muscle machine.

And to make things just that much more awful, he'd brought up her marriage.

Her defunct marriage, she reminded herself. Under normal circumstances, remembering she was divorced was usually enough to give her spirits a lift.

These were not normal circumstances.

She slanted the speedometer another glance, then wished she hadn't.

"Let's talk cars," she said abruptly. Cars were her business with Quinn Younger, cars and Wilson.

"You mean the cars I stole from Vince Branson and sold to your grandfather?" he asked, downshifting around a curve in the road.

"Yes. Those cars," Regan said, gritting her teeth. She couldn't help herself, as they went into the turn she clutched the door panel and held her breath, but the car stuck to the road, all four tires gripping asphalt, and she had to wonder how in the hell he managed to do it. He shifted up again, bringing them out of the turn, and by the time they hit the straightaway, he was running the Camaro at full throttle.

God, he drove like a . . . *a fighter pilot.*

Of course, she thought, the realization coming to her from out of the blue. Whatever kind of lousy, low-life car thief he'd become—*if* that's what he'd become, and the jury was still out on that one—he was still one of the most highly trained and highly skilled pilots in the world. Surely he could drive a car better than most, even at a hundred and twenty miles an hour.

"What kind of cars were those again?" he asked, ratcheting the speed up another notch, so help her God.

She dug her fingers into the car's upholstery. "Huh?"

"The cars I stole, then sold to your grandfather."

Oh, right. "A . . . uh, 1967 Dodge Coronet, with red paint and a red leather interior with hot pink piping." Nikki had loved that car. Regan had thought it looked pretty cool, too, just not cool for her seventy-two-year-old grandfather who seemed to be losing track of some of his marbles. "And the Porsche he disappeared with, a silver one with a black interior. He only had the Coronet for a couple of days before trading it in on the Porsche."

"Hot pink piping?" he repeated, sounding a little incredulous and none too pleased with the color scheme.

"It had a lot of power. He liked to sit in the driveway and run the motor." *What in the world had Wilson been thinking?* she wondered for about the millionth time, to drag home a candy-apple-red car to their sedately historical, upper-middle-class neighborhood and then sit around in the driveway revving up the engine like some sixteen-year-old kid. It had been embarrassing and distressing at the time, but now she wished she were sitting in that driveway again, listening to the neighbors complain. She'd rather be embarrassed than dead, and that's what she was going to be if Quinn didn't slow down. She'd also rather have Wilson back. "The Porsche was a little quieter."

"Yeah," he said, his voice tight. "It would be. So what tipped you off to Cisco?"

Okay, she thought. It was time to put her cards on the table, or rather her card. She'd only had one reason for coming to Cisco. Lifting her hips off the seat, she searched in her pocket for the piece of paper that had sent her on her doomed mission. Unfolding it, she smoothed the page open on her leg.

"This is from Wilson's calendar, a page from June. At

the bottom, on Saturday, it says 'Pick up Betty. Contact Quinn Younger, Cisco, Utah, for nine-one-one.'" She glanced up at him. "That's the kind of Porsche he went off in, a nine-one-one."

"A nine-eleven, yeah," he said, his expression growing even darker.

She hated to ask the next question, but she had to know. "So . . . uh . . . do you know this Betty lady?" As impossible as it had seemed, she hadn't thrown out the possibility of seventy-two-year-old hormones being the catalyst for the crazy happenings in her grandfather's life.

"Betty," Quinn repeated with a short laugh, giving his head a disbelieving shake. "Betty is the candy-apple-red Dodge with the pink piping." And it was SDF's baby, the most cherried-out machine in their Steele Street garage, a car so reeking of girly-girlness, the only one of them with enough balls to drive it in daylight was the boss, Dylan.

Son of a bitch, Quinn silently cursed. Dylan really had done it. He'd contacted old Doc McKinney and brought him in on the operation—for reasons Quinn was damn well going to find out—and then he'd paid McKinney off with free rides in Betty and one of the Porsches.

And the 911? He wasn't going to tell her, but "Contact Quinn Younger in Cisco, Utah, for 911" didn't have a damn thing to do with a Porsche 911 and everything to do with what the old man should do if he found himself in trouble and needed help. Dylan was the only one who could have told Wilson about Cisco.

He'd been wrong. Things weren't looking up. They were going straight to hell, and if they all weren't damned careful, they were going to take Regan McKinney, her grandfather, and her kid sister right along with them.

Chapter 6

Work, work, work. They were going to work him to death—and it would almost be worth it. He had a whole warehouse full of dinosaur bones to catalogue and identify.

Wilson McKinney hummed to himself as he moseyed from one plaster-covered fossil to the next, his glasses low on his nose, checking the numbers against his clipboard.

The men running around had really gone after the femurs and the tibias, looking for their missing guns. Yes, he'd figured that much out, that the guys at the warehouse had lost a bunch of guns, though why in the hell they thought someone would be hiding guns in dinosaur bones was beyond him.

Foolishness, pure foolishness. It was a good thing they'd called in an expert—namely him.

Of course, it was too darn hot to really be working with nothing but a darn fan blowing on him. All a
darn fan did was blow the darn air around. Air-
conditioning was what the darn warehouse needed. Air-
conditioning.

Not that he couldn't take it. He'd been in a lot hotter places than a warehouse in . . . in—well, wherever the
hell he was. Hell, yes, he'd been in hotter places than
this. Spent his whole darn life in hotter places, digging up
bones.

Though, swear to God, he'd never dug up anything
even half so interesting as the three-hundred-pound
peach of a fossil he'd found over near the generator, on
table four.

His face split into a broad grin. Just wait until Regan
got a look at number 42657. By God, he ought to just
give her a call—and he would have, by God, if his darn
phone worked, but he'd forgotten the darn charger. There
was a phone in the warehouse. He heard it ringing every
now and then, but he hadn't figured out where the darn
thing was. He would, though, and by God, then he'd give
Regan a call.

Oh, well. He'd be home soon, and he could tell her all
about it. He ought to be telling a lot of people about it.
There were still a couple of folks left in the warehouse,
and if he could remember any of their darn names, by
God, he'd call them over and show them a thing or two
about dinosaurs.

But who could remember names, when it was too
darn hot to remember anything?

A particularly round specimen caught his eye on table seven, and he wandered over to give it a closer look. He was sure he'd opened it up, but he'd better check it, just to make sure.

So you did sell him the cars?" Regan asked, and Quinn found the disappointment in her voice heartening. Somehow, after the last wild hour, she must have still been harboring a hope that he wasn't quite as bad as he seemed.

Interesting.

He shrugged. "Let's just say he got to borrow Betty for a while."

"And who would let him do that, if it wasn't you?"

Quinn wasn't about to give her Dylan's name, not yet. "One of my partners" was all he said.

"Who?" she demanded, but he just looked at her. "Okay, then what about the Porsche?"

Yeah, what about the Porsche. He was still thinking about the Porsche, too. "We did have one we were looking to unload, but your grandfather isn't exactly a regular on our client list."

"Of course not," she said, sounding thoroughly offended again. "He never—" She stopped suddenly when the computer came to life.

A series of numbers flashed on the screen. Quinn hit a kcy, and a message scrolled across the monitor at the same time as it came through a speaker.

"*Skeeter here. All clear in Boulder,*" a young voice said.

Quinn adjusted the volume. "Did you get a visual?"

"*That would be affirmative.*"

"Nikki's fine," he interpreted for Regan. "Skeeter, I need you to call Superman, tell him we're coming in. I'll call the boss myself." *Or not*, he thought, already knowing what Dylan would think of him and Kid breaking cover.

"*Copy that.*"

Quinn hit another key. "Kid. What's your ETA?"

"*Seven o'clock tonight.*"

"Great." A quick smile curved Quinn's lips. "I'll have Regan call you in."

At least that had been the plan, but when he glanced over at her, she didn't look in the mood to cooperate.

"Skeeter is our . . . office manager," he said with a smile. An encouraging smile, he hoped. "The computers are Kid's. Something he's been fooling around with, a wireless laptop with internal cell phone components on a closed satellite network with GPS. Do you want to call Nikki and tell her Kid Chronopolous is going to stay with her until you get home?"

"Why shouldn't I call the police instead?" she retorted, sounding like her mind was already made up, lifting her chin just enough that she could look down her nose at him, and suddenly he was back in that tent in Rabbit Valley. She'd been surprised when he'd walked in on her, but no more surprised than he'd been, and he never could have said who had recovered first—though his money had always been on her and the princess-to-pauper gaze she'd leveled at him. She hadn't been frightened. He'd realized that real quick. Badass jokers on the streets were afraid of him—but not the professor's granddaughter. No, she'd just looked down her prissy little nose and stared at him.

He'd loved it, absolutely loved it—there she'd been, practically naked and giving him attitude. He'd noticed her before, had been watching her, but that was when he'd fallen in sixteen-year-old love. Letting his gaze take a quick trip down her body and back had turned that split-second, initially pure and breathless feeling into molten lust. For an encounter that couldn't have lasted more than a minute, it had had one hell of an impact on him.

He'd pretty much ricocheted between love and lust the whole rest of the summer. Both reactions had made it impossible for him to work up the guts to talk to her. Every time he'd seen her, in his mind he'd seen her naked.

Some things never change, he thought, mildly disgusted with himself. He wasn't a kid anymore, and she certainly deserved better than him continually imagining her without her clothes on, but there it was anyway.

Her skin was amazingly soft, though. Any guy who had touched her would notice—which made him wonder what had happened to her husband, a story he probably wasn't going to get any time soon.

"I asked you a question."

"Yeah, you did," he said, stalling until he could get his mind back on what she wanted to talk about. "Why shouldn't you go to the police? Because the police don't have a clue where your grandfather is, and I do."

The answer to her question was as simple as that. He hadn't known before—not about the doc and not about the contents of those crates—but Betty had clinched it for him. Old Doc McKinney was working for SDF. There had been dinosaur bones in those crates, and Dylan had gone to the dinosaur man for help.

"So where is he, damn it?" she demanded. "Is he okay, or what?" The faint tremor in her voice stole some of the force out of her question and made him feel guilty as hell.

"If he's where I think he is, he's fine."

She was quiet for a long minute on her side of the Camaro, but he could feel her looking at him.

Turning his head, he slid his gaze over her. Her hair was falling down all over the place, her lips were pale, and her skin was flushed with heat. Most women would look like train wrecks under those circumstances. He'd never seen anything more sexy in his life.

"And if he's not where you think he is?" she asked.

"Then I'll find him."

And that was a promise.

WELL, *that settles it*, Christian Hawkins thought, slipping his cell phone into the back pocket of his jeans and pulling out a lighter and a pack of cigarettes. His whole day had just gone to hell. His boss at SDF, Dylan Hart, had just confirmed it.

Leaning back against the old warehouse where he was working with Doc McKinney, Hawkins, sometimes known as "Superman," knocked a cigarette out of the pack.

Uncle Sam was pulling the plug on them. Dylan's trip to Washington, D.C., to plead SDF's case on a bunch of dinosaur bones had come to nothing. Not even General Grant had been able to save the mission. Hell, Quinn had almost died stealing the damn things, and now the government didn't want them—not that Hawkins blamed them. Who the hell would want a bunch of old dinosaur bones, except old man McKinney?

Guns. That's what they had been looking for in the Burlington Northern and Santa Fe rail yards two weeks ago. They had been looking for a stolen shipment of cutting-edge military assault rifles commissioned by the Pentagon.

Hawkins bent his head low over the flame of his lighter and inhaled until his cigarette was lit. Then he snapped the lighter shut and shoved it and the pack back in his pocket with his phone. He took a long drag and looked over the warehouse's parking lot. The place made him uneasy, and not because of the rusting piles of gutted cars, abandoned shipping crates, and junkyard trash.

The warehouse was too isolated. They were sitting on the interstate with Denver twenty-five miles to the south, Boulder fifteen miles west, and nothing but endless prairie to the east. A single FBI agent was inside the building, watching Doc McKinney sort his way through all those tons of bones. Two weeks ago they'd had three agents working in shifts around the clock, and in about five more minutes, they weren't even going to have the one.

Hell. Dinosaur bones. They were a logistical pain in the ass and the most unlikely method of smuggling any of them had ever seen. They'd had to cut each plaster jacket to see what was inside, and McKinney was refusing to have the fossils moved until they'd finished replastering all of them.

They'd traced the wooden crates back to Seattle, but where the bones inside had come from was a mystery. Old man McKinney predicted it could take months, years, or maybe forever to figure out where the fossils had originated. To top it all off, the old doc had fallen in love with a three-hundred-pound specimen he'd made clear he wasn't going anywhere without.

Hawkins didn't have time to baby-sit either the doc or the bones. As far as Roper Jones knew, Hawkins was still working for him, and he'd been called in for the night shift. Hawkins could use Quinn and Kid right about now, but Quinn's cover as a low-lifer named Jeff Frazier had been blown all to hell, and if Roper had his way, the all-American hero was as good as dead the minute he stepped back inside Denver city limits.

The bones and Quinn—Roper wanted both of them

back, and he wanted them bad, which was why Quinn had been shipped to Cisco with Kid to baby-sit.

Leaving only Skeeter in SDF's Steele Street office.

Hell, Hawkins hadn't even gotten through the last time he'd tried to reach the little nerdzoid. So much for the dashboard-laptop-phone combo that should have connected him to Skeeter's Jeep. It didn't work. His gadgets never worked. Kid said it was because Hawkins let off too much electromagnetic energy, whatever the hell that meant.

Kryptonite, Skeeter had further explained. "You're like raw kryptonite, giving off an interstellar force of exponential power and frying the heartsheath of the laptop's unprotected motherboard."

Sometimes Hawkins wondered if Skeeter's lightbulbs were screwed all the way in.

Alerted by the sound of a metal door opening, he pushed off the wall and flicked his cigarette onto the asphalt.

Special Agent Tom Leeder, a big, burly guy in a dark suit, walked over to him. "Sorry, Hawkins," the FBI agent said, lifting his hands and shrugging in resignation, "but this is it. I'm outta here. If the old man finds anything tonight, let me know, and I'll have agents all over this place."

"Yeah. Thanks." The old man wasn't going to find anything. They'd already cut open all the plaster jackets and come up with nothing. One case of assault rifles, that's all he'd wanted. One frickin' case of OICW prototype assault rifles. Was that too much to ask for a lousy four months' work? With the FBI working from the top down and Steele Street working from the bottom up, they should have found them by now—if the guns had ever actually been slated for an exchange in Denver. Hawkins was beginning to have his doubts.

"We'll have a crew up here from Buckley Air Force Base in the morning to get everything packed up and shipped out."

"Where are the bones being sent?" Maybe with a little bit of the right wheel-greasing, Doc McKinney could still have a chance at his three-hundred-pound fossil. Steele Street owed him that much for dragging him into this.

"Into the abyss of bureaucracy." Leeder flashed him a grin. "An official warehouse someplace where even the guy who loads them off the forklift won't know where they are." Lifting a hand in farewell, the agent turned to leave, then stopped. His expression sobered. "Things are heating up all over. If the cops can get that pimp on Wazee Street to talk, Roper Jones is going to get nailed for killing that whore a few weeks ago. And then the shit's really going to hit the fan. Watch your back."

Hawkins nodded, appreciating the tip even though Leeder's warning was not exactly a news flash. Hell, Hawkins knew the situation was heating up. Roper's primal nerve endings were fraying right down to their synapses over the missing crates. It was a dangerous condition for a guy who was at best a meaner-than-hell sociopathic son of a bitch. The question they hadn't been able to answer was *why*.

Why was Denver's newest crime lord fretting over a bunch of old bones?

As for the pimp, Hawkins knew Benny-Boy Jackman personally, and he didn't care what the cops threatened or promised, Benny-Boy wasn't going to talk. Desiree hadn't been the first girl Benny-Boy had ever lost. She'd just been the first he'd lost to a knife. It hadn't been pretty.

Watch your back. Hawkins's mouth curved in a mocking grin, and he knocked another cigarette out of his pack. He hadn't lived as long as he had and survived two years in the pen without watching his back.

When Leeder drove away, Hawkins glanced back at the metal door and reached for his lighter. He couldn't leave the old man alone, not all night. He'd been watching McKinney for the last two weeks, and the doc's mind wandered...a lot, maybe too much. He didn't drive, either. One of the first things he'd done after showing up at Lafayette was hand over his car keys. There'd been no explanation offered, and Hawkins hadn't asked. Hell, the Porsche the old guy had been driving was Dylan's.

Hawkins pulled his cell phone out of his back pocket and punched in a number. As it rang, he checked his watch. Johnny Ramos should still be at SDF's garage in Commerce City.

"Yo," Ramos answered on the third ring.

"Johnny, it's Hawkins. I need a favor." He could almost see the younger guy's grin come out in full bloom. Johnny "the negotiator" Ramos ought to be his name.

"Sure, Superman," Johnny said, already sounding overly confident.

Superman. "I'm at a warehouse just off the Lafayette exit. How soon can you get here?" He bent his head to the lighter and lit up the cigarette.

"Depends what I'm driving."

Hawkins could have called that one the minute he'd decided to tag Johnny.

"You'll be driving your pickup. I'll need you all night, watching an old man and a dozen crates." He took a drag off the cigarette, before taking it out of his mouth and flicking off the ash.

"Roxanne," Johnny said succinctly, naming his price. "Next Friday night."

Okay, he'd seen it coming, and he might have to bite the bullet—but not without some negotiating of his own.

"Betty's the one you want for Friday-night cruising. All the girls love Betty. Roxanne will just scare them off."

"Not the girl I'm thinking about."

Well, that was actually a little bit alarming. Any girl who wasn't scared off by Roxanne was probably more than a seventeen-year-old boy could handle, even if that seventeen-year-old boy was Johnny Ramos.

"How's school going?"

"I finish classes next week and I'm back at East High in the fall."

"Probation? How's that going?"

"Clean as a whistle," the boy said easily. Maybe too easily. It was hard to give up the cash of a few quick deals, harder yet to stay away from your old buddies in the 'hood.

"You know what I'm getting at, don't you?" Hawkins knew Johnny better than Johnny knew himself, knew what it was like to get a chance to get off the streets, and knew, too, what it was like to screw that chance up.

He also had a fine appreciation for Roxanne. He knew why the boy wanted her.

"Yes, sir."

That sounded more like what Hawkins was looking for.

He rubbed a hand across his brow, thinking, weighing his choices, weighing Johnny. He lowered his hand and absently noted the blue tattoo arcing up the length of his arm. It went from the back of his hand to under his T-shirt, then it tracked across his back and worked down his other arm to just past his wrist.

What he didn't know about misspent youth hadn't been written.

"No racing," he told Johnny, making his decision. "No high-octane even if you're not racing, and no leaving the state."

"Agreed." The boy didn't hesitate, which Hawkins didn't find in the least bit reassuring.

"No track racing. No street racing. No drag racing. No racing your grandmother to the end of the block."

"Dusk to dawn," Johnny vowed.

"Okay," Hawkins said with effort, knowing he didn't have much of a choice. "I'll see you in an hour."

He hung up and shoved the phone back in his pocket,

his gaze going to the Sublime Green low-slung beauty sitting in the hot summer sun, the steam rising around her tires. Roxanne. She was a 1971 Dodge Challenger R/T. He'd bought her a few months ago off a dealer in Naperville, Illinois, who'd only raced her on Sundays, invariably in the low-thirteen-second zone. At Steele Street, he and Skeeter had already knocked another second off that. Roxanne was a verifiable earthbound cruise missile—and he was going to let Johnny Ramos drive her on Friday night.

If he'd needed any more proof of his commitment to Uncle Sam's welfare, he'd just gotten it. No matter how many rules he laid down, Ramos and Roxanne were a combination guaranteed to smoke.

"Skeeter to Superman. Skeeter to Superman," a faint voice came to him from inside Roxanne.

I'll be damned, he thought, pushing off the building and heading over to the car. His laptop gizmo was working.

CHAPTER
7

FEEDING HER HAD BEEN a good idea, Quinn thought, watching Regan pick her way around a hamburger and a plate of fries. She wasn't eating much, but she did have a little color back in her face. The temperature had started dropping with the sun and their ascent into the mountains, so she'd changed out of her wet clothes in the restaurant's bathroom. He couldn't complain. The pale yellow shirt she'd put on was pretty, especially on her, real pretty, with short, lace-edged sleeves and a lace-edged collar. This morning, if anyone had asked him if he'd liked lace, he'd have told them only if it was black, skimpy, and coming off.

Now he was expanding his horizons.

The same went for little buttons. He was ready to prostrate himself at the baptismal font of little pearly buttons like the ones running all the way down the front of her shirt, ready to sacrifice himself on the altar of her mid-thigh-length jean skirt. He'd never gotten so much mileage out of a bag of ice, had never imagined pleasantly erotic possibilities even existed in a five-pound bag of frozen water.

He needed to get over it. Regan McKinney probably hadn't given him a second thought after the Rabbit Valley camp, and the only reason she was with him now was because of Wilson. She'd come to him with a problem, obviously against her better judgment. He made her nervous as hell, and he didn't blame her. The situation they were in made him nervous as hell, too.

He'd caught a couple of her sidelong glances while they'd been driving. He'd noticed every time she'd wrapped her arms around herself, taken a deep breath, and tried to steel herself against the craziness of the day—the slight lifting of her chin, the forced straight-ahead gaze. She'd be good for a few minutes before the façade would start crumbling, before her chest would lift on a heavy sigh and her hand would rise to her hair, trying to tuck in a loose strand here or there. Then she'd take another deep breath, tighten her arms, and start building her defenses all over again.

She was tired. She was scared. She was worried about her grandfather.

She was breaking his heart, and he still thought she was sexy, sitting in a corner booth with a picture-window view of Vail and the valley behind her. He hoped the food would help her relax, maybe make her drowsy enough to doze off. If his driving made her uneasy in broad daylight, rocketing over the mountains in the dark was guaranteed to give her a new religion. He'd offered her wine with her dinner, but hadn't been surprised when she'd turned him down. She was careful. He'd figured that much out, careful with what she said, careful with her buttons, and her clothes, and her modesty, careful with her accusations, too damn careful with the decision she hadn't yet made about what she was going to tell her sister, Nikki—whether to run or stick. So no. Drinking wine in the company of a gun-toting car thief was not a careful thing to do.

He wasn't used to explaining himself, but he needed to explain a few things to her. He needed her to call Nikki, and had figured getting her out of the car for half an hour could only help. God knew she'd needed a break. Jeanette was no Cadillac. She was a beast, and riding in her meant riding hard. By the time they'd reached Vail, Regan had looked like she was coming apart at the seams, so he'd pulled off at Jake's, the first place he'd seen with good food, fast service, and a parking lot in the rear.

"Andy's fries are famous from one end of the valley to the other," he said, watching her push another french fry to the side of her plate.

She looked up. "Andy?" The simplicity of the question couldn't hide her wariness.

Yep, he definitely made her nervous. He was sure she was going over everything in her mind and still couldn't exactly figure out how in the hell she'd ended up with him and Jeanette. Things had moved pretty fast in Cisco.

"Andy 'Jake' Johnson, World Cup downhill racer. He took the Big Three a few years back. Homegrown Colorado boy. He owns this place."

"Jake Johnson." The delicate arches of her eyebrows drew together, her brow furrowing. "I remember him. He's from Boulder. Everyone thought he would take gold in the Olympics. Then he quit the team. You know him?"

"We shared a house in West Vail one winter." He grinned. "Damn near killed me."

Her eyebrows rose, and with good reason. Jake Johnson was notorious for high living, fast women, and the kind of shenanigans that would, and did, land lesser mortals in jail. There had been one incident with an aging movie star's young wife that had been tabloid fodder for weeks.

"Yes, well, that's a pretty fast life," she said, trying to hide her surprise and maybe a little relief. Under normal circumstances, Jake Johnson would probably not be considered much of a character reference. At least not one who would impress her, he was sure.

"The people who live it think so," he said, his grin turning into a wry curve.

"And you don't?"

He shook his head. "Fast is twice the speed of sound above thirty thousand feet."

He watched his words sink in, saw the flicker of understanding cross her face, saw her tension ease, and knew he was on the right track. U.S. military hero was more in her comfort zone. He'd figured as much, but he hated to lead with his trump card in the credential department. His only trump card.

"You drive like a fighter pilot," she said. It didn't sound like a compliment the way she said it, but his grin broadened anyway.

"Yeah, but Jeanette and I have never been shot down." And they hadn't, not ever, not on the streets, not on the track, not in the quarter-mile.

Her head came up, the gray of her eyes bordering on violet as they met his, and for the first time her expression lacked the wariness she'd worn all day.

"You were all over the news," she said, leaning slightly forward, her own predicament suddenly forgotten. "We couldn't believe it at first. That it was you. It was amazing, really, that you survived."

"It was one hell of a ride," he admitted. He didn't mind talking about his last great flying-ace disaster, if it helped her relax a little.

"We read all the stories. Wilson even had the *Newsweek* cover framed. He keeps it in his office at home."

He let out a laugh. "I definitely got my fifteen minutes' worth of fame out of losing a twenty-million-dollar jet."

Her brow furrowed again. "They didn't blame you for what happened, did they? None of the news reports we saw mentioned anything about pilot error."

"No." He reached for his coffee. "The investigation

cleared me of any wrongdoing. The missile had been fired without radar. By the time I knew I'd been targeted, it was too late. The damn thing was only a couple of seconds away from my fuselage. When it hit, the whole plane came apart around me."

"I can't even imagine what it must have been like, to be blown out of the sky." She leaned even closer over the table, her voice softly sympathetic, her gaze darkening with concern—her breasts pushing toward the scoop top of her little lacy shirt. She'd fixed her hair in the bathroom, gotten it all back up in a tidy ponytail, but as she spoke, an errant strand slipped free and fell in a silken curve to her chin.

Something inside Quinn turned over, and it was all he could do not to lean over and take her mouth with his, to slide his fingers up into the silver and gold silk of her hair and bend her into his kiss. He wondered if there was a name for this kind of reaction to a woman. Obsession might cover it. Horny certainly did. When she looked at him all gray-eyed and tenderhearted, like she wanted to take care of him, make it all better, he wanted nothing more than to give her the chance—every chance.

Telling himself to slow down, way down, he stayed put on his side of the table and did no more than hold her gaze. He did have a point he was trying to make, and maybe he better just make it.

"Kid was one of the Marines who dropped behind enemy lines to rescue me," he said.

"The boy wonder?"

A quick grin turned the corner of his mouth. "He was

only eighteen, but I can guarantee you he didn't think of himself as a boy then, and he sure as hell doesn't now. He carried me out of there on his back, under fire. You can trust Kid with Nikki, Regan. He's smart and effective, and one of the most highly trained weapons experts in the world. If protecting her is his mission, somebody would have to kill him to get to her."

Her face paled again at his words. "And you think this Vince Branson is the kind of man who might try to harm my sister?"

"Branson will hurt anybody who gets in his way."

"Because of you and those cars." It was a flat condemnation.

"No." He shook his head, his decision already made. At seven o'clock, he wanted Kid glued to Nikki McKinney, whatever it took. If Roper's goons were on the hunt, there wasn't any room for second guesses. "Because of a load of dinosaur bones I stole off the Burlington Northern."

For a long moment, she just looked at him.

"What?" she finally asked, as if she thought she must have misunderstood him.

"We were looking for stolen goods, but I think there were fossils in the crates."

"Fossils? Stolen goods? What kind of stolen goods? And what do they have to do with my grandfather?"

He could tell by the look on her face that none of what he was saying made sense.

"Some government stuff, very hush-hush. I could tell

you more, but…" He let the sentence trail off with a grin and a lift of his eyebrows.

"Then you'd have to kill me?" She didn't look worried. She looked like she thought he was nuts.

"The stuff we've been looking for was stolen in April, and two weeks ago, we thought we'd found it all on a train in Denver."

"But you ended up with dinosaur bones instead?"

"I think so, yeah. And one of my partners must have asked Wilson for help with the fossils."

"No." She shook her head, adamant. "Impossible. No dinosaur bones came into Denver two weeks ago. No dinosaur bones were scheduled to come to Denver two weeks ago. I would have known."

"You?" Now it was his turn to be surprised. "Why you?"

"I'm a fossil preparator for the Denver Museum of Nature and Science. If there were bones coming into Denver, they would have been coming to us."

Quinn sat back in the booth, intrigued. So that's what she did all day, scraped away at little flecks of rock, millimeter by millimeter, exposing two-hundred-million-year-old skeletons. He had to admit it was a good job for a careful person—and enough to drive anyone else crazy.

"Unless the fossils were being used to pay for a stolen shipment of government goods," he said. "You wouldn't have known about those."

"Dinosaur bones as illegal tender?" She looked extremely doubtful. "It doesn't make sense. Dinosaur fossils, especially unprepared ones, aren't exactly a top black-market item. They can weigh hundreds of pounds, are sometimes nearly impossible to free from the rock, and aren't necessarily worth much except in the scientific sense, unless they're a spectacular or unique find. They're not pre-Columbian pottery. You've seen them. You were there that summer at Rabbit Valley."

"Yeah," he agreed. "I saw a lot of things that summer."

He shouldn't have said it, shouldn't have let a slow grin curve his mouth when he did, but the soft wash of color staining her cheeks was worth it. He'd never seen a prettier shade of pink.

*R*EGAN felt the heat flood her face and would have given anything not to be blushing like a schoolgirl. Anything. Damn him. She'd wondered exactly how much he remembered about the night he'd walked into her tent, and now she knew. Everything. And all of it was showing in his cat-in-the-cream smile.

He was impossible, utterly impossible, with his wild story and wilder Camaro. Dinosaur bones and stolen government goods, and Jeanette and Betty, for crying out loud. She'd never known anyone who named his car, let alone every car he owned. And he was dangerous, unquestionably dangerous. He'd slipped on a shoulder holster and covered it with a denim shirt before entering the restaurant. She was eating dinner with a man carrying a concealed weapon—who had seen her naked.

A second wave of mortification rolled through her, and

she wanted nothing more than to excuse herself, incredibly graciously, and walk away from him and never, ever, have to see him again.

But she still had to find Wilson, and every time Quinn Younger opened his mouth, she knew that no matter how awful the day had become, she'd been right to go to Cisco. If she was honest with herself, she also had to admit the truly awful part of the whole mess was that she remembered plenty about that night, too. Plenty.

Embarrassed enough by her own memories, let alone his, she shifted her gaze from the table to the window and the mountains beyond. He'd been sixteen, pure adolescent renegade, and in her whole life, no one had ever looked at her as hotly as he had that night, standing there in her tent with his lazy, hip-shot stance and heavy-lidded gaze. His T-shirt had been white and clean, his arms hard and browned by the sun, the veins running down his forearms to the backs of his hands readily visible. His eyes had been so green, green fire, and they'd touched her everywhere, licked her skin like a flame, frightening her and exciting her at the same time. It had been better than sex. Better, at least, than any sex she'd ever had—which she well knew was a pitiful comment on her marriage. Her fault, Scott had assured her with his ego and arrogance intact. She just didn't have what it took—whatever the hell that meant. He'd been a little short on particulars.

She probably ought to thank Quinn Younger for being living proof that at one time she had been able to hold a man's attention—except he hadn't been a man yet. He'd been a boy whose threadbare jeans hadn't done nearly enough to hide what she'd done to him. She'd noticed just before he'd turned to walk away, and if he hadn't ducked out of the tent, she might have asked him to stay. Not for sex, she hadn't been ready for sex, but the way he'd looked at her had definitely made her long for a kiss, her first kiss, a French kiss. That's what she'd wanted from him, to feel his arms around her and to look into those impossibly green eyes and taste him, to run her tongue over his oh-so-white teeth and feel his tongue in her mouth. To slide her fingers up into his silky dark hair, to touch his skin and feel his warmth surround her, and maybe to feel safe. Though how she'd thought she'd feel safe with a juvenile car thief doing time with her grandfather was something she'd never quite figured out. When he'd shown up in *People* magazine shortly after her divorce, it had all come back to her, how much she'd longed for the boy he'd been.

Now he was back in her life, and he was pure trouble wrapped around a face she'd been going to bed with every night for the last five years—a situation that made her feel painfully ridiculous. He didn't know, of course, but it didn't matter. Just looking at him made her feel foolish. Physically, he was even stronger, harder, his face still perfect, even with the scar on his cheek and his too-long, mussed-up, windblown hair. Any normal woman would have outgrown her infatuation years ago. But, no, desperate Regan McKinney had clung to hers. What she should have done, she admitted, was take his picture off her closet door a long time ago, instead of letting it become a permanent fixture. Better yet, she should never have put it up in the first place.

Regardless, she'd tracked him down because of Wilson, not out of some timeworn crush. Memories or no memories, she had a responsibility in her current situation, a responsibility she had no intention of forgetting.

Forcing herself to lift her chin, she met his gaze.

"How did my grandfather get involved in this mess? Did you call him?"

He shook his head. "I've been out of action for a couple of weeks. One of my partners must have contacted him."

"Kid?"

"No. Kid's been with me."

"Hiding out in Cisco." Like the outlaw she was sure he still was.

"Laying low," he corrected, flashing her a grin straight off her closet door—all mischief, pure promise, and too damned familiar for comfort.

"Are you still with the Air Force, then?" If he was looking for stolen government goods, it seemed a distinct possibility.

"Not directly, but we're on the same side, and we will find what we're looking for."

Okay, she thought, not precisely appeased by his too careful explanations, but reassured enough to let go of one layer of panic and half a layer of doubt.

"So are you with the CIA or something?"

"No." He reached for his coffee cup.

"FBI?"

He held her gaze and took a drink, but said nothing.

"Secret Service? U.S. Marshals?" She was running out of ideas.

When he still said nothing, she felt herself floundering. "Police? Sheriff's office?" Silence. "The Boy Scouts?"

His grin flashed again. "Nothing that official, but we're behind the motto one hundred percent," he said, putting his cup back on the table.

Okay. So they liked to be prepared. Which meant exactly what? she wondered.

"But you're still one of the good guys?"

"I've always considered 'good' a relative term." When she glared, he laughed and leaned forward over the table. "Yeah," he assured her. "I'm still one of the good guys. Kid's one of the good guys, too, Regan, and I really need you to call Nikki and tell her to let him in and to stick with him."

"Can't you tell me who you *do* work for?" It wasn't too late to warn her sister off—but the thought of Nikki being watched or followed by someone like Vince Branson made Regan very much want to believe in Kid Chaos.

To his credit, Quinn's hesitation was so brief as to be almost imperceptible. "Sure," he said. "It's a company called Steele Street. We deal in cars, mostly rare iron, Mopar muscle, pony cars, street machines. Porsches when we get a line on a good one. Every now and then we put a car on the track."

"So you're a used-car salesman who races the merchandise and tracks down stolen government goods on the side?" She couldn't help it, every ounce of her disbelief ended up in the question.

He laughed, a surprised sound. "Pretty much," he agreed, his grin returning.

Right, she thought.

"So why do I get the feeling you're not telling me much, let alone everything?"

His smile broadened even more. "Because you're a smart lady," he said. "It's one of the first things I noticed about you."

"Before or after I fainted in the barn?" she asked dryly, well aware of a whole day's worth of shortcomings on her part. There was a reason she stayed tucked away safely in her lab. It was safe, quiet, and eminently controllable, just her and some old bones locked in stone. This past year, her grandfather had joined her to coordinate the senior brigade, as they called their older volunteers. Their young and dynamic director, Dr. Houska, was too busy trying to find a *Tyrannosaurus rex* nest in the badlands of Wyoming to spend much time at all in the museum between April and September.

"Way before," Quinn said, the natural mischief in his smile taking on a whole new meaning.

Oh, brother, she thought, feeling her stomach tighten. He was doing it again, thinking about the night in her tent, when he most definitely had not been staring at her intelligence.

"Call Nikki for me, Regan," he said, leaning even closer over the table. His smile faded. "I don't know how you showed up on Branson's radar, but you did, and we need to control the damage. If Kid's with Nikki, she'll be safe. Your only other option is to tell her to run, and that's the last thing I'd want my little sister doing, especially on her own."

He was right. Regan hated it, but he was right. She had to call Nikki. She had to warn her sister about the trouble headed her way.

God, what a mess. Her gaze slid away from his. Suddenly the faintest curve of a smile threatened the corner of her lips.

Nikki wasn't the only one in for a wild night.

Too bad there wasn't anybody to warn the boy wonder.

CHAPTER

8

QUINN'S CELL PHONE rang on their way across Jake's parking lot.

"Quinn," he said, holding the phone to his ear while reaching for the passenger door of the Camaro.

"Kid is more than halfway home, and I've got McKinney with me in a warehouse on the Lafayette exit," Hawkins said. "Where the hell are you?"

"Vail. How's McKinney? All in one piece?" His hand fell away from the door, and he looked up at Regan. The wind had come up, and she was holding her hair back off her face in an intrinsically feminine pose, the soft curve of her arm limned by the sun. Her eyes, gray and intense, were focused on him.

When Hawkins answered "Fine," Quinn gave her the okay sign.

"What's Kid clocking in at?" he asked.

"He isn't saying, but he must have pushed one-forty at least once before he hit Glenwood Springs."

"So there were bones in the crates?"

"Seven tons and nothing else, but don't get any ideas. Dylan wants you out of this, Quinn. Roper Jones is after your head."

"Cisco is no good."

"Then stay at Jake's. You still have a key. Hell, everybody from L.A. to Denver has a key."

Quinn didn't answer, just waited for Hawkins to realize what he'd just said. He didn't have to wait long.

"Hell, even I've got a key. Okay, so Jake's won't work."

"What about Branson? How did he get into this?"

"McKinney is pretty high profile in the dinosaur business, and Roper is missing a bunch of old bones. He must have put two and two together and taken a pretty damn accurate stab in the dark. I had Skeeter do some checking, and the oldest granddaughter is in the dinosaur bone business, too. Given nothing else to work with, following her must have looked like a good bet to Roper."

That was the way Quinn had figured it had all gone down. McKinney was *the* dinosaur man. Anyone looking for missing fossils would have put him on their short list.

"Maybe we ought to start getting our intel from Roper's guys. Their batting average looks a hell of a lot better than ours on this deal."

"Yeah." Hawkins didn't sound any happier about the fact than Quinn did. "Roper's looking for you hard, Quinn, you and the fricking bones, so find a place and hole up. Give me a chance to get this all sorted out, and—"

"Bullshit." The damage was already done. It had been done the minute Regan had pulled into Cisco with Branson on her tail—and now he was back in, all the way in.

Turning away from the car, he stuck his hand in the front pocket of his jeans and dropped his gaze to his boots.

"I'm not holing up anywhere. I'm going hunting," he said into the phone. "Should be good game, if you want to come along." Inside his pocket, he wrapped his fingers around the tracking device Kid had taken off Regan's Taurus hours earlier. A high-tech GP M21, it was the perfect calling card. All he had to do was pick his place, switch it on, and wait.

Somebody was bound to show up.

Hawkins swore, one succinct word. "Dylan's going to have all our heads if something happens to yours."

"Probably." Quinn knew exactly what he was worth to SDF and the rest of the team at Steele Street. He was Dylan's ace up his sleeve, General Grant's national-hero card, something they both could play to put a pretty face on dirty deeds when the feds turned up the heat or some Congressman got his panties in a wad.

Hawkins swore again, and Quinn heard the click of a lighter and Hawkins's quick intake of breath.

"The FBI pulled out this afternoon," Hawkins said, exhaling. "They don't have much use for dinosaur bones."

"Neither do we." Quinn knew Superman wanted

Roper as badly as he did. The bastard was a plague on the streets of Denver, which made the problem personal to a couple of guys who had grown up on those streets. The rest of it, the assault rifles, was a no-brainer. Roper had to be stopped. The terrorist market would inhale Uncle Sam's wonder weapon and turn it back on him from every hovel and unmapped back alley in the Third World. It was time to stop playing undercover cop and start playing bad cop.

"So what do you say we give the bones back to Roper," Hawkins said.

That's exactly what Quinn had been thinking. "I'll stop at Steele Street and pick up one of Kid's trackers." They could set Branson's tracker in the Lafayette warehouse, drawing the bad guys in, and have Kid's tracker already in with the fossils. After that, piece of cake, they'd follow the bones—hopefully right to the assault rifles.

"We've only got tonight," Hawkins told him. "The Air Force is coming in tomorrow morning to ship the bones out."

"Then tonight."

"What are you going to do with the woman?"

"Take her home." He glanced up and found the woman in question watching him—*woman* being the operative word. She wasn't a fifteen-year-old girl anymore, and the longer he was with her, the more intrigued he became with the change and the curious but undeniable fact that she still had a powerful effect on him. He was so *aware* of her, of the way the sunlight and the wind played with her hair, of her whole body, her breath, of the intensity of her gaze and her barely hidden distress.

"You could have sent her with Kid in the first place."

"Could have," he admitted. But he was glad he hadn't.

"The McKinney house might not be the best place to wait this thing out, not until Roper gets his bones back and calls off his dogs."

"Yeah. I've been thinking about having Kid and the women check into the Southern Cross Hotel." He saw her eyebrows rise at the mention of the very expensive resort nestled in the foothills above Boulder. "It's a good safe house, and it keeps both of them out of the way."

"Good idea. I'm on my way to Roper's now. I'll see what I can find out about Branson and the other guy."

"What about Doc McKinney?"

"He's finishing up. Johnny's on his way to take over, and I think I'll have the two of them stay at Steele Street for the night. No sense in keeping all our eggs in one basket."

"Roger," Quinn said.

Hawkins chuckled. "Right." Then he hung up.

Quinn flipped his phone closed and slipped it back in his shirt pocket, his gaze going to Regan.

"My grandfather?" she demanded.

"He's fine, practically down the street from your house, in Lafayette." The big mystery turned out to be no mystery at all, except for whatever reason Doc McKinney had for not checking in with his granddaughters.

"Lafayette?" she repeated, her brow furrowing. Then

she tucked her chin, and her hand slid up to cover her eyes. A soft curse left her mouth. "Lafayette."

"I just confirmed there were fossils in those crates my partners and I took off the Burlington Northern. They're in a warehouse in Lafayette near the interstate."

She nodded and leaned back, resting her hip against Jeanette, her other arm wrapping around her waist. He'd expected her to be relieved, but he wasn't seeing relief.

"We'll be stopping at Steele Street. Your grandfather should be there by the time we hit Denver," he said, continuing to watch her. She'd gone very still. Too still inside her makeshift cocoon.

She didn't answer, and after a moment, he realized she couldn't. She was trying too hard to control whatever emotion had caused her to pull in on herself.

"Hey," he said, moving a step closer and bending his head to better see her face. "Are you okay?"

"Yeah." The lie was barely a whisper. A tremor went through her. He saw it in the brief trembling of her shoulders, in the nervous adjustment of her fingers across her brow. "Yeah. I'm fine. Thanks."

She turned toward the car and reached for the door handle. Her shoulder accidentally brushed against his chest, and the contact brought her to a sudden halt. Her head came up, and their eyes met.

She was close, very close, her scent coming to him on the hot summer air, all overheated woman and soft sweet musk.

Intoxicating.

He found himself breathing deeper just to have more

of her. *Crazy, crazy, crazy*, the word went through his mind. He was certifiable, trying to breathe her in—but, God, he loved the way she smelled. He didn't know what to make of the shadowed expression in her eyes.

"What's wrong?" He reached out and gently took hold of her upper arm.

She hesitated before answering, her gaze dropping. "Nothing. You said you would find him. And you did. Thank you."

Gratitude. It was a hell of a lot better than wariness, but it wasn't even close to what he really wanted from her.

He slid his thumb along the edge of her sleeve, feeling the silken softness of her skin and the texture of lace, and took another step closer.

"Captain Younger, I—"

"Quinn," he corrected her. He was going to kiss her. The least they ought to be was on a first-name basis.

"Quinn," she conceded, making a small dismissive gesture, part shrug, part turn of her hand—but he wasn't about to be dismissed, not yet. "This has been a crazy day. Absolutely crazy, and you haven't exactly made it better, except for actually finding Wilson." She paused, her jaw tightening for an instant. "I just find it hard to believe I drove halfway across the state and back, and he was in Lafayette the whole time. God, things are bad . . . or worse—" She stopped herself short and her hand came back up to cover her face. "I mean, he doesn't seem to think straight all the time anymore, but I can't believe he didn't call or...I don't know what your partner was thinking, to involve an old man in such a..."

Now Quinn did know the answer to that. Dylan was thinking of the win, the best way to win. That's what Dylan did. He won. Every time. It was what made him the best, the absolute best.

"Or those damn cars. I should have known better than to let..."

He'd opened a floodgate, and he let it all wash up against him, all her barely concealed frustrations and worries, and suddenly he got a glimpse into what it was like being Regan McKinney, all practicality and responsibility, taking care of an old man who was losing his grip on reality.

"...and my car, now. Gone."

"I'll have your car back to you by the end of next week," he promised her. "You can drive Betty until then."

"Betty?" Her head finally came up. She'd been mostly talking to his chest and the pavement but he had her attention now.

Women loved Betty. They couldn't help themselves. Hot red leather, all buttery soft, wrapping around them. Hot pink piping to add some flash. A mirror-finish paint job so clean you could put your lipstick on looking in the fender. Whitewalls.

"Betty," he confirmed, bringing his hand up and smoothing his fingers along the curve of her jaw, letting her think about what was going to happen next for a moment, but just a moment, just long enough for her eyes to widen with the knowledge before he lowered his head and opened his mouth over hers.

She let out a soft gasp, which was perfect, and her hand came up to hold on to his waist, which was even better. She might have been thinking of pushing him away, but he didn't think so, and she didn't do it. In fact, it only took about two seconds flat for her to tighten her grip and sigh into his mouth.

God. He knew exactly how she felt. Her lips were as soft as they looked, the inside of her mouth even softer. She tasted like Coca-Cola and heaven. It was amazing, kissing her.

He turned her deeper into the kiss, pressing her back against Jeanette, wild Jeanette who was hot in the summer sun, hot enough to make Regan McKinney melt into his arms. He hadn't expected such a soft giving way, such surrender, and it went straight to his groin in a wave of pleasure so intense, he groaned.

Cupping the back of her head with his hand, he slowly increased his assault on her mouth, delving deeper with long, lazy strokes of his tongue and feeling her response in the subtle tightening of her body.

Sweet Christ. His fantasies had nothing on reality. For all their wonderful, intoxicating crudeness, he didn't spend much time kissing her in his fantasies. In truth, he didn't spend any time kissing her in his fantasies. He always skipped ahead to the good parts.

Big mistake.

Kissing her was a great part, and if they hadn't been standing in a parking lot with bad guys behind them and bad guys ahead of them, he would have slid his hand up to her breasts to feel their weight and softness, knowing it would push them both a little closer to the edge. If it wasn't for Vince Branson and Roper Jones, he would definitely give in to the urge to press his hips against hers, pinning her more solidly to Jeanette, and he would have kept kissing her—kept kissing her until she was too hot to stop.

Even the thought of it made him hard.

Oh, great—He stopped, right then, right there. Stopped and for a few seconds didn't move, not an inch, just tried to catch his breath and find his brains.

She didn't move either, just stood with her mouth on his, her breathing ragged, her body trembling—and he knew they were going to make love. For real, real physically, real soon.

She'd kissed him like she was drowning and he was the rope that could save her. And once was not going to be enough, not when everything he'd ever dreamed of shattered in the reality of having her in his arms with her mouth hot on his, her body moving against him, all curves and softness and need.

The need had surprised him, but he'd felt it as surely as he'd felt her tongue slide along the length of his, as surely as he'd felt her hand clutching at his waist. He had a feeling she'd been just as surprised by her reaction as he'd been.

Gently, because he couldn't resist, he kissed her again, brushing his mouth across hers in a light caress, more of a good-bye than a hello, trying to take them both down one level from being ready to crawl inside each other's pants before he raised his head.

It didn't work. Looking down at her, her face flushed, her mouth wet, feeling her breasts rise and fall against his chest with every breath, he still wanted to get inside her pants. He dipped back down for another taste, then one more before he was actually able to let her go and retreat half a step.

Her eyes fluttered open, her gaze slowly clearing from a slumberous shade of confusion to a thunderstruck, oh-my-god gray. A wash of color rose in her cheeks as she stared at him, suddenly wide-eyed.

"Oh, my God."

He'd second that.

"We have to go," he said, his hand still cupping the back of her neck, his thumb stroking the soft skin behind her ear. "We can't stay here."

"No. Of course not," she said. The color in her face deepened, but her gaze didn't waver from his, not for an instant. She was as transfixed as he was, her pulse racing beneath his hand.

God save him.

"Or maybe we could get a room." The words were out, husky and heartfelt, before he had time to think. He wanted a room, a room with a bed and her naked in it. He wanted the rest of the night and into the morning. He wanted to know what turned her on and the chance to drive her out of her mind, just the chance.

The look on her face said he could do it. She would

come undone for him, completely undone. It was a hell of a temptation, to take her and make her his.

"No." The word was barely a breath of sound, but he heard it loud and clear.

"No?" He slowed the movement of his thumb across her skin, his brows drawing together. What part of what he was feeling wasn't she feeling?

She gave her head a small shake and turned toward Jeanette, her movements jerky, her voice strained. "No, I . . . uh, don't think, well, I . . . uh, I have to call Nikki, and I need to make sure Wilson is okay, and then what about those other guys, Branson and the man with him?" He let her go. There was no need to push. She'd melted for him with a kiss. He could take it from there—take it all the way home. A grin curved his mouth. He was going to like chasing her just fine, little Miss McKinney with her careful buttons and careful job and completely wild kisses.

"Christian Hawkins is checking them out," he reassured her, reaching around and opening the door. "He'll call when he has something."

She whirled back to face him. "Christian Hawkins? That's who you were talking with? The one who went to jail for life?"

"Actually, they only held him a couple of years." Just long enough to change him forever. To change his nineteen-year-old streetwise toughness into pure tempered steel with a razor's edge. Nobody fucked with Christian Hawkins anymore. Nobody fucked with Superman.

"But he murdered a senator's son." The accusation was flat, chiseled in the granite of common knowledge.

That was the damned thing about the media. They were more than happy to splash a man's sins all over page one, but his redemption barely made the paper, especially when someone powerful wanted the truth kept quiet.

"No, he didn't, but not much got printed about his release." And that was an understatement if Quinn had ever heard one.

"He was innocent? Good God." Her hand came up to her mouth, then dropped to the base of her throat. "The papers crucified him."

Quinn would never have used the word *innocent* in connection with Hawkins even before prison, but he hadn't deserved what had happened to him for being a street kid in the wrong place at the wrong time.

"He survived," he said, summing up the salient facts in two words.

"I remember him," she said, her embarrassment momentarily forgotten. "I remember talking with him at Rabbit Valley. *Survivor* is a good word to describe him."

"You spent time with Hawkins?" Son of a bitch. Hawkins had never mentioned talking with Doc McKinney's hot granddaughter.

She nodded. "We were actually together quite a bit. Wilson liked him, put us both on supply crew a number of times. It was hard for him, thinking one of his summer boys had committed murder."

"Yeah," Quinn said absently, imagining it had been

hard, but mostly he was remembering supply crew, the damned elusive supply crew. He'd never gotten assigned to it, not once. Regan and Hawkins had been assigned to practically every one. But what he remembered was Regan sitting in the truck cab with the graduate students, and Hawkins always being in the bed of the pickup, going along as muscle to hump the supplies into the truck.

Now he was wondering how many times Regan had ridden back from town in the bed of the pickup with Hawkins.

Son of a bitch.

"Well, there's a good chance he'll be coming by your house sometime, maybe even tonight. He might need to talk to you, or Wilson again, or catch up with Kid." Damn. He was jealous. What a kick in the ass. It was ridiculous, especially after that kiss. But there it was, because he knew Hawkins, and he knew the effect Superman had on women, especially classy women looking for a dangerous thrill, looking for a walk on the wild side.

Hawkins had given it to more than a few.

Damn.

"Maybe you better warn Nikki she might be having a lot of company tonight," he said, repressing his jealousy.

"Nikki. Right." A faint trace of her blush returned. "I'll call, and maybe you should talk to Kid and tell him..." She stopped in mid-sentence, as if she'd suddenly thought better of what she'd been about to say.

"Tell him?" he prompted.

"Tell him, well..." She hesitated a moment longer.

Her hand came up to brush at a straying tendril of hair. "Well, Nikki kind of has this thing about men, kind of an artistic compulsion thing with her art and . . . men. It's not a personal thing." A pained expression crossed her face, as if she really weren't at all sure it—whatever "it" was—wasn't more personal than she wanted to admit. "Well, just sort of an art thing, something to do with never really knowing her father, I think, and I wouldn't want Kid to get wrapped up in something that might compromise his ability to do his job. I mean, well, he's kind of young and maybe if he was warned, you know, that Nikki can be a handful . . ." Her voice trailed off.

Fascinating, Quinn thought, watching her stumble over her words, trying to explain something that didn't make much sense to him. He wasn't overly concerned.

"So Nikki's an artist?"

"Yes."

"And how old is she now—I'm thinking twenty-one, twenty-two?" He remembered her younger sister had just been a little kid back at Rabbit Valley.

"Twenty-one," she confirmed.

Quinn grinned. "Don't worry. Kid is a pro. There isn't a twenty-one-year-old girl on the planet who could wrap him up in anything he didn't want to be wrapped up in." And Quinn was including silk sheets right along with trouble.

The doubt on her face only made his grin broaden. He thought it was sweet of her to be concerned, sweet and totally illogical. Kid was rock solid, honed by the Corps's finest into an elite combat weapon, trained to think two steps ahead of the enemy while under fire, underwater, and outmanned. Unless an army had declared war on Boulder since this morning, there wasn't anything in northern Colorado Kid couldn't handle, on his own, with one hand tied behind his back.

Absolutely nothing—least of all little Nikki McKinney.

CHAPTER
9

KID WATCHED Skeeter's Jeep drive away from the McKinneys' house before he reached inside the Porsche and lifted a black duffel bag and a pack out of the back seat. Skeeter had done a good job watching the place. Stayed cool. Laid low. Kept the intel flowing between them. If any of Roper's men had shown up, she would have called the police. Now any bad guys would have to deal with him.

Kid slipped the duffel and pack straps over his shoulder, then reached back in for his sport drink and took another look around. The McKinney house was big and old, the first floor built of stone, with a wooden wraparound porch complete with a swing and more windows than he wanted to know about. Four huge spruce trees nearly overwhelmed the place, and years ago some gar-

dener had gone nuts. The yard was a jungle. Kid could
have put a whole platoon in the front alone and nobody
would have ever been the wiser. In the back, beyond the
gazebo, a small stone cottage could barely be seen hidden in the undergrowth.

The garage was detached. There was no fence, and a
stripped-down Jeep was parked in the alley between the
McKinneys' and the brick two-story house behind them.
The vehicle was little more than a roll bar with two seats
and four wheels, but the back was full of stuff, good stuff
from what Kid could see, ropes and climbing gear. From
his position in the driveway, he could just make out the
license plate: SRCHN4U. If Nikki McKinney had company, Skeeter hadn't mentioned it, but she wouldn't
have seen someone arriving from the alley. Or the Jeep
could belong with the brick two-story. Finding out
would be his first order of business.

He looked back to the house and took note of no
fewer than three doors opening to the outside, one of
them French—and that was just on the ground floor.
The upper balconies had at least another two doors
opening out.

A definite challenge if anything started to go down.

Kid finished his drink, and tossed the empty bottle
onto Nadine's floor with all the other junk he hadn't
bothered to clean out of the Porsche lately, including
half the sand in Utah. For fifty bucks, Skeeter would get
her cleaned up, a real bargain. Nobody detailed a car like
Skeeter.

He grabbed the laptop before locking the car's doors

and heading on up to the house. The temperature had been 104 in Cisco, and even at seven o'clock was holding at an easy 99 in Boulder. It was going to be hot all night long. He could tell. Swelteringly hot. A beer and a little ESPN would be a nice break after two weeks of camping out in a barn, but he wasn't going to get either tonight, not as long as he was on his own with two women to watch. Quinn had said he and Regan were about an hour behind him.

Kid didn't know what to think about that. An hour? What the hell had the two of them been up to? Quinn should have been right on his ass the whole way.

The doorbell itself was his first clue that this was not exactly cold-beer-and-ESPN territory. It was a naked angel—a highly detailed, metal-casted, anatomically cor-rect naked *guy* angel with wings spread, tips touching, standing on a fiery sun. The doorbell button was the sun, and it looked hot and molten, the depths of its amber crystal lit from within.

His finger hovered for a second, then two, before he pressed it. From somewhere inside the house, a guy screamed.

Shit! He jerked his hand back. Then he felt like a fool.

Shit. No wonder the old man had left home.

Damn. He grinned and pressed the button again, holding it in.

Yeah, the guy was screaming in there all right, but it wasn't a fearful scream. It was more primal, more like Tarzan, or the sound he'd made the last time he'd lofted himself off a half-pipe on a snowboard.

His grin broadened. Yeah, that's what it sounded like—some bozo doing something really stupid.

The door opened, swinging inward to reveal a woman on the threshold. For another incredibly long second, he didn't take his finger off the button. With the temperature sweltering and the guy screaming away, all he could do was stare. It took another second before he realized his jaw had dropped open.

He shut his mouth and dropped his hand from the doorbell at the same time. Then he spent yet another embarrassingly long moment trying to remember something to say. Something simple like ... like "Hello." It finally came to him, but instead of hello, when he opened his mouth, years of training and mission readiness took over and what came out was "Ma'am."

Worse, immeasurably worse, his voice cracked when he said it. *Geezus.* His voice hadn't cracked since he'd been sixteen.

"Hey," she said, her voice sweet and cool, like liquid silver.

He didn't believe in love at first sight, honest to God, but something really awful and wonderful was happening to him on that porch.

"Nikki McKinney?"

"As charged." She offered her hand, her voice still very liquid and very cool.

She didn't look like her sister, nothing at all like her sister. She couldn't have been over five foot two or a hundred pounds. Her hair was black ... and purple, cut short and spiky. Her eyelashes were black, and long enough to cast shadows at the corners of her eyes.

And her eyes—he swallowed softly—her eyes were the clearest, most crystalline gray he'd ever seen, like river water with sunlight shooting through it.

He suddenly remembered she was holding her hand out, and he finally took it with his own. She had delicate bones, a single silver band around her middle finger, and paint caked into her fingernails, electric blue and glitter green. Her skin was soft, her hand very small inside his, but she was stronger than he'd expected. Her firm grip on his hand was proof of that. He looked back to her face—and swallowed again. God, she was beautiful. Not pretty. Not cute, but freaking fucking beautiful, like a Victoria's Secret model, but without the push-up bra.

Without any bra.

His mouth went a little dry at the realization, and he had to force his gaze back to her face—which was no hardship. She had a smear of electric blue paint on one cheek. He had a serious urge to lick it off, but—God—if he ever once got his tongue on her, it was a pretty sure bet he was going to lick more than her cheek.

"And you would be?" she prompted with just enough amusement in her voice to let him know how long he'd been standing there with his tongue hanging out.

"Kid . . . uh, Peter Chronopolous," he stammered.

"Chronopolous," she said, his name sounding lazily

silken on her tongue. "Also known as Kid Chaos?" One dark, winged brow arched in question.

"As charged," he managed.

"Regan called a little while ago. She said you were coming. She said Grandpa was fine, camping out in Lafayette."

"Yes, ma'am."

Those crystal-gray eyes held his for a long, considering moment. "She said I should be careful with you."

"With me?" People weren't careful *with* him. Some people might be careful *of* him, but not *with* him. That was his job, to be careful with people, to make sure they didn't get killed—except when he was on the other side of the equation, when his job was to make sure someone did get killed.

He was good at both. The best.

"She told me you were a sniper, an ex-Marine with a gun," Nikki McKinney said. "Very dangerous."

Well, hell. He never knew what to expect from civilians, but this was his least favorite response. He wasn't only a sniper.

Who the hell would ever have thought the retrieval operation for a bunch of guns would come to include someone like Nikki McKinney—this incredibly gorgeous, black-Lycra-miniskirted woman wearing a tiny, torn white T-shirt, who was currently short-circuiting his brain and whose hand he'd been holding for far too long—and whose sister had told her he was dangerous. Given the way he'd met Regan McKinney, she could have said worse. Hell, she probably had.

"Actually, ma'am, I'm the least dangerous person with a gun you are ever going to meet." It was the truest truth he knew, and he knew it down to the marrow of his bones. No one had more respect for the killing power of a gun than a Marine sniper.

"She said to let you in." It was a simple statement, but Kid got the feeling the question was still under debate in Nikki McKinney's mind.

"I would appreciate it."

Still she hesitated.

"Sooner rather than later would be better, ma'am."

MA'AM. Nikki wondered if Kid Chronopolous knew how somber he sounded when he called her ma'am. She wondered if he knew how incongruous his frat-boy party looks were with what her sister had said about finding him armed and dangerous with Quinn Younger in Cisco.

He didn't look dangerous, though his duffel bag probably held the gun Regan had warned her he'd be bringing with him. Nikki supposed it only made sense that a sniper would have a gun. She didn't like guns, but neither was she going to make a fuss over it. Regan had been very insistent that she treat Mr. Kid Chaos Chronopolous with a healthy measure of respect. He was wearing a pair of wraparound Oakley sunglasses, and she wondered if his eyes would be dark like his hair, richly dark.

Boy Wonder, Regan had called him, and he was a boy wonder—a wonderful, beautiful boy, a psyche on the cusp in a body fueled by pure testosterone. Perfect. Or at least he looked perfect standing on her front porch. She wouldn't really know until she got him out of his camouflage pants and rumpled blue parrot-printed Hawaiian shirt. It would all have to go, including his scuffed sneakers and black T-shirt, until she had all six feet of him—six feet of warm, smooth skin wrapped around converging layers of ironbound muscle, sinew, and bone—naked and under the lights.

Then she would unwrap him, layer by layer, through her lens and beneath her brush. For model material alone, she decided to let him in.

She loved Regan, but anyone who knew her older sister knew Regan was wound a little tight, especially when it came to her and Wilson. In Regan's view, Grandpa was too old to get anything right and Nikki was too young. Between the two of them, they'd formed a silent pact not to panic every time Regan had a meltdown.

Like last night, when Regan had found the entry on Wilson's desk calendar.

Nikki had stayed cool. Wilson wandered. That's what he did. All summer long. And if he had run off with a woman named Betty, all Nikki had to say about it was "Great."

She wasn't flippant about her grandfather's welfare. He was getting old. He needed a little looking after, but he was far from incompetent. He could handle himself.

When she'd called, Regan had said there was some

kind of trouble, and Nikki didn't doubt it. Trouble was everywhere, expected and unexpected. Her big sister had spent a lifetime building walls around herself to keep the trouble out.

But every wall Nikki had ever tried to build had crumbled, every single one, leaving her naked and un-protected. So she'd long ago learned another way.

"Would you like some iced tea?" she asked, stepping aside, the movement inviting him in. It was still hot, pushing a hundred, and she knew he had to be feeling every degree. She and Travis were melting in the studio.

"Yes, ma'am. I would."

"I have some work to finish up before Regan and Cap-tain Younger get here. There's a small kitchen in the cot-tage, well stocked, if you're hungry."

"Thank you. I made a pretty fast run from Cisco. There wasn't time to stop for...uh...dinner." He'd come to a halt in the entryway, his gaze ricocheting from one corner of the living room to the other, his mouth agape.

"I call it *Narcissus by Night.*"

Kid called it incredible, stunning, and the strangest freaking thing he'd ever seen in a living room. Someone had stretched huge sheets of canvas on the walls and had been painting on them. Someone damned good with a brush, and who had a fixation on men—totally ripped, bare-assed naked men. They were everywhere, each one partially painted, partially composed of line draw-ing, all of them exuding strength and a real out-there sexuality—especially Narcissus, who bore a striking resemblance to the naked angel on the doorbell, from his broken nose to his six-pack abs.

Jesus, Mary, and Joseph—Kid felt like he'd just walked into a cathouse, a tomcat house. The Narcissus guy had one wall all to himself, stretched out on his side along the length of a dark pool with thunderclouds and bolts of lightning all around. He was gazing into the water, just the way old Mrs. Vernon had told the story in tenth grade English, except old Mrs. Vernon hadn't said anything about the guy's hand sliding along his thigh.

There was no doubt what this Narcissus was thinking, or which direction his hand was heading. It made Kid nervous as hell to be looking at him while he was thinking it and getting ready to do it—not the act, but the rawness of the desire behind it. The artist had stripped him bare, filleted him like a fish. The guy was more than naked, spread out there on the wall like that. He was way too hot for himself, sexually desperate—which was more than Kid wanted to know about the guy's problems, and a whole hell of a lot more than old Mrs. Vernon had ever told them.

So who had dreamed up such a masochistic, homoerotic twist on the story?

The answer hit him before the question even finished forming in his mind.

She'd done it. Nikki McKinney.

I call it Narcissus by Night, she'd said. It was her work.

Quinn had said she was an artist, but sweet Christ. He slanted her a look out of the corner of his eye. She didn't look old enough to know anything about what he was seeing on the wall.

And who was the guy?

Kid wouldn't let anyone paint him with that look on his face. Hell, he couldn't even get that look on his face, not on command, not without some serious incentive, like having the woman of his dreams stretched out naked beneath him and the two of them well into the most incredible sex of his life.

Someone like Nikki McKinney ought to do the trick.

The immediate visual he got cleared up the mystery. All he had to do was put her naked in the pool, and suddenly the whole painting made perfect sense—unless the Narcissus guy was gay.

He could only hope.

"It's amazing," he said, telling the truth. Subject matter aside, the walls looked like something out of a museum.

"Thank you."

"So you . . . uh, know all these guys?" He had to ask.

"Not in the biblical sense," she said in passing, throwing him a coolly artless look over her shoulder.

He grinned. He couldn't help himself. Then in the next instant, his grin faded completely away.

She'd walked on by, leading the way through the living room, leaving him to follow behind the black Lycra miniskirt, behind the languid movement of bare feet, bare naked legs, and the smooth rolling motion of her hips, behind the most perfect ass he'd ever seen— perfectly curved, perfectly tight. And he was dying, the awful, wonderful feeling from the porch rearing up again and swamping him in one big crashing wave.

Pure lust had never come so close to dropping him to his knees. Never. He could handle lust, so this had to be something else, but he'd be damned if he was going to put a name to it. He didn't dare. Whatever it was, it didn't relent, not all the way through the dining room, through the kitchen, or across the back porch and out into the yard. It was like a fist around his heart, a cold knot in his stomach.

She kept up a casual, mostly one-sided conversation about the weather. He heard himself agree—*Yes, ma'am, it is definitely hot*—all the time trying to tear his gaze away from the sway of her butt and the little scrap of black cloth trying to cover it—and failing. The only victory he could claim was the struggle he won to keep his hands to himself and his tongue in his mouth; he didn't jump her. Yeah, that was a victory, a pitiful, embarrassing victory.

She made him feel like a hound, and he'd never dogged a woman in his life. He liked to think he was a classier guy than that, smarter—but she was taking him down with every step she took.

They were headed toward the stone cottage he'd noted earlier. With an effort of pure will, he forced himself into sniper mode. He checked out lines of sight and potential weaknesses in the building. On the upside, he didn't find many of the latter. The place was a fortress; the walls looked to be two feet thick at the windows.

Concentrating on the business at hand gave him a bit of a breather, eased up on the tightness in his chest. He started to relax just a little—right up until she opened the cottage door and he followed her inside.

Then all bets were off.

Work, she'd said. She had work to do. He'd seen the living room, seen the doorbell, and he should have been better prepared—but he wasn't. Nothing on earth could have prepared him for Narcissus in the flesh, in the raw, in angel wings.

SRCHN4U. He flashed on the Jeep in the alley and knew he'd just found the person with the ropes and gear, Nikki McKinney's favorite naked guy. The angel definitely looked like he could pull himself up the side of a cliff with just his arms and a solid finger jam.

Kid could do it. He knew what it took, and this guy had it.

Pushing his sunglasses a little more firmly onto his face, he checked out the rest of the studio. The place was a junk jungle: paint junk, camera junk, molds-and-plaster junk, computer junk, easels, frames, and rolls of canvas jammed in every cranny from the floorboards to the rafters. One wall was covered in black-and-white photographic portraits.

But inevitably, his gaze landed back on the angel. It sort of gave him the heebie-jeebies to know he'd practically seen the guy get off on himself. The sunglasses helped a little, like maybe he'd only *half* seen the guy's package.

Right, like if Narcissus turned around he wouldn't be staring right at it.

Geez. He'd grown up in and around Denver and had always heard Boulder girls were the wild ones, but this—this place, these guys everywhere, and Nikki McKinney the reason for all of it. This was really something else.

"Hey, it's looking good, Travis," Nikki said, breezing into the studio.

"Yeah." Without turning around the angel stepped back from where he'd been painting a dark, ragged maelstrom on a canvas backdrop. He tilted his head to one side, studying his work. Shoulder-length blond hair slid over the high arc of one white-feathered wing. "Yeah," he said again. "That's the best eternity-sucking vortex of hell I've ever seen."

Kid had never seen anything like this just-shy-of-six-feet, blond-haired, naked angel with a paintbrush in his hand. He'd never seen a guy wearing nothing but white wings curving higher than his head and draping all the way to the floor, powerful, muscular arcs of feathers and form. He'd never seen a guy with electric blue and glitter green shooting stars painted on his body, with blue and green comets streaking down his legs and across his back—the same electric blue and glitter green paint caked into Nikki McKinney's fingernails. The same blue paint smudged on her cheek.

Damn.

He got turned on just looking at her, and she'd spent the afternoon finger-painting some other guy—not exactly a hit on his top ten sexual fantasies playlist.

Top forty, maybe, but not top ten.

Shit.

It was going to be a long, hot, strange night, and he had a feeling he was going to wish he had some backup before it was through.

CHAPTER 10

*H*OLY MOTHER OF GOD, Regan thought for the millionth time, working hard to keep from constantly looking over at Quinn while he drove. He'd kissed her, slanted his lips over hers, licked the inside of her mouth and consumed her, and she'd gotten wet. Instantly. Just like that.

She couldn't believe it.

Neither would Scott—not that her ex-husband was ever going to find out.

Five years of fantasizing about Captain Younger must have preconditioned her for a response. She couldn't explain it any other way. Five years of dreaming about his kiss, of imagining how it would feel to have his tongue in her mouth and his body pressing into hers, of how he would taste, had cross-wired her sense of reality—and reality had won, hands down.

In her fantasies, she hadn't imagined his mouth being so hot, or that the sheer physical heat of his kiss would wash down her body like a flood tide and make her ache for more. She hadn't known her breath would catch and her heart would race, that her hips would rise toward him and her body would yearn for his, before her mind had even registered the facts, let alone analyzed them and formulated a plan.

She needed to get a grip on her emotions—a highly unlikely occurrence when she was still using everything she had to keep her grip on Jeanette. Though he'd slowed it down considerably, the Camaro was still eating up the highway, coming off the last mountain pass, sliding in and out of the lanes and cruising through the traffic. They were heading for Steele Street and the lights of Denver on the plains below, miles and miles of luminous lights spreading all the way to the horizon.

"So you work for the natural history museum," he said, surprising her out of her thoughts. "With the dinosaur bones. That must be very interesting."

The way he said "very interesting" sounded a little like "drier than dust," but he was obviously too nice to put it quite like that.

Nice? She did a mental double take.

No. *Nice* was not a word she associated with him. Dangerous, devastating, an explosion going off in her life—that's what he was, not "nice."

"It's quiet work, at least on my end of the museum." Nice. My God. The man was carrying a gun. She must be crazy.

"Do you still go out to Rabbit Valley every summer?"

"No. Fieldwork isn't my strong point. I like working with the bones in the lab." She liked it a lot, but had long ago learned that other people seldom shared her boundless enthusiasm for dragging the past up through millions of years of stone. Everyone loved the idea of bone hunting in the wilds of Wyoming or Argentina. Everyone loved the final product, a big dinosaur skeleton mounted in the hall of a museum. But the preparation of the bones, the scraping away of the rock with a dental pick, square inch by square inch, was not most people's idea of excitement.

They were wrong, of course. It was all amazingly exciting, actually riveting, watching the bones unfold from the stone.

"What are you working on now?"

She looked at him again. He was actually starting to sound pretty interested. That he was even attempting conversation was interesting. With Jeanette's low-pitched, rumbling snarl as background noise, there weren't exactly any awkward silences that needed filling. She could hardly hear herself think.

Of course, given the track of her thoughts, that had been a blessing. She'd practically devoured him when he kissed her. The more she thought about it, the more embarrassed she became all over again, which had made it tough for her to come up with anything to say or a good enough reason to say it.

"Slow down" had crossed her mind a few times,

though. So had "Could you pull over and kiss me again, because I really can't believe what your kisses did to me."

She'd kept both thoughts to herself. Played it safe. That's what she was good at, playing it safe.

"Well, we've got the *Seismosaurus* phalanges from New Mexico I've been working on for the last three years."

"Long-term project, huh?" He flashed her a grin. For a moment she forgot all over again that he was dangerous. When he smiled, all she could remember was that not so very long ago he'd been America's hero and one of the fifty most beautiful people in the world.

Good Lord, he'd shaken hands with the President of the United States. What in the world was she doing sitting in a car going ninety miles an hour with him, talking about dinosaur toes?

She took a breath and did it anyway.

"It is taking a while, but the sandstone is like concrete, and there's only so much time I can devote to it. We have a lot of fossils in storage. I don't know if you've been to the museum lately, but the dinosaur exhibit is incredible. Dr. Houska, our curator of paleontology, is a phalanx expert, and he'd like to highlight some of our more spectacular fossils. Of course, what he'd really like to be known for is finding a Cretaceous carnivore's nesting site."

She did a surreptitious check to see if his eyes had glazed over yet. Surprisingly, they hadn't.

"Isn't that what Wilson was always hoping to find at

Rabbit Valley, a *Tyrannosaurus rex* nest, or egg, or a juvenile, or something?"

Regan's eyebrows lifted, her estimation of him skyrocketing, guns and bad guys or no guns and bad guys. Thanks to Spielberg, most people thought of Tyrannosaurus as a Jurassic dinosaur. Quinn seemed to know it belonged to the Cretaceous period.

"Well, yes. It's his dream, actually. I'm surprised you remember." Shocked was more like it.

"I remember everything." He smiled again, albeit a little more wryly. "And not just about that summer. It's how I got through college after almost flunking out of high school. Photographic memory. Of course, by my junior year at CU, I realized I actually had to start learning how things worked together, not just memorize facts."

"You went to school in Boulder?" He was a wellspring of surprises.

"My last two years of undergrad work. I spent the first two at UC Denver."

"And you never came back by the house to say hello?" She didn't know why the thought was so disappointing, but it was.

"We weren't exactly friends," he said with a shrug. "And by then you were married. Scott Hanson, wasn't it?"

"How did you know that?"

"He's still a professor at Boulder, right? In the engineering department. That first semester I was at the university, right after I'd gone to see Wilson, everyone was talking about Dr. Hanson getting married. That he'd left his wife for some really young girl who was barely out of high school."

Regan had been wrong. She hadn't been embarrassed before. She was embarrassed now, shamefully embarrassed. Mortified.

"It took me a while to put it all together," he continued, his tone perfectly normal, perfectly conversational, as if he weren't saying the most awful things. "You getting married that fall, and him getting married that fall. I never would have put the two of you together, but your name came up, and there it was—Professor Hanson was marrying old Doc McKinney's granddaughter. Just so you know, I aced his class. I was the only A he gave that whole semester."

"Congratulations." The word was as stiff and cold as she felt. He wasn't nice. He was despicable.

"All the other students were hoping you'd show up one day, bring him his lunch or something. Even the girls wanted to get a look at the sweet young thing Hanson had snatched out of the cradle. Not me, though. I was glad you never came."

So was she. It would have been horrible to have walked into one of Scott's classes and seen Quinn Younger— her middle-aged husband and the fantasy crush of her youth. It hadn't taken her long to realize she'd made a terrible mistake in marrying Scott—not nearly as long as it had taken her to get out of the marriage. It had all been so stupid and awful, the way he'd treated her like a child instead of a wife, telling her what to do and whom she could see, when she had to be home and what she should wear. He hadn't treated her like a child in bed, though, and given her lack of experience, the whole sex thing had been a disaster right from the very first time to the last.

To be fair, she'd made plenty of mistakes, too. By the time it was over, neither one of them had looked like much of a bargain.

Damn Quinn for dragging up the whole sorry mess. She didn't owe him an explanation, no way in hell, but her pride demanded one.

"Just so *you* know, I was a sophomore in college when I got married, a long way from being fresh out of high school, and whatever problems Scott and his first wife had didn't have anything to do with me. He had filed for the divorce before I ever went out with him, and I never slept with him before our wedding night. Never."

"That's interesting," he said in a tone that all but called her a liar.

"No." She turned angrily in her seat and glared at him. "That's true. Believe me, if I had slept with him, I would never have marri—" She cut herself off and sank back into her seat, so furious she could barely speak.

"Well . . . he *was* old enough to be your father." He turned on his blinker and switched lanes, moving toward an exit ramp. They were still in the mountains, overlooking the city below.

"Which was obviously the whole point of my getting married in the first place," she snapped back. "I was looking for a father figure. I didn't need a rocket scientist or a therapist to tell me that then, and I sure as hell don't need you to tell me that now."

A hundred yards off the exit, he pulled onto a dirt track heading into the trees and turned off the Camaro. After all the roar and rumble, the silence seemed sudden and complete. Slowly, the night sounds intruded. Wind blowing through the pine trees and rustling the leaves on the aspen. The muted sounds of traffic on the highway they'd left to the north.

"Look, I wasn't making a judgment."

"You most certainly were," she fumed.

"I was only—"

"Stop it. Just stop it." She cut him off again, her words sharp-edged with emotion. "You don't know anything about my marriage. Not anything."

"So tell me."

"Go to hell."

GREAT, Quinn thought, sinking back into his seat, both hands draped over the steering wheel. He hadn't meant to make her angry.

Or maybe he had. God knows he'd been angry. It was crazy, but after he'd kissed her and they'd gotten back on the road, he'd started thinking about her husband, a subject he'd thought he'd thrown out of his memory banks years ago. But there they'd been, cruising down I-70, and he'd suddenly gotten an image of old Hanson kissing her like Quinn had just kissed her but without having to stop. That had gotten Quinn pissed off.

Really pissed off.

But he still hadn't meant to bring up the subject—and that was the God's truth.

It had just happened.

"I'm sorry," he said, and wondered if it was true.

Shit. Professor Hanson—he really shouldn't have started thinking about the old buzzard.

"You don't know me. You don't know *anything* about my life." Her voice trembled, and underneath his anger he felt a twinge of alarm. He'd be damned if he wanted to make her cry.

"You're right. I don't." So why did he care so damn much? A thousand other women could have shown up in Cisco that afternoon, and he would have treated them with the utmost professionalism. But Regan McKinney was different and always had been.

A moment later, he heard her gasp.

"*You*," she exclaimed. "It was you."

She swiveled in her seat, staring at him aghast, suddenly not sounding like she was anywhere near to crying.

He had a feeling he knew what was coming.

"*You* stole Scott's car."

"Guilty." He couldn't help it. He grinned. God, he'd been such a moron. He'd stolen Hanson's prize 1966 Mustang. It had been street-punk jerk adolescent revenge. Revenge against Professor Hanson for having what Quinn couldn't have: Regan.

"How could you?" She sounded appalled. "How could you steal his car?"

Somehow, he didn't think she wanted the technical answer.

"He loved that car. It was a classic, totally unique."

"Trophy car," Quinn admitted, turning his gaze on her. "Trophy wife. Did he love you, too?"

Even in the darkened interior, with only the moon to light her face, he saw her blush.

"I am not going to discuss my marriage with you. Not now. Not ever."

"Fine."

Damn it. Eighty-four days—that's how long he'd spent in Wilson's bone beds at Rabbit Valley. Eighty-four of the most important days of his life, even though he'd only been sixteen at the time. Without ever saying a word directly to him, hardly making eye contact, Regan had ruled every one.

She and Wilson had changed him that summer. She'd come and gone a number of times, breaking his heart every time she'd left to go back to Boulder, giving him a thrill every time she'd returned, but Wilson had been a constant presence, always talking and teaching and pushing.

Baking in the hundred-degree heat and digging old bones out of the sun-baked dirt had not been fun, not by any stretch of the imagination. It had been more like torture, punishment for all the bad deeds he'd piled up as the car thief king of Steele Street.

Quinn's motto before that summer had been: If a man could afford a Porsche, he could afford to lose one—or a Mercedes, or a BMW, or a Lincoln . . . or a 1966 Mustang.

As an adolescent he'd actually stolen a lot of cars out of Boulder, he and the guys cruising up to the university town and raiding the streets, culling out the finest machines and racing them back to Steele Street.

Then Steele Street had gotten busted but good by the Denver cops, and all the street rats had run for their lives. Most had gotten away, but the inner core—Quinn, Dylan, Hawkins, Rivera, Prade, and J. T.—they'd gotten their butts landed in the city jail. From jail they'd gone to "juvie," and from "juvie" to court, where Judge Campisano had sold them down the river to Wilson McKinney for his Job Training Partnership program.

A damn fancy title for slave labor, he'd thought at the time. But he would have dug those dinosaur bones out of the ground with his teeth to avoid going to the state penitentiary. It was the first time Quinn had ever been caught, ever actually been picked up by the cops—and he'd known he wanted it to be the absolute last time.

And yet, four years later, he'd still gone after Hanson's pony car.

It could have cost him everything, college and ROTC, his way out, his freedom. But he'd been so cross-eyed angry over the idea of Professor Hanson with Regan. What he'd wanted, he couldn't have, and the rest of it—hell, the rest of it hadn't seemed important in comparison, not right then when he'd been hurting.

"Don't we have someplace we're supposed to be going?" she asked, none too nicely.

"Yeah." They did, but he wasn't ready to leave, not just yet.

He heard her sigh over on her side of the Camaro, a heavy—very heavy—much maligned sigh.

Denver.

It was a good place to be.

Wilson looked out the window of Johnny Ramos's pickup truck and absently nodded his head. The Denver Center for the Performing Arts was all lit up. On the other side of Speer Boulevard, the Auraria Campus was busy with students going to night classes.

He'd lectured there many times over the years and had always received a warm reception.

Denver was good.

Getting away from the warehouse before the Air Force showed up was good.

He twisted around in the seat as best he could and checked the crate he and Johnny had tied down in the bed of the truck. He didn't want the crate careening all over the place, and even though he'd packed it himself and carefully moved it with the forklift, he was worried about it. He didn't want to forget what he was doing with it, with the fossil inside. He didn't want to forget what he'd already learned about it or what he'd found in the surrounding plaster, and he certainly didn't trust the Air Force to ship it off somewhere and take good enough care of it.

He'd heard Hawkins and another guy talking, and he'd known he had to do something. The Air Force certainly hadn't taken good enough care of Quinn Younger, letting him be blown out of the sky like that. He hoped the boy was okay.

He stopped for a minute, stopped thinking and back-tracked a bit. Then it came to him and he remembered. Quinn Younger had been rescued. He was fine, a hero, still friends with Christian Hawkins, who—it turned out—wasn't the cold-blooded murderer he'd been made out to be all those years ago. Both of them worked for Dylan Hart.

He was working for Dylan now, too, and he was sup-posed to tell Dylan everything he found, but Dylan was gone, so he'd told no one. It was important, though, what he'd discovered embedded like riprap in the *Tarbosaurus*'s plaster jacket. It was important and strange, and he needed to remember.

A *Tarbosaurus* nest. *My God*. He had two, maybe three eggs—with embryos!—of the fiercest predator ever to walk the planet, a toothier Mongolian version of North America's *Tyrannosaurus rex*. His young com-petitors were out beating the badlands again, and he, washed-up old Dr. McKinney, had had a fossilized Cretaceous carnivore nest practically dropped right in his lap.

Of course, *Tarbosaurus* was just his first guess. It could be a *Tyrannosaurus*. He needed more comparisons, tests, X rays. He needed Regan with her light touch and her dental pick to clean away the detritus and stone. He needed to get the nest someplace safe and find out where it had come from. Provenance would quickly tell him if it was *Tarbosaurus* or *Tyrannosaurus*. The bureaucratic abyss of a nameless federal warehouse was not a safe place, and the place he and Johnny were supposed to be going, Steele Street, couldn't possibly be safe either.

He remembered it. The bust on Steele Street sixteen years ago had hit all the papers, closed down the city's biggest car theft ring, and netted him most of his first summer work crew.

There was only one place safe enough for a find of this magnitude, and it wasn't too far from where they were heading.

"Turn here," he said to Johnny, pointing left, using his most professorial tone of voice, one no undergraduate had ever dared to gainsay. It had also worked pretty well on a dozen years' worth of juvenile offenders, and as he'd hoped, it worked on this one, too. He knew the look of hard living on the streets, and this kid had it.

The boy cast him a quick sidelong glance, but he made the turn.

"Sir," he started. "Superma—I mean, Hawkins told me to take you to Steele Street tonight."

Yes, he'd heard the orders, but he needed to go someplace else first. He looked back out the windshield. Their next turn was just up ahead.

Johnny Ramos reminded Wilson of Christian Hawkins a little bit. They were both dark-haired, with tall, rangy builds, but for all his machismo, the boy wasn't as hard-edged as Christian. Wilson doubted if he'd ever seen a man with harder edges than Christian. He was all angles and toughness and maybe a streak of mean.

Christian carried a gun, sometimes more than one. He

also had a knife, not a useful knife like a Swiss army knife, but a switchblade, a killing knife, and most of the time he dressed like someone who knew how to use it—someone who *had* used it, with a bandanna tied around his head and wraparound sunglasses, in T-shirts and low-slung jeans and two-hundred-dollar Nike Airs. After Wilson's initial shock at seeing him, he'd recognized enough of the boy he'd once known to be comfortable working with him.

Still, he wished Dylan would return. Wilson wasn't good at keeping secrets, not anymore. He wasn't afraid of accidentally telling someone. What he was afraid of was that the secret would simply drift away.

So many things drifted away from him.

But not the crate. He wasn't going to lose the crate.

"Take the next right."

"Sir—"

"This won't take long," he assured the boy. "We're only going a few miles. You know where City Park is, don't you?"

Johnny gave the old man another long, dubious look.

But he made the right-hand turn.

CHAPTER 11

"Hᴏᴡ ᴡᴏᴜʟᴅ ʏᴏᴜ want to go to hell? Blindfolded or eyes wide open?" Nikki McKinney asked.

Question number 308 by Kid's count.

"Eyes wide open, ma'am," he said, as he finished hauling Travis, in harness and rigging, into the air. He secured the rope to the wall. Travis had said eyes wide open, too, but she'd blindfolded him anyway.

She'd also tied him up, gagged him, and put more paint on him, a hellish concoction of black and red.

It hadn't exactly been the erotic episode Kid had imagined it would be.

She was too intense, too intensely focused on the art. She was a little pushy, and tougher than she looked—and without actually coming out and telling him to back off, she'd made it damn clear that if he was going to be hanging around her studio, watching her, he was going to do it by her rules.

Kid didn't want to actually come out and tell her to back off either. But he hadn't busted his hump getting from Cisco to Boulder so he could spend the night watching Nikki McKinney put a naked guy through hell—literally. She wasn't actually hurting Travis, but she wasn't gentle with him, either. If Kid hadn't been there, Travis would have been at her mercy.

In her case, size was deceiving. She was damned relentless. Wherever she was trying to take Travis, helpless and naked, she was going to get there. For a hundred dollars an hour, Travis was perfectly willing to go.

Maybe Travis had been there before. Nikki had other angel prints and sketches stacked around the walls. Kid figured it was just his own bad luck not to have been called up on a night when she was photographing or drawing a female angel—not that he saw any female angels in her lineup. But watching her finger-paint another woman's body, a naked woman, would have definitely made his top ten sexual fantasies list.

Yeah. A brief grin curved his mouth. Definitely top ten material—unless she'd bound and gagged the woman the way she had Travis. Binding and gagging were for-sure turnoffs in Kid's book. The other angels were all flying free, but she'd definitely headed into some new territory tonight.

He was only going to give her about another ten minutes. He'd done a couple of perimeter checks; everything had looked fine, but he wanted fresh intel, or he wanted out of the house.

So where in the hell were Quinn and the sister? An hour at the most, Quinn had said, and they were kicking that hour in the back. Kid checked his watch. Ten more minutes max, and he was putting in a call.

"Have you been there?" she asked.

"Ma'am?" He looked up to the platform where she stood behind her bank of cameras. Whatever else Nikki McKinney was, she was a bona fide gearhead. A snake pit of cables and cords connected her to the ton of equipment stacked on the platform, and she ran it all from a handheld control board.

Sweet. Very sweet. He was itching to get a better look at her setup, find out who had built it, and probably improve it. That ought to impress her.

Or not.

He'd never met anyone like her. Never even imagined anyone like her. He didn't know what in the hell impressed somebody who painted calendar boys on her living room walls and tied up guys like Travis on Friday nights.

"To hell and back with your eyes wide open," she said.

See, that's what he meant. Who in the hell asked questions like that?

"Yes, ma'am," he answered after a slight hesitation, because to deny it would have been to deny who he was. Still, he had no intention of elaborating.

"And what do you think? Am I close?" She gestured at

the scene she'd created with the backdrop and Travis, with all her ropes and wings and paint and complicated lighting.

He followed the gesture with his eyes, looking the whole thing over, then told her straight-out. "I think you're naive."

Incredibly naive.

"And you're not?" she asked with more curiosity than heat.

"No, ma'am. I'm most definitely not." Long, hot, strange night, all right, he thought. The guys back in the 24th would never believe it.

Without a word, she ducked under the black cloth hanging off the back of the biggest camera and began setting off her show. She had eight versions of the lighting rigged up and went through them one by one, taking what she wanted. With the lights set, she sent some heavy punk rock music blasting through the sound system, four tracks of it all at once, two of them playing backward, fighting it out. Then she started the fans blowing—thank God. They were all drenched in sweat, and he figured she'd done that on purpose just to add another level of misery to Travis's appearance.

He didn't know why the guy did it, not even for a hundred bucks an hour. Double the going rate, Travis had told Kid, but then Nikki asked for a lot.

With the studio lights dimmed, Kid slipped off his sunglasses and stuck them in his shirt pocket.

"Travis," Nikki said from under the cloth. "Whenever you're ready, I'm good to go."

Kid had to give the guy credit. He seemed oblivious to the fact that he was naked, and for someone who had been tied up, blindfolded, gagged, and raised and lowered half a dozen times while she'd finished setting everything up, he was amazingly loose, amazingly calm—until she told him she was good to go.

Then he started changing, slowly and torturously, from a laid-back Boulder slacker dude into a fallen angel being pulled into the eternal sucking vortex of the inferno, lured and beset by the wretched demons flying off the canvas backdrop, bound by hopelessness. It was weird, watching it happen, knowing the guy was faking it and yet believing.

In his real life, Travis had told Kid, he was an EMT with the Boulder County Search and Rescue Squad. Given the pay scale of the job, modeling for Nikki was how he paid the mortgage on his place up the canyon.

Kid hoped to hell Nikki McKinney was getting what she wanted out of him, because this shot—*Geezus*—this shot made the fillet-o'-fish Narcissus pose look like a piece of cake.

Cameras were going off all over the place, at least two of them eating a constant whir of film, and Kid was mesmerized. For the first time since she'd opened the front door of her house, he wasn't focused on her. And as he watched the whole endless ordeal, with the music screeching and screaming and the lights flashing, with the wind blowing hot and acrid and Travis disintegrating in pain and despair, he realized her version of hell was closer to his than he'd thought.

It was the red paint. It looked like blood, as if the angel had been tortured.

Shit. Kid felt his jaw tighten. He was starting to feel a little fucked by her game. Where in the hell was Quinn? It was time to get out of there. He suddenly felt it down to his bones.

*F*ROM beneath her black cloth, Nikki tripped her shutters again and again, over and over, capturing Kid Chronopolous completely. She had five cameras on Travis, who was worth far more than she paid him—and two cameras on the ex-Marine, who was giving her everything for free.

Travis was amazing, and later, she would go through the whole session frame by frame, both video and stills, and print what she needed for the piece of work she had in mind.

But the ex-Marine. She watched him through the zoom on her Nikon, working carefully, breathing softly. She'd thought she'd take a few shots of him, record his reaction, take his portrait for her studio wall, all standard stuff—but there was nothing standard about him. He'd taken his sunglasses off when she'd started the show, and suddenly she was seeing him for the first time, really seeing him, and she couldn't tear her gaze away.

His eyes were dark hazel, bordering on brown with streaks of moss green, and so very serious, so very watchful of everything going on around him.

So very fierce.

It fascinated her, his fierceness, the way the high arch of his cheekbones fascinated her, and the lean angle of his jaw. He had a short nose, which added an incongruous level of cuteness to his chiseled features. His eyebrows were thick, dark lines, his skin flawless, something she seldom saw even in her fashion work. His mouth was wide and firm, and made her wonder how he would taste—and that was the most disconcerting thought she'd had in weeks.

She'd been wrong about getting him out of his clothes. He wasn't one of her college boys, despite the similarity in age, not even close. He was carrying a gun beneath his rumpled Hawaiian shirt, not in his duffel bag as she'd supposed, and his expression was nothing short of a warning to beware. She'd set something off in him, something he didn't like—which was the whole point of the piece, *Pathos VII*. Everybody had their own personal hell.

She pulled back through the lens, bringing more of him into view. No, she thought, he most definitely was not one of her football players, mountain climbers, or starving-art-student models.

Sniper. Bodyguard. She could see those things in him now, the heightened awareness, the physical readiness, and the predatory alertness of his expression. He was tuned for trouble—and he was not to be fooled with, not to be unwrapped for mere artistic indulgence.

Which made her want to do it just that much more. She wanted to paint him, bad, even if she had to do it with his clothes on. It was a curse, her stubborn dedication to artistic impulse—and every impulse she had was telling her to keep him for a while, not to let him go until she'd had a chance to explore him more thoroughly. And that simply fascinated her. She didn't keep anybody, for any reason, for any length of time.

How much trouble could one seventy-two-year-old man have possibly gotten into? she wondered. Wilson had definitely lost a foothold on some of his memory banks, but surely he couldn't have done anything that required armed guards for the house. Nothing that could have required a warrior of Kid Chaos's caliber.

Yet there he was, a warrior in her studio, an avenging angel.

She'd never had one before, but as she watched Kid, she found herself wondering what it would be like to have him.

To really have him.

And that was damned disconcerting.

Idle fantasy was not her realm. She imagined something; she created it. Going around imagining making love with an ex-Marine her sister had sicced on her for the night couldn't be good for her. Actually doing it—with a sniper, for God's sake—could lead to nothing but disaster, no matter how fascinating she found him.

Regan had been so wrong about him. He was no boy wonder, no boy.

He turned then, fixing his hawklike gaze on the Nikon's lens, and fearless Nikki McKinney, who had stripped down and painted over fifty men in her studio and never so much as blinked, felt an electric current of attraction sizzle all the way down from her head to her toes. Her cheeks grew hot, her heart damn near stopped, and she had to look away.

Ho-lee mo-lee. She stepped back from the Nikon and swore under her breath. Then swore again and quickly tripped the shutter, hoping like hell she hadn't missed the shot. Flustered, she forced her concentration back to the video camera she had on Travis.

Damn. Regan had been right about one thing: Trouble was definitely happening, right here, right now.

CHAPTER 12

WE CAN'T STAY here all night," Regan said, sounding incredibly put out by the whole situation and still furiously angry with him.

Quinn didn't blame her, and, no, they couldn't stay parked on this nowhere dirt road under the pine trees all night. He had to stop at Steele Street and then take her to Boulder, where Kid would take over keeping her safe. If everything went according to plan, Roper would have his dinosaur bones back by midnight, and the heat would be off the McKinneys. She could go back to her nice, quiet life, and he could go back to looking for the Pentagon's guns, feeling like he'd just been hit by a cyclone.

Regan McKinney, good God. How in the world had his day come down to arguing in a car with Regan

McKinney? And really being hot under the collar about it?

He let out his own to-hell-and-back sigh and cut his gaze across the Camaro.

"You're wrong," he said, because he believed it. He'd been sitting there thinking it all through, and she was wrong. "I do know you."

He might have been pissed off about the wedding, and freaked out by whom she'd married, but he hadn't risked ending up in the state pen for someone he didn't know.

He might not know the circumstances of her life, or whether or not she liked a *venti* soy chai latte or a fucking double-shot cappuccino.

But he knew her.

"No, you don't," she said in her high-handed tone.

"An eye for an eye," he said.

"What?" She turned and stared at him.

"An eye for an eye," he repeated, reaching for the ignition. "He stole something from me, so I stole something from him."

With a twist of the key, Jeanette roared back to life, the growl starting deep in the engine block and rumbling through the headers.

She instinctively clutched the door handle even though her gaze stayed riveted on him. He was pretty sure Scott Hanson had never stolen so much as a penny piece of bubble gum in his whole life, which left only one thing for her to think he was talking about: her.

"That's . . . that's crazy."

He couldn't argue the point. Stealing the car had been crazy as hell, almost as crazy as giving it back, almost as crazy as caring enough to take the risk in the first place.

"The Mustang was never the same, after it was returned. Wh-what did you do to it?"

"I fixed it up for him."

"Fixed it up?" Her voice rose on a doubtful note. "It wasn't even drivable after it showed back up in our driveway."

"I drove it," he contradicted her. "I drove it a lot. Made about twelve grand racing it around and up at Bandimere that year." Which had covered his costs and then some. Then he'd given it back. Taken the Mustang up to Boulder one morning about two A.M. and parked it in Dr. and Mrs. Hanson's driveway.

She was right. The whole thing had been crazy. Going to so much trouble, all over a girl he hadn't seen since she'd been fifteen.

He hadn't seen her that night either, though there had been lights coming on in their house and every other house on the street as he and Rivera had roared off in Rivera's supercharged Chevy. There was nothing like 375 horses and a set of tuned headers to wake up a neighborhood at two o'clock in the morning.

"Scott's mechanic said it was dangerous to drive the way it had been altered."

"And I bet he offered to buy it and take it off your hands," Quinn said matter-of-factly. He knew mechanics, and there wasn't a gearhead in the world who wouldn't have salivated over the 466-cubic-inch 385-series block he'd dropped into the Mustang along with a Holley Dominator carb and a Hurst shifter. *Altered* didn't begin to cover what he'd done to that car. He'd out-and-out fucked with it, turned a classic pony into a street monster.

Yeah, it had been a lot of engine to handle, but mostly it had been too much engine for old Professor Hanson to handle—and that had been the point, the whole muscle-car metaphor taken to a new low. Not enough balls to drive the car, Prof? Then not enough balls to fuck the girl.

Quinn had wanted to fuck her. He'd wanted to make love to her. He'd wanted to roll over in his bed—just once, please, God—and have her lying next to him, all soft and blond and reaching for him. He'd wanted to take her dirty and take her sweet, take her any way he could get her and every way he could dream up—and in those four years between sixteen and twenty, he'd dreamed up plenty of ways and gotten off on every one.

And now she was here with him, and it was all coming back, how much he'd wanted her.

Hell, he still wanted her, bad, especially since she'd melted all over him back in Jake's parking lot. He wouldn't have given good odds on reality holding up to his fantasies, but the sweetness of her mouth and having her amazing body laminated up against his had definitely blown some of his fuses.

"Well, yes, the mechanic did want to buy the car, but Scott...Scott—" She stopped abruptly on an indrawn breath, then turned away, facing the side window.

He eyed her from across the front seat. Scott had what? he wondered. He knew for a fact that the professor hadn't totaled the car and died in a flaming ball of fire. Professor Hanson was still listed as faculty at the university. Maybe he'd only crashed, maybe just broken both his legs and been crippled for life.

"Scott what?" he asked aloud. Hell, he had enough sins and misdemeanors on his conscience without adding getting her husband hurt.

"I can't believe you stole his car," she said, her voice shaking again. "I really can't believe you stole his car because of me."

In the next second, she pushed on the handle and swung the door open, scrambling outside before he could grab her.

Shit. He jerked on the parking brake and leaped out his own side, ready to give chase.

But she hadn't gone far enough to need chasing. She was only a few feet away, one arm wrapped around her waist, the other covering her face in what he now recognized as the Regan McKinney classic pose of distress. He figured he ought to be ashamed of himself, and he was. They said no bad deed went unpunished, and eleven years after he'd stolen Scott Hanson's Mustang, the chickens had finally come home to roost. And after what had to be six of the most hellacious hours of her life, he was afraid he might have finally made her cry.

She looked very small, standing in a pool of moonlight and shadows with Douglas firs towering up on both sides. The road he'd followed into the trees had petered out into little more than an overgrown track, and farther up, he could tell even that disappeared beneath a covering of pine needles. They were definitely on a road going nowhere.

"I'm sorry," he said, approaching her. "I'm sorry about the car. Are you okay?" God, he seemed to be asking her that a lot today.

The night was growing cooler. A mountain wind blew through the trees, soughing through leaves and pine boughs, while Jeanette rumbled softly in the background.

Then he heard her laugh, a short, breathless sound of disbelief, but definitely more of a laugh than a sob.

"You stole Scott's Mustang." She suddenly turned and looked at him, dropping her hand to her side. "You turned it into one of your muscle cars. Drove it around for the better part of a year. Raced it at Bandimere Speedway, for the love of God. And then just dropped it off in the driveway in the middle of the night?"

Yeah, that pretty much summed up the whole episode.

"Because of me?"

Before he could say anything, she threw her hands up and stalked back to the car. She didn't get inside, though. She sat back against Jeanette's hood, her arms crossed over her chest, and stared at him with an utterly perplexed gaze, her eyebrows furrowed above her dark gray eyes.

"He had everybody looking for that car, every cop on the Front Range, and you drove it around right under his

nose without getting caught?" She let out another disbelieving laugh. "What are you, the Shadow or something?"

"No," he said, walking over to her. She was a little
jumpy, and if she got it in her head to dash off again, he
wanted to be ready to catch her. "I'm just careful, maybe
a little lucky. So what did Scott do with the Mustang?"
He really did want to know. After all these years, and
despite thinking Scott Hanson had been nothing but a
dirty old man for marrying a nineteen-year-old girl, he
hated to think the guy had gotten himself hurt driving
the car.

She gave her head a short shake. "In the end, he did
sell it. He didn't want to, but he couldn't even get the
damn thing out of the driveway without killing half the
neighbors." Her hand came back up to cover her face on
a soft curse. "He always said I'd ruined his life, and
you . . . you just had to go and prove him right."

Now they were getting somewhere, he thought,
though he didn't think much of where they were going.

"Nineteen-year-old girls don't ruin forty-year-old
men's lives," he told her flat out. "Forty-year-old men do
that all on their own."

She shook her head behind her hand. "He was only
thirty-eight."

"Twice your age."

She looked up. "Which still doesn't explain why you
stole his car. Why you really stole his car."

Why he'd really stolen her husband's car? He wasn't
sure he could explain it any more than he had. He'd
been twenty years old, with a sappy, romantic dream in

his heart and a chip on his shoulder—and she'd been in the middle of all of it.

"Knee-jerk reaction," he offered. "I've stolen a lot of cars."

"How many?" The wind picked up, dropping the temperature another few degrees, and he saw her shiver.

"Close to a hundred, I suppose," he said, shrugging out of his denim shirt and closing the final distance between them.

"And you never got caught?"

"Just the once," he reminded her with a brief grin, putting his shirt around her shoulders. He straightened the front to cover her better, then didn't let go.

Her gaze slid away from his, her mouth tightening, and she started to push by him, but he still didn't let go of her. He didn't dare.

Damn it.

"Hanson got to sleep with you, and I didn't," he said, his own jaw a little tight. "So I stole his car." It was as blunt a confession as he'd ever made to anyone, and there wasn't a damn thing about making it that made him happy.

She went very still between him and the Camaro, her head still down. All he could see was her hair and ponytail and the bright flash of her yellow shirt in the opening of his denim shirt.

"You were jealous?"

To put it mildly. "Yes."

They were very close, her head barely reaching his

shoulders, his shirt falling almost to her knees. He could feel every breath she took, feel the hesitation in her.

"You never even spoke to me that summer."

"Yeah." He knew it, and in about thirty more seconds, he was going to start feeling like a real idiot. He'd fallen hopelessly in love with her at sixteen, and for all his cool and street bravado, hadn't had the guts even to say hello. Even in retrospect, it was an unnerving assessment. "Look, I'm sorry if stealing the car made anything hard for you, if it made your life difficult."

"He was pretty upset," she admitted.

"The Mustang was the last car I ever stole." He just wanted her to know. "And it sure as hell was the only one I ever gave back."

"Guilty conscience?" She looked up, her eyes meeting his. Her expression was unreadable, part wariness, maybe, part curiosity, but her mouth looked soft in the moonlight, and it struck him how very, very easy it would be to kiss her again.

"A little," he confessed, "and a little bit just growing up." There was more, but he wasn't about to tell her that making love with the flag girl up at Bandimere in the backseat had sort of cured him of his sexual obsession with the Mustang and her. After he'd smoked the competition in a 10.7-second quarter-mile run, he and the girl had spent half the night in the car, steaming up the windows. By the time they were done, he was done with the car. The girl's name had been Lindsay, and she'd been beautiful, blond, and stacked. In the darkened backseat of the Mustang she'd looked just enough like Regan to suit his needs. And if she hadn't been using him as much as he'd been using her, he might have felt guilty about never calling her.

"Scott would be the first to say you'd gotten the better part of the deal," she said, her gaze slipping away from his.

"Scott's a fool."

"Maybe," she conceded. "Or maybe you should have kept the car."

No way in hell. The only way he would have kept the car was if it had been her in the backseat. Then he would have enshrined the damn thing.

But it hadn't been her. It hadn't been Regan McKinney with her smart mouth and her lofty opinions, and her oh-so-intellectual discussions with the graduate students. She'd used words he'd never even heard of, and each and every one of those words had come out of the most beautiful, take-me-now mouth he'd ever seen. She'd been so blond—the curves, the hair, the eyes, the cheekbones—everything about her so ditzo gorgeous, and then she'd opened her mouth and out had come words like *Saurischia* and *Ornithischia, placental mammal* and *multituberculates*. He'd sat down and listened to her lecture on the cladistic system of biological taxonomy, and he'd fallen in love.

He'd always been smart. Smart enough to steal cars, stay out of jail, and keep from using any drug that was going to use him—but she'd inspired him to do better.

When he'd finally gotten to college, engineering and aeronautics had grabbed him a lot harder than paleontology, but he'd known it wasn't the particulars that were important. It was the education. A guy couldn't be a dumb-ass car thief and walk off with a girl like Regan McKinney.

The trouble was that by the time he'd gotten a little education under his belt, it was too late. She'd already walked off with Dr. Hanson.

But not anymore. Hanson was long gone—which just left him and the definitive object of half a lifetime's unrequited affection alone in the dark on a dead-end road in the middle of the woods.

It was enough to make a guy think.

Jeanette didn't have a backseat, but on a night like this, they didn't need one, not really, not for what he had in mind.

You are so fucking crazy, he told himself, even as he tightened his hold on the denim shirt and pulled her closer. It was crazy to kiss her after making her so mad. Crazy to kiss her after confessing how much he'd wanted her. He didn't have the high ground here, no tactical advantage, no good reason on earth to kiss her, except for the low ache in his body that could only be relieved by getting close to her—really close. He wanted to get inside her, even if it was just a little bit, even if it was just his tongue in her mouth.

He couldn't just hand her over to Kid and walk away.

He pulled on the shirt until her hips came up against his. Then he backed her up against the car, and all thoughts of advantages, tactical or otherwise, disappeared. He held her dark-eyed gaze, and heat coiled low in his belly. Better part of the deal, his ass. If Hanson had made her think that, then the man had been worse than a fool.

She was more beautiful as a woman than she'd ever been as a girl, the angles of her face more delicately carved, not so softly rounded, her body even more lush. He let his gaze drift over her face, memorizing every curve. When his attention settled on her mouth, she knew it. He felt her soften, heard the slight intake of her breath. Whatever else was going on between them, however angry she'd been with him before, she wanted his kiss as much as he wanted hers.

She wanted to get inside him, too.

Well, she could have him any way she wanted him, and if she ran out of ideas, he had enough for both of them.

Pulling her even closer, tighter to him, he lowered his head and took her mouth, slanting his lips across hers and seeking entrance with his tongue. Her response was immediate, a soft gasp of pleasure, and he took the kiss home, slipping inside and finding his own piece of heaven. God, she was so sweet.

Her hands came up around his neck, her fingers tangling through his hair, and he opened his mouth wider, taking more of her—and knew a single kiss wasn't going to be enough.

Her mouth was made for love, for kissing and making love, so soft and lush and enticingly erotic. She moved against him, her breasts pressing against his chest, her mouth angling over his and creating a brief moment of suction, and as quickly as that, heat shot to his groin. He felt his control slip, a quick jerk of it out from under him.

Suction opened up a whole new field of possibilities, one he was more than happy to play in. In his fantasies, she loved going down on him, couldn't get enough of him, and it was always incredible. He'd imagined it a thousand times, her head in his lap, her blond hair draped like silk across his thighs and belly, her mouth on him, driving him wild, and him returning the favor.

But her kiss . . . God, tonight her kiss was enough to undo him. They'd barely begun, and he was already primed to take her to the edge. She made a sound in the back of her throat, the kind of sound guaranteed to focus a man's attention and get him hard, and his body heeded the call in spades. She felt so good.

Instinct slid his hands up under her shirt, one smooth sweep of his palms up to her bra, and for a second she stopped breathing. He rubbed his thumbs across her nipples, making them hard and feeling the wonderful, soft weight of her breasts in his hands and the amazing texture of lace over silken skin. She groaned in his mouth.

The sound shot through him like wildfire. *Geezus.* It couldn't be this easy. Not to see her for all these years and then just have her fall into his arms—but it was easy, and nothing had ever felt more right.

He knew lust, and it was running hot through his veins, but there was something more. Something beyond the burning ache he felt for her. Something fiercer, with an edge of desperation he was trying to ignore and could barely comprehend. If it was love, he didn't want it. He'd given up loving her a long time ago. The emotion had been too demoralizing, too defeating, too god-awful naive, and it had made him a little crazy.

Kissing her was making him crazy. Her mouth was hot and wet and had gone from sweet to demanding. She wanted more, and he obliged, gently sucking on her tongue, setting a rhythm he matched with his hips. If she'd had any doubts before, she knew now what he wanted from her: everything.

R*EGAN* was drowning. Drowning in desire and confusion—and desire kept winning, every second, every heartbeat. She wasn't proud of it. She should be made of sterner stuff. She was so angry with him for stealing Scott's car, for passing judgment on her marriage, for even daring to have an opinion on what she and Scott had tried and failed to make between them— and despite his having found Wilson, she was angry with the whole mess that had dragged her to Cisco.

But what he was doing with his mouth made anger a slippery commodity. The taste and smell of him made a hash out of her righteous indignation. Who wanted to be right, when she could be kissed?

She'd lasted all of 0.5 seconds when he'd looked at her mouth, but had truly been lost the minute he'd said he'd stolen the Mustang because Scott had gotten to sleep with her and he hadn't. Through all those strained encounters and halfhearted standoffs of her marriage bed, Quinn Younger had wanted her. He'd wanted her like this: passionately, his tongue halfway down her throat, his hands all over her, his breathing ragged. No rules and nobody in control. They were outside on a dirt road, for the love of God, and she could hear traffic going by on the highway below.

The realization added a dark thrill to the whole heart-stopping experience of having Quinn make love to her mouth. She didn't know what else to call what he was doing. It was more than a kiss, more than any kiss she'd ever been given, except for the one he'd given her at Jake's. The slow, deliberate sucking on her tongue was meant without doubt to make her think of a far more intimate act.

And she was—shamelessly. The feel of him in her mouth, the taste of him, was intoxicating, dizzying. He set her on fire with his kiss, made her gasp, and every inch of her wanted more. It was crazy. Crazy and hot and utterly sexual in a way she'd thought she would never know except in her fantasies—but the reality of it, *God*, the reality of it was so much more intense, the silkiness of his hair sliding through her fingers, the rough edge of his jaw beneath her palm, the strength of his arms wrapped around her. In her fantasies, everything was safe. She was in charge. With him, nothing was safe. The pure physical energy of him was a force to be reckoned with. He was powerful, dangerous, and unpredictably seductive. She didn't know what was going to happen next—but she should have.

He slid his hand up under her skirt, and a moment's

panic stirred in her veins—too late. He had been unerring, his hand moving between her legs, where he cupped her with his palm—and at that point he knew as well as she just how much she wanted him.

She was slightly mortified, but too aroused to pull away, especially when his fingers slowly slid beneath her underwear and began moving over her so very, very gently. The kiss came to a sudden, heart-catching stop, leaving both of them standing so very still, breathing into each other's mouths, hardly daring to move.

People fall in love for this, Regan thought through the haze of her arousal. They fall in love with a person who can give them so much pleasure. She was entranced by it, by the sheer eroticism of Quinn's touch and her own physically wanton response.

"God, you are so soft," he murmured against her lips. "So beautiful."

His words worked like a magic elixir poured over her senses, and she knew the touch of his hand would not be enough, would never be enough. She wanted him the way she had him in her most carnal fantasies. She wanted him filling her up, driving her to the pinnacle of release. She wanted him to make her feel more like a woman than she ever had with Scott—and if he couldn't give her everything, she still wanted him.

God, she wasn't even sure she liked him. He was wild. He was practically a stranger. He drove too fast and lived on the edge, and his work was a mystery, a dangerous mystery that had already caused her a boatload of trouble. But the connection they were sharing, the seduction—for all its raw power and reckless disregard for even her most dearly held rules of safe comportment, it felt like a gift, like the most precious of gifts, her rules be damned. He was the haven and the storm. She'd wanted his kiss forever, and now she wanted more.

QUINN felt the last ounce of tension drain from her body, felt her soften against him in a thousand yearning ways, and he knew the battle had been won, if there had even been a battle. She was like honey, wild honey, the kind that drove men mad—and she was his for the taking.

The truth put a fierce edge on his desire. Breaking off the kiss, but holding her where she stood, he leaned over and reached inside the passenger window. A quick rap on the dash popped the glove compartment open. "Be prepared" was one helluva motto, but when he found what he wanted, he knew he'd mostly been damn lucky.

"No surprises, Regan." His voice was husky as he held up a packet of condoms. "I want to be inside you and feel you come all over me."

"No surprises?" she said softly, her hands slipping up under his T-shirt as her gaze slid away from his. "Well, then, I, uh, usually don't. Not really, and I know this can be . . . upsetting . . . for a man, but I want to be with you, Quinn." Her confession was barely a whisper, and it was with obvious effort that she lifted her eyes back up to meet his. "I really do. When you kiss me, I . . ."

Get hot. She didn't have to say it. He knew. He got hot, too, when they kissed, really hot.

She was blushing again. He could tell, even in the silvery glow of the moonlight. She didn't come with a man inside her? She'd all but said her sex life with her husband hadn't been good, but that was pitiful—but neither did it matter, not really, not tonight. If she didn't come with him inside her, he'd try something else. He wanted her to get off on him. He wanted her sweating, and moaning, and *his*, and if one thing didn't work, they'd go to the next—and he'd make damn sure she loved every minute of it.

Holding her gaze steadily with his own, he gently rubbed his thumb across her mouth and said, "Maybe I can help." Then he leaned down and licked her lips.

It wasn't a kiss. He simply got her wet, ran his tongue over her like she was ice cream melting on a hot summer day. Then he moved to her jawline, her throat, across her collarbone, and all the while he was pushing her shirt up under her arms, exposing her breasts. When he got to her nipple with his tongue, she stiffened on a gasp, and when he covered her with his mouth and began to suck, she melted back onto Jeanette.

He could feel the Camaro rumbling through both of them. It was as erotic as hell, but not nearly as erotic as having Regan in his mouth. The lace of her bra was incredibly delicate. He could feel it disintegrating, almost melting away beneath his tongue and the gentle suction of his mouth.

God, he wondered if her panties would do the same, if he could literally lick them off her.

He slid his hands up under her skirt again, cupping her bottom and lifting her onto the hood. Stepping between her legs, he pulled her against his crotch, seating her firmly against him, and reached for his belt. He needed some relief; he needed her.

When her hands came down to help, he let her take over and moved back up to caress her breasts and take her mouth in another soul-shattering kiss.

Oh, yeah, this was how it was supposed to be—her small hands working his belt buckle, unbuttoning his jeans. Her fingers pulling the tab on his zipper, grazing his erection, every move she made turning him on and winding him up tighter.

When she pushed his pants down low on his hips and took him in her hand with languorous, rhythmic strokes, he groaned with the pure, mindless pleasure of it. Sliding his hand back up between her legs, he returned the favor, playing with her ever so gently, teasing her and exploring. It was heaven.

She'd been wet all day, with sweat and melting ice, but this is what he'd wanted, her soft folds slick and swollen, her most primal response all in readiness for him—all because he was touching her. He'd known they would be good together. He'd known it even at sixteen. But he'd be damned if he'd ever thought there would be a chance to prove it.

"Quinn," she whispered, her mouth moving over his face, leaving a trail of kisses. "Oh, Quinn." Her voice was soft, her words nearly lost in the purring rumble of Jeanette's low growl.

Working her panties off with one hand, he threw them inside the Camaro. Then he sheathed himself with the condom. When he entered her, she sighed in his ear, a sweet, shuddering sigh, as if at long last she, too, was coming home. He thrust, and she clung to him. She was warm and loving, and whispering in his ear—soft words and his name, over and over, like a litany of her most secret desires.

It was erotic, and arousing, and strangely unnerving. *Oh, God*, he thought, wary as hell, but so turned on he couldn't stop—*please don't let me fall in love*. This was sex, wonderful sex with a beautiful woman he'd wanted since time had begun, and he had to have it. This was sex like breathing, but he didn't need love.

He just needed sex, and the soft catch of her breath. He just needed the fullness of her breasts pillowed against his chest, his hands hot on her bare bottom and hot between her legs, taking her higher and higher with each of his thrusts. She was going to come for him. He could feel it in the tightening of her legs around his waist, in the arch of her back, in the straining grasp of her hands on his upper arms. She was reaching...reaching, her breath coming in short, ragged pants. When her release hit, it hit him like a riptide, dragging him under on a wave of intense, searing pleasure as she contracted around him. He jerked against her, deepening their contact, burying himself to the hilt inside her, and he came, endlessly, pouring into her, until he was drained.

It was all he'd wanted.

All he'd ever wanted. He found her mouth and took it with a long, lazy, devouring kiss, his heart racing like a freight train, his breath coming hard, the soft, ambient ripples of her orgasm playing over him like the sweetest torture.

Easing her down onto Jeanette, he bared her shoulder and pressed another kiss to her skin. Then he kissed her neck, and her cheek, and her eyebrows. She was beautiful, so beautiful, her body hot beneath his, still pulsing with the pleasure he'd given her.

And Jeanette—good God—she was like the world's biggest vibrator. How could he never have thought to make love on the hood with 383 cubic inches of pure power rumbling in idle beneath him?

Regan stirred, and he quieted her with another kiss.

"Shh," he murmured, stroking her with his hands, long, gentle sweeps from her waist and up over her breasts. "Don't move. Not yet."

Her lashes rose, revealing the gaze of a slumberously satisfied woman, and heat coiled in his groin.

Ten minutes, he thought, leaning down over her, running his tongue over her skin, ten more minutes—or, God, maybe five, or one—and he'd be ready to go again. He loved the way she smelled, the way she tasted. Her skin was so soft, silken, everything he'd ever dreamed it would be.

"Shh." He kept kissing her—and thinking Scott Hanson must have been the most sexually inept man on the planet. God, she'd come for him, effortlessly, like a wave coming to shore.

When she ran her foot up the back of his leg, he slipped free of her long enough to do away with her skirt and change condoms. Then he started making love to her all over again, unbuttoning her shirt and undoing the front closure on the bra he'd practically devoured, getting her naked.

This was his fantasy, having her spread out before him, the perfect picture of bare breasts and smooth skin. She didn't have a tan line on her, just one creamy curve after another, starting with her shoulders and going all the way down to the silky calf he held wrapped around his waist. He'd been here before—sated and yet still horny for her. It happened all the time in his little daydreams.

But this was real, and the combination of coming down from a world-class rush while simultaneously getting turned on to take another ride was mind-blowing. He was afraid that just like in his fantasies, he wasn't really going to get enough of her—and suddenly, there it was again, that fine edge of desperation he didn't want to think about. He toed out of his boots and pushed his jeans and underwear to the ground. Then he pulled his T-shirt off over his head and slipped back inside her.

Perfect. She was so perfect, like silk around him. This time they took it slow, which in no way lessened the intensity. They both ended up sprawled on top of Jeanette, the engine growling, and him ready to howl, and when she came, he didn't stop. He just kept pumping into her, letting her ride her high for as long as they both could take it.

Geezus. He collapsed on his side when it was over. He kept one arm around her, holding her to him. He'd snapped one of Jeanette's windshield wipers clean off the hood and was holding it in his other hand. Regan's bra was missing—or so he thought until he noticed it was hanging from his wrist by a single silky strap—but her shirt was still half on, draping off her left arm, a handful of yellow lace trailing across Jeanette's black steel. The logistics of her clothing situation were beyond him. He just hoped to hell they hadn't lost her skirt.

"Quinn," she said softly, smiling at him, an utterly lazy, satisfied smile that appeared almost to take more effort than she could muster, and he grinned back. What fun she was, he thought, sliding his hand over her hip and rolling her toward him. She flowed into his arms, her leg coming up between his. What incredible fun, the kind of deep-down, frisson-up-your-spine kind of fun he hadn't had in a long time—or maybe ever, not like this.

His hand stilled in its absent caress, his gaze sliding over her. She was so lovely.

Slowly, he moved his thumb along the curve of her hip. He didn't think he'd ever used the word *lovely* in his life, but she was lovely, so lovely it made his chest tight.

"Regan." He whispered her name, and she opened her eyes again, a drift of dark lashes rising, and the tightness in his chest got worse.

He was going down—hard. Just like he had in his F-16.

But, God, the landing this time—the landing this time was so incredibly soft. Her eyes darkened as he watched, her mouth parted, and he leaned down and pressed his lips to hers. The rest of his body had given out, but they could still share a kiss.

It wasn't going to be enough. Nothing they did would ever be enough. No wonder he felt a little desperate. He was never going to get his fill of her.

Never.

CHAPTER 13

As soon as the shoot was over and Travis was safely back on the ground, Kid Chaos had slipped outside the studio—much to Nikki's relief. She wasn't used to having her heart race just because a man looked at her—but she'd never had anybody look at her the way the ex-Marine had.

She hoped to hell she'd gotten it on film.

God, he was such a piece of work, and she meant that in the nicest, most wonderful way. She *was* going to paint him.

She was *not* going to get involved with him—if the opportunity even arose. That was crazy. She didn't know a thing about him, except he was the complete opposite of everything she had ever known. A warrior. Not a gridiron warrior, or an MBA shark, but the real thing, a soldier who had put his life on the line for what he believed in. God, country—she wasn't sure. Her parents had done it for Incan ruins in the Peruvian highlands, and she'd always thought they'd paid too high a price for what they believed in. Or maybe it had been she and Regan who had paid too high a price.

Damn, she wished Regan and Wilson were home, where they belonged, instead of out running around, getting into trouble with a bunch of stolen dinosaur bones, which by all rights shouldn't have had a thing to do with them. It was so unlike either one of them, but especially Regan. Nikki was the one who pushed boundaries, who lived a little on the edge. She was the one with the wild teenage years behind her, not Regan.

"The guy's got a gun, Nikki," Travis said, wiping off the last of the paint before slipping on his shorts. "Do you want me to stick around?"

She looked up from where she was taking film out of the cameras. She wasn't surprised Travis had seen Kid's pistol. He'd probably noticed it before she had.

"No . . . uh, he's a friend of Regan's, in some kind of law enforcement. She'll be home pretty quick. She just asked him to stop by and check on me. You know how careful she is." It was sweet of Travis to offer to stay, but if she was going to get any work done the rest of the night, the last thing she needed was two caged wolves prowling around her studio. One was more than enough.

"Too careful," Travis agreed with a rueful grin, walking over and helping himself to a bottle of water from the refrigerator. He liked older women, and he had a definite thing for Regan, who so far had managed to resist his repeated offers to sexually reimprint her. It was his own New Age specialty.

Regan had been horrified at how much her baby sister had revealed to Travis about Regan's less than satisfactory marriage—but not nearly as horrified as she would be if she ever found out how Nikki had gotten Travis psyched for the Narcissus painting. Somewhere up the canyon, tacked on the wall in a hand-built and only half finished cabin full of climbing gear and skis, was a life-size poster of her sister in her morning dishabille—her hair tousled and backlit by the sun, her silky sleep-shirt falling off one shoulder, way off, the hem hiked up to reveal the perfect curve of her derriere and a pair of sheer lavender panties.

Oh, the wonders of a zoom lens and a sister prone to falling asleep on the sunporch while reading the Sunday funnies.

The whole panty thing had really worked for Travis.

Nikki was shameless. She'd be the first to admit it, but she'd gotten what she wanted, and it was the Narcissus piece that had gotten her a showing in September at the Toussi Gallery in Denver, one of the city's most exclusive art galleries and a guaranteed stepping-stone to L.A. and New York. She wanted *Pathos VII* finished for the show.

"Okay, then, if he's a friend of Regan's. You've got my number," Travis said, walking toward the back door. "There's a meteor shower tonight. I'll be up till dawn, so don't hesitate to call, if the mood strikes."

The look he slanted her from across the studio said he didn't care if the mood struck her or not; if there was trouble, she better damn well call.

Nikki blew him a kiss and watched him walk out. As soon as he closed the door, she furrowed her brow. Damn. She was getting a lot of rescue offers tonight. At some point, a girl had to start wondering if she might actually need to take somebody up on one.

THEY were fucked.

Standing by the pool table in the back room of the Jack O' Nines Club in downtown Denver, Hawkins didn't so much as alter his breathing or raise his eyelids. He didn't so much as blink or let his lips twitch. But with every word Roper Jones spoke, he knew they were fucked.

Vince Branson and Gunnar Linberg, the two guys who had tailed Regan McKinney to Cisco, had called Denver to report that their quarry had taken off with a man in a black 1969 Camaro, and one of Roper's home-boys had connected the car to Quinn.

Jeanette had given him up.

Roper now knew it had been Quinn in Cisco, Quinn whom Regan McKinney had gone running off to find. The dinosaur lady had run to the man who had stolen Roper Jones's bones, which brought Hawkins to the really awful news: Nikki McKinney sitting in the McKinney house in Boulder. Suddenly, she was Roper's prime target for getting back what was his.

Hawkins had to get her and Kid out of that house, and in order to do that, he had to get out of the Jack O' Nines. A quick *adiós* and walking out the door was not an option, especially with Roper's rottweilers hauling their ugly asses to their feet. Neither was flipping open his cell phone and making a quick call. Which left him doing a lightning-quick search for Plan C.

"Cristo," Roper called out from where he was sitting eating his dinner across the room, and Hawkins scratched Plan C.

It was time to rumble.

"Yo." He stepped forward, loose and ready, his attention totally focused on Roper and the dogs. If he went down, he was taking all three of them with him.

"Kevin says he saw this Camaro at a garage up in Commerce City. You're a Commerce City boy. Go with Kevin here. Check the place out. Bring me what you find, and if Younger's there, bring me his head." A broad grin split Roper's face. "You think you can handle that?"

"No problem."

Roper's grin hardened into a cruel curve. "Yeah, that's what I like about you, Cristo. You're the guy with no problems. *No problemas. Verdad?*"

Hawkins shrugged, not at all sure which direction the conversation was going. Probably straight to hell like the rest of the night—but so far he was one hundred percent behind Roper's plan, minus the ten percent about Quinn's head.

"Yeah, you bring me his head, but I still want it attached. *Comprende?* I want to talk to the fucker before I feed him to my boys. If he's not there, you stay put until you hear from me. I don't want him slipping through any holes."

From anyone else, the threats might have been euphemistic. But Roper didn't deal in euphemisms. When he said head, he meant just the head, and when he said feed somebody to the boys, he was talking about the rotties.

Quinn should have stayed in Cisco and shot it out with Vince and Gunnar. With Kid on his side, they could have easily won the gunfight, and then Roper would be wondering where his guys were, instead of getting all excited about killing Quinn himself.

"Yes, sir. I'll keep him in one piece." *And you can bet the fucking bank on it, asshole.*

"Yeah, you do that." Roper narrowed his gaze and pointed with the knife he was using to cut his steak. "You do that for me, Cristo, and I'll do something for you. Now get outta here."

Roper dismissed him with a jerk of his head, and Hawkins gave Kevin a heads-up on his way by. A clean and fast getaway, that's what he wanted, before Roper decided to send a third guy along on this joyride. Checking out a garage that was probably empty didn't have to be a full-blown gang bang. Hawkins appreciated the fact and wanted to keep it as low-key as possible, just a couple of guys cruising up to Commerce City to loot the place and stake it out for the night.

Of course, in his plan, only one of them was actually

going to know where they were. The other one was going
to be out cold.

Outside the Jack O' Nines on Seventeenth Street, the
traffic had slowed down from rush hour and the city was
settling in for the night shift. Bars were busy, restaurants
were gearing up for dinner, and shops were shutting
down. A few blocks south, Hawkins could see the Denver Center for the Performing Arts all lit up. He'd been
there four months ago for *La Traviata* with the cochair
of the Denver Opera Guild, a very classy lady named
Vanessa Sattler, who was still leaving messages on his answering machine. The gig with Roper had effectively
sidetracked their relationship. Hawkins didn't mix business with pleasure. When he was undercover, he stayed
undercover, and he doubted if Vanessa would let "Cristo"
park her car, let alone do what he'd done to her after
he'd taken her home.

A quick grin curved his lips. Yeah, he knew why she
kept calling.

"Man, that was sick," Kevin said, having to hustle to
keep up. "Did you see that knife, man? That's one cold
son of a bitch, to do that whore up on Wazee and then
eat his fucking steak with the same fucking knife."

"Yeah, that was rough, man, real rough," Hawkins said.
And that was no lie.

He led the way down the nearest alley to a nondescript late-model Buick known affectionately as Sheila.
She was solid, no flash, built to run, topping out at one-
twenty, and one in a long line of similar Sheilas. Steele
Street traded their Sheilas out every year. The big muscle

cars like Jeanette and Roxanne were too damned distinc-
tive to drive around when a guy was trying to maintain a
low profile. A point just proved in the Jack O' Nines.

Hawkins slipped in behind Sheila's steering wheel and
leaned over to get a pack of cigarettes out of the glove
compartment. Right on cue, Kevin got in the passenger
side, and in one smooth move, Hawkins coldcocked him
right between the eyes with his elbow, then reached over
and slammed the passenger door shut.

Kevin slumped down in his seat.

Hell. The kid was about as sharp as a button.

Sheila purred like a big cat when Hawkins fired her up
and started down the alley. With one hand on the wheel,
he knocked a cigarette out of the pack with the other,
then tossed the pack on the dash and flipped open his
cell phone.

The first call was a speed dial to Kid.

The second was to Quinn.

CHAPTER 14

FIVE MINUTES.

It had been five minutes since Hawkins had called. Five minutes since Kid had told Nikki McKinney to grab what she needed, they were heading out.

And she was still in the bathroom.

What in the hell could she be doing in a bathroom for five minutes?

As a sergeant in the United States Marine Corps, when he'd said move out, men had *moved out*.

She was—what? What was she doing? He didn't have a clue. The shower wasn't running. The toilet had flushed about a minute after she'd closed the door. He didn't begrudge her use of the latrine—not much, anyway—but the other four minutes were pressing him hard.

Too damn hard.

He'd asked her twice to hurry things up, and twice she'd called out "Okay."

But it wasn't okay. She was still in there.

He stopped his pacing in front of Narcissus in the living room and looked up the stairs. A line of light shone from under the bathroom door.

With a soft curse, he took the stairs three at time. His M40 and extra ammo were in the duffel bag slung over his shoulder. He had a short shotgun in his hand and his pistol holstered under his arm. He was ready to rumble, and she was . . . what?

He didn't have a clue.

A sharp rap on the door announced his presence. "Ma'am. Ms. McKinney. We have to leave *now*."

Hawkins had called right after Travis had left. Kid had still been outside, and everything had looked fine—but that had been over five fucking minutes ago. If Nikki McKinney had been a man, he would have cut this scene real short about four and a half minutes back.

"It's open."

Open? What in the hell did that mean? Was he supposed to just walk in?

He didn't second-guess it any more than that. He didn't have time. He wanted out of the house with her in tow. Roper Jones had identified Quinn leaving Cisco with Regan McKinney. Or rather, Roper had identified Jeanette. Either way, that left Nikki as the most accessible target—and he'd be damned if he'd let Roper Jones get ahold of her. No fucking way.

Opening the door, he stepped inside and stopped cold. *Sweet Jesus.* No wonder she was taking so long. The bathroom looked like a grenade had gone off in it, a grenade full of little tiny bottles and underwear. Bras of every shade and shape were hung on every available rod, dowel, doorknob, and window latch, each with a matching pair of underwear. Panty hose were draped over the showerhead like skinny water snakes. A thousand doodad makeup thingies were piled on every flat surface and in boxes on the floor.

The floor!

Geezus. He couldn't even find the toilet. Then he spotted it in the corner. The tank was covered with a beaded scarf and set with an artistic display of fat candles and fresh flowers.

He wanted to tell her right then and there that her grandfather was never going to come home, because a man couldn't live in a bathroom like this. A man needed clean surfaces. A man wanted his bathroom to smell like nothing. Hers smelled like a combination cinnamon pastry shop and flower stall, with a side of fruit salad.

"I can't find my cherry lip gloss," she said.

No shit, he thought.

"Don't ever tell my sister I let you in here," she went on, sorting through a silver box full of lipstick tubes and tiny containers. "She doesn't like the guys I work with to come in here and see her underwear, but she's always hand-washing everything."

Hand-washing. Right. Kid gave the bras another look, then slanted a glance at Nikki's chest, confirming what she'd said. No way were those her bras. The cups were full-size, and she was definitely half-pint.

She didn't have to worry. The last thing he was likely to do was tell Regan McKinney that he'd stood in her bathroom ogling her underwear. But, criminy, she had a lot of it, every color imaginable and then some, every piece made of lace and silk, a whole lot of it sheer, as in see-through.

Oh, man, Quinn. You're a goner, he thought, beginning to get an idea of what might be taking the captain so long.

Turning back to Nikki, he took hold of her arm and started hustling her out of the bathroom. "Take the whole box," he said. "We're outta here."

"But . . . but I don't have— What's that?" She balked, pulling back, and he nearly upended her down the stairs.

"What?" He looked back. She was staring at the gun in his other hand, the one he'd locked and loaded while he was waiting for her to get her things. "It's a shotgun." Specifically, it was a pistol-gripped Mossberg 12-gauge Cruiser 500 shotgun, but he really didn't think she wanted to know all that.

Or maybe she did. The expression on her face was pretty much a mystery to him.

"What's wrong with your other gun? The one under your shirt?"

O-kay, he thought, wondering what in the world she was really talking about.

"Nothing," he said. "Every single firearm I own is in perfect working order." He could A-1 guarantee it, but she was still staring at the Mossberg like it might spontaneously explode.

He gave the gun a quick glance.

"I think I've changed my mind about—"

"No, you haven't," he interrupted, all of a sudden getting the picture. As long as everything had been on her terms and on her turf, she'd been fine with the Marine invasion. But the tables had turned now, and he was in charge—and instead of having a discreet pistol tucked under his shirt like a television cop, he was carrying a much bigger gun that looked exactly like what it was: a serious, close-quarters, get-the-fuck-out-of-my-way man-killer.

"Yes, I have, and I'm not—"

If there was one thing Kid was *not* in the mood to hear, it was what she *wasn't* going to do.

"Look," he interrupted her again. "I am here for one reason, to keep you alive—and if there's only one thing you can count on tonight, it's that I'm damn well going to do it. If it will make you feel better, you can call your sister as soon as we're in the car, but *this* is a done deal."

His ultimatum delivered, he had a powerful urge to do the caveman thing, just pick her up, throw her over his shoulder, and clear out. It was the quickest way he could think of to get her out of the house—and to get his hand on her butt.

Shit. He had to stop thinking like that.

He'd always considered himself one of the best, one of the very best, but the whole "girl" thing with her was making him stupid. Maybe if he just kissed her, he could get on with the job.

He looked at her mouth—and instantly knew that was just another shit-for-brains idea. One kiss was not going to be enough.

"Come on," he said, dragging her along behind him. At the front door, he killed all the lights and waited for his eyes to adjust.

"I thought we were in a hurry," she whispered, standing next to him. She was still holding on to her little box of doodads and had a cloth purse thrown over her shoulder.

"We are," he said, scanning the yard and the street, and remembering what he'd thought about hiding a platoon in the shrubbery. "When I say go, we're heading straight for the car." He didn't see anything, and the clock was ticking in his head.

Five minutes.

Shit.

He scanned the area one last time, then made his move.

"Go." They slipped outside, and he kept pace with her, searching the area as they ran, looking for targets. When they made the Porsche, he stood by the passenger door until she was inside.

He'd loaded his personal gear during the interminable five-minute bathroom break Nikki had taken, so once he dropped into the driver's seat, they were good to go.

Or so he thought.

"Oh, geez." She let out a short gasp and turned in her seat. "What's that?"

He'd unzipped his duffel bag between them and pulled the stock of his M40 up and out, readying it for an easy grab. The whole operation had taken him about three seconds—just long enough, apparently, to freak her out.

"My sniper rifle," he answered. He turned Nadine's key and fired up her engine. Glancing over his shoulder, he reversed out of the driveway.

"Just how in the hell many guns do you have?" she asked incredulously.

He met her gaze for one piercing moment.

"Enough." It was a guarantee.

Jamming the Porsche into first gear, he took off, and a block from the house, he turned onto a cross street. He hit his lights just before he merged into the Friday night traffic. Finally, thank God, they were outta there.

As a last precaution, he checked the safety on the pistol-gripped Mossberg and eased it into a scabbard behind the passenger seat. If he needed it, he wouldn't have to reach far to get it.

CHAPTER

15

STEELE STREET didn't look anything like Regan had imagined. She'd expected a car lot full of cars, some of which they probably couldn't sell on their best day, the ones that looked like Jeanette. But there were no cars. There wasn't even a car lot.

Steele Street was an iron door in a dark alley in a bad part of town, with no sign, except for the numbers 738 above the door, and an ancient freight elevator that crawled up the side of the old brick building like a vertical catwalk, its steel beams exposed. Quinn had driven Jeanette right into the elevator cage and onto the lift platform, after keying in a code. The gears ground and the cables groaned as the lift started up and began hauling the car to the seventh floor. Quinn was still inside the Camaro, talking to Skeeter via the laptop, but Regan had gotten out and was watching the night skyline of Denver come into view against the mountains as the freight cage rose higher and higher.

While they'd still been in the woods, trying to find their clothes, Hawkins had called. Quinn was to ditch Jeanette and not go to the McKinney house; Roper was on the prowl.

Nikki had called shortly after—very shortly after— and told Regan she was on her way to the Southern Cross Hotel with a perfect specimen of male pulchritude and no paints, thank you very much. Oh, and by the way, did Regan know he was a walking arsenal?

Other than her expected distaste about the guns, Nikki sounded to be in good shape, which Regan found very reassuring. The part about male pulchritude was a bit unnerving. Yes, Kid Chaos had been relatively good-looking and—the clincher—in very good physical condition.

Regan just hoped Kid had enough sense to keep his clothes on. Being painted by Nikki was *never* what most of her first-time models thought it was going to be. Nicole Alana McKinney put those boys through the wringer. She was demanding and pushy, and operated strictly by her own rules, which was certainly what had gotten her where she was in her career, on the verge of her first major show. Regan had never condoned naked men as an appropriate subject matter, especially when Nikki had first started at the ripe young age of sixteen. If Regan could have convinced her little sister to paint flowers, landscapes, or just about anything else instead, she would have. God knows, she'd tried.

The freight elevator screeched and shuddered over a particularly rough spot, and she braced her hand on Jeanette's rear spoiler. From through the car windows, she could hear Quinn still talking to Skeeter. His voice was deep and sure, and just hearing it made her feel all funny inside.

She must be out of her ever-loving mind. In fact, she was sure of it. She felt awkward, and uncertain, and yet still connected to Quinn, this man she'd all but absorbed through her pores on the hood of his car.

Oh, geez, it sounded worse every time she thought about it.

Maybe she'd just snapped from the pressure and completely lost her mind. It happened. Her friend Suzie had just snapped one day and run off with a bronc rider she'd met in a cowboy bar, leaving a perfectly good lawyer boyfriend in the dust. Five months later, Suzie and the cowboy were still on the professional rodeo circuit, living out of the back of his pickup truck and a string of cheap motel rooms, and by all accounts, still madly in love.

The last two weeks of searching for and worrying about Wilson had been difficult for Regan, extremely distressing, and the whole day today had just been one disaster after another. She could have snapped just like Suzie had snapped.

But despite the boots, Quinn was no cowboy, and if she'd just snapped, maybe she should have just snapped years ago. One hour on the hood of Quinn's Camaro had been a more emotionally involving, sexually intimate experience than the whole six years she'd spent in Scott's bed. God, she'd been so clueless. She'd had no idea what she'd really been missing. She'd thought the world had stopped while they'd been making love on that mountaintop, outside, naked, and completely lost to decency and decorum.

It had stopped for her, and she still wasn't ready for it to start back up. But it had, beginning with Hawkins's phone call.

She was a jumble of emotions, riding up the old elevator. Her sexual state had rather suddenly and unexpectedly gone from a coma into overdrive, with a man who was practically a stranger even if she had been nursing a crush on him for close to fifteen years, a situation she wasn't even close to sorting out on such short notice. Meanwhile, in a few minutes, she'd finally have Wilson back. She needed to be careful not to throttle him before she had a chance to cry all over him.

"It's about fifteen minutes of elevator ride to the top," Quinn said, coming around the side of Jeanette.

She'd heard him get out of the car, heard the door shut, but still felt a rush run through her when he came and stood next to her.

"I can't believe you'd drive a hundred and twenty miles an hour to get from Cisco to Denver, and then spend fifteen minutes to get from the street to the seventh floor," she said, grateful that she didn't sound half as breathless as she felt. He wreaked havoc on her. There was no doubt about it.

He grinned. "There's another elevator on the other side of the building. It'll get you there in sixty seconds flat, but..." His voice trailed off as he moved in closer and wrapped his arms around her, drawing her into his embrace. "But once we get to the seventh floor, we'll have company."

His mouth came down on hers, softly and gently, as he sucked on her lips and slipped his tongue in her mouth. Then he opened his mouth wider and lightly grazed her with his teeth.

"I've been wanting to do that since we got back in the car." His voice was rough with emotion, his words searing her heart.

She knew exactly what he meant. She'd wanted to kiss him again, too, be close to him again...have him inside her again.

"I *really* want to take you upstairs, lock all the doors, and throw away the keys." His hands moved over her back underneath the T-shirt she was wearing, his WEATHERPROOF T-shirt. The only other thing she had on was her skirt. Her panties had been lost, and her bra had been, well...eaten, just enough that wearing it felt slightly more indecent than just going without.

"I'd like that." She met his gaze, and what she saw made her feel like she was on the edge of a precipice. His hands slid down her torso, his thumbs grazing the sides of her breasts, and Regan felt it starting all over again. A deep thrill coursed through her body and settled between her legs—and he knew it. She could see it in the smoldering green depths of his eyes.

A guy could die from this, Quinn thought, taken aback by what he saw reflected in her gaze—a hunger as deep as his own—*just up and die from making love to her and forgetting to eat or sleep until there was nothing left of him.*

"Are you okay? From before?" he asked, bringing one hand up and tunneling it through her hair. Whatever had been holding her ponytail in place, they'd lost it, and her hair was all down around her shoulders, windblown and falling through his fingers, soft and silky. She was wearing his shirt and a skirt and nothing else. Once he'd gotten her out of her clothes, she hadn't been nearly so careful about them.

He liked that. He liked it a lot.

"Yes." A wash of color stained her cheeks. "Are you?"

He grinned at that.

"Yeah. I'm fine." He loved the way she blushed.

Fourteen minutes max, he thought, wondering if he could make it good for her in fourteen minutes. Sometimes slow was good. Sometimes fast was even better. But knowing exactly what she didn't have on under her skirt was enough to derail his decision-making process straight into the "fast is better" column. Fast was certainly better than letting her go and doing without. Way better than that.

Fourteen minutes. It wasn't much, but it was enough,

if a woman was willing—and she looked very willing, her lips softly parted, her gaze drifting from his mouth, to his chest, and back to his eyes, telegraphing the simple fact that she wasn't going anywhere without him.

He reached for his belt buckle and saw her eyes widen slightly, then darken, heard the little catch in her breath.

That was it, that little catch. She did it every time they crossed the invisible threshold from maybe into definitely, and it was like lighting tinder into flame. Every cell in his body responded to that little catch in her breath. It was amazing. Profound. Absolutely irresistible. If she was going to catch her breath, he was going to take her all the way and back again.

With his other hand, he reached into his back pocket and pulled out his last condom. Sticking it between his teeth, he tore the top off the package and held it up between them. Despite her willingness, he wasn't sure what she'd do with his offer.

A shy, slightly embarrassed smile curved her lips as she took it out of his hand. "Thank you, for . . . um, opening it," she said so very politely, not quite meeting his gaze.

He laughed—thank *you*—looked once at the wall, then leaned down to kiss her and went back to undoing his pants. Her response was to melt into his arms and kiss him back, a real soul kiss, as if there were no way on earth for her to get enough of him, either.

The elevator, he'd noted, was just sliding past the large white numeral 2 painted onto the wall.

"We've got five floors to make this happen, sweetheart," he told her between kisses, his voice growing rougher as the kisses got wetter and deeper and a little more frantic. Finally, his pants were open and he was free.

"Five floors, honey. Come on," he urged, lifting her against the Camaro and leaning into her, holding her while she took care of him. She was sweet and gentle, rolling the prophylactic down on him, kind of tucking him into it, and she absolutely set him on fire.

When she was finally finished, and he was sweating bullets, he pushed up inside her, and, oh, God, she felt good. So good, her legs wrapping around him, holding him tight against her.

Sliding one hand up through her hair, he tilted her head back, baring her throat for the track of his tongue up to her mouth. He ran his nose down the side of hers, loving the softness of her skin, the feel of her breath against his cheek, and he reminded himself to breathe with her.

She started to move down on him, and he pressed deeper up into her, giving her more of himself. It was an exquisite sensation, entering a woman, always, every time he'd ever done it, but with Regan... God, making love to her was incredible.

He stopped after his first few thrusts, just stopped and held himself still, dropping his head on her shoulder and trying to catch his breath. He needed a minute just to hold her, just to fill her up and fill himself with her scent and her softness. She was wrapped in his arms. He was buried deep between her thighs, and he still didn't feel close enough to her. Whatever he was after with her, whatever it was going to take, he was afraid it might drive him crazy before he got it.

"Quinn," she gasped his name, and it was like a benediction. He loved hearing her say his name when he was inside her.

Lifting his head, he met and held her gaze. She was so lush, her skin so smooth. As he watched, a sigh shuddered through her and her lashes drifted closed.

Bands of light and shadows slid down across her face as the elevator rose higher and higher, the bars on the freight cage bisecting the light from the street lamps. Her cheeks were flushed, her mouth free from lipstick, but still ripe and full, and softly pink.

He knew what she tasted like now, and it was better than he'd imagined. A man would never, could never, get his mouth on anything softer or more gut-wrenchingly addictive than a woman. He'd never felt the truth of it more than with Regan McKinney. Next time, he promised himself, they were going to do this in a bed, and he was going to taste the rest of her.

Oh, yeah. Just the thought of having her with his tongue and mouth was enough to shoot his temperature up a couple of degrees and make his next thrust a foregone conclusion.

"Quinn," she whispered his name again in a soft, shuddering sigh, moving against him, needing more.

He felt it, too, the heat building between them, the long seconds dragging out, the tension winding up. He thrust once more, and she groaned. There was too much he wanted to do with her, and not nearly enough time to do it all—but this was good, *very* good, trying to stay still, dying a little inside and letting her kiss his neck and throat, her hands sliding up under his shirt and then sliding back down, way down, pressing against his buttocks. She wasn't big enough to make him give her what she wanted, to move him, except in the was-it-good-for-you kind of way. She moved him like that. Moved him real good, hard and deep right down to his core.

"Please . . . Quinn," she murmured, her words pleading, her breath hot against his skin. "Please . . . please."

That's what she said, but what he heard was far more succinct and a hundred times more crude. He knew exactly what she wanted, exactly what she wanted him to please, please, please do.

Please fuck me, Quinn—that's what she meant. That's what she wanted, and, finally, when he couldn't hold himself back anymore, he did it, one long, slow thrust at a time, each one taking them higher, each one coming faster and harder than the one before. He opened his mouth on her neck, filling himself with the taste of her.

The freight elevator slid steadily upward, shaking at each floor passage, marking the time. He was lost in her, lost in the soft panting of her breath in his ear, in the love bites she was leaving with her teeth along his jaw and down the length of his neck. He moved his mouth to hers, and she sucked on his tongue, her hips arching into his, trying like him to get even closer.

It was getting wild again, completely out of control.

She arched back over Jeanette, reaching for the spoiler, and in one move he pushed her up onto the trunk of the car and was on top of her.

God*damn*, he wanted a bed. He shook his head once, hard, trying to clear it—but she was sweet and tight and so *hot* for him. His fuse was lit and burning down fast, but the trunk space on a Camaro was an oxymoron, and the absolute last thing he wanted was for them to go sliding off and crashing onto the floor, so a part of him had to stay sane and it was driving him crazy. Why hadn't he thought this through a little better?

The answer was just too damn easy—with her, he didn't think. How could he think when just the smell of her was enough to get him hard? He had a death grip on the spoiler and his other arm around her, anchoring her to him, and he was the one silently pleading . . . *please. Please, please come,* because he was right on the fucking verge and it was too late for anything to stop him from going over it—and then he was over it, his body rigid with the sudden, powerful rush of his release, and, oh, sweet miracle Mother of God, she was with him, her soft cry tearing through him, her body shattering around him. He felt her pleasure as surely as he felt his own, the throbbing heat of it, the sweet ecstasy coursing through her. She was holding him so tight, her ankles locked at the small of his back, forcing him deeper and deeper, until he thought he could die from the pure mind-blowing pleasure of it.

When she finally released him, her legs sliding off to either side of him, he was spent, completely spent. He wanted nothing more than to roll over and fall asleep, and he would have, if there had been even a square inch of space to roll over in. She'd gone so quiet, her body so relaxed beneath him, he thought she might have beaten him to it. Then her hand slid up his thigh and over his hip.

"*This* has been an amazing day," she murmured, sounding as wrung out as he felt, completely done in. Her hand continued up his body, until her fingers were sliding through his hair.

He lifted himself up enough to look at her, resting his weight on his forearms. Her eyes were dark, her face utterly serene. He wasn't sure he'd ever seen anything like it. She looked transported, like a sated angel with kiss-swollen lips and a cloud of blond hair.

"Amazing," he agreed.

A slow smile curved her mouth, and her eyes drifted closed as she adjusted her hips ever so slightly, while he was still inside her, still between her legs.

His eyes damn near crossed. He did let out a hoarse groan, short and guttural, using up the last ounce of energy he had in his body. *Christ.* He'd just had her and he still wanted her. Not sexually. After tonight, he probably wasn't going to be able to get it up for a week—or at least until morning. She'd done him in, but he still wanted her, wanted something. He brought his forehead down to rest on hers and let out a short breath. He was going to have to marry her. Yeah, that made sense. He didn't see any way around it.

He couldn't let her go. That was out of the question.

And he didn't want another man within five feet of her, ever. She'd taken his most cherished adolescent imaginings of a fantasy fuck and thrown them into the stratosphere, and he was never going to be the same again.

CHAPTER 16

A FEW MINUTES LATER, when neither of them had yet made a move, he started wondering if they ever would. It was possible the trunk of a Camaro, clinging to the spoiler, could become one of his favorite places to relax. He felt completely drained.

"You've been hurt." Regan's voice was soft and languorous in his ear, barely a whisper as she lightly traced a path across the top of his shoulder with her fingertip, pushing his shirt back as she did.

On a scale of one to ten, getting shot was about a negative four on the list of things he wanted to talk about right now.

He looked off to the side of the Camaro. Bands of light and shadow were still sliding through the freight cage, giving the whole scene a somewhat surreal film noir look—which, interestingly enough, was how he'd felt in the alley off the rail yard after the bullet had gone through him. Up until then, the day had been going down in full Technicolor, even the bad parts, but by the time he'd dragged himself into the alley, bloody and beaten, his knee swelling to the size of a cantaloupe, his shoulder on fire with pain, everything had started looking real black and white with the edges fading to gray.

No. He didn't want to talk about it, not when he was still in a postcoital haze. The moment was just too damn good to mess up with the lousy memory of his last big mistake.

"Mmmm," he murmured, deliberately *not* committing to the conversation. He eased himself out of her and nuzzled his face down into her hair. He loved the smell of her shampoo, her skin.

Come to think of it, he did have something he wanted to talk about: old Scott Hanson and what had gone on between her and her husband, because the two of them were setting some kind of record for good times in a horizontal position. Unlike her, he realized this was probably the last damn thing she wanted to talk about, so he kept his questions to himself.

"This scar is new, like the one on your cheek."

Okay, she wasn't taking the hint. He was going to have to tell her something.

WHAT happened?" Regan asked, refusing to be put off, if that's what he was doing. She'd just made incredible love for the third time with the man, and she wanted to know more about him. Everything. She needed to know. She didn't feel like a one-night stand, but by all rights of definition, if he dropped her off at the hotel and she never saw him again, that's exactly what she would be— and she still wouldn't have missed it for the world. Whatever she had given him, she'd gotten far more in return.

He'd thrown his denim shirt on for the drive into Denver, but hadn't bothered to button it, and while her one hand was being oh so careful checking out his shoulder, the other was doing a sensory exploration of his chest. He was a wall of hard muscle covered with soft, dark hair. Touching him, sliding her fingers across his skin, was heaven. She flattened her hand close to his heart and felt the deep, solid rhythm echo through her palm and into her awareness, and she knew he'd given her more than just sensual pleasure.

Since the death of her parents when she was twelve, she hadn't had much of feeling safe. She'd *been* safe; Wilson would never have let anything bad happen to her. But she'd seldom felt entirely safe or secure.

She felt safe with Quinn, cocooned within the open drape of his shirt, the warmth of his body surrounding her. It didn't make sense, but her instincts all those years ago had been right-on. They'd broken some sort of barrier, she and Quinn, and on what was actually the most dangerous night of her life, she felt safer than she had in years. She didn't even know if she liked him, let alone loved him, but she knew she was crazy for him. They'd made love in an out-of-control, over-the-edge way that had sent her someplace she'd never been before, into rapture, utter, unequivocal rapture, and nothing had ever felt more right, more safe, or more freeing—certainly nothing she'd ever done with Scott.

After a long, silent moment, when she was about to give up on him answering her question, he brought his hand up to smooth his thumb along her jaw. They were lying rather precariously on Jeanette's trunk, held in place by the Camaro's spoiler, but she wasn't about to move, not if there was any hope of his telling her what had happened.

"Are you sure you want to know?" he asked, looking down at her. His eyes were impossibly green in the low light, his lashes thicker and darker than any man should be allowed to have.

Her answer was a simple nod. She needed to know something about him besides what she'd read in *Newsweek* and *People* magazine.

"I got caught in a vise the night we stole the bones," he started. "Bad guys on both sides and me not quick enough to get out of the middle, not all the way. Hawkins, Dylan, and Skeeter had already left with the truck, and I should have left with them, but I went back to make sure we'd cleared out the railcar. Something had caught my eye, a piece of paper, maybe a waybill. I never got close enough to find out. They were waiting for me when I got there. I took down the guy with the knife, but not until after he'd caught me on the face. That was crazy. He should never have come at me like that. There were a few more of them, and it's just lucky for me that the one who finally got me in his sights was a lousy shot."

She swallowed softly, appalled by what he'd told her and trying not to show it, trying not to think about what he meant by "took down." She'd asked, and now she knew.

"This is a gunshot wound?" She gently ran her fingers over the scar. She was in over her head with him, way over. Maybe she was only fooling herself, and nothing about the two of them together made sense. Maybe she was just so pitifully desperate she'd mistaken the realization of her most perfect fantasy for something more.

But, God, who would ever have dreamed she would ever actually make love with Quinn Younger? Three times, no less. In one night.

Not her, not in a million years.

"Not much of one," he assured her. "It just kind of tore across the top there, caught a little meat, nothing serious. The bad part was—" He stopped and gave her a shrug and a grin. "The bad part was that Hawkins had to come in and save my ass, and he's never going to let me live it down."

"So he's still pretty tough?" She loved being this close to him while he talked. She could feel the rumble of his voice through her hand on his chest.

"Tough enough." He nodded, his grin flashing again. He was so beautiful, his features chiseled to near godly perfection—straight, narrow nose, deep-set eyes, hair a fall of black silk on either side of his face.

"Was one of the guys Branson? The ones who hurt you?"

"No." His smile faded, and he pushed himself to a sitting position. "Come on." He offered her his hand, and she took it as he slipped off the side of the Camaro and helped her down. She wasn't sure her legs would hold her, but they did. She only wished they had a week and a bed to spend it in—a thought that had never crossed her mind in six years of marriage.

"Branson and his partner are new in town," he continued, hitching up his jeans and walking over to a trash bin in the corner of the elevator. "They work for a real psycho mother—" he stopped suddenly and switched gears, ". . . uh, guy out of Chicago. But Chicago keeps coming up clean on the goods we're looking for."

"Is the psycho named Roper?" She probably should have looked away as he cleaned himself up, but she couldn't take her eyes off him. He was tall and lean and broad shouldered, with a lanky kind of grace when he moved. It was all she could do to keep her hands off him.

No one would believe this about her, about Miss Straight-and-Tidy McKinney. She hardly believed it herself. She should probably at least feel a little shame. But she didn't, not one iota, nothing, *nada*. She felt wonderful, like he'd handed her the keys to the Magic Kingdom. She wasn't a frigid sexual disaster case, far from it. She was *hot*—Quinn had told her so, whispered it in her ear as he'd driven her out of her mind, and she believed him. He made her feel exquisitely female, desirable, beautiful.

And in love.

The thought came from nowhere and froze her to the spot.

He came back to the car, zipping his pants, his gaze narrowing on her. "Where did you hear that name?"

Love?

She *had* lost her mind.

"In the...uh...parking lot at Jake's. You told Hawkins you should be getting your intel from Roper's guys, and at the barn in Cisco, Kid mentioned the name. I figure he's your main bad guy, the one Branson works for."

He bit off a curse. "You're damn quick, aren't you?"

"Top of my class." She couldn't possibly be in love. She barely knew him. Of course, what she did know was more than she'd ever known about any other man. She knew how much he wanted her. How it felt to be consumed by him, and how he'd never forgotten her, any more than she'd ever forgotten him.

He leaned back against Jeanette, a flicker of a grin returning to his mouth.

"Which brings us back to the stolen goods," she said, "which even you don't believe can be bought with the bunch of dinosaur bones you have my grandfather working on." She needed to take a deep breath, get a grip. Fantasizing about someone, even for years, was not love. Having sex with someone was not love, even great, oh-my-god-I'm-dying sex. Of course, marrying someone and living with him for six years hadn't turned out to be love, either. So what in the hell did she know about love?

"No, it doesn't bring us back there at all." The freight

elevator came to a jarring halt at the seventh floor, but he ignored it, his attention focused solely on her. "You're out of this, Regan. With luck, you and Nikki will have a great night at a world-class hotel and never have to think about this situation again."

Nikki, she thought. Nikki was love, and Wilson. She would go to the ends of the earth to keep them safe. She knew that much beyond doubt.

Looking at Quinn, she realized she didn't want him hurt either, ever, and it was more than a slight possibility that she would go to the ends of the earth to keep him safe, too.

Damn, oh damn.

"I could help you." The words were out before she considered them. Then she considered them a lot, real quick. Helping men with mysterious jobs and gunshot wounds was definitely out of her depth. Way out, as in no way in hell should she be offering to help him out.

"No." He was adamant.

She, on the other hand, was simply crazy. Just like Suzie, she'd snapped for great sex, just snapped. Obviously, guys like Suzie's cowboy and Quinn Younger should come with warning signs: WOMEN: BEWARE. THESE ARE THE RULE BREAKERS, AND IT'S YOUR RULES THEY'RE GONNA HAVE YOU BREAKING.

"I know at least as much about dinosaur fossils as Wilson, and I've probably forgotten a lot less. Maybe you should let me have a look at them." And maybe she needed her head examined.

Okay, she definitely needed her head examined. Once

she got back to her regular, dry-as-day-old-toast life, today—and especially tonight—was going to look like a seriously dangerous aberration.

"No. You're out of it. The bones are out of it. We're giving them back. Then Roper has no reason to remember your name, let alone come after you."

It was the perfect solution, she was sure, to all her problems except one: what kept happening between the two of them.

"You never actually mentioned what's been stolen." It was terrible, but the more she thought about it, the more sense it made for her to look at the fossils. He'd been hurt very badly stealing the damn things, and her life and Wilson's and Nikki's lives were apparently on the line because of the damn things.

"And I'm not going to. Roper Jones plays for keeps," Quinn said. "Everybody is a little nervous. If he's got our stuff, he's upped his ante significantly."

"Who is everybody?"

"The alphabet soup contingent—FBI, CIA, DOD, DIA, NSA, BSA," he went on and on, being deliberately obtuse, she was sure.

"The Boy Scouts of America?" She let out a disbelieving laugh at his last acronym, and he grinned. She knew that DOD stood for the Department of Defense, and she guessed DIA was the Defense Intelligence Agency, and NSA could only be the National Security Agency; given the company he kept, she was pretty sure she had it right.

"They're good guys," he defended himself. "Always prepared. We like that, remember?"

She didn't doubt that they did, but it begged the question. "What about Steele Street? Are you guys nervous, too?"

"Nah," he said. "We're not nervous, we're double-D'ed."

"Double-D'ed?"

His grin returned, broader than before. "Destructive and Dangerous for you, if you're one of the bad guys."

"Are you classified?" she asked, tilting her head and giving him a very considering look. It was the only thing that made sense.

He didn't so much as blink. "Honey, we're a bunch of car salesmen, and other than that, we don't exist."

Classified, she decided for herself. So far, the "car salesmen" at Steele Street included a highly decorated Air Force captain and a Marine sniper who had probably won a couple of medals for rescuing Quinn out of northern Iraq. Hawkins was a convicted felon, so she doubted if he had any military service, but from what she remembered of him, he probably pulled his weight just fine with the two glory boys. He'd been very savvy about himself and the world and his place in it at sixteen, very insightful, and even a little poetic—and he'd been tough, more than tough enough. She'd been as shocked as Wilson when he'd been arrested and then convicted for the murder of Senator Traynor's son.

As for the rest of it, she'd done enough government work to know the labyrinth of regulations and departments was big enough to hide anything that somebody didn't want to be found. Something like she was beginning to imagine Steele Street might be wouldn't be too hard to hide.

"What about the other guys?" she asked. "There was a whole group of you from the chop shop. You already mentioned Dylan Hart, I remember him well, and Skeeter, who I don't remember at all. Hawkins I definitely remember. There was also that skinny kid, Cesar Raoul Eduardo Rivera. You all called him Creed. And then there was J. T. Oh, my God." She stopped suddenly, her eyes widening. "J. T. *Chronopolous*. Kid Chronopolous."

"Yeah," he said. "Kid is J. T.'s little brother."

"So does J. T. work for Steele Street, too?"

He just looked at her and shook his head. "Do you ever forget anything?"

"No."

"Does the word *precocious* mean anything to you?" he asked, walking over to open the cage.

"I'm too old to be precocious."

"How about too damn smart for your own good? Are you too old for that?" With a pull on a long lever, the door to the elevator began grating open.

"Absolutely." In her book, there was no such thing as being too smart for your own good. "The world needs more brains, not less. So what about Dylan? What does he do?" In a group of very intelligent, very young car thieves, he'd been the ringleader, the guy who knew how to work the angles—though all the angles he'd tried to work on Wilson had come to naught.

"*Capitán! ¿Qué pasa?*"

Regan turned at the sound of the voice and saw a young Hispanic guy coming across the cavernous opening that was the seventh floor, working his way through a line of very expensive cars. They were all sleek and shiny: Betty, looking pretty in hot pink and candy-apple red, a couple of Porsches and Corvettes, maybe a Jaguar, and something so high-tech-looking she didn't have a clue what it was called.

Then she saw the car in the corner, a sleek, lime-green, muscle-car monster, and knew she'd just found Jeanette's best friend—the pretty one.

"Johnny!" Quinn called out, giving the kid a wave before turning back to Regan. He took her hand in his and spoke quickly, quietly. "I've got to meet Hawkins tonight, finish up a few things, but I'd like to see you afterward. I could come to the hotel, spend the night . . . sleep with you." He let out a short laugh and linked his fingers through hers. "Wake up with you. We could have breakfast together, waffles and whipped cream."

"Waffles?" What in the world was he talking about?

"Okay, just the whipped cream, then." His grin explained everything, and despite what they'd just done, she felt herself start to blush.

"I . . . uh . . . we're moving awfully fast." Which in her heart of hearts she had to admit was a whole hell of a lot better than coming to a screeching halt. She wasn't ready to give him up, not just yet. On the other hand, spontaneously combusting on his car three times was significantly different from taking full, clear-eyed responsibility for her actions and agreeing breathlessly to meet him in bed with as much whipped cream as room service would allow.

Significantly different, especially for a woman who had never worked with so much as a single dairy product while making love.

"Definitely." His grin broadened. "Very fast."

And that's the way he liked things, she realized. Very fast—jets, cars, women, and probably love affairs. If she wasn't careful, he would be done with her before they'd even gotten properly started, the operative word being *properly*. Improperly, they'd broken the land speed record.

Her blush deepened, much to her dismay. After tonight, how was it possible to blush? Then again, how was it possible not to blush?

Before she had a chance to answer his question, the teenager he'd called Johnny arrived at the elevator. "Hey, *Capitán*. Superman said you'd be here about an hour ago. What happened?"

Regan turned toward Johnny, and that's when she saw him—the reason for the whole crazy night and two weeks of desperate worry.

Behind the teenager, a tall, broad-chested man was slowly making his way down a short flight of metal stairs from a bank of offices with windows looking out on the main floor. A lion's mane of white hair swept back off his face. His skin was tan and leathery from a lifetime of working the badlands of the West from New Mexico to

Montana and all the wild places in between. He was wearing his regulation khaki pants and an open-necked blue oxford shirt, looking as imposing and regal as ever— except for the hesitation in his steps and in the careful way he was maneuvering his way down the stairs.

"Wilson," she whispered, her hand coming up to her chest to hold in the sob forming there. She'd found him. Through the grace of God and Quinn Younger, she'd finally found him.

CHAPTER 17

KID KNEW THEY WERE in trouble when he gunned Nadine's engine up to a death-defying ninety miles an hour on the winding mountain road leading up to the Southern Cross Hotel, and the two cars behind him did the same.

Son of a bitch, this was all his fault. He should never have let Nikki lollygag in that freaking bathroom.

He slammed the Porsche back down into fourth, then third, and slewed around the next curve. Kid was intimately familiar with the approach to Southern Cross—a dead-end road to the hotel and nowhere else. There was a passing lane about another half a mile ahead, and if he used it correctly, it could be their ticket out of this mess—unless, of course, one of the drivers behind him was capable of doing a bootlegger's turn in a narrow space at a very high rate of speed with a cliff wall on one side and a sheer drop-off on the other.

He was betting neither one of them was crazy enough to try it.

Hell, he wasn't crazy enough to try it. No, he was just going to damn well do it, and he was going to do it clean and fast.

He'd checked his rearview mirror all through Boulder, and he hadn't seen the tail until they'd hit the mountain road—and that bothered the shit out of him. The bastards had to have picked them up at McKinney's, and he'd been—what? Getting off on the smell of Nikki McKinney's perfume filling up Nadine? Noticing how her nothing scrap of a skirt rode all the way up to her ass when she sat down in a bucket seat? Even stupider yet, hadn't he thought, more than once or twice, mind you, just how damn good she looked in his car?

What the fuck was up with him?

He needed to get laid more often. There was no doubt about it. But now he wanted her, with her spiky black-and-purple hair and those silver-gray eyes and that mouth that seemed to say "Kiss me, Kid" every time he looked at it. But if he didn't start thinking with his head instead of his dick, he was going to get them both killed, and he could just kiss off any chance he had of making love with the most beautiful, totally incomprehensible woman he'd ever met.

And *that* was not going to happen.

"Get down, stay down, and put your hands over your ears," he told her.

"What's going on?" she asked, without, he noted, following a single order.

Geez. Women. No wonder they didn't let them go into combat.

"We're being followed, and if they shoot at us, I'd rather you didn't get hit."

"Hit? You mean with a bullet?" Nikki sounded incredulous, and rightfully so. As wild as she was, getting shot at was not part of her normal working day.

"Nadine is partially armored, so if you'll just put your head down on your knees, ma'am, you'll be safe." Well, safer anyway, providing he didn't get hit, and they didn't crash, and providing everything else went according to plan.

Then he remembered he didn't exactly have a plan, except to jerk on the parking brake, turn the wheel, and ride the skid through a head-snapping 180-degree slide guaranteed to flip them ass-backward in the opposite direction. If they lived through all that, he'd hit the lights and, power-shift his way back up to a balls-to-the-walls rate of speed heading down the mountain. Nadine was painted flat black with no chrome showing. Stealth Porsche, that's what she was, and on a night like tonight, with only a sliver of moon hiding behind the treetops, it was possible the guys following them wouldn't even see her as they flashed by. Instead, they'd be looking for a pair of taillights they'd be thinking were just around the bend up ahead.

"Armored? Did you say this car was armored?" Nikki

asked, finally finding her voice. She definitely sounded nervous, but her head still wasn't down around her knees. "Why?"

"I bought her off a guy who had her in Panama during Noriega's regime, and you've got about thirty seconds before this baby comes to a screeching halt and turns on a dime. Do not, I repeat, do not lift your head until I tell you to, because if the guys tailing us shoot, I'm going to shoot back. Twenty seconds."

He pushed Nadine even harder, screaming around the curves, looking for those extra few seconds to put them out of sight when they hit the passing lane and made the turn. The acceleration was enough to hammer his point home. Out of the corner of his eye, he saw her duck down.

He checked his rearview again, and when it came up blank, nothing but black, he readied himself and downshifted. Then the white lines of the passing lane started slipping beneath the Porsche, and he executed the maneuver like a fucking Duke of Hazzard. Nadine spun around, tires squealing, brakes burning. Kid hit the lights, slammed her into first, sidled her up to the canyon wall, and lay there, catching his breath and lurking on the narrow shoulder of the road in the dark.

Shit. His heart was pounding. Sweat was pouring down the sides of his face and under his arms. His heart was in his throat, but he didn't waste a second. He reached for the Mossberg and laid the shotgun across the open window frame. The first car zoomed past; the second car followed half a dozen heartbeats later. Both of them had been Mercedes, which fit Roper's MO.

He eased up on the clutch and rolled Nadine back onto the road. Once he cleared the curve going back down, he punched the lights on and hit the gas. A quarter of a mile later, he knew his ruse hadn't worked. Or more correctly, it had only half worked.

A pair of headlights loomed up in his rearview, but only one pair. Divide and conquer: that's what Roper's guys had done. That they'd done it so quickly told Kid they had radio communications. When the first driver had failed to catch up with the Porsche, they'd obviously decided to send the second driver back down the canyon.

A three-burst *ping, ping, ping* and the shattering of Nadine's driver's-side mirror wiped any last doubt out of Kid's mind about who was following them. Bits of glass flew as the mirror disintegrated, leaving only a part of the shell hanging from the car.

"Oh shit. Oh shit. Oh shit," he heard her swear. She was in a damn near fetal position now, her legs drawn under her, her shoulders hunched around her knees.

Roper always played for blood. The rest of his slimy-assed crew weren't any better, but one car full of submachine-gun-toting goons was better than two. Kid could outrun them.

He shoved Nadine back up into fifth and came around the next curve—almost head-on into the rear end of a freaking minivan in his lane. A humongous RV was approaching in the other, both of them poking along. He tapped the brakes, hard, then double-tapped 'em, then triple-tapped 'em, until he was damn near tap dancing on them.

Where in the hell, he wondered, had a minivan come from? There'd been no other traffic forty seconds ago, when they'd been racing up the canyon. Then he remembered the access road that led up to a lone cabin just before the passing lane. The minivan must have come from there, puttering down onto the highway at the absolute *worst* time.

The RV's timing sucked just as badly. It slowly rumbled forward, blocking off any escape. Nikki McKinney was still huddled down in her seat. It crossed his mind to tell her to prepare for a crash landing, but there wasn't time to voice the warning. The truth was, she was never going to know what hit her. They were going to annihilate the minivan and themselves in about two fucking seconds with the Mercedes close behind, as in right up Nadine's tailpipe.

Everything was happening in split seconds. He held on to the wheel, played the brakes, and prayed and cursed at the same time. Just a millisecond from impact the RV rolled far enough past the minivan to create the narrowest of openings, and Kid shot through. The fit was so tight, the rear light of the RV went by him less than six inches from his window. The shattered remains of Nadine's left side mirror were history.

They rode two wheels into the narrow shoulder over the drop-off, overshooting the road by two feet, before he was able to muscle the Porsche back onto the highway in front of the minivan. The Mercedes held on to the road by the same hairsbreadth, sending up a plume of dust before screeching in behind the Porsche.

More shots dinged into Nadine's rear end. Now it was a run for the money, and it was no contest. There was a half a mile of straightaway up ahead, the only straight stretch on the whole damn road. If it was empty, Kid was taking Nadine out of there.

"Hold on," he warned as they flew up a small rise. At the top, one look proved the straightaway was clear of traffic. He didn't hesitate. With the flip of a bright-red switch on the console, he unleashed a ten-pound bottle of nitrous oxide into Nadine's carburetor—and they disappeared down the road in a rocket blast of power.

IT was good to see her, Wilson thought. Good to see Regan. It had been a long time. Too long, maybe. He couldn't quite remember.

"Did you have supper tonight?" she asked, straightening the perfectly straight sheets on a bed in one of the suites above the garage where he'd be spending the night. Most of the suites were used as offices, but three were set up to accommodate overnight guests. They all had outside windows facing the street, and inside windows looking out over the garage. The decor was very sleek, very modern, especially in the offices, which were full of high-tech gadgetry that went beyond even some of the science labs at the university. The bedroom suites were more user-friendly, with dark paneled bookcases, leather chairs, discreet lighting, and private, well-appointed bathrooms. Efficiency seemed to be Steele Street's overriding theme— and cars. There were cars everywhere, all through the building, floors of them.

"Yes." He did remember supper. "The boy and I stopped for burritos." He loved burritos smothered in green chile, and the boy had known a great place to eat, Mama Guadalupe's.

He and the boy—whose name he couldn't quite re-call, but he'd be darned if he asked again—had parked on one of the lower floors when they'd arrived at 738 Steele Street, which was actually more of an alley than a street. He didn't remember which floor, though, darn it.

There had been a bunch of cars down there, most of them torn apart and in pieces. Big engine blocks had hung down, hoisted on pulleys and chains. One whole wall had been nothing but tires. The car Dylan had first given him was here, the one he'd called Betty. That was the one thing he *did* remember. The car was a beauty, but Wilson had decided his driving days were behind him. He was getting too darned forgetful to trust himself behind the wheel of a car.

He was tired, too. He'd been sleeping poorly, he and Hawkins roughing it on cots at the warehouse most nights, though a few had been spent in the comfort of the Steele Street guest rooms.

And the Porsche had gotten away from him outside Lafayette. Besides almost outright killing him, the inci-dent had darn near scared him to death, and probably the driver he'd nearly had a head-on collision with as well. When he'd finally reached the warehouse, still badly shaken up, he'd given the keys to Hawkins.

Forgetful, tired, careless—driving was a risky business for an old man suffering from what he feared was a terminal lapse of memory. He hadn't told Regan, but he'd been seeing the doctor. No diagnosis had been made other than old age catching up to him with a vengeance, but it felt like more to Wilson, especially lately.

Where was Hawkins? he wondered.

And where was Dylan?

He couldn't remember either of those things, any more than he could remember the boy's name, and that bothered him like so much of his forgetfulness bothered him. So many things floated just out of reach of his memory. Sometimes a piece of information would land, and he would wonder how something so clear had ever eluded him. But the boy's name was not one of those things, and neither were the whereabouts of Dylan and Hawkins, or when they were coming back.

"I wish you'd called," Regan said, turning down the bed and fluffing up the pillows. "Nikki and I have been very worried."

"Worry's no good, honey," he told her, moving into one of the chairs with a book he'd picked from the bookcase, one he'd started a week ago. "But you do seem to like it more than most."

He heard her sigh, but he didn't retract his statement. Regan worried the same way Nikki painted—distressingly well. She always had. Nikki was a scandal, without a doubt. If they'd lived anywhere except Boulder, he would have had to shut the house up. But Regan was the one Wilson had always worried about.

Nikki had been little more than a baby when Robin and Lisa had died. She'd hardly known her parents, what with them spending so much time in South America that last year. Regan had known them, though, and she'd felt their loss even more keenly than Wilson had himself, devastated that his beautiful son had died, along with his lovely wife, in an earthquake in Peru only three years after Wilson's own wife had passed on, his own dear Evelyn.

Too much tragedy, he thought, and wished he couldn't remember that part of his life so well. Yesterday and even this afternoon were a bit of a blur, but twenty years ago was crisp and new, and still painful.

"You have a cell phone, Grandpa."

"Yes, but I forgot the darn charger," he finally had to admit. "Darn thing ran out of juice early on." He'd meant to call her, he was sure. It was just hard to keep everything straight.

"I went to the police."

Oh, hell. Of course she had. Count on his girl to look under every rock.

"Well, that's no good," he grumbled, settling into the chair. "The whole thing is supposed to be very hush-hush. Top-secret stuff. The FBI was there."

"The FBI?" Her voice rose in surprise from the end of the bed, where she was putting his suitcase on a porter's bench. "And Christian Hawkins? Together?"

"Yes, yes. I know what you're thinking, but Hawkins turned out okay. Never could believe that other, about him murdering that senator's son. You know, your grand-mother was a worrier, so you come by it naturally enough." And wasn't that the truth. Evelyn had worried about him all the time. He reached up to turn on the reading lamp next to the chair. The boy had already set out a pot of tea and a few cookies, just the way he liked, the tea from England, the cookies from a French bakery on Sixteenth Street. The chop shop boys had definitely come up in the world.

"Quinn told me Hawkins had been exonerated, but still, the FBI? He didn't tell me you were actually work-ing with the FBI."

"Doubt if the boy knew. He hasn't been there, I don't think." He had Quinn's address, that was it, but he didn't think he'd actually seen him at the warehouse. "I meant to be in Vernal by now, with Stan Ryan, chipping away at that big old *Stegosaurus* he found this spring."

"You missed your presentation up at Casper."

He had?

"Darn." He leaned forward, resting one hand on his knee, and looked at her. The Casper speech at the Tate Museum was the highlight of his whole darn year—and he'd missed it.

Well, shoot. He'd have to call Vic Sutter and reschedule. That's all there was to it.

She'd opened up his suitcase and was staring at the contents, clearly surprised. She glanced back at him over her shoulder. "Somebody has been taking very good care of you."

He grinned. There was nothing like a suitcase full of

freshly pressed and wrapped laundry to impress a woman. The laundry service Hawkins used even pressed and wrapped his darn socks.

"And I'm getting paid a consultant's fee of a thousand dollars a day." He was far from being used up and put out to pasture, even if he couldn't remember every darn thing that happened.

"A thousand dollars a day?" Her eyebrows lifted almost up into her hairline.

He'd really surprised her with that one, and it gave him a good chuckle. It was hard for him to get one up on his girls anymore. Nikki had always run circles around him. She was all energy, and creation, and lightning strikes coming from unexpected angles. Regan was just the opposite, always organized, doing things by the book, step by step, brilliant in her own way, but never reaching her full potential, because she always played it safe.

Wilson took some of the blame for that. He'd raised a son pretty much in his own image of the rough-and-tumble field researcher first and professor second. To say Wilson had been unprepared for taking on his little granddaughters was an understatement. Not that he ever, even for one second, had considered an alternative. Nikki and Regan were his, all he'd had left after the Peru disaster. Still, he could have done better by Regan than just being content to let her tag along in his footsteps. Nikki had just exploded in her own direction, but he'd always felt he should have exposed Regan to more options, encouraged her more to try different things.

He sure as shoot should have put his foot down with

that idiot Hanson. One of the biggest regrets of his life had been letting her marry Scott. She'd been almost immediately miserable. But if he hadn't been ready for little girls, teenage girls had completely hog-tied him. Emotional hadn't begun to describe Regan at seventeen, eighteen, and nineteen. Hormonal tornado would have been more accurate.

He'd actually, briefly, once, hoped marriage would settle her down a bit, and it had—too much. By the time of the divorce, she'd gotten so miserably settled, it was as if her spark had gone out.

She seemed to have a little spark left in her tonight, though. Not now, not while she was organizing him for bed, and no doubt getting ready to give him the third degree on his meds, and probably figuring out how to lay into him again for not calling her, but earlier, when she and Quinn Younger had first shown up. She'd been practically glowing, she'd had so much spark.

He looked at her more carefully, noticing things, unusual things. She was wearing an overlarge T-shirt, which was not Regan's style at all, ever, and it was only half tucked into her skirt, which was even more out of character. She liked feminine clothes, the girlier the better. Her hair was a mess, an unheard-of circumstance. Personal tidiness was a religion to Regan. Nikki, on the other hand, spent hours on her grooming to *ensure* that she looked like she'd just walked out of a blender. Between the two of them, Wilson never had figured out which end was up. He only knew the downstairs bathroom was the only safe one in the house.

But Regan, tonight . . .

Something flipped over in his brain, and he knew he had to tell her something tonight.

Something of incredible importance.

He furrowed his brow and let his gaze drift to the floor, thinking, thinking.

"What is it, Wilson?" He heard the concern in her voice, heard her walking back across the room. Then she knelt by his side, her hand coming up to hold on to his. "What's wrong?"

He couldn't remember. He was too tired to remember, too weary. It had been an awfully long day. He shook his head and looked at her, but it wasn't coming back. He did remember the soft gray of Evelyn's eyes, and Regan's were the same color, the same beautiful color. His wife had been blond, too, and small-boned, just like Regan. Though Evelyn most definitely had not had Regan's other attributes. The girl's figure had been a cross to bear, with him trying to keep her covered up and buttoned down, and giving his evilest evil eye to every boy who had ever come calling.

Maybe that had been the problem. He'd scared off all the young ones who'd wanted a chance with her when, if he'd had more sense and less panic to work with, he might have spent his energy scaring off Scott Hanson.

"A thousand dollars a day. That's incredible, but not a penny more than you're worth," she said, giving him an encouraging smile.

A thousand dollars? For a moment, he wondered what she was talking about, then he remembered—the money.

He wouldn't go so far as to say he was worth more

than a thousand dollars a day. Dylan had been very generous with his offer, but then, he'd not only been buying expertise, he'd been buying silence. The whole operation at the warehouse in Lafayette had been very secretive. Besides the FBI, a couple of military types had shown up every now and then doing God knew what besides looking serious and acting officiously. He certainly hadn't been able to tell if they'd accomplished anything or not. Then, over the last few days, the whole atmosphere had changed, going from "red alert" to "the party's over," and he'd been left pretty much on his own.

"Don't zone out on me, Grandpa." She tightened her grip on his hand, her voice bringing him back to the present. "We're in a lot of trouble because of those dinosaur bones you've been checking out for Dylan Hart, and I need to know if you found anything."

That was it. His mind cleared in one brilliant flash.

"Yes!" A broad smile curved his mouth. "I did find something. Something remarkable." Excitement edged his voice. "Regan . . ."—he leaned close, his voice falling to a whisper—"there was a nest, a *Tarbosaurus* nest, a real Mongolian monster. It's all there, a fully developed embryo, broken eggshells, and a couple of eggs still intact, and I'm sure it's a *Tarbosaurus*. When I cut open the plaster, the whole thing smelled like the Gobi Desert. The sand, the wind, the heat, it was all there. The other fossils didn't have that sense about them, but this one did, and the skull inside the egg was pure carnivore, with serrated teeth and the shape of a *Tyrannosaurus rex*."

She tightened her grip on his hand, utterly speechless.

He understood. What he'd just told her was as close to im-possible as finding a four-carat diamond in a cereal box.

He paused for a second, his mind caught on some-thing, but the moment passed, and then his attention was back on Regan, who was clearly stunned. His smile got even bigger, almost as big as her eyes, which were damn near bulging.

"A—a *Tarbosaurus* nest?" she finally choked out. "My God, you disappear for two weeks and come up with a *Tarbosaurus* nest? With a visible embryo?"

"Yes, yes, I know," he said, still excited, despite her ob-vious doubts. Heck, who wouldn't doubt such a find? "But it's there, Regan, and it's real."

It was enough to make a person's head spin. It had made his head spin—the mighty Cretaceous carnivore he'd always wanted had appeared from out of nowhere and been waiting for him in a warehouse in Lafayette? Stranger things had happened in science, but this was definitely one for the books, definitely one to set young Dr. Houska back on his heels.

"Mongolia," she murmured in a tone filled with awe. "Grandpa, this is *amazing*. My God. We have a Mongolian *Tarbosaurus* nest right here in Denver?"

Yes, he was sure. He might have been old, and he might have been forgetful, but by God, Wilson McKinney knew his Cretaceous carnivores.

She grinned up at him, her smile going from ear to ear. Then, as suddenly as it had appeared, her smile disap-peared. She swore softly, and rose to her feet, then paced back toward the bed.

"What's wrong?"

"Well," she hedged, drawing the word out before coming to a stop and turning to face him. "We have to give it back now, don't we?"

Well, yes, eventually, probably. Okay, for sure, someday, but . . . but not yet. They didn't even know yet who to give it back to, and there was something else she needed to know.

"Does anyone else know what you found?" she asked, interrupting his train of thought, and for a second he was confused. He hadn't told her yet what else he'd found.

Or had he?

"Did you tell Christian Hawkins?"

He shook his head, knowing the answer to that question at least. "Hawkins hasn't been around much, and I'm supposed to report to Dylan, but Dylan . . . left." That's what he knew. Dylan had left, so he'd kept his report to himself, but he'd written up part of it, the part about the *Tarbosaurus*. He'd only found it two days ago, after most of the FBI guys had left, after Dylan had left. For hours there had been no one there to share the news with. Then Hawkins had come, but they hadn't had time to talk much before another FBI guy had shown up.

The two of them had pretty much left him on his own, and then this morning he'd found something else with the *Tarbosaurus*. Something . . . odd.

"Grandpa?" Regan was back by his side, shaking his knee, trying to get his attention.

That was the whole darn problem, of course. His darned attention kept wandering.

He focused on her, wondering what had upset her. He'd just given her great news.

"Grandpa. I have to leave now, but you're going to be safe here. I'm going to go check on Nikki, make sure she's okay. We'll both be at the Southern Cross Hotel tonight. Call if you need me, and I'll come back. Hopefully, by tomorrow, we can all go home."

That's where he wanted to go: home. Working was stressful, having people depending on him, trying to meet a schedule, being part of the hustle and bustle, answering all their darned questions all the time. It was enough to rattle anybody's concentration. Giving up driving hadn't been easy, either. As a matter of fact, it scared the hell out of him. If he couldn't drive, what was going to happen to him? Was he going to be housebound, a real old man? Washed up at seventy-two?

"We should take a vacation," he said, suddenly getting an idea. "Use the money I made and just go." That's what he loved, just getting up and going, traveling around, seeing what was out there. He didn't want to give that up. "Maybe the three of us could go to Rabbit Valley for a month." Just the thought made him feel lighter, younger.

SURE, Grandpa," Regan said, unable to say anything else even though she knew when push came to shove she was lying through her teeth.

God, she had always been such a disappointment to him, but there was nothing on earth she hated more than camping in a pup tent in one-hundred-degree heat, in the middle of Desolation Nowhere, USA, with a five-gallon container of tepid water they'd had to haul from forty miles back. No showers, no toilet, no sink, no bed, no shade, but plenty of sandy grit, and flies, and skin-sizzling sunshine—the list went on and on.

Both her parents had loved that kind of life, roughing it in the desert or the jungle. She must be some kind of genetic throwback to some long-lost ancestor who'd spent her life in a day spa. A vacation was the Caribbean, Hawaii, a week in New York.

Rabbit Valley was an endurance test—and it didn't take the thousands of dollars he'd made to get there. A tank of gas, a bag of groceries, and a stick to poke around for snakes with would do the trick.

He looked good, though, well cared for, and for that she was grateful. At a thousand dollars a day, she couldn't exactly say the guys at Steele Street had taken advantage of him—not hardly—and he was safe. Steele Street was a fortress. Even the rickety old freight elevator had a state-of-the-art security system. She'd seen other signs of security around the building—cameras, keypads for all the doors, alarms. More than any of that, the place had a feel about it, a very tight feel, as if with the push of a button, one man could lock the place up tighter than a drum. She'd never been in a building where she'd gotten such a feeling of impregnability.

"It'll be wonderful." Wilson was practically beaming.

Okay, help me, God, she silently prayed. She'd go, but not for a month. For a weekend—max.

Of course, none of them were going anywhere until

they got out of the mess they were in with Dylan Hart's fossils. *My God*. A *Tarbosaurus* nest.

"Sure, Grandpa," she repeated. "It'll be wonderful." She had to talk to Quinn before he made any more plans. "Do you have everything you need for the night?"

He glanced at the bed and nodded. "Yes, a real bed and air-conditioning. Is the boy staying around?"

"Johnny?"

"Yes, *Johnny*," he said, putting emphasis on the name, his smile broadening.

"Yes. He'll be here all night, if you need anything. He'll stay with you tomorrow, too, until Nikki and I come and get you, or until he can take you home." She rose to her feet and leaned down to give him a kiss. "Good night, Grandpa."

Leaving him for the night, she closed the door behind her and walked across one of the most beautifully decorated offices she'd ever seen. Her mind was racing, but not beyond the point where she didn't recognize the exquisitely appointed furnishings—exquisitely expensive. Everything was sleek and creative. There was nothing hodgepodge or mundane. The beautifully crafted leather chairs had simple, modern lines. The rugs were thick-piled and artful on a clean oak floor. The desks were Scandinavian, in pale hardwoods. The office equipment was simply mind-boggling, all state-of-the-art, from computers to phones to the surround-sound CD system and wall-size movie screen.

The only incongruous piece in the suite was a two-foot-by-three-foot metal sign hung between two of the

windows with the word WEATHERPROOF on it, the same
as the logo on the T-shirt she was wearing. She was going
to have to ask Quinn about it. WEATHERPROOF showed
up all over Steele Street. There'd been a long row of
WEATHERPROOF bumper stickers stuck to the wall inside
the iron door off the alley. There was a WEATHERPROOF
decal on the window of the door separating the garage
from the office, and there had been license-plate-size
WEATHERPROOF signs in the freight elevator.

Actually, she was going to have to ask Quinn a lot of
things. He was no car salesman. No one at Steele Street
was. Not even close. This was a million-dollar suite of
offices—which didn't exactly bring government work
to mind, either.

Whatever he was up to, they needed to talk and re-
group, right now, immediately. The *Tarbosaurus* nest
changed everything. It could not be given back to Roper
and Vince Branson and all the other criminals breathing
down their necks. The nest was an unprecedented find, a
vital piece of the fossil record, and she'd be damned if
she'd let Quinn and Hawkins give it to those thugs. Now
more than ever, she needed to see those stolen bones.

On the other hand, if they didn't give the fossils back,
all the fossils, she and Nikki and Wilson would still be
targets.

"So now what," she whispered to herself.

"Regan?" Quinn walked in from an adjoining suite.

"You startled me," she confessed, feeling her heart
slow back down from the jump it had taken. All in all,
she guessed her nerves were just about shot. The last

twenty-four hours, since she'd found the note on Wilson's desk calendar, had been the wildest of her life.

"I'm sorry." He walked farther into the room and pulled her into his arms. He held her and kissed the top of her head. "Did you get Wilson all tucked in?"

"Yes." He felt so good, so solid, so warm. She felt warm, too, especially across her face. She'd made love with him three times and she still hardly knew a thing about him. "He had some information that changes everything."

"What was it?"

Her smile returned. Wilson's news truly was amazing. "One of the fossils he's been working on is a *Tarbosaurus* nest, one of those Cretaceous carnivores he's spent his whole life hoping to find. I know it's unbelievable, but you have a seminal, rare treasure in your possession that's probably worth whatever else was stolen and then some. You can't possibly give it back to Roper, not at least without letting me—"

"Oh, yes, I can," he interrupted, his gaze darkening.

Okay, she'd expected him to say as much, given the very persuasive reasons for giving the fossils back. She cared at least as much about everyone's safety as he did, and probably more.

"Then you have to at least let me see it." That was her backup plan. She hated it. She wanted the damn nest, every little bone, in situ, in toto, intact. "I'll need to photograph it, before you give it back—oh, God." She stopped abruptly and squeezed her eyes shut. *No, no, no.* The backup plan sucked. Big-time. "We can't give it back," she said, holding up her hand as if to ward off any possible argument. "No, we just can't. Not if it's what Wilson thinks it is. Not if it's a Mongolian *Tarbosaurus* nest. Honestly, Quinn. There's got to be another way. It's that important."

"Mongolian?" His voice was suddenly very serious, very quiet. "We have Mongolian dinosaur bones?"

She nodded. "If Wilson is right in his identification, you have at least one Mongolian fossil."

"Does anyone else know?"

"No. I don't think so."

He looked at her for a long, silent moment.

"Okay," he finally said. "I'll take pictures for you."

"I should take the pictures," she insisted. "I'm the one who knows what to look for."

"No. You're going to the Southern Cross."

"But—"

"No." He was adamant, and she was just about ready to tell him she didn't take orders from anybody, thank you very much, when his expression softened. "Look, Regan. I'm sorry, but it has to be this way. The bones are the bait for Roper. I don't want you anywhere near them."

The look on Quinn's face told her there was absolutely no way she was going to change his mind. It was a done deal. She was going to the hotel, and he was going to set a trap for a man who had already nearly gotten him killed.

She didn't even want to think about it.

But, damn, despite the danger, she wanted to get her

hands on the Mongolian monster, the Cretaceous carnivore of every paleontologist's dreams. She wanted to get her hands on it, get the museum's claim on it, and get it locked up in her lab—all without getting anyone killed.

There had to be a way.

CHAPTER
18

WELL, WELL, WELL, Kid thought, completely flabbergasted by the sheer torrent of conversation gushing out of Nikki McKinney. They were still on the run, headed southeast out of Boulder, away from the Southern Cross Hotel, and he could absolutely guarantee nobody was following them. He'd taken every evasive maneuver in the book. Twice.

But Nikki McKinney—*geezus*, there was obviously nothing like a little danger to put a nickel in her. He'd stopped trying to actually understand what she was saying, or God forbid, *respond* to it, quite a while back. It was an incredible amount of verbiage, sort of a life story soliloquy, and he was afraid she might just fry something, like her brain or her vocal cords, if she didn't get a break. She was so freaking *wired*, and maybe still scared.

It wasn't every day a person got shot at. And it wasn't every woman who could render him speechless, or with one look, one smile, make him think about stuff he'd never thought about. Like what she would look like in the morning, or twenty years from now. *Geezus squared.* What in the hell was going on with him? He didn't think about women in those terms. Morning after. Down the road.

"Of course, Regan just about died when she walked into my studio, which was really still the garden shed back then, before I finally got it cleaned up and con- vinced Grandpa to put in a pair of northern exposure skylights, because the light is so important, especially for painting, and I was doing a lot of painting, before I started using photography and printing techniques to create some of my bigger pieces. But Travis was there, naked, of course, and I was only sixteen, and Regan thought all the worst possible things, him being older and all, but not by much, two years is all. And it was re- ally weird, but Travis practically fell in love with her that day as she was standing there, trying so hard not to stare at him and practically fainting from the shock. It was ter- rible really, she was struggling so hard not to overreact, and you know Travis, he doesn't even notice if he's naked or not, and Regan was thinking the worst—oh, I guess I already said that."

She paused for just a bit longer than usual, and that was probably his cue to say something, but before he could think of anything, let alone spit it out, she jumped back in the breach.

"Of course, there *wasn't* anything going on. Travis and I just don't find each other attractive—well, I guess I shouldn't say that, because of course I find Travis incredibly attractive. He's gorgeous, the most physically gorgeous, unbelievably photogenic man I've ever seen in my whole life."

Perfect, he thought grimly, trying to concentrate on the road in front of him and continually checking the road behind him. Travis James was her ideal man, and Kid didn't look anything like Travis James. He was not blond-haired and blue-eyed. He did not have that dreamy, artsy thing going for him, and he didn't have a fucking clue if he was photogenic or not—or why, all of a sudden, he cared.

"But poor Regan, her husband must have been like the world's worst lover, because she was so miserable with the whole bedroom scene, and then to literally expose her to Travis like that, who quite frankly just *exudes* sensuality. I think it was a serious shock to her system."

Hell, Travis's exuding sensuality was starting to be a bit of a shock to Kid's system, and he most definitely did not want to hear about Regan McKinney's love life, not after seeing her underwear, and not after seeing the look on Quinn's face when she'd fainted into his arms.

No, sir-ree. Quinn would not want him hearing this.

"And don't you know, she started divorce proceedings just a few weeks after that?"

She came to a full-out stop and after a second or two, he realized that, unbelievably, she was actually waiting for an answer.

"Uh . . . no." He hadn't known.

Apparently satisfied with his comment, she started up again at full tilt. "I'm sure it was seeing Travis naked that made her decide there had to be something better out there for her than musty old Scott Hanson, and I like to think my work with him has the same effect on the women who come to my shows, and I don't just mean that he's beautiful on the outside. Travis is beautiful on the inside, and that part of him, that more feminine part, just glows. I think women really respond to it."

Shit. Now the guy was *glowing?* And what was this about Regan seeing him naked and deciding to leave her husband? That made no sense. He'd seen Travis's package and it was just a regular guy package, a few working parts, everything in the right place, like—

His brain came to a screeching halt, and really, he had to take a breath and ask himself just what the fuck he thought he was doing, and how in the hell she'd gotten him off on such a freaking weird train of thought. He did not go around thinking about other guy's dicks, at least not since he'd been fifteen and realized he was okay in that department.

He shifted uncomfortably in his seat and tried not to listen anymore, but that was impossible. The sound of her voice, like everything else about her, was irresistible.

"I think he makes women question their position in life through their association with the dichotomy of his physical power and his whole feminine mystique. That's the part of Travis I'm always trying to capture. The tension. You must have felt it in the studio."

She was serious. He could tell by the tone of her voice. And again, unbelievably, she was waiting for an answer.

"Uh...no." Oh, yeah. He was scoring points all over the place with this conversation.

He flipped on his blinker and gunned the motor for the highway entrance ramp ahead. With the Southern Cross compromised, Kid had decided she needed a fortress, not a safe house. They were headed to Denver. He was taking her to Steele Street. He'd called in his change of plans, catching Quinn halfway to the Southern Cross from Steele Street, and Hawkins halfway to Steele Street from Commerce City. Neither had liked hearing how fast Roper's men had moved in on them.

"You didn't feel the tension?" She sounded like he couldn't possibly be telling her the truth.

O-*kay*, he thought, doing a quick about-face.

"Yeah, there was tension. I just didn't realize it was the dichotomy of Travis's physical power and his, uh, feminine mystique creating it. I thought it was the paint and the hellish death motif, not to mention the, uh, sheer demonic luridness of the eternity-sucking vortex." God, he was skating on thin ice here, damn thin.

"Well, yes, that's the obvious interpretation," she said, a shade of relief in her voice, which just left him even more flabbergasted. She'd bought his line. "But the whole piece is powered by the duality of man's nature, innocence and evil, male and female. Didn't you ask yourself what an angel was doing in hell? I mean, what awful thing could he have done to have fallen so terribly from God's grace?"

No, he hadn't asked himself those questions. He'd been too distracted by her, but now that she mentioned it, he didn't have to look far for the answers. That poor freaking angel didn't have to have done a damn thing to lose God's grace. Sometimes it just happened, between one breath and a man's last. He'd seen it in combat. Grace died. Death won, and for a while, the whole world felt like hell.

There was nothing easy or simple about Nikki McKinney—but she was definitely naive.

"Do you know what the angel did?" he asked. Yeah, he had his own answers, but he wasn't going to rock her boat with them, not when she was so damn close to going under. To hell with Travis's tension, she was wound tighter than a boatswain's knot, with tension rolling off her in waves. Everything about her was giving off caution warnings—Woman on the Edge of a Meltdown—in big red, flashing neon letters. Her hands were nearly white where she had them clasped around the little box of doodads in her lap. Her shoulders were stiff, and her posture ramrod straight, a near impossible feat in a bucket seat.

Worse, he wasn't doing much beyond holding on for the ride and hoping she wouldn't explode or something. Or even worse yet, cry. It was damned frustrating, and more than a little unnerving. She needed help, and he was clueless. That's what came from growing up with a bunch of older brothers and no mother: incompetence, pure and total. She was going to self-destruct, and he was going to be left picking up the pieces.

But, God, she was a steamroller, and as afraid as he was of her melting down over there all on her own, he was even more afraid of saying the wrong thing and being the cause of her collapse.

"No. I actually don't know why the angel fell." She shook her head. "I should, but I don't, but it's one of the things I'm trying to do, expand the work beyond the boundaries of the canvas. Of course, it's only been the last year or two that I've learned to take a piece all the way to the edge. I think Travis knows what the angel did, and I think he uses that knowledge to get where he goes, but he hasn't told me. He never *tells* me much of anything, but he's not afraid to *show* me, and more than any other model I've ever had, he understands the innocence of his sensuality and the feminine power inherent in his own masculine nature. He lives the dichotomy of the fallen angel."

Kid stifled a heavy sigh. The dichotomy of the fallen angel? What in the hell, he wondered, was she talking about?

For a second, he'd hoped to get home without having to hear too much more about Travis, his exuding sensuality, or his feminine mystique, or any more of his freaking dichotomies. One more gushing comment, and it was quite possible he was going to be sick. He was already starting to feel a little woozy.

Food, he realized, was a big part of the problem. Having half a gallon of adrenaline unloaded into his system in about 0.2 seconds on an empty stomach always made him hungry. The food she'd mentioned being in her studio had never quite materialized, and he was reaching critical nonmass. He needed food, a lot of food, and less Travis. The EMT was actually a nice guy, but Kid was going to hate him in about five more minutes if Nikki couldn't find another subject. She'd gone through about eight subjects since they'd done their nitrous blast out of the canyon, but she seemed to have gotten stuck on Travis the glowing wonder stud.

One thing he'd figured out while she'd been talking nonstop was the absolute necessity of never, ever posing for one of her paintings. Models were weighted down with some pretty heavy freight in her book, and the freight made them untouchable. He wasn't even sure she saw them as real men, and he definitely did not want to be put in an untouchable, not-real-man category by her.

No way. He wanted to be touched by her, a lot, like in full body contact with sweaty skin and open mouths, but at this point he realized that was probably thinking way ahead of the game. *Way* ahead. She had hardly so much as looked at him since they'd met. It had all been about Travis, who, twenty bucks said, wasn't her lover.

So who was? he wondered for about the millionth time, and hoped like hell the answer was nobody. The way she talked about Travis made him think there wasn't anybody else in her life.

"Travis—"

Exactly, he thought.

"—has a small business on the side, where he sexually imprints women who have had bad experiences, putting the innocence of his sensuality to a really super good use. He's doing quite well. It's very pure, very cool, but Regan refuses to take him up on his offer of unlimited free sessions. It's crazy, of course. I'm sure he could help her, just the way he helped a friend of mine last year, whose boyfriend was having a, uh, problem, you know?"

No way could she expect him to answer that. But she'd gone dead silent again, leaving an expectant pause hanging in the air, torturing him, probably on purpose.

"No," he ground out. "I don't know." Nor did he want to know. Yet at the same time he was morbidly fascinated with what else she'd said. The guys back at the 24th Marines would love to get their hands on an idea like sexual imprinting, and he'd bet they'd all be happy to offer all the free sessions any woman wanted. Of course, there wasn't a Marine on the planet who could be described as innocent. Neither was there one who didn't already think of himself as a first-class sexual imprinter.

A broad grin split his face. What kind of racket was Travis running?

The boyfriend problem was something else, and he hoped to hell she would show some discretion and keep the details to herself.

"I'm hungry," he said abruptly, and hoped his panic didn't show. "Are you hungry?" Eating always made him feel better. Maybe it would work for her, too. Honestly, he was such an idiot. He should have been feeding her the minute they'd gotten out of the canyon. He'd been hungry since way before that, and the odds were good that she was hungry, too. "There's a bunch of fast-food places up ahead at the next exit. Mexican, Chinese, a sub sandwich place, hamburgers if you want one. We'll be fine, if you want to stop and get something quick."

"Uh, no, thanks," she said after a slight cough, or maybe a choking sound, and a moment's hesitation. "I don't, uh, think I could eat right now."

And she didn't sound like she could. Maybe it was the fast-food idea that turned her off.

"If you want an organic soybean-curd fajita or something, I'm sure I can find one." Actually, he wasn't at all sure he could, not off the turnpike, but if it would help her relax a little, he'd whip one up himself at Steele Street.

"No, that's…uh…fine. I don't really like soybean curd."

Go figure, Kid thought, an artsy Boulder chick who didn't like soybean curd.

He downshifted on the off-ramp, exiting the highway for the shopping malls, gas stations, and fast-food joints of the north Denver suburbs. If the choice was going to be his, it was gonna be cheeseburgers all the way, and if he was lucky, maybe he could get a few french fries or some milkshake down her. Anything, he was sure, could only help.

F*ROM* her side of the car, Nikki looked at him, aghast.

Eat? Was he crazy? The only way she could keep breathing was to keep talking, and he wanted to eat? She might never eat again in commemoration of the most freaking awful experience of her whole entire life.

If she hadn't gone to the bathroom before they'd left the house, she would have peed her pants. Under normal circumstances the very thought would have been mortifying—but not now. Oh, no. She was way beyond being embarrassed by a small physical dysfunction.

And hadn't he been sitting right here in the very same car with her? The one with the side mirror that had been shot off in a wave of bullets?

Bullets!

Just before it had actually been scraped clean off the car by a gigantic Winnebago going full speed, head-on, up the canyon? Hadn't he been sitting right next to her as he'd taken them to certain death in a game of chicken so close she still didn't believe they hadn't gone up in a ball of twisted metal and flame?

Oh, yes, she'd peeked over the dashboard and looked death in the face, and wasn't that all just seconds before they'd almost gone straight off the cliff, just before he'd flipped that awful red switch, the one she still couldn't bear to look at, and turned his already dangerously powerful Porsche into an Atlas rocket with a built-in fear factor that made the Dreaded Drop of Doom at Six Flags look like a baby buggy ride?

And he wanted to *eat*?

God, the very thought made her feel faint.

And feeling faint made her hyperventilate, and hyperventilating made it hard to breathe, and having difficulty breathing made her want to talk and talk and talk, until she had distracted herself enough to keep from fainting.

It was a vicious circle, and it was wearing her out at an alarming rate, and once she got worn out, she was going to cry, and she did not want to start crying just because she was so scared, not in front of him, not when she was so aware of him. And that was something she'd been avoiding thinking about at all costs. He was so . . . so everything.

No. It was better to talk, which would be a helluva lot easier if he would just talk back a little. Damn it, it was like pulling teeth to get him to say anything.

Like right now. He'd gone completely silent on her again, leaving the ball in her court, where the ball had been for the last half an hour, ever since they'd done that unbelievable Dukes of Hazzard thing up in the canyon. Couldn't he help her out a little?

Oh, God, she was going to cry, and for the first time since she'd been sixteen, she wasn't going to be able to save herself. What in the hell had Wilson done? And was he okay? Was Regan? Or were they getting shot at, too?

Oh, please. She couldn't bear the thought.

"I never had a pony when I was a kid," she blurted out, feeling a sob welling up in her throat. "I wanted one. I begged for one, but Regan and Grandpa wouldn't let me have one. They knew I wanted it to take to South America, to Peru. That's where my parents died, in Peru, in an earthquake, and I always thought if I could just get there with my pony, I could ride up into the mountains and find them, and the pony and I could dig them out, and bring them home, and then everything would be okay. It never occurred to me that they would still be dead. I was so sure that if I could just get them out from under the rubble, they would be fine. Funny, isn't it, the way kids think?"

After a moment, when he didn't say anything, she bit back her irritation and the sob stuck right in the middle of her throat, choking her, and she looked over at him.

He was watching her, his face very still, betraying nothing, and she realized he'd stopped the car. She didn't know when he'd done it, but they were stopped in a shadowed area of a shopping mall parking lot.

"You're crying," he said.

"Oh, damn." She checked her face and discovered he was right. Her cheeks were wet. Tears were running into the corners of her mouth. She wiped them away with the back of her hand, wondering what in the world had compelled her to tell him about the pony. She'd never told anyone but Regan and Wilson about the pony, and the whole idea had done nothing but freak the two of them out, especially Regan, who'd been afraid she actually would run off to Peru, whether she had a pony to take with her or not.

"How old were you when your parents died?" His voice was very calm, his question very straightforward, as if she hadn't just told him something really pitiful about herself.

God, the pony story. What had she been thinking?

"Three." She inhaled a breath, deeply, and hoped it would somehow get past the knot in her chest. "I, uh, don't remember them, my parents, not personally, I mean, because they were gone a lot that last year, and it wasn't until I was around ten or so that I realized *my* parents were dead. I'd always known Regan's parents were dead, and that was always so awful, the burden we all bore, the great family tragedy. It was what made us different from everybody else in the neighborhood. She cried a lot for them, but for me they were just people I couldn't remember—up until I was ten and it hit me that they'd been my parents, too."

"That must have been hard," he said, still so calm, his voice a little sad, surprisingly empathetic. "Hard to realize your parents were gone, and then realize you were really late in figuring it out."

She slanted him a quick glance, startled by his insight. She'd never told anyone that particular twist on her grief. She'd felt so stupid, and foolish, and alone. Not only had she missed her parents' lives, she'd missed their deaths, which had made her even more of a weirdo than she already was, which according to every housekeeper they'd ever hired was pretty damn weird—a situation that had not improved with the live-models-in-the-garden-shed incidents. Her first piece with Travis had garnered her national recognition in the Cooper-Lansdowne competition, but she'd never had to talk so fast in her life as she'd had to talk to keep Regan from sending her to a psychiatrist for professional help. She hadn't slept with Travis. Regan had made her swear it on their parents' unmarked graves—and to this day, she'd never slept with any of her models.

In fact, she'd never slept with anybody, not the full-contact, welcome-into-my-body type of sleeping with somebody, and seeing as how she'd just turned twenty-one last week, that was probably the weirdest thing about her of all. It was certainly the least known. Everyone thought she was such a wild thing.

"Were your parents' bodies ever recovered?"

"No." She shook her head and gave him another careful, slightly amazed look from across the Porsche. No one in her whole life had ever had the guts to ask her that.

"You might feel better about it if they were."

She didn't doubt that she would, had never doubted it, not since she'd first come up with the stupid pony plan. A part of her was utterly compelled to go to Peru, but she hadn't done it, and she wasn't sure exactly what kind of fear it was that kept her from going, whether it was the fear she wouldn't find them—or the fear that she would.

They'd be nothing but bones now. She wasn't sure she could bear that, to see their bones. She'd spent her whole life around bones. Wilson and Regan dragged them home by the truckload. It was the reason she worked with live models, living, warm-blooded, muscular, fleshed-out men who breathed and sweated. And when she painted them, they breathed and sweated on the canvas as well. Life pulsed from them. They were angels and demons and powerful creatures of psychic mythology—and they lived. In her work, she put the flesh on the bones. She didn't scrape the dust away and leave them all bare.

She hated bones.

"Wilson went to look for them once," she said. "But he couldn't find them, couldn't locate the bodies. Everyone he talked to had a different story about the *norteamericanos* and where they'd been when the quake had hit. He came home feeling worse than when he'd left, and I guess I always figured if he couldn't find them, I wouldn't have a chance." She gave a small shrug and rearranged a couple of the eye shadow containers in her silver box. "I wouldn't even know where to begin." It was an excuse, but an excuse she'd clung to for years.

"I would."

Dumbstruck, she lifted her head and stared at him. Had he just said what she thought he'd said? And who was he, she wondered, to even offer such a thing?

"If you ever decide you want to try, call me," he continued. "I'll see what I can do. Steele Street has a lot of connections in South America. I'm down there all the time. Quinn and I just got back from Colombia a few weeks ago, and my brother is still there."

He was serious. It was hard to believe, but he was actually serious.

"What's Steele Street?" she asked, swiping the back of her hand across her face, then lifting the hem of her T-shirt to do a better job. "The place where you work?" She kept her gaze on him.

"Uh, yes," he said, after clearing his throat. His gaze had dropped quickly to her bare midriff, before flicking back up to hold hers, and if she wasn't mistaken, a little color had washed into his cheeks.

That was interesting, she thought. Very interesting. It was the most emotional thing she'd seen him do all night. He hadn't so much as flinched during their ordeal in the canyon. Nor had he hesitated, not once. He'd been in complete control of their imminent destruction, right down to his lightning-quick reaction in drawing that wicked-looking shotgun in the middle of it all.

Hell, he'd even aimed. And now he was affected by her midriff? Was it possible he was feeling a little of what she was feeling? And wouldn't it be great if she could figure out exactly what that was?

"We do a lot of, uh, international business as well as domestic."

She read men for a living, and Mr. Thank You, Ma'am, but I'm in Charge was just a little bit flustered by her flash of skin. It was subtle, amazing, and definitely there. And in the odd way of things, it made her realize she wasn't having any more trouble breathing, and that she'd stopped crying, and that he truly had a remarkably soothing voice and incredibly beautiful eyes—which was about the millionth time she'd noticed that particular fact. They were thick lashed and deep set, with the most wonderfully stark, hawklike eyebrows.

She needed to paint him. Not on canvas, but put the paint right on him, her fingers on his face, sliding color across his skin—and if that flustered him a little more, all the better. She kind of liked him flustered.

"What kind of business?" she asked, and gave the edge

of her shirt a quick glance. Dark streaks of mascara dirtied the white cloth, giving her a pretty good clue as to what she must look like: a mess. The smudge of blue swirled next to the mascara didn't look promising, either. As usual, she must have had paint on her face the whole night, and as usual, no one had bothered to tell her.

Dang it.

"Cars, mostly. Specialized cars and security."

"You mean cars like this one, with armor?" And there they were, having a little old regular conversation, without her talking her head off. What a relief, even if the conversation was about armored cars.

But what in the world, she wondered, had Wilson been doing with those dinosaur bones to get them all in so much trouble?

"Yes."

"And is that where you learned how to drive like you were doing up in the canyon?" Which had been utterly insane, but she wasn't going to put it in those words. He'd probably saved her life driving like a madman.

"Actually, we go out to California, to a tactical driving school, every few months and burn up a few sets of tires."

Ex-sniper, ex-Marine, tactical driving, private company, bought his car complete with armor from a man who'd lived in Panama—finally, it was all starting to make sense. "So you're a bodyguard?"

"Sometimes. Yes, ma'am."

Ma'am. The man had offered to help her find her parents' remains, been blatantly sidetracked by her midriff, and he was still calling her ma'am? God, who would ever have believed that a sniper could be so sweet? Sweetly fierce like he'd been in her studio, sweetly sincere in the offer he'd made, and so sweetly beautiful, it hurt.

Yeah, she liked him flustered all right. She liked him flustered, because he flustered the hell out of her. His hair, short as it was, was standing on end. A trace of beard stubble darkened his jaw and upper lip. His clothes were rumpled and damp from the ungodly heat, and he was still beautiful, with cheekbones she wanted to slide her fingers over and a mouth she wanted to kiss—thoughts even more disconcerting now than they'd been an hour ago, when she'd been safely behind her camera.

"Have you been to Peru?"

He shook his head. "Colombia, Venezuela, Brazil, and all over Central America, but not down into Peru."

But he would go there? For her? To find her parents?

"I just about drove Grandpa crazy asking questions about Peru," she told him. "Where he'd gone. Who he'd talked with. I took notes in a special notebook. I wanted to know everything for the trip. I had maps and snacks, and a backpack full of winter clothes. Regan was terrified I was going to run away, and then one day, I just quit talking about going, quit planning the whole, big, awful adventure. I wasn't curious anymore. I was just angry, and I pretty much stayed angry."

"Until?" he asked.

"No until," she admitted. "I'm still angry." She knew the fact didn't throw her in a very mature light, but it was the truth. She was angry at her parents for hurting Regan, and for hurting Wilson, and for not even bothering to hang around long enough to find out who she was, before they'd gone and gotten themselves killed. She'd seen her grandpa crying, when he thought there was no one around.

Poor Wilson and Regan, they should have both learned a long time ago that she was always around, usually with a camera connected to a long lens. Shameless Nikki McKinney who spent her days painting beautiful, naked men. She couldn't imagine that her parents would have found her any less interesting than the other people who knew her. Every woman she knew wanted her job, but none of them had the talent, or the obsessive passion that took her work out of the prurient into the divine. Her men were beautiful, because she made them so. They were real, because she didn't let them keep their secrets.

"I guess I'd be angry, too," he said, and she looked up again to find him still watching her. The low light in the car cast him in the gray halftones of muted nighttime colors—making his face a study in silky ecru and velvety soft shadows.

So touchable. That's what he was, and if he showed her even one more ounce of sensitivity and compassion, she'd probably fall in love with him for life.

"What about you?" she asked, ignoring the soft wave of heat rolling through her body, turning in her seat to face him more fully. This was comfortable, being here with him in the dark, cozily tucked in his car. "Have you ever explored your feminine mystique?"

The question took him by surprise; she could tell by the way his eyebrows drew together, one lifting slightly higher than the other.

"I don't have one to, uh, explore," he said after a second more of confusion.

"Every man has one," she said, and watched his expression go from confusion to extreme doubt. "Honest. If you'd like to come to my studio sometime, let me paint you, I can guarantee you'll find yours." Oh, and wasn't she just so smooth—for all the good it was going to do her. From the look on his face, his feminine mystique wasn't something he particularly wanted to find.

"I don't think I'd make much of a model, ma'am."

Ma'am again. He was in perpetual politeness mode, and she wanted to take his clothes off.

"What about your folks? Where do they live?" she asked, giving him a break and changing the subject.

The relief on his face was so obvious, it was almost comical.

"My mom's in L.A. still trying to make it in the movies, which as far as any of the rest of us has been able to tell, isn't going to happen. She left when I was eight. Us boys stayed with Dad in Denver."

"Do you have any sisters?"

"No. All guys. My dad, my two older brothers, me, and usually two or three other kids who just always sort of ended up at our house for days or weeks on end. Quinn was there a lot, and a couple of other guys who are with Steele Street now. It was like growing up in a locker room, both the good and the bad."

"There's a good side to a boys' locker room?" she asked skeptically, but with a humorous edge, feeling better, safer, by the minute.

"Yeah, but you have to be a guy to appreciate it." He grinned, a flash of white teeth in a boyishly lopsided curve, and without any warning, her heart careened off into a slow, uncontrolled, 360-degree skid. He had dimples and slightly crooked lower teeth, and when he smiled he was absolutely devastating.

Oh, my God.

She was in such deep trouble.

A short laugh that had nothing to do with humor and everything to do with the nameless emotion tightening into a knot inside her chest escaped her on a surprised breath.

A Marine sniper.

God help her. She'd been so wrong. She didn't want to paint him; she wanted to inhale him.

CHAPTER 19

CHRISTIAN HAWKINS PULLED INTO Steele Street just before ten o'clock, pretty disgusted with the whole night.

The Pentagon's guns, which they should have found weeks ago, had disappeared off the face of the earth, leaving them with nothing but a bunch of dusty dinosaur bones in a Lafayette warehouse, and a whole bunch of people running around getting shot at. Regan McKinney's side trip to Cisco had started an avalanche that was picking up speed as the night wore on. The enemy had now been engaged, up close and personal, shots fired, and evasive action taken. But they were no closer to finding the Pentagon's assault rifles than they'd been four months ago.

He hoped to hell everything was about to change.

His footsteps echoed hollowly as he crossed the dim, open space, winding his way through the cars. This building on Steele Street was SDF's secret headquarters. Only nine people on the face of the earth had the fingerprints necessary to open the doors, or run the elevators, or access the building in any way, shape, or form. Most of them lived there at least part of the time. Hawkins kept a loft on the eleventh floor across from Skeeter's apartment. Quinn had the tenth, and Creed had taken the jungle loft on the ninth. J. T. had dibs on most of the twelfth along with Kid. Dylan, the boss, commandeered the top floor, the thirteenth, and there were enough nooks and crannies in the rest of the building to accommodate anyone who needed a place to store their stuff or themselves for a while.

As Hawkins neared the east side of the garage, he could see Jeanette parked in the shadows to the left of Roxanne. Great, he thought. At least one part of the night was going down right. Quinn had traded Jeanette for a less conspicuous ride.

Or so he first thought. When he looked around, he realized Quinn's idea of less conspicuous was none other than a candy-apple-red 1967 Dodge Coronet with hot pink piping.

Quinn had taken Betty, which was damned interesting since he had about forty-two cars to pick from. The one time out of a hundred he would pick Betty would be the one time he had a woman with him. It was the only reason any guy would pick Betty over something with a lot more muscle, because women loved Betty.

They loved her paint, her whitewalls, her tuned headers, and they really loved her hot pink piping. She was a babe magnet. He'd seen Betty charm females from Creed Rivera's seventy-eight-year-old great-grandmother to Johnny's thirteen-year-old little sister.

So what the hell was up with Quinn and Regan McKinney? He remembered her from all those years ago at Rabbit Valley. She'd been built even at fifteen, and cutely blond, fun to talk with, and nice—too nice to hold his interest beyond friendship. He didn't remember Quinn ever having much to say to her, but he definitely remembered Quinn watching her.

Shit.

The closer he got to the two cars, the clearer it became that Jeanette had been ridden hard and put away wet.

But how in the world had her windshield wiper been broken off? Quinn made a point of keeping Jeanette looking dirty and mean, but he treated her with kid gloves. She was an ultrahigh-performance machine who could turn on a dime, damn near break the sound barrier, and fall apart at the drop of a hat if her specs weren't met. So how in the hell had she lost a wiper?

He reached out to smooth his hand over her hood, then leaned down to take an eye-level gander. Sure enough, she'd been dented.

What the fuck? he wondered.

The rest of her body was in good shape, and he

ducked his head through the driver's-side window to check her out on the inside. Everything looked good, if *good* was the right word to describe the stripped down, bared bolts and snake-pit look of Jeanette's interior.

He started to duck back out of the car, when something pink caught his eye. Leaning in deeper, he reached out and picked up a scrap of cloth from between the passenger seat and the gear console.

It was a pair of lace underwear. Not very big. Pink. Torn.

Scented with expensive perfume.

He arched a brow. Regan McKinney's?

He brought the scrap of lace closer to his nose. Hell. Quinn had never had a chance. The guy just wasn't that strong when it came to smart, beautiful blondes built like Jack O' Nines strippers.

And wasn't that just great. He was so fucking glad to know *somebody* was having himself a real good time tonight.

IT was official, Quinn decided. They'd hit disaster status. The Southern Cross Hotel in Boulder had been compromised, and Kid and Nikki right along with it. Kid hadn't gone into details, but Quinn knew him well enough to read between the lines, and what he'd figured out wasn't anything he wanted to discuss with Regan right now. Better for her to have her little sister close at hand, all safe and sound, before she heard the particulars of Kid and Nikki's ill-fated attempt to reach the hotel.

Quinn pulled off the Boulder side street where Betty had been idling while he and Regan had been arguing for the last five minutes in between phone calls from Kid and Hawkins. She wanted to go to Lafayette. He wanted to ship her as far away from this mess as he could get her. She wanted a chance to study the dinosaur bones. He didn't give a damn about the bones.

And somehow, she'd won. Thanks to the last phone conversation with Hawkins, who had pointed out that Regan might spot something about the bones that her grandfather had missed. Quinn turned the car east, heading toward Lafayette and the warehouse, instead of Denver and Steele Street, where he should have been taking her.

"You won't regret this," she said, her voice full of excitement, but she was wrong. He already regretted it, and they hadn't even gotten there yet.

"Thirty minutes. That's all. Then we tie the whole thing up," he said. "And Hawkins better be right about bringing you in."

The clincher had been time. They were running out. Hawkins had weighed in heavily in favor of using everything they had to get some sort of edge on Roper and get their dead-in-the-water operation back on track—now. If they didn't handle this right, the McKinneys were going to be prime candidates for the Federal Witness Protection Program, or they were going to be dead.

It was a chance nobody wanted to take, which had put Quinn's back flat up against the wall and left him doing the exact opposite of what every instinct in his body was telling him to do. He was taking Regan to Lafayette to look over the damn bones, and probably taking her straight into a whole lot of trouble.

Shit. The absolute best day of his whole life had just taken a real bad turn for the worse.

CHAPTER

20

ONCE HE'D DELIVERED Nikki to Steele Street and left her with her grandfather, Kid found Hawkins on the eighth floor, in the armory, picking out a pair of HK MP5 submachine guns with four extra thirty-round clips.

"Expecting trouble?" Kid asked, crossing the room where SDF kept their weapons and assault equipment.

"Looking forward to it, if it gets this far," Hawkins said, loading a magazine into one of the guns. "We either finish this thing up, or it starts coming down around our ears even more than it already has. Where's the girl?"

"Nikki? With her grandfather."

"When I checked, he was asleep." Hawkins slipped the extra clips into a hip pouch on his belt.

"Still is, but she wanted to see him, make sure he was okay. It's been a rough night."

"Johnny still asleep, too?"

Kid nodded. "You going to need another shooter in Lafayette, or do you want me to stay here?"

"Here. We're going to set the bones up as an easy snatch-and-grab for Roper and his guys, if anything about seven tons of rock can be called easy." He flashed Kid a weary grin. "What a fucking mess. This thing has been crazy from the get-go. I want the guns, and I want out."

"What about Regan McKinney?"

"Quinn is taking her to Lafayette to look over the fossils." Hawkins picked up an extra pistol magazine and slipped it in a separate pouch. "Seems the old man found something he forgot to tell me about. I knew he was pretty excited about this one chunk of rock. But he pretty much got wound up about every chunk of rock we had. Then when I'd push him on it a little, he'd kind of forget why he was so excited. I think the pressure has been too much for him. He doesn't forget how to button his shirts or anything, but he does forget what he's doing, even while he's doing it. He might not have been Dylan's best call for the job."

"Dylan usually doesn't make mistakes."

"Yeah, well, he usually doesn't get very damn sentimental, either."

Kid understood Hawkins's complaint. He knew SDF's and Steele Street's history as well as any of the guys who had lived it, starting with the street gang of car thieves who'd worked out of this very building, and the Bust, as they always called it.

He also knew about the subsequent summer they'd all spent baking in the desolate badlands of western Colorado at the misnamed Rabbit Valley. Not a one of the busted juvies had seen a rabbit the whole damn time they'd been there, though Hawkins had told him about a run-in he'd had with a rattlesnake. Wilson McKinney always figured pretty heavily in the stories, kind of a curmudgeon-with-a-heart-of-gold type, but no one had ever mentioned his granddaughters. Of course, Nikki couldn't have been much more than a little kid back then. Regan would have been more the guys' age, though, and Kid was betting Quinn had noticed her—plenty.

"Skeeter says Wilson has got a good reputation with dinosaur bones and stuff."

"So does his granddaughter, apparently. Now it's her turn." Hawkins checked the load on his pistol before returning it to its holster. "By the way, Dylan called about twenty minutes ago. He'll be in tonight. Something's come up in Colombia."

Colombia, Kid thought. His brother J. T. and Creed were in Colombia.

"He said he'd have better intel by the time he got here." Hawkins glanced up at Kid. "I need you to get some sleep. Once Roper gets the bones, we're not letting them out of our sight. Quinn and I will finish up the night shift, but I'm going to need you for the A.M. stakeout."

"Quinn shouldn't even be here in Denver, let alone be chasing Roper's merchandise around, not with the price Roper has on his head," Kid said. As for whatever had come up in Colombia, his brother and Creed were on a hostage rescue mission that didn't have anything to do with the Roper Jones operation. Maybe they'd finally gotten their guy away from the rebels who had kidnapped him.

"Yeah," Hawkins agreed. "Dylan is going to kick all our asses if we lose the poster boy, but Quinn is ready to rumble, and quite frankly, I think *he's* gonna kick *Roper's* ass—which works out a whole lot better than if I do it."

Kid agreed with a nod of his head. ALL-AMERICAN HERO TAKES OUT CRIME LORD played a whole hell of a lot better than EX-CON MURDERS CRIMINAL SUSPECT IN GANG-LIKE SLAYING, even in the brackish backwaters of Capitol Hill where SDF's orders originated out of the underbelly of the Department of Defense.

"You ever hear of feminine mystique?" Kid asked.

"Betty Friedan?" Hawkins said, without so much as a lift of his eyebrows when the question came out of the blue. "Yeah. I read it. Pretty damned depressing book. I think they put it in the library at the state pen just to mess with our minds."

"No, I'm not talking about a book. It's a...I don't know, a way of thinking maybe. Or a way of... glowing."

That got Hawkins's attention. He looked up from the ammunition bench, where they made their custom loads.

"Glowing?"

Kid shrugged self-consciously. "Yeah. Nikki McKinney, she's an artist, only paints men, really out-there, spectacular stuff, but one of the things she really likes in a guy is his feminine mystique, the way he kind of glows with the tension inherent in the masculine/feminine dichotomy."

Hawkins blinked, then said, "Okay." To Kid's surprise, he didn't sound the least bit incredulous or confused—only slightly curious.

Great. He knew he'd come to the right place. Kid's brother J. T. wouldn't know feminine mystique from beans, but Hawkins, well, the guy just knew stuff.

"Well," Kid said hesitantly. "I . . . uh . . . don't have any."

Hawkins gave him a sidelong glance. "No feminine mystique?"

"Nope."

"And you need some, because you like this girl?"

"Yeah. I guess I do. She says she can help me find mine, but—I don't know." He shrugged.

"Go ahead and let her." Hawkins turned back to the bench and finished loading another magazine. "Hell, you might be surprised with what she comes up with."

Let her? Kid studied Hawkins's face. He was serious. Okay. He supposed there were worse ways to spend time than posing naked for a beautiful woman who might possibly finger-paint your body, and he was pretty sure that would be Nikki's way of helping. A grin split his face. Definitely top ten material there.

"Okay. Maybe I'll do just that."

"I remember her from Rabbit Valley," Hawkins said as he shoved another ammo mag in his belt. "She was a cute kid. I guess she turned out okay."

"More than okay." Kid's grin broadened. "She's amazing."

"Right. Another amazing McKinney woman." Hawkins let out a short laugh, then went back to loading magazines. "Look, I'll call you about four o'clock to tell you where we are."

Kid checked his watch. It was almost eleven. Buoyed by the new plan, he helped Hawkins finish up. When Hawkins left for Lafayette, Kid went back to the office to check on Nikki.

She was alone and asleep. The minute he saw her, curled around a pillow on the bed in one of the guest suites, he knew he couldn't do it. He couldn't be naked in front of her while she painted him or took his picture, or tried to dress him up in angel wings or anything else. It was a great fantasy, but the reality of it was impossible.

First, he'd probably embarrass himself with a raging hard-on, which Travis had not done. He didn't know how, but the guy had been totally placid during the whole shoot. Kid just didn't have that kind of disinterest. He hadn't been able to think of much besides sex since she'd answered the door back at her house.

Secondly, he just couldn't do it. Couldn't bear the thought of her looking for something in him that just wasn't there, and missing *him* in the process. Not that she was likely to miss his guaranteed hard-on. He was more than okay in that department. No ego. Just the facts, and given her artistic expertise, so to speak, she would definitely notice.

So, great. He was standing there, watching her sleep and thinking about his equipment—and the equipment was rising to the occasion.

It was pathetic. She was just lying there, fully clothed, breathing, and he was getting turned on. It didn't make sense. She wasn't even his type, not even close. He liked tall, willowy blondes and brunettes with long hair and even longer legs. Girls who were athletic, liked extreme sports, and were preferably stuck on him. Colorado was full of these beautiful outdoor girls whose only makeup was a tan and whose idea of fixing their hair was winding it up in some kind of a knot and sticking a chopstick or a pencil or both through it. They wore cargo shorts and T-shirts that said SAVE THE ESCALANTE, and their mountain bikes cost more than their cars.

Nikki still had mascara smears on her face, and her little silver box of makeup doodads was right next to her on the bedside table. She had five earrings in one ear, and three in the other, and her hair was black and purple, neither color anywhere near a natural shade. Her T-shirt had almost as much Lycra in it as her little black skirt. It clung to her, leaving nothing to the imagination—as if his imagination needed any help.

She stirred on the bed while he watched, stretching with sleepy grace and absolutely riveting him to the spot. He couldn't take his eyes off her, and when her eyes opened, her gaze went straight to him.

"I missed you," she said around a small yawn, her hair a wild tousle of pure bed head, her T-shirt riding up just enough to give him a heart attack.

Yeah, right, he thought, his pulse skipping a beat. He'd known her a little over four hours, been gone less than twenty minutes, and he'd missed her, too, a lot. This was so pitiful, feeling this way, but there didn't seem to be a damn thing he could do about it. She was so freaking beautiful. How could any guy not stare?

"How's your grandfather?" He already knew, had just checked on the old man, but it felt like the polite thing to ask.

"Asleep"—she yawned again—"just like the boy watching him. What's his name again?"

"Johnny Ramos."

"He's cute. Almost pretty, with those delicate Hispanic features," she said, dragging her hand back through her hair, making it stick up even more wildly from her head. "How old is he?"

Kid just stared at her, then expelled a burst of laughter. "No way," he warned her, and laughed again. "No way. He's only seventeen."

A sleepy, teasing smile curved her lips. "Okay. He's

jailbait. How about you? Have you changed your mind about modeling for me?"

"Maybe," he admitted, and wondered just how true it might be.

"I was dreaming about you."

Well, that pretty much froze him to the floor.

"I was so scared tonight," she continued, her smile fading into another yawn. She rolled onto her back and covered her mouth until the yawn was finished, then turned back to him. "Sometimes I talk too much, when I'm scared. I'm sorry I went all motor-mouth on you."

"Not a problem," he assured her, knocked senseless by the way she moved. He'd never seen so much unconscious grace in such a small package. Everything about her was so smooth—mesmerizing. "I think I've got your whole life story now."

"How awful for you." She propped her head up on her hand and gave him the full benefit of her undivided attention.

Even with the mascara smudges, he'd never seen more beautiful eyes, such a clear, sun-shot gray, her lashes so thick it occurred to him they might not be real, her eyebrows like two perfect sparrow wings. Everything about her was perfect. She was pedicured, manicured, and probably bikini-waxed.

Whoa, what a dangerous thought to have pop into his mind.

He cleared his throat. "No. It was fine, really, except that you were scared."

"Weren't you?"

"A little," he confessed. "In places." Especially for her.

She stared at him for a long, quiet moment.

"I found my cherry lip gloss."

"Uh, great." Cherry lips. Right. That's just what he needed to know—that her mouth was all glossy soft and sticky sweet with the taste of cherries.

"Are you going to be around for a while? Doing the bodyguard thing?" she asked, sitting up on the bed. A long, sinuous stretch followed, complete with another yawn.

"Yes, ma'am." The words came out sounding like something he'd swallowed. His heart beat heavily in his chest. He was going to have to kiss her. He couldn't possibly get through the night, or even the next five minutes, without kissing her. His body was nearly electrified with the need to touch her, to somehow draw her close and bury his face in the curve of her neck and shoulder, to open his mouth on her skin and run his tongue all the way down her body from her throat to between her legs.

Geezus. He was going to fry a circuit board if he didn't get out of the room.

He cleared his throat again. "I'll be out in the office, if you need anything." Amazingly, the statement came out fairly controlled, as if he were actually in charge of himself—which he wasn't at all. She breathed, and his pulse raced. She glanced at him, and his blood surged.

"No," she said quickly, half coming off the bed, a trace of panic in her voice. Then she blushed and sat back down. "I mean, I was hoping you would stay, for just a while. I thought, well, you don't have to take your clothes off or anything, but I thought I could do your face."

"Do my face?"

"Yes." She gave him a small smile and scooted back on the bed, making room for him at the same time as she reached for her box of tiny makeup containers. "Just your face, I swear. Please. It'll help me relax. I've never been shot at before."

Yes. Of course. Perfect. He owed her that much at least. He'd be happy to sit on the bed with her and have her hands all over him.

All over his *face*—anything to get close to her.

And when he died from pure and abject sexual frustration, it would at least be an artistic death. He would keel over looking like God knew what by the time she was finished with him.

No, he told himself, *use your head*. It was impossible. He simply wasn't to be trusted on a bed with her.

"Sure," he said, walking over as casually as possible and consigning himself to a few minutes of glorious torture.

But it wasn't a few minutes. A half an hour later, Nikki was still "doing his face," and he was floating someplace between heaven and hell.

She smelled wonderful, not like perfume, but a little like makeup, a little like her studio, and a lot like warm skin and soft breath, and up close he'd figured out that her eyelashes were real. She'd gotten an expression on her face, the same look he'd seen when she'd been

278 ◆ TARA JANZEN

working with Travis, and he was fascinated by it. He'd never thought anyone could be so intensely focused on his face.

What was she seeing? he wondered, when she would lean back and narrow her gaze, taking him all in before she started in anew. He might have doubted it was him at all, except that now and then she would meet his gaze, and color would rise in her cheeks.

He loved it, her awareness. Personally, he was going for a Bronze Star in awareness. She was using her fingers on him and lots of brushes, dabbing out of her tiny pots and compacts, spiking his hair and putting color there, and every time she touched him, another pint of blood drained out of his brain and pooled in his groin. It was the most perfectly awful and wonderful sensation, a real challenge to his integrity and everything he believed in. He was holding himself so still, he was hardly breathing to keep from rising up and pressing her back down onto the bed and consuming her.

"There," she finally said, sitting back on her heels.

Reaching out, she took his chin in one hand and turned his face to either side, surveying her handiwork.

"Do you want to see?"

"Sure." God, he was so smooth. He'd actually managed a word without his voice cracking.

She took a small digital camera out of her purse and leaned back to take a picture. When she turned the camera around and gave it to him, he glanced down and was instantly taken back.

He looked up and met her gaze, amazed.

"Do you know what you are?" she asked, an excited smile playing about her lips.

"Yes." He knew what he was, what she'd made him. He knew exactly what she'd painted on his face, and it did nothing short of astound him.

"Well?"

"A goshawk." Not a Cooper's hawk, or a red-tailed hawk, not a gyrfalcon or a golden eagle, but a goshawk— the largest, deadliest hawk. They were fierce predators, skilled hunters coveted by falconers all over the world. "I had one as a kid. We called him Gus."

"Gus the goshawk?" She wrinkled her nose. "That's not very regal."

"Gus was a goofball," he said, grinning. He looked back to the digital photo. It was all there on his face, the bird's dark crown and cheek patches, a yellow stripe across the bridge of his nose, a dark gray beak, his eyes done in a narrowed, raptor gaze. "You are so good."

"Do you want to do me?"

Oh, yeah. His gaze snapped up to meet hers. He wanted to do her all night long.

"I mean, my face," she hurriedly explained, a faint wash of color coming into her cheeks. God, she was pretty.

His own cheeks had to look the same way, but she would never see it through the mask she'd brushed on his face.

His instinct was to say no, he wasn't much of an artist, but for once, he didn't follow his instincts. He needed to expand his horizons if he was going to keep up with her, and he definitely wanted to keep up with her, maybe even get ahead of her if he could. They were at Steele Street. They were safe. He could let down his guard a while longer—long enough to play her game, even if he didn't have a clue about the rules.

"Sure," he said, reaching out and taking her chin in his hand, the way she'd done to him. He turned her face from side to side, acting as if he knew what he was doing, when all he really wanted to do was touch her. Her skin was so soft, her bones delicate within his light grasp. "Close your eyes."

That was better, he thought, when she did. Now he could look his fill.

"Don't forget the base," she said.

"Right." He picked up the biggest brush and dusted it off on his pants, getting rid of any color. Then he dragged it across her cheeks, first one and then the other, down the length of her nose, across her forehead, letting the soft bristles fan out on her skin. He took his time, covering her whole face in gentle sweeps, and suddenly he understood what Hawkins had said. He was sinking into feminine mystique faster than snowballs melting in hell, playing makeup with a girl. And he liked it. A lot.

He'd be the first to admit he'd grown up in a rowdy, raucous, and sometimes sexually crude household, lots of guy jokes, a few—okay, more than a few—pinups here and there, and he'd be the first to admit that he'd been known to approach sex as sort of a two-person team sport with a definite goal in mind and the whole point being to score.

But this.

This was wildly different.

He hadn't known he liked this sweet, teasing sensuality and the way it was wrapping around him from a thousand different directions.

He switched brushes, to something smaller, and made sure to wipe all the color off on his pants. With small, measured strokes, he started feathering invisible lines down each side of her nose and across the tops of her cheeks to the corners of her eyes.

"Are you doing a bird, too?"

"Mmm-hmmm." He leaned in to studiously and invisibly color in the area beneath her eyebrows. She had the sexiest eyebrows.

"What kind?"

"Sparrow." He reached for her tube of cherry lip gloss.

"Don't goshawks eat sparrows?"

"Yes. They do. Open your mouth."

And she did.

Wow.

He twirled up the lip gloss and touched it to the center of both her lips.

"Sparrows don't use lip gloss," she said quietly, trying not to move her mouth too much.

"This one does." He twirled the tube back down and tossed it aside, then smeared the little dabs of gloss with the pad of his thumb, giving her soft, glossy, cherry, cherry lips. They felt like wet satin.

His breath caught in his throat, and his thumb drifted to a slow stop in the middle of her lower lip.

"Are you finished?"

"No." His gaze slid over her, from the thick sweep of lashes lying across the tops of her cheeks, down the delicate symmetry of her nose, to her cherry lips. This was it. He'd reached the absolute end of his rope. His whole body was pulsing. He felt hot everywhere, and the only thing that could possibly save him was to make love with her.

"No," he confessed again, leaning in closer. "Just getting started."

He lowered his mouth to hers, just his mouth, and tasted her cherry lips. God, she was sweet and as ready for a kiss as he'd been. She instantly softened, flowing toward him, touching her tongue to his. Her sigh escaped into his mouth, and Kid felt the whole world shift on its axis.

With one arm firmly around her, he lowered her back onto the bed, kissing her the whole time, and more by miracle than design, he ended up between her legs.

Geezus.

"Oh," she said, when he lifted his head.

He knew what she meant. There was no mistaking how turned on he was, not when he was pressed up against her, right where he'd dreamed of being.

"Don't worry. I won't, uh, you know..." His voice trailed off in embarrassed confusion. She turned him around more than any girl he'd ever known.

"Force yourself on me?" she finished for him, a small smile turning up the corners of her mouth.

He nodded, totally turned around now. She simply upended him.

"Don't worry. I won't force myself on you, either." A teasing light lit the soft gray depths of her eyes. "At least I don't think so. I've never done it before."

Of course she hadn't. Girls never did—well, except once he remembered a girl getting a little sexually aggressive with him. Not that he hadn't been able to fend her off or anything, but it had been a real eye-opener, and he'd been real careful after that to make sure he never . . .

Wait a minute.

"Never?" he asked, picking up on a subtle inflection in what she'd said. He wasn't embarrassed now. He was focused, fascinated, and he didn't want to misunderstand her in any way.

"Never," she said, her gaze turning oh-so-serious. "Not once. Not with any of them."

Well—he took a breath—there was no way to misunderstand that. He knew who she was talking about, all those ripped, naked guys in her studio and on her living room walls.

"You're a virgin," he said, and even to him his voice sounded oddly flat, but she'd done it again, completely turned him inside out. The wild girl who painted naked men was a virgin? What did that mean? Had she seen enough of them and just wasn't interested? Hell. He'd let one kiss go to his head and give him all sorts of ideas. Okay, that was a lie. He'd had all those ideas long before he'd kissed her. Damn.

"Does that bother you?" she asked.

Okay, take a breath. That one had trick question written all over it. *Don't lose your head,* he told himself. *Think.*

"No . . . no, not really," he could honestly say. She was saving herself for someone special, and he had to admire that, even if it broke his heart, not to mention a hundred other places in him he couldn't even name. "Actually, I think that's pretty cool." Cool for some lucky guy who he didn't think was going to be him. Hell, all he'd done was drag her around and get her shot at. She barely knew him—and yet he felt like he knew her.

He felt like he knew her through and through, as if she were a piece of him he'd never known he'd been missing. When she'd opened her door, the connection had been that sudden, that intense.

Looking down into her eyes, he smoothed his hand up the side of her face and ran his fingers into her hair. It was hard to imagine she hadn't felt something of what had hit him so hard.

She shifted beneath him. It was a small movement, but it was enough to send a bolt of pleasure shooting straight through his body. God help him.

"Nikki, I . . ." What could he say?

"Would you look in the makeup box for me? On the bottom?"

No. He didn't think he could. He was done playing with makeup. Now all he wanted to do was play with her. But a virgin—he wasn't sure what she wanted.

He glanced at the box anyway, past all the doodads,

and a disbelieving grin slowly curved his mouth. How could he have missed it earlier, tucked into the bottom like that? And how could he get this lucky?

"Are you sure?" he asked, looking back at her, not daring to believe what he was seeing in her eyes and hearing in her voice. Not figuring he could possibly be this lucky, this—Holy Mother of God—this blessed, that she, the woman of his dreams, could want him as much as he wanted her. A virgin. Sweet Jesus.

"Will you call me ma'am and take *all* your clothes off for me if I say yes?"

His grin broadened even as his pulse raced. She wanted him. "Yes, ma'am."

She laughed at that, a soft, giggly laugh, and he kissed her, lowered his mouth to hers and simply indulged himself. She touched him with her tongue, tasting him, and he returned the favor, letting himself just get high on her kisses, her mouth so wet, and warm, and lush. Easing onto his side, he pulled her close and slid his hand down her back, molding her to him.

He didn't mean to move too fast, but her skirt was damned short, and his hand ended up under it before he even knew that's where he was headed. God, it was heaven to touch her. He wanted to touch her everywhere, naked, but told himself to take it easy, to slow down. Then he felt her hands at the front of his pants, felt her fingers undoing his belt, and he gave up all thoughts of going slow.

"Take off your shirt," she murmured, breaking off their kiss.

With her hands on his zipper, he was only too happy to comply, shucking out of his clothes even as he helped her remove hers, skimming the skirt down her legs and her T-shirt up over her head. She giggled a couple of times when one thing or another got stuck, but by the time they were done with each other, all her laughter had turned to sighs and soft sounds of encouragement, soft words of love.

"You're so beautiful, Kid." Her hands were all over him. His mouth was all over her. Every place he kissed her, she tasted like a promise kept. Every place she touched him, she left a trail of fire.

When he'd taken all he could, he emptied the makeup box on the bed and retrieved the condom from the bottom. He wanted inside her, and she was whispering in his ear that she wanted the same.

"I'll be careful." He sheathed himself with the prophylactic before settling over her. Leaning down, he kissed her cheek.

"I know, and I'm not worried, really, even though . . ."

He met her gaze and grinned, and felt shy even as he did. "Yeah. I know." He was big, but he *would* be careful—and she was so ready for him. He'd made sure of that.

He entered her in careful degrees, kissing her the whole while, being careful not to put too much of his weight on her, or too much of himself inside her too soon.

"Kid—" He heard the note of panic in her voice, felt her tighten her grip on his waist.

"Shhh. It's okay," he murmured, pulling back out and trying again, taking it even easier.

He'd never made love to anyone so slowly in his whole life. He felt like they'd fallen into a time warp— but every breath was filled with the scent of her, and every kiss was filled with the taste of her, and he never wanted any of it to end.

Her first time—*oh, yeah.* He was finally in deep enough to thrust. When he did, he felt a slight barrier give way and heard her gasp.

Holding himself perfectly still, he nuzzled her ear, kissed her cheek. "Are you okay?"

"Mmmmm." She moved against him, lifting her hips ever so slightly, and relief flooded through him. He pulled almost all the way out of her, before slowly sliding back in. She arched her head back on a soft purr, and he ran his tongue down the length of her throat. She was so beautiful. Her breasts small, her nipples softly pink. He leaned down and captured one with his mouth—and sucked, so gently. She groaned, and the sound went straight to his balls, making them tight. God, this was heaven. She was so responsive, so languorous, and so incredibly hot. She was melting for him, and she was so wet.

The briefest grin curved his lips, and he slid his mouth up to nuzzle her throat. She wasn't weatherproof. It was one of the wonderful things about girls. When they got wet, they melted like sugar in the rain. The first time he'd heard J. T. and Quinn discussing this amazing phenomenon, he'd been way too young to understand, and they hadn't been the least inclined to explain girl stuff to J. T.'s baby brother. But he hadn't forgotten, and in a few more years, he'd gotten a pretty good idea of what they'd been talking about, especially from the guy's side, the weatherproof side. When guys got wet, they were vulcanized. They got hard and stayed hard, and the wetter they got, the harder they got. They were weatherproof.

He was the living truth, vulcanized right down to his soul by her body's response. No melting for him. Oh, no. Except in his heart, where she'd turned him into mush, and his brain, which was operating strictly on autopilot. She was so beautiful—her nose so delicate and refined, her cheeks so soft, and her mouth ...

God, her mouth.

He slanted his lips over hers and thrust into her again. It was her first time, and he wanted her to come. He wanted to feel it. He wanted to know she'd come for him—and he wanted to give her pleasure, mind-blowing pleasure, because he wanted her to stay.

To stay with him for days, and weeks, and months, maybe forever. She rocked his world hard, and he wanted to know everything about her. She could paint all the naked men she wanted, because he'd been the first to make love to her. Maybe he would be the last. Maybe.

Carefully pulling all the way out, he moved down her body, kissing her softly on her belly, following her itsy-bitsy tan line down to the silky insides of her thighs. His heart was racing. She must cause riots at the pool.

Sliding his fingers through her dark curls, he opened her for his kiss. She caught her breath on a shocked gasp, then released it on a soft whimper when he licked her, his tongue gliding over the soft, silky, hot, sweet center of her arousal again, and again, and again. She stiffened, and a rush of pleasure so intense it made him groan shot through him. His hand tightened convulsively on her waist, holding her still for his delicate assault.

She cried his name and opened her legs for him even wider, surrendering to his mouth, to his fingers sliding in and out of her so very, very gently. It was her first time, and he wanted to push her right to the edge and take her down the other side in a long, long fall. He wanted it to be exquisitely sweet for her, more pleasure than she could ever have given herself. He wanted to give her a guaranteed, soul-shattering orgasm she would never, ever forget, not if she lived to be a hundred.

Caressing her, he slid his hand up her torso and down her arm, taking her hand in his and bringing it to his mouth. He sucked on her fingers, then moved back up her body to suck on her mouth. He kissed her over and over again, loving being with her, being on top of her and feeling her getting more and more turned on.

Cradling her head with one hand, he took hold of himself with his other and checked to make sure his condom was still in place, before he fitted himself back inside her. He pushed in just a little way and held himself still.

"Mmmm." She murmured a soft sound deep in his mouth, her hips lifting toward his, and he pressed himself deeper, dying just a little, but not going all the way, not yet. The torture was too sweet. He wanted to play with her and tease her for as long as was humanly possible, with no rules save one. He wanted her to come. He wanted her to have that for her first time, for every time.

He lifted himself above her, resting on his forearms, and moved himself in and out of her in a lazy, heat-inducing rhythm. They smelled like sex, the two of them, warmly animal, their skin damp with sweat and pleasure. She was small, so slight, and yet so female. She was taking him easier now, her body having adjusted, and when he gave her all of himself, she took all of him with a groan of longing, not pain.

"Kid." His name was barely a breath, uttered with such need he leaned down and kissed her cheeks, her brow. He was here, with her. He wouldn't leave her, not ever. Her leg came around his waist, holding him more closely to her as he pumped, and she groaned his name again.

God. He felt it, too, the edge of pleasure turning sharp and sweet.

"Kid." She tossed her head, her hands grabbing him on either side of his waist, pulling him deeper, holding him tighter.

He hesitated, then thrust, making her wait for a heartbeat or two in varied intervals, slipping his hand between them to stimulate her. It didn't take much before her body went taut beneath him, his name sighing from her lips, urgent and wanton.

"Kid . . . don't . . . please, yes."

He was in such a haze. He understood her perfectly, his mouth wet on hers, her body slick and balanced on the edge. He slid his other hand up the length of her arm, twining his fingers through hers, rocking into her again and again, until she came, her breath catching, her body pushing up against his, holding him deep. She gasped his name, and he went rigid, releasing on wave after wave of the purest, sweetest ecstasy. It rolled through him, making it hard to breathe, impossible to think.

At the end, he felt transported, his body in some sort of limbo. He rested his forehead on hers, but other than finding his breath, didn't even try to come down. He was so high. His muscles were twitching with latent pleasure, his mind floating in the ozone of total physical and mental relaxation—and he would have stayed there for as long as he could have possibly ridden it out, if he hadn't bent down to kiss her and tasted her tears.

"Nikki?" He rolled to his side and wiped her cheek with his thumb. He knew he hadn't hurt her. She'd been with him, right there with him, every single second. "What's wrong?"

"Nothing. Oh, Kid." She sighed, kissing his face, his mouth, her hands sliding over his chest.

Yeah, he thought, understanding dawning on him. He was just lucky he wasn't crying, too. He'd never felt anything like what had just happened between the two of them. Never. She was hot and sweet and soft and smart, funny and tender and wild, and he was in love. Crazy in love.

He kissed the top of her head where she was snuggled up against him, relaxing into sleep, the movement of her hand slowing into a lazy caress.

He should tell her about being in love. Feeling what he was feeling, there was no way to keep it inside. Yeah, he needed to tell her, and he would—tomorrow.

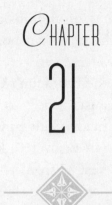

CHAPTER

21

No GUNS. Just bones. Nothing but bones. Quinn stood
in the middle of the Lafayette warehouse and couldn't
believe he'd almost gotten himself killed over a pile of
old bones that even Regan seemed to find disappointing.

"It's not here," she said again, examining one of the
fossils for the second time. She'd been through them
all in a quick search for the Cretaceous carnivore nest
Wilson had thought he'd found. They'd been at the
Lafayette warehouse for more than half an hour, and her
time was up. She knew it, he knew it, and all they
needed now was for Hawkins to show up so they could
bait the trap.

"Wilson seemed so sure," she said, walking down the
side of a long table, her fingers sliding from one fossil
to the next, some still half plastered, some with their

jackets removed. Most of the fossils were crated on pallets on the floor, the ones that positively weren't the *Tarbosaurus* nest.

Neither were they the Pentagon's OICW assault rifles, he thought with disgust, trying to remember exactly what it was that had made General Grant so damn sure this was the shipment to steal.

"Maybe it was all just wishful thinking on Wilson's part," Quinn said to her, getting carefully down off the forklift he'd been using. His knee was starting to hurt like hell. He'd spent his half hour organizing the "reject fossils" for easy loading. Hell, he'd practically gift wrapped the damned things. When Roper did finally show up—and Quinn knew he would—Quinn wanted things to move fast and smooth. He wanted the bad guys in, and he wanted the bad guys out. No screwups. Not when Regan was going to be there—a risk he should have known better than to take.

Damn it.

"You think he's delusional?" she asked, looking up from the table.

"Your grandfather? I haven't seen him in years, but from what you've said, it's possible." He didn't want to add to her worries, but here they were, and there wasn't a damn dinosaur nest in sight, or anything else that changed their situation. "What do you think of the rest of the fossils?"

"They're a mess." She looked around at the crates she'd checked and the few fossils still on the table. "No two bones seem to be from the same species, let alone the same animal. They weren't jacketed very carefully. There aren't any skulls, no teeth, no vertebrae. You seem to have somebody's discard pile of bone fragments without the map to tell you where they were found and how they were laid out."

Great. He'd dragged her into this for nothing.

"What's wrong?" she asked, coming around the side of the table.

"Nothing," he lied, making an effort to get the scowl off his face. "Look, I guess I should have told you this before, but you can have another chance at these bones if you want it."

"What do you mean?" Confusion marred her features.

"We're going to let Roper have the fossils tonight, but we won't let him keep them if that's not in our best interest."

Her brows furrowed even deeper.

"You'll steal them back," she said after a moment. A small smile threatened the corners of her mouth. "You haven't changed at all, have you?"

He smiled, too. "No."

He hadn't changed, not one iota, from the shaggy-haired sixteen-year-old juvenile delinquent she'd first seen all those years ago. Neither had Hawkins changed, or Dylan or any of the guys her grandfather had taken under his wing. After all the years, and all the miles, in their hearts and by trade, they were still thieves. Only now they stole for the government.

"So you stole a hundred cars before you got caught,"

she said, settling back against the table and crossing her arms over her chest. "Why?"

He'd been seeing that one coming all night, since he'd first confessed to her up on that dirt road above Denver, and he'd already decided to tell her the truth.

"Stress."

"Stress?" Her brows lifted. "What stress?"

"Going-hungry stress, freezing-your-ass-off stress, and getting-kicked-out-of-the-house stress. We had it all."

All traces of her smile faded away, and her eyes went dark and serious. "Who's *we?*"

"Me and my mom."

"What about your dad?" It was a fair question, or would have been if his father had had any bearing on their situation, which he hadn't.

"You know," he said, walking over to her and pressing a brief kiss to her mouth. "He's not such a bad guy. Guess he actually turned out pretty good when you consider that he was a father at fourteen. I never knew him, until he looked me up a few years ago. Has a nice family, two more boys, Jesse and Eric, and runs his own tire shop. Steele Street gets all their tires from him. We've been a real good account." And wasn't that sweet how it had all worked out. Hell. He'd given up being angry a long time ago. How in the hell did you stay angry at a fourteen-year-old kid who'd just gotten lucky one night?

His jaw tightened just a bit, and inside he admitted it was probably still all too easy to get angry, not for himself, but for how casually that boy had used his mother, who obviously hadn't known any better either.

Well, he'd sure as hell kept his pants on at fourteen, and fifteen, and sixteen, and seventeen, which was probably just one more reason he'd become so incredibly fixated on Regan McKinney—whose face, he noticed, had paled.

"Fourteen?" she said, her voice rising in disbelief.

Yeah, it was pretty damn young.

"How old was your mother?"

"Fifteen," he said, telling her that unvarnished truth as well. "I used to tease her about going for younger guys, until I realized that making her cry was just too damn easy, and that even when I was at my absolute worst, she still loved me. It's the only thing that saved me, that she loved me no matter how rotten and wild I was."

He'd shocked her, he could tell. His parents' ages certainly hadn't been in any of the newspaper articles about him. He'd made damn sure of that, for his mom's sake.

"I didn't know."

God, she was sweet, her voice trembling for a little boy who had obviously turned out pretty well.

"If you cry, I'm not going to tell you any more." He lightened the threat with a smile, but he meant it. There was one more box of fossils to crate up, the smaller ones on the table, and he picked up the closest and moved it over to the last wooden crate.

"I'm *not* going to cry," she said, swiping the heel of her

hand across her cheeks, then reaching for a hand-sized bone encrusted with rock. She followed him over to the last crate. "So go ahead and tell me everything. It's not like I haven't wondered a million times how you ended up on Wilson's work crew. Who kicked you out?"

"My mom's dad. He was always kicking us out of the house. It was either his way or the highway, and at about thirteen, I started choosing the highway every time."

"Where's your mom now?" she asked, going back for another load.

"In Boulder. She married a dentist when I was sixteen. I've got two half sisters, Jessie and Lynne, sweet kids."

"Two Jessies?" She gave a little laugh, stopping and turning back to look at him.

"Yeah." He grinned with her. "My mom and dad didn't exactly keep in touch. Funny how that turned out, both of them naming a kid Jessie."

"What about your grandfather?"

He shrugged. "Who knows? I don't keep track, and I don't ask Mom."

He knew how that must sound to someone who adored her grandfather, but Bart Younger had not been Wilson McKinney, not by any stretch of the imagination. He'd been an alcoholic asshole who'd beaten Quinn's mother, but Regan didn't need to know all that, not tonight.

The sound of Roxanne's 426 Hemi pulling up outside brought both their heads around.

"Hawkins," he said, relieved. He started for the door, but she caught his hand and held him back.

"Thanks," she said, rising up to kiss his cheek.

He kissed her fingers, before taking her hand in his. "Let's get Hawkins and get this show on the road."

Regan's memories of Christian Hawkins were very clear in her mind as she and Quinn stepped out of the warehouse, and at first sight of him getting out of a sleek green muscle car with a black racing stripe running up the hood, she realized she would have recognized him anywhere.

He hadn't changed, except for being taller and broader through the shoulders. His hair was still so dark as to be almost black. He still had the most intense gaze she'd ever seen, and a face made up of angles, not curves. Amazingly, he still dressed in worn-out jeans with a worn-out T-shirt, though he'd added a long-sleeved, striped cotton dress shirt that undoubtedly hid a shoulder holster and gun. The lines in his cheeks when he smiled were deeper and longer than they'd been, and she remembered thinking he was cute, too experienced for his age, and dangerous in a way she couldn't quite pin down.

Well, *cute* didn't begin to encompass the man he'd become. *Handsome* wasn't the right word either, not if it conjured up images of pretty-faced, square-jawed, shaving-cream models. Christian Hawkins was not pretty. He was striking, serious even when he smiled, and looked like he'd been to hell and back since she'd last seen him, and that he might have enjoyed the trip, or at least learned plenty along the way.

The air of danger was still there, along with an animal magnetism she'd known better than to succumb to even at fifteen. At thirty, she had a much better idea of where all that animal magnetism was coming from and where it could take a girl, and the knowledge made her grip Quinn's hand a little tighter.

"Regan," Hawkins said, reaching out to shake her hand, his smile broadening.

She responded automatically, and when their hands clasped, she felt not only his warmth and strength, but his subtle awareness of her as a woman. It was in the ease of his grip, the light pressure of his fingers, and the unspoken appreciation in his eyes. As a greeting, it was both unnerving and charming, and she got the impression that she was very much in the company of a gentleman—and a rake, a description she wouldn't have quite thought was even in her vocabulary.

"Christian," she replied with a smile, surprised at how glad she truly was to see him.

After releasing her hand, he glanced at Quinn and lifted one eyebrow a fraction of an inch.

"An hour, tops," Quinn said, "unless you want to call Roper with a personal invitation."

In reply, Hawkins rattled off a phone number beginning with the Denver area code.

"Yeah, that probably works better," Quinn agreed, but

Regan didn't know to what. It was obvious, though, that the two of them worked together a lot.

That impression was only confirmed as they went through the warehouse together. Quinn set the tracking device Kid had taken off her car, and placed it in one of the crates. That was for Roper Jones to follow to Lafayette. The device he'd picked up at Steele Street was turned on and placed in a different crate. That was for Quinn and Hawkins to follow to wherever Roper took the bones. The idea, she assumed, was that the bones would lead them to whatever they were really after. He still hadn't told her what that was.

The two of them spoke in a virtual shorthand, but Regan did understand how disappointed Hawkins was about the *Tarbosaurus* nest or something similar not being a reality. Apparently, Roper Jones was berserk about the bones, and not even the great Wilson McKinney had been able to give them a reason why.

Maybe Wilson *had* gotten a little delusional, she thought. Especially if he'd known how badly Hawkins and Dylan had wanted him to find something special.

Hawkins's arrival had bought her a little more time, and she was working her way back up the table while they loaded the remaining fossils, hoping she'd missed something. She wasn't trying to be quiet, and she certainly wasn't trying to eavesdrop, which didn't make what she heard any less startling.

"He wants your fucking head, Quinn. Just your head, and I told him I could get it, especially for the fifty grand he's ponied up."

"And the rest of me?"

"You know him. To the dogs. Hell, he'll probably sell tickets."

"We could—" Quinn turned suddenly, warned, she was sure, by her quick intake of breath.

She couldn't believe what she'd heard, and yet she did, every word.

"You've got a price on your head? Just your head?" The thought was so awful, she could hardly breathe.

Quinn looked back at Hawkins and, with a silent exchange, apparently laid a course for the rest of the evening. She didn't know how they did it, but neither did she protest when Quinn took her by the arm and led her outside to Christian's car.

"I know what Hawkins said sounded bad, but it's nothing to worry about." He opened the trunk and pulled out a very dangerous-looking gun. She didn't know what it was, but it wasn't a pistol. It was bigger, more deadly, like something she'd seen in the movies, with a big clip of bullets curving out of the bottom—and it looked like exactly what they might need.

"How can you say that?" she asked, and damn him, he actually chuckled.

"Somebody is always out to get me, or get Hawkins, or Kid or J. T. or Creed. That's just the way it is. Steele Street only gets sent out on the tough jobs. We do them, and then we move on," he said, leading her around to the back of the warehouse, slinging the gun's strap over his shoulder.

They were making their way around piles of metal

scrap with the day's heat still radiating off them. When they'd first arrived, she'd been filled with excitement about the bones, but now the whole place looked depressing and run-down, like an awful place to meet someone who would pay money to have someone else decapitated.

She glanced over at him and felt her anger shift into dread.

What had she done? She'd had no business falling in love with a man whose work put him in such danger. No business at all.

"And where do you move on to?" Her voice was tight, but she couldn't help it.

They rounded the corner of the warehouse, and in the next step, he backed her up against the wall, his body just inches from hers, his hands on her waist, holding her.

"Nowhere without you," he promised, moving the last step closer. "Ever," he added fiercely, his mouth coming down on hers.

She gave in to it, was helpless against the longing he incited with his kiss.

Lifting his head, he kissed her once more, then said, "Come on."

Taking her hand, he led her up a back stairway. It was built like a fire escape, and he pulled the last section of stairs up behind them before they ascended to the top. Inside, they walked along a catwalk to a narrow room hidden in the shadows of the rafters.

"We'll wait here. Hawkins will come up in a minute

from the other side and wait over there. After the bones are picked up, I'll take you back to Steele Street. Okay?"

"Where are you going to go?"

"To meet Hawkins. He'll follow Roper and let me know where they take the fossils." He opened the door into the room. There was a long desk inside, a couple of chairs, and a filing cabinet. There wasn't any glass in the windows, only louvered steel blinds that were open.

He sat down on the desk, and she sat down beside him. Taking his cell phone out of his pocket, he punched in a number with his thumb.

After a moment, he spoke. "Tell Roper to check his receiver. I want the fifty K off my head." He hung up before anyone would have had a chance to answer, his message brief and to the point.

So that's what the phone number was for, she thought.

"I'm scared for you," she confessed, when he'd repocketed the phone.

"You don't have to be." He slid off the desk and walked over to the windows to look out through the louvers. The main floor of the warehouse was brightly lit, as was the front outside, but the upper level was all in shadows. They could hear Hawkins moving the forklift, and when the sound stopped, Quinn came back to the desk.

He stood in front of her, his hands on either side of her arms. "I can take care of myself. I promise."

She looked away from him, wrapping one arm around her waist, and covering her face with her other hand. This was awful.

What kind of sick person would put a bounty on

somebody's body parts? And how in the world had she gotten into this thing up to her neck? God, she was in a broken-down warehouse in Lafayette, in the middle of the night, waiting for a bunch of horrible criminals to steal a bunch of Class B fossils, which she could absolutely guarantee were not worth somebody's life. Anybody's life.

But especially Quinn's.

"Hey," he said, moving in closer.

A tremor went through her, and she prayed, *Please God, don't let me cry.*

"Hey, everything's going to be okay," he promised. "I'm not going to let anything happen to you."

"It's not me I'm worried about." Her voice came out as a whisper.

"Shhh. It's okay, Regan. I'm here." He kissed her forehead, and then each of her cheeks, and finally her mouth, and even with that awful gun lying on the desk beside her, and the whole night going to hell around her, she felt herself start to melt for him.

She'd never known a man could taste so good.

"You've already been hurt once," she reminded him, between kisses.

"Bad judgment on my part, I admit, but I always learn from my mistakes." With his hands sliding up from her knees, he opened her legs enough for him to slip between her thighs, and she wondered just how far it all could go—in a warehouse, on a stakeout, in the middle of the night, and her with no underwear.

Far enough and then some, she realized, as he kept

kissing her, going lower with each soft caress, until he'd pushed her back on the desk and was kissing her knees and working his way back up the insides of her thighs.

At the hem of her skirt, he lifted his head. His eyes glittered darkly in the shadows of the office.

"Wanna have some fun?"

Oh, God, whatever he was thinking, it was crazy.

Still leaning over her, he lifted her leg and pressed another kiss on the inside of her knee as he pushed her skirt up higher and higher, until she was intimately, utterly exposed to that glittering green-eyed gaze. A thoroughly satisfied smile curved his mouth.

"This is crazy, Quinn." Even to her ears, it was a weak defense.

"Uh-huh," he agreed, bending his head back down. "Totally crazy."

Oh, God. A shuddering sigh went through her. If this was what people were doing to each other, she didn't know how her marriage had lasted a week.

She wanted to stay with him forever, to feel like this forever, but didn't think that was prudent, or even possible. In fact, the very thought scared her to death. Tonight had been the wildest night of her life, but it was only one night, and she was absolutely positive it would be better to keep it that way, just one night—one incredible night.

Tomorrow she would go back to her regular, perfectly safe life, wiser for the experience—but remembering this, how he made love, and discovering that the taste of his mouth was enough to drench her in desire. She still didn't feel like she knew him. She *didn't* know him—but her body did. Her body knew his, and her mind had been more than willing to follow its lead—which was so unlike her. Regan McKinney did not take her clothes off in the great outdoors, and she most certainly did not have sex on the hoods of cars, or on the trunks—and she did not, *did not*, let a man do to her what Quinn was doing under her skirt, not, dear God, in the rafters of an old warehouse in Lafayette.

His mouth slid another inch up her thigh, and it was all she could do not to beg him to go higher, to beg him, *please*. She was paralyzed with anticipation, her breathing shallow, her body trembling. He palmed her again with his hand as his mouth strayed up onto her belly, kissing her, licking her, tantalizing her with the lazy tracings of his tongue across her skin—driving her out of her mind.

She was on a slow burn, his other hand molding her breast, teasing her nipple.

"Quinn," she pleaded, breathless. "Quinn, please."

He responded by sliding down—down until he was there, where she needed him, his mouth so hot, his tongue so sweet, and quick, and clever between her legs. A tidal wave of pleasure surged up her body, making her gasp.

IN the rafters on the other side of the warehouse, Hawkins dropped his head into his hands. God*damn*, he couldn't possibly be hearing what he thought he was hearing. They were at it again?

What in the hell was Quinn thinking?

No, he quickly told himself. *Don't go there. You do not want to be thinking about what Quinn is thinking about.*

Damn it. This is unfuckingbelievable.

He heard another soft groan, a woman's groan, and his imagination started filling in all sorts of pieces whether he wanted it to or not.

This was torture.

He didn't know how much noise they thought the generator was making down on the main floor, but it wasn't making enough.

Great. He gritted his teeth and checked his pistol, a Glock 9mm he'd already checked twice. He checked his watch, then rolled over, aimed, and checked his line of fire.

Slowly, but inevitably, those sweet sounds she was making fell into a rhythm that without a doubt spelled his doom. Christ save him. He absolutely, positively, did not want to be part of some long-distance, voyeuristic, ménage à trois, and—oh, great, he was getting hard.

Perfect.

He was going to kill Quinn.

He would have thought a former Air Force pilot, a decorated hero, for God's sake, could have kept his hands off her for thirty or forty lousy minutes.

Was that asking for so much?

In Quinn's defense, Hawkins admitted that he himself

was one of those rare people who could hear a pin drop at fifty yards over two lanes of fast-moving traffic, let alone a woman on the verge of orgasm who was definitely less than thirty yards away.

He was going to kill Quinn.

Down on the main floor, the refrigerator running off the generator kicked into its hourly On cycle, bringing the noise level in the warehouse back up to normal, and as quickly as that, he was saved. If he couldn't hear them, he didn't have to think about them.

If she and Quinn were in love, and from the way he'd seen them looking at each other, he couldn't imagine they weren't, he was all for it. Quinn had been working off a full dance card for years, hoping to find someone to share his happily-ever-after. He was such a romantic sap, always had been, even as a kid, and he was the last person Hawkins would expect to show a little restraint once he'd found the woman he loved.

Thank God for the refrigerator.

He had plenty else to think about, like how he was going to get back into the Jack O' Nines and explain to Roper about Kev-boy screwing up and getting himself arrested.

Anger, he decided. He'd go in real pissed off about having to work with such a jerk-off idiot. Roper respected anger. He understood it.

If things went down even half right after the Jack O' Nines, some phone calls would be made, the deal struck, the exchange set up. With the bones back in Roper's possession, it would be time for somebody to rumble up with the guns—if that was even the deal.

Hell, Hawkins didn't know anymore. Government intel wasn't a hundred percent reliable.

He checked his watch again and hoped to hell Quinn was checking his.

CHAPTER

22

KID OPENED HIS EYES, instantly awake and aware of his surroundings. Steele Street. Past midnight. Bed.

Nikki.

She was still wrapped around him, her leg over his, her arm resting lightly across his chest, her breath, so soft and warm, falling in the curve of his neck. It was as close to heaven as he'd ever been, having the silken length of her body resting against him. And he never wanted to leave her—but he had to, because he'd heard something.

Careful not to wake her, he slipped out from under the covers. She stirred, a sigh falling from her lips as her shoulders relaxed deeper into the bed. He reached for his pants, letting his gaze linger on the curve of her hip beneath the sheet, the length of her naked back, and that wild tousle of purple-and-black hair spread out on the pillow.

They'd been asleep for a couple of hours, and if possible, he was even more in love now than he'd been when they'd drifted off in each other's arms. She had a hold on him that half fascinated him and half scared the hell out of him. He hoped Quinn and Hawkins had gotten lucky tonight and closed the whole damn Roper Jones file for good. He wanted some time off, starting now, to spend with her and figure out what was happening between the two of them.

Not bothering with his shirt, he padded across the carpet and slipped out into the hall leading to the office. He was awake, alert, and on guard, but not too worried. Steele Street was as damn near impregnable as a building could get, which meant someone could still get in, but it would have to be someone damn good—better than anybody Roper Jones had working for him—and they'd have to have a damn good reason to go to so much trouble.

Nobody that good had a reason, not this month—and his sixth sense was telling him it was Dylan. He was expected, and the noise Kid had heard had been no more than a snick of sound. Neither Hawkins nor Quinn moved with that kind of silent grace.

When he reached the open area of the office, he stopped. He hadn't seen Dylan since before he'd been sent to baby-sit Quinn in Cisco, but he recognized him instantly, not always an easy task with Dylan.

A guy of medium height, with a medium build and an

unremarkable face with plain brown eyes, glanced up from the computer monitor he was standing over. His hair was ill-kempt, shaggy, sparse, and dishwater blond. He was wearing a poorly tailored, dull brown suit with a beige tie and a rumpled off-white dress shirt—not exactly power dressing in Washington, D.C., or anywhere else, which made Kid wonder what else Dylan might have been up to on the East Coast.

Dylan didn't look up, but Kid knew the boss of Steele Street knew he was there.

"Kid," he said after a minute, his attention still on the monitor, his voice anything but indistinguishable. "I'm glad you're here."

Dylan's voice was deep, with a soft raspiness Kid had once heard a woman describe as "pure sex on a dark night under a magnolia tree," except it had come out sounding like "pyooah sayx on a dahk naht unda uh mugnolya tray," which was exactly how he would have described *her* voice.

Kid didn't get it himself, but the description had made an impression, as had the woman—especially the woman, an elegant and sultry New Orleans beauty who had dismissed him with one glance as a boy too young to hold her attention, let alone her interest—not at all the way she'd looked at Dylan, who had held her attention just fine.

"Dylan." He nodded in greeting. "What's up?"

In response, Dylan glanced over at the far corner of the office to a rumpled figure snoring on the couch. "What's Johnny doing here?"

"Watching Wilson McKinney. We had to pull everybody in. Quinn and Hawkins are out at the warehouse in Lafayette right now."

Dylan finally looked over at him, and one eyebrow lifted. "You're wearing camo-cream to bed now?"

Damn. The goshawk makeup. Kid wiped his hand across his face, knowing he must be a mess, while Dylan continued, "Skeeter updated me about an hour ago, but didn't mention the girl. Who is she?"

"Nikki McKinney." Damn. The sound he'd heard must have been Dylan closing the guest suite door.

"Ah, look, Kid...I'm going to need you in Colombia with me ASAP." Dylan slanted him an unreadable glance. "We have a military transport standing by at Peterson."

Kid felt his heart stop for a second. There was only one reason for Dylan to send him to Colombia. Something must have gone wrong with his brother J. T.'s mission. He tried to keep the panic from his voice. "Trouble?"

"Maybe." Dylan deftly removed a pair of dirt-brown contacts and placed them in a container he'd taken out of the desk's top drawer. "Creed and J. T. missed their check-in four days ago, and this morning in D.C. we got a report of a wounded American being held at a village in northern Choco, near the Panama border."

"Choco? That's the Darien Gap. What in the hell are they doing up there?" The Darien Gap was the most impassable stretch of jungle in the whole western hemisphere.

A pair of cool gray eyes were leveled at him from across the room. "We're not sure it is them. That's why we need to get down there. They should have been in Cartagena on Wednesday." He turned back to the computer and hit a couple of keys.

A series of grid maps began scrolling down the monitor. Dylan loosened his tie, then reached up and peeled the dishwater blond wig off his head and tossed it on the desk.

Thick brown hair cut in a style that only British schoolboys, Japanese *anime* characters, rock-and-roll stars, and Dylan Hart seemed to be able to pull off fell in a flattened, cheekbone-length swath down the right side of his face. He dragged his fingers back through it, and for the most part, except for a few strands, it stayed in place.

"What else?" Kid asked. There was something else, something worse. Kid felt it down to the marrow of his bones.

"There was another man with the wounded American, a dead man the villagers described only as having *tres cicatrizes*."

Three scars. Kid felt the world fall out from under him. His pulse slowed to a near stop with dread. J. T. had three scars in a neat row near the top of his left arm.

He met Dylan's eyes, saw compassion and concern and the steady regard of a man who also loved his brother. "I can take someone else," Dylan said.

Kid shook his head, gathered himself. "Give me half an hour."

"Half an hour, then."

Kid washed his face and threw his things together faster than that and had his bags at the office door before Dylan had finished downloading whatever information he'd been able to find about northern Choco, using the Defense Department's files.

"The CIA has run a couple of operations out of there over the last four months," Dylan said, popping a disk out of one of the drives, "though it's hard to tell if they're working for or against the NRF."

Kid knew he was talking about the National Revolutionary Forces, a rebel army operating out of northern Colombia that spent a lot of time blowing up the country's oil pipelines, using money they earned through selling drugs, kidnapping oil executives, and extortion.

"I'll find out who's still there. If we need them, maybe they can back us up." Dylan paused, nodded toward the door. "Tell her good-bye if you want to."

"Five minutes," Kid said, then turned and walked back down the hallway to the room where he'd left Nikki.

Shit. His pulse was racing. His mouth had gone dry. *Tres cicatrizes.*

Nikki was still asleep when he reached the guest suite. He knelt down next to the bed and ran his fingers through her hair, smoothing it back off her face.

"Nikki? I need you to wake up," he said quietly.

Even with the low throb of fear pounding through

him for J. T., watching her drift up from sleep proved to be one of life's more profound pleasures. She stretched, and the sheet slipped off her breasts. She yawned and smiled and lazily opened her eyes, and his heart turned over in his chest.

"Kid," she murmured, and closed her eyes again.

"Nikki, I have to go. I'm sorry, but I can't tell you— Nikki? Are you awake?"

"Hmmm," she sighed.

"Nikki." He rubbed his hand up the length of her back and gave her a little shake. "Nikki, I have to go. I wanted to stay with you tonight, but I can't."

Soft gray eyes slowly reopened and focused on his. "Go?"

"Yeah. There's a plane waiting for me. I don't know when I'll be back."

"Does somebody else need a bodyguard?"

He hesitated, swallowed back the fear for his brother and his reluctance to leave her. "Yeah." That was as good an explanation as any he could come up with and actually tell her. "I might be gone awhile, and I . . ." His voice trailed off. What could he say? *Wait for me? Don't forget me? Don't, for God's sake, run off and have Travis sexually imprint you while I'm gone, because I think we've got it down perfectly?* "I'm going to miss you."

"I don't want you to go, Kid," she murmured, sliding her hand up his chest. A soft smile curved her mouth. "Tell them to get their own bodyguard. I want to make love with you again, and again . . . and again." She raised up enough to kiss him, and he couldn't help himself. He opened his mouth over hers and bore her back down on the bed. His hand slid up to palm her breast, so warm and sweet.

God, he felt torn in two. He didn't want to leave her, not for a minute, but every fiber in his being was telling him to get to Colombia *now* and find his brother. The one thing he'd learned in the Marines was never to assume anything, and he wouldn't believe J. T. was dead, not without a body right in front of him. Not J. T., no way.

What in the hell could have gone so terribly wrong? J. T. and Creed were the best.

A wave of fear rolled through him, and he slowly broke off the kiss.

"Nikki. I have to go, but I'll be back. I swear."

"I'll be right here." She sighed, sinking back onto the bed in a way that made him wonder if she was even truly awake. "Don't be late. Okay?"

"Okay," he said, watching her curl herself back around her pillow as he rose to his feet. Hell. He didn't know if she was going to remember a word he'd said.

But he had to go, and with a final kiss to her brow, he turned and walked away.

ROPER Jones had the face of evil, pure and simple, nothing more and certainly nothing less. Regan could see him clearly in the bright lights below her in the warehouse. He was bullying the men he'd brought with him, shouting curses and curt commands, and the men were stumbling over themselves to respond, making short, sloppy work of loading the crates.

It was a face she would never forget, at first glance handsome, but with each successive expression becoming an object of fear and loathing. He had blond hair, thick and straight, and cut to accentuate his finely chiseled features. His smile was wide, revealing perfect, blindingly white teeth. His nose was narrow, his eyes blue slits. He was thin, almost emaciated, an aesthetic model for what even she could see was a very expensive pale gray suit, and even in the dust and detritus of the Lafayette warehouse floor, his shoes were still shined.

But those blue slit eyes were heated with a frantic energy that seemed to spill out of the pores of his body. Worst of all, he'd brought his dogs, a matched pair of rottweilers who fed on that selfsame energy, the animals Hawkins had said would feed on Quinn. The thought had been too bizarrely horrifying even to register properly, until she actually saw Roper with the beasts. The warehouse was in a frenzy with him and his dogs at its vortex, and the sight of all that manic, malevolent energy struck terror in her heart.

Neither she nor Quinn had spoken a word since Jones had first pulled up to the warehouse with his trucks and gang of street toughs. She'd been warned to keep her silence, but the warning hadn't been necessary. She was hardly breathing for fear of drawing attention to herself, or to Quinn. The last place on earth she wanted to be was in the middle of the frightening chaos Roper Jones was orchestrating around himself.

His men had already dropped two of the crates in their hurry to get everything loaded on the trucks. Bones had spilled out onto the floor, crashing into the cement, some of the fossils cracking, a few out-and-out disintegrating.

Roper had cursed and raged with every mishap, and then forced two of his men down on their hands and knees to sweep the floor with their hands, leaving hardly a dust smear behind by the time they'd left the warehouse.

He had to be insane. Certifiable.

Thank God the *Tarbosaurus* nest had been only a figment of Wilson's imagination, she thought. Eggshells, even fossilized eggshells, wouldn't hold up long under such rough treatment. Whatever Roper Jones wanted with the bones, she couldn't imagine that there would be much of them left by the time he was finished with them, nothing but the dust and crumbles he seemed so hell-bent on not leaving behind.

When the storm of chaos had passed, and Roper and his thugs had roared away, Quinn turned to her.

"Well, he got what he wanted, and now we'll see if he leads us to what we want," he said grimly. "Wait here. Hawkins and I will check out the warehouse, and then I'll take you to Steele Street to be with your sister and your grandfather."

"And where are you going to be?" As if she didn't know he was going after Roper.

"Staying out of trouble," he promised her with a smile, and then he disappeared out the door.

Damn. She turned back to the louvered windows.

She'd never known such horrible people existed so close to her world. She wasn't naive. She knew there were criminals and murderers, rapists and kidnappers everywhere. She'd just never knowingly seen one before, nor had a connection with one.

Seeing Roper Jones had given her a glimpse into Quinn's world, and what she'd seen frightened her.

But it was over now.

She rubbed her arms, feeling a shiver course over her skin even in the ungodly heat of the warehouse rafters. Maybe she'd feel safer once they got to Steele Street.

Turning from the windows, she glanced around the office where Quinn had made such sweet love to her. Scattered papers littered the floor. An out-of-date calendar had fallen open onto the seat of the desk chair.

What in the world had happened to her today? she wondered. What had happened to Regan McKinney, mild-mannered fossil preparator, sexually shy organizational freak, and all-around Goody Two-shoes? Had she lost her ever-loving mind?

Without a doubt, came the answer, which she didn't find in the least comforting. Nothing about the whole night had been comforting, except for the way she felt in Quinn's arms. For all the intense sensuality and passion of their lovemaking, he was a comfort, an ease to the loneliness she spent far too much time ignoring. He was the connection outside herself she'd given up hoping to find—but at what cost had she found him?

Her gaze strayed back to the louvered windows and the now empty warehouse floor. Yes, she assured herself. The whole thing was over, but if it was over, why didn't she feel safe?

CHAPTER

WILSON WOKE WITH a start. Hell, he always woke with a start nowadays. He seemed to have only two speeds left in his old age, dead stop and wide awake.

It was dark in the room, with only a faint line of light coming from the bathroom. The boy, Johnny, had gotten into the habit of leaving the bathroom light on for him, so he could find his way in the dark if he needed to get up.

Johnny. A brief smile curved his lips. That's right. He remembered now. Johnny was the boy's name, and the two of them had come to Steele Street for the night, where Dylan and Hawkins and Quinn Younger kept all their cars.

His smile broadened. Everything upstairs in the old noggin was working for a change. Sleep always brought an improvement in his memory, but this morning he seemed to be particularly lucid, just like in the old days, by God.

Except it wasn't morning yet.

The clock said two, when he looked, and when he glanced toward the window, he could see it was still dark outside, with only the street lamps to cut the gloom.

Darn it. He hated it when he woke up in the middle of the night. Hated to waste his brightest moment on nothing but worrying about how, or if, he was going to get back to sleep.

Forget that, he thought. He had too much to do to waste time or brainpower worrying about anything. He had a *Tarbosaurus* nest to explore, and a whole heck of a lot of rough-cut diamonds to pick out of the nest's plaster jacket.

Diamonds! My God. That's what he'd been trying to remember. The whole darn nest was encrusted with diamonds, and he was pretty darn sure they were stolen. Why the heck else would they be hidden in the plaster jacket surrounding the fossil? No self-respecting paleontologist would have stuffed diamonds in a fossil's plaster.

Only a smuggler would do that.

Yes, he'd had it all figured out a few days ago, then gotten all rattled again, but if the fossil was a *Tarbosaurus*, then it had come from Mongolia, and there was no shortage of smugglers in Mongolia or over the border in Russia. With the diamond mines of Siberia directly to the north, it wasn't inconceivable that some Russian had decided to export some resources for personal gain. Heck, the whole of Russia was made up of nothing but bandits anymore, with everyone out for themselves and a quick ruble, or better yet, a quick American dollar, if they could get it.

From what he'd seen in the nest, some smart Ivan had been set to make a whole lot of American dollars, or something else equally as lucrative.

Well, the smart Ivan wasn't looking so smart now. He'd been foiled, but good, by the Steele Street boys. All Wilson had to do was get his wrinkled old butt down to the museum and start working on the fossil, digging out those diamonds. Heck. Right when he needed a darn car, he didn't have a darn car.

Regan would just have to take him down to the museum. She was a good girl. She always did what she was told, and the museum was just a couple of miles down the street.

Except Regan wasn't at Steele Street, he remembered. When she'd left earlier in the evening with Quinn, she'd told him she was going to go to the Southern Cross Hotel to stay with Nikki.

Well, darn. He'd just have to wake up the boy, Johnny.

Swinging his legs over the side of the bed, he got up and made quick work of getting dressed. There was nothing like getting a start on the day with all the old cerebral lightbulbs burning bright.

Once dressed, he went looking for the boy. No one answered his knock on the door next to his, but he'd no sooner gotten the door open than a big grin spread across his face. Turning back around, he closed the door behind him. His luck was definitely on the upswing. Only one person on the planet had a mop of purple-and-black hair that stuck up all over, and that mop was peeking out from under the covers in Steele Street's second guest suite.

If his granddaughter Nikki was here, no doubt Regan was, too. She watched her little sister like a hawk.

Chuckling at his good fortune, Wilson hotfooted it down to the next room, and sure enough, when he knocked, Regan called out.

"Come in."

He opened the door to find her sitting on the side of the bed, still fully clothed and looking as tired as she sounded.

Well, that was no good, but he hadn't spent years getting two teenage girls off to school every morning without learning a few things about motivation.

"Come on. I need you to take me down to the museum, so I . . . uh, *we*, can get to work on that *Tarbosaurus* nest."

"It's two o'clock in the morning, Grandpa," she said, blinking owlishly. She looked a little like hell warmed over. If possible, her clothes were even more wrinkled and mussed up than they had been earlier in the evening, and her hair was an out-and-out mess.

"Which doesn't leave us with much time, honey. Come on. We've got to get going."

"For the *Tarbosaurus* nest," she said blankly, lifting her head and staring at him from across the room again, as if she didn't quite believe what she'd heard—and implying that if he had half a brain, he wouldn't believe what he'd said, either. "I just got back from the warehouse, and there is no *Tarbosaurus* nest."

"Not at the warehouse, no," he explained, frowning. Regan was usually quicker than this. "Johnny and I took it to the museum and put it in your lab before we came to Steele Street tonight. Hawkins was going to have it shipped out with the rest of the bones he's been having me work on these last couple of weeks, but I couldn't let him do it. So come on. We've got work to do, and by God, we've got to get on it."

Her eyes grew big and round. She blinked and blinked again.

"You stole a stolen fossil and put it in my lab?" She sounded a bit incredulous, and not at all happy, but she'd change her tune once she saw the thing—and all those diamonds.

"Not just a fossil, honey, although a find like that is a miracle in itself, but somebody stuffed the plaster jacket full of crystallized carbon. *Diamonds*, honey! And I think we ought to get them all out of there," he said, letting his enthusiasm spill over into his smile.

"Diamonds?" she repeated woodenly, going all owlish on him again.

Well, that was his girl all right. Strictly by the book. He let out a sigh. Someday she was just going to have to let herself get a little shook up. She couldn't spend her whole life following the rules. She needed to live a little, have a little adventure—and today was the day.

"A *Tarbosaurus* nest chock-full of diamonds, and we've got to get them out of there. I don't want some cop coming down and confiscating our nest just because it was used to smuggle stolen gems."

"No," she said slowly, maybe coming around a little bit. "I guess we wouldn't want that to happen."

She narrowed her gaze at him, and he narrowed his gaze right back at her.

"Time's a-wasting," he said carefully.

"Are you sure, Grandpa?" She was looking directly at him, right into his eyes, giving him her own version of the old steely-eyed stare. "Are you sure you took the fossil to the museum, and that the packing was full of diamonds?"

"I know I've given you reason to doubt me lately, but on this I'm absolutely positive."

Regan sat back a little on the bed, mulling over her grandfather's impossible story. In the end, she decided the story was too impossible not to believe. Well, maybe not the part about the diamonds, but the rest of it, yeah. She believed him. When he smiled like that, and his eyes twinkled, how could she doubt that he knew exactly what he was doing, where he'd been, and what he needed to do?

But diamonds? Where in the world would he have come up with that if there weren't— She stopped in mid-thought, his explanation suddenly making more sense than anything else that had been going on all night.

This was what Roper had been looking for all along,

she realized with a start. He didn't want old dinosaur bones.

Roper Jones wanted diamonds.

"Okay, Grandpa," she conceded, feeling excitement pump into her veins even as she wondered if she, too, was losing a little bit of her mind. "Let's take a run down to the lab."

It would just be a short trip. Just a little zip down the street and a quick in-and-out into the museum and then back to Steele Street. If he was wrong, there'd be no harm done.

But if he was right—holy cow.

CHAPTER

24

SOMETHING WAS WRONG, Hawkins thought, walking into the back room of the Jack O' Nines, staying well into the shadows. The fit Roper had thrown out at the Lafayette warehouse had been classic Roper Jones: a little theatrics, a little fuck-you-all bullying, and a whole lot of frayed nerves.

But Hawkins didn't like what he was seeing in the Jack. Roper was still as a stone where he sat at his table, nothing moving but his cold blue eyes now and then, and the knife he was flipping in his hand. Roper's main man, Louie Lazano, was nowhere to be seen, and the two trucks full of dinosaur bones were sitting in the alley.

Hawkins checked to see who else was in the room and saw two guys at the bar who had to be the Chicago boys Roper had sicced on Regan McKinney.

Hawkins took a long drag off his cigarette. It had sure taken Vince Branson and Gunnar Linberg a long time to get here from Cisco. They didn't look too happy about having followed their own tracker—the one Quinn had put in with the dinosaur bones—here to the Jack.

They'd been duped, and everybody in the Jack O' Nines knew it—especially Roper.

"Cristo," Roper called out, and Hawkins swore under his breath.

"*Jefe*," Hawkins responded, calling Roper the boss and walking toward his table.

"Where's Kevin?" Roper caught his knife one more time and simply held it in his hand—ready.

Shit, Hawkins thought.

"He went to his girlfriend's house, after we checked out the garage." It was a reasonable lie.

Roper grinned, and it was not a pleasant sight. "He's going to find himself on the street—in pieces—if he doesn't quit fucking around."

Hawkins shrugged. "*Es una verga.*"

"Yes. He's a stupid prick all right, but you're not. What did you find?"

"A couple of leads. Maybe a couple of places where Younger hangs out. I'd like to go and check them—"

"Yeah, yeah," Roper interrupted, holding up his hand for silence. His gaze had gone to the door.

Louie was entering the room, brushing white dust off his fancy suit, looking angry enough to explode. White dust coated his bald pate, and it didn't take a rocket scientist to know Louie had been in the trucks with the bones—a fact Hawkins found curious as hell. Louie was not a hands-on type of guy.

"Nothing," Louie said to the unasked question in Roper's eyes, when he reached the table. "We've got *nothing.*" His voice was low and dangerous. Threatening—and that was a helluva new twist, for Louie to threaten Roper. "You lost control over this deal weeks ago, and now we've got nothing. You've blown the whole thing."

"I didn't blow anything, Louie," Roper spat back, the knife coming back to life in his hand. "We'll go with what we've got."

"And that's what I'm telling you. You've got nothing. Nothing but a couple of truckloads of dinosaur bones and plaster dust."

There was a trick to being invisible, and Hawkins was working it overtime, not moving, barely breathing, listening like hell, but looking off to the side, as if he weren't completely focused on the two men.

"If the Russians fucked up the shipment, that's their problem. Stupid Russians. I'm giving Chicago what we've got, and I'm taking the big fat cut I've earned."

"All you'll get is all of us killed," Louie growled back under his breath. "The bones have been missing for two weeks. What do you think, Roper, that Younger wasn't all over them? That he didn't find—"

Louie shut himself up and glanced at Hawkins. With a jerk of his head, he told him to back away.

Hawkins did just that, wandering back toward the

pool table, but keeping all his attention focused on Louie and Roper.

Russians and Chicago. Shit. Roper was no more than the middleman in this deal.

At the table, Hawkins turned sideways and managed to hear plenty.

"The boss in Chicago didn't set you up out here to make this kind of mistake," Louie growled. "You were supposed to broker a deal, Roper, a real simple deal. The Chicago bosses send you the Pentagon's guns, and the Russians send you the payoff. All you had to do was get those two things to line up in Denver. The Russians get their fancy new guns to sell to all their Middle Eastern friends, and Chicago gets rich. But you blew it, you idiot. You blew it."

Roper leveled Louie a killing look. "Screw you," he said, not bothering to keep his voice low. "I'm tired of being in the middle of these guys. I don't care who owed who a favor." He was getting a little white around the gills, maybe going into berserk mode, which, having seen it more than once, Hawkins wasn't looking forward to seeing again. People got hurt when Roper went berserk.

Louie leaned in close to whisper in Roper's ear, and Roper flushed.

"Yeah," Roper said, agreeing with whatever Louie had just said, suddenly sounding calmer. "Yeah, you're a real smart guy, Louie, real smart. That's probably exactly what happened." In one fierce, vicious move, he rose to his feet and struck, burying his knife into Louie's abdomen up to the hilt. "Real smart, and real dead."

Louie let out a strangled gasp of agony, grabbing the knife, but Roper didn't let him have it. He twisted the blade in deeper, and Louie fell to his knees, with Roper crouching in front of him, still holding in the knife.

Holy shit, Hawkins thought, inadvertently taking a step back.

"Don't ever threaten me, Louie. Not ever." Roper looked up at two of his men who had been watching him and nodded toward the bar. Before Vince Branson and Gunnar Linberg even knew what was coming, Roper's guys leveled their guns and shot the two Chicago men—clean hits.

Fuck. His heart racing, Hawkins did a quick scan of the room. Every guy in the Jack was frozen in place. No one had seen a triple homicide coming down the pike.

Hawkins let out a slow breath, trying to keep his heart from pounding out of his chest, and told himself it might be time to be looking for a new line of work. This sucked, big-time.

"Danny, Brad, grab your crews. You're going with me," Roper called out. "I've got a stop I need to make. The rest of you, clean up this mess, then get your asses out to the hangar."

Out of the corner of his eye, Hawkins saw four guys bend down and drag Branson and Linberg toward the back door.

"Cristo," Roper said.

Fuck.

"Jefe." He strolled across the room.

"Go get this Younger asshole for me. Check out those places you found and bring him out to the Avatrix hangar at the old Stapleton Airport. I'll meet you there. If he stole from me, I'm gonna turn him into beef jerky. If you don't find him, I'm gonna turn *you* into beef jerky."

Great. That was just the sort of incentive he and Quinn liked—the fucking beef jerky threat.

Rᴇɢᴀɴ had been in the museum at night many times over the years, helping to host fund-raisers, chaperoning the yearly Dinosaur Campout, and often just working extra hours to get a job done, or to get a time-sensitive piece ready for shipping or display. She'd never once felt nervous. Never. Until tonight.

Her hand shook as she tried to fit the key into the lab door. She'd had the same trouble with the keypad on the outside door, fumbling the code twice, before Wilson had just taken over and gotten them inside.

She'd had less trouble getting Betty out of Steele Street. Johnny had been pretty skeptical about helping them, but he'd also been half asleep and no match for two very insistent adults used to being in charge.

When she finally got the door open, she hit the bank of switches on the wall and flooded the lab with light. For the last few weeks, she'd been working in the glassed-in lab where the public filed by and could watch the preparators at work. She and everyone else were always careful to make sure any displayed work in progress was labeled for easy identification—but she'd be damned if she knew what to call the fossil now commandeering the middle of her worktable—"Possible *Tarbosaurus* nest stolen by my grandfather from a man who stole it from a criminal who stole it from somebody else who stuffed it full of stolen diamonds, but please don't call the cops" seemed a bit wordy.

But, oh, God, what if it really was a *Tarbosaurus* nest? And what if it really was stuffed with diamonds?

"Ah, yes. Right where I left it." Wilson chuckled and went straight over to the rocklike fossil lying on the table. The chunk of stone and plaster, and hopefully, fossilized eggshells and bones, was about four feet wide and three feet across, and despite the danger it represented, it beckoned to her.

But Regan found herself hesitating. It occurred to her that getting her fingerprints all over the damn thing might not be in her best interest. But then, she hadn't stolen it; she was retrieving it. She doubted if Steele Street would press charges against Wilson, either, considering how they'd gotten themselves into this mess by hiring him in the first place.

Somewhat reassured by her train of logic, she finally let a measure of her excitement seep through, and seep through it did, making her fingers tingle with anticipation. As far as she knew, this was the first Cretaceous carnivore nest ever discovered. It was certainly the first she'd ever gotten her hands on.

Wilson was well into removing the hastily reassembled plaster jacket he'd put on the fossil, before she allowed herself to get in on the action. The two of them had always been a team while Regan was growing up, and they easily fell back into the familiar rhythms of working closely together.

As they pulled the plaster away, the fossil inside appeared, including what appeared to be eggs, two broken open and one still intact. Regan wanted nothing more than to work on those eggs, to scrape away at the surrounding stone and free them, to check for embryonic skeletons and the bones of prey that might have been left in the nest.

Then Wilson pulled out the first diamond, and then the second and on to the third, until he quickly had a pile of ten. Good God. It was just like he'd said. The whole jacket was full of diamonds, hundreds of them. Regan could hardly believe her eyes.

Most were no bigger than marbles, some much bigger, each one looking more like colorless glass than a potential brilliant cut. Some were still embedded in a matrix of kimberlite. Some were round, others more squared off, some triangular, all of them together worth a fortune, a bloody fortune.

My God, she thought, picking out another diamond and putting it in a small canvas bag Wilson had gotten out of one of the lab's cupboards. Nothing about working on fossils went quickly, not even a diamond harvest. For her, and for Wilson, too, the greater treasure was underneath the plaster and the gemstones, the nest with the fossilized eggs. Years of study would go into the nest—along with a fair amount of glory.

Visions of *National Geographic* and *Smithsonian*

flashed through her brain. Maybe even a television documentary.

As they worked, Regan found herself finally relaxing into a controlled state of excitement. This is what she did. This was her life, the quiet confines of the paleontology lab, bones millions of years old fossilized into stone, and mysteries to be unfolded from the rock—and this time, diamonds. *My God.*

She loved the work. It kept her life on a smooth track. There were surprises, delights, and epiphanies aplenty even in her normal working day, but they all came at a slow, manageable pace. Absolutely nothing happened at a hundred and twenty miles per hour. It was contemplative work not given to startling or heart-stopping moments of terror.

Except...

She held herself suddenly still, catching a movement in the darkened museum out of the corner of her eye. The hair on the nape of her neck slowly rose, sending a purely fear-induced bolt of panic down the length of her spine.

Something was out there.

Or someone.

Wilson chatted obliviously along beside her, giving her an unnecessary lecture on rough-cut diamonds concurrent with a recap of Jack Horner's famous discovery of hadrosaur nests in Montana, and the naming of the genus *Maiasaura*, "good mother lizard."

Good mother lizard, indeed. If someone had broken in to the museum, why weren't alarms sounding all over the place? And if it was a guard, why was he lurking about in the dark? Or was the whole thing just her imagination?

She was too scared to go over and simply look out the window. Something was telling her not to give away her hand like that.

She glanced at the phone on the desk in the corner next to the lab door. Taking a deep breath, she started over. It was well past time when she should have called Quinn. She'd made the mistake of allowing herself to get sidetracked by the nest, letting her excitement override her common sense.

Her legs felt stiff as she walked, a dead giveaway, she was sure, if someone was actually watching, not only for where she was headed and why, but that she was scared senseless.

On the other hand, she tried to reassure herself, what—or who—could possibly be out in the museum? She was probably being ridiculously silly, just jumping at shadows, because the whole day had been nothing but one momentous, life-altering event after another, and at some point a girl just had to yell "uncle."

Sleep is what she needed, not a million dollars' worth of rough-cut diamonds and the world's most exclusive dinosaur nest.

Fine, she decided. She would call Quinn, and then she and Wilson were heading back to Steele Street just as fast as Betty could take them, and given the engine in the red Coronet, Regan would bet that would be pretty damn fast.

All she had to do was make her call.

Finally reaching the desk, she stretched out her hand for the receiver—and froze, her gaze locked on the cruel face leering at her through the window in the laboratory's door. Her fingers trembled in sudden paralysis; her arm refused to move. So did her mouth, and her vocal cords, for if they hadn't, she most definitely would have let out a bloodcurdling scream.

CHAPTER

25

ONE THING ABOUT QUINN, Hawkins thought as he pulled Roxanne to a stop on the corner of Fifteenth and Curtis in downtown Denver. He was always where he said he'd be. Getting out of the green Challenger, Hawkins approached Jeanette from the front.

"Hey." He leaned against the Camaro's door panel. The heat of the night had hit him like a furnace blast when he'd stepped out of the Jack O' Nines. The club had air-conditioning. Of course, it also had three dead bodies in it, which definitely detracted from its dubious charms.

Hawkins sure could use a drink, about a pint of twelve-year-old Scotch ought to do it, a feeling that had only grown stronger when he'd seen Jeanette waiting for him on Curtis Street.

Hell. Jeanette was nothing but trouble out on the street tonight. Quinn should have stuck with Betty after dropping Regan at Steele Street.

"What's the situation report?" Quinn asked, cutting straight to the chase.

"Well, for starters, you've got a lot of balls parking Jeanette this close to the Jack O' Nines." Hawkins knocked a cigarette out of its pack, stuck it in his mouth, but didn't light it. Not yet. "Balls that I would have thought would be at least slightly deflated from that stunt you pulled in Lafayette," he said wryly, reaching for his lighter.

"Stunt?" Quinn repeated, then laughed. "Oh, right." He had the grace to look embarrassed, but not for long. "Hell."

"Yeah, hell is right. Roper just offed Louie and the Chicago boys in the Jack."

"Shit." Quinn sat up straighter. "You're sure they're dead?"

"God, I hope so. Louie was knifed and was still trying to hold himself together when I left. Branson and Linberg were shot point-blank. This night has gone from bad to worse and from worse to completely fucked faster than any night I can remember, and damn it, Quinn, I want both of us to walk out of it in the morning in one piece."

"Fair enough," Quinn agreed easily. "Look, I'm sorry, but Regan's out of it now. No more distractions. I swear."

"Right. Out of it. So let's see what we've got."

Hawkins wasn't going to belabor the point, but he'd definitely felt a need to make it. He needed Quinn to be a hundred percent focused on the job, something he couldn't remember his friend ever having a problem with until Regan McKinney had gone looking for him. "From what I gathered from eavesdropping on Roper and Louie's conversation in the Jack, Roper's in the middle of the deal. He's the broker, not one of the players, with the Chicago mob and the guns on one side and the Russians and something missing in the dinosaur bones on the other."

"Russians. Shit. We should have known it was Russian mafia buying the fucking guns. They've got every terrorist in the Middle East on their doorstep, looking to buy guns."

"Yeah, and it looks like Chicago is only too happy to be selling them." Dylan had a long and checkered past with the ex-KGB guys who ran the Russian mafia. It was one area no one at SDF liked to delve into too deep.

"So what's missing?"

"I don't know. I only know Roper expected to find something in the dinosaur bones he didn't find."

"So we call Wilson?" Quinn asked. "Russians tie in real nicely with him thinking he had a Mongolian fossil."

"A Mongolian fossil we couldn't find," Hawkins reminded him. "Hell, he struggles to remember stuff in the middle of the day. Waking him up in the middle of the night is a long shot. No matter what he says, we'll have to check it out, and we don't have time to run down bad leads. Not now."

"What do you want to do?"

"Finish this fucking mess before it finishes us. The deal is going down tonight, real quick, in the Avatrix hangar out at the old Stapleton Airport. Roper wants me to meet him out there with you, so he can turn you into beef jerky."

"He'll have to get to me before I get to him," Quinn said, an edge in his voice Hawkins didn't misinterpret for a second. There wasn't a guy at SDF who didn't want Roper Jones to go down hard.

"Yeah, well, before you two get to each other, I'm calling in the FBI for backup. We all go out to the Avatrix hangar, wait for Roper and the Russians to put their cards—and the guns, and whatever—on the table, and then bust the whole lot of them. Bad guys lose. End of story. As a bonus, I'll have Special Agent Leeder send someone over to Steele Street to question Wilson. If they come up with something, great. We'll use it. If not, we haven't wasted our time. Where's Kid?"

Quinn didn't say anything right away, but the look on his face was enough to trouble Hawkins.

"What the hell else has happened in the last fucking hour that I need to know about?"

"Dylan made it back to Steele Street while we were in Lafayette, and picked Kid up. They're both on their way to Colombia."

Okay, that didn't sound good. Whatever intel Dylan had gotten must have been all bad news. "Did he say why?"

"J. T. and Creed missed their check-in, and a couple of

Americans in bad shape have been reported up by the Panama border."

"Okay," Hawkins said, tamping down his concern and deliberately not asking for more details. They had a job to do, right now. "One thing at a time. Once we get the guns, we'll let the FBI sort the rest of it out. This damn thing has taken too long as it is. One of us can be heading to Colombia by morning to back them up."

Quinn agreed with one word. "Avatrix?"

"Avatrix," Hawkins repeated.

RIDING through the murky darkness of predawn, captive in the back of Roper Jones's Mercedes, Regan didn't have an ounce of heat left anywhere in her body. She was frozen numb with panic. *Terror* was really too mild a word to describe the talonlike emotion that had taken hold of her heart. Terror implied a certain heated chaos, or at least it always had to her.

Her only consolation was that whatever Roper Jones had in mind for her, he'd left Wilson out of it. He was safe, unharmed. One of Roper's men had tied her grandfather to a chair in the lab, and Regan knew it would only be a matter of hours before he was found.

For herself, she held out no such hopes. Since she'd reached for the phone in the lab and seen Roper Jones's face staring at her from the other side of the lab door, she'd lost all hope.

They'd driven east out of Denver, sticking to the city streets, and just moments before, she'd recognized the old Denver airport, Stapleton. One sign in particular was looming bright in neon against the night sky above one of the old hangars: AVATRIX.

It looked like a terrible place to die, but with no one knowing where she was, she was sure her fate was sealed. Roper didn't need her. He'd gotten both the *Tarbosaurus* nest and all the diamonds. He had it all. Everything. He'd won.

Never in her wildest dreams could she have imagined ending up like this, that her life would end in a grimy airplane hangar in a deserted airport in the middle of the night. That she would die at the hands of a criminal maniac. Even after just having had the wildest day of her whole life, it was hard to piece together how it had all come down to this.

"H-how did you get into the museum?" she asked Roper, who was riding in the backseat with her. The question had been torturing her. The museum was secure. She'd counted on that security without question, and it had let her down.

"My dearly departed friend Louie guessed where the diamonds might be, so my men and I came out to see if he was right. We didn't have to wait long before you showed up, and Brad here"—he gestured to the driver— "watched the old man finally punch in your code through a pair of night vision goggles. Couldn't have been simpler. Any idiot could have done it." He squeezed her arm, then stroked it, and Regan wished she hadn't asked. Her skin crawled where he'd touched her, and she knew, deep in her heart, that he might do far more than touch her.

She had to escape if she could. So help her God, she had to escape.

The Mercedes pulled up in front of the hangar and was instantly flanked by another, matching sedan. Even before Roper pulled her out of the backseat, she had a bad feeling about the other car. Shadows were moving inside the sedan, shadows she couldn't pin down, until the doors were opened.

Suddenly, even rape paled in contrast to what she feared would be her final fate.

Two huge rottweilers bounded out of the car, unleashed, unchained, their bodies rippling with slabs of muscle beneath sleek, black-as-hell coats. But it was their heads that demanded her attention, large heads with drool gathered in the corners of their mouths. Gaping mouths lined with teeth. Massive jaws designed with one overall purpose in mind: to crush bone, tear flesh, and destroy life.

Roper called the beasts to heel, and as they padded past her, each one cast her a soulless glance filled with a single primal need to assuage: hunger.

Don't do it."

Quinn heard Hawkins's warning, felt his hand on his arm, keeping him from taking aim at the men hauling Regan into the hangar, but his blood was running too cold to register the fear the sight had put into his heart.

They'd both parked a couple hundred yards away, but were watching the Avatrix hangar from closer in, from behind a stack of empty fuel drums.

"We need Kid," he said, and truer words had never been spoken. Quinn wasn't a sniper, and neither was Hawkins. Both were good shots, but neither of them could hit a cold zero in the dark, on a moving target who was too damn close to the hostage to give them a clear shot—let alone hit five targets and two dogs.

"Leeder and the FBI will be here soon," Hawkins said. "I'll call and have them bring in a sniper team."

Soon wasn't going to be soon enough, and once Roper got her inside the hangar, it was going to take more than a sniper team to get her back out alive.

"We need to do better than that, and we need to do it right now." Quinn knew it. Hawkins knew it, too.

"You know he's not going to hurt her until after the deal is made," Hawkins said, his voice tight, the voice of reason. "You know it and I know it. He's going to wait for the guns to show up—which I highly recommend we do as well—and after all the wheeling and dealing is over, he'll have his fun. Except we'll go in, and we'll get the guns and save the girl and all go home happy."

"Fuck you," Quinn said.

After a long moment, he heard Hawkins sigh. "Yeah. Fuck me. I suppose you want me to turn you in to Roper and collect the fifty K he posted for the bounty."

"Demand it, then use it to get Regan."

"Fifty thousand dollars for a woman? You really think Roper is going to believe I'd pay fifty thousand dollars for a piece of ass?"

He held Hawkins's gaze steadily with his own. "Pay what he asks, just make him believe you'll pay anything. Don't leave without her."

"Aw, hell, Quinn." Hawkins looked away, shook his head, then swore again under his breath, before looking back up. "Okay, but don't come looking for me later, when you decide we could have done it my way and saved us all a whole lot of trouble."

"Cuff me."

Hawkins swore under his breath, gave him a baleful look, then reached into his pocket and pulled out a flex cuff. "*Kee-rist*, I hate this idea."

CHAPTER 26

THE INSIDE OF the hangar was jammed full with freight—boxes, cartons, and containers—all of it haphazardly organized. Regan saw lots of electronics: flat-screen televisions, in-home theater components, computers, DVD players, and everything in between. There was a whole fleet of Mercedes-Benz sedans parked on the east side, and racks of gasoline barrels. Two large refrigerator compartments held God knew what, but they walked past stacks of crated caviar and wines, cigarettes and cigars. More than a warehouse, she realized. Avatrix was Roper Jones's commissary.

They continued on toward the back, to a place with a couple of desks sitting out in the open. Sweat was beading on her brow, even though she felt frozen.

At the desks, Roper had them all stop, but only the

dogs got to sit. The men with him spread out, looking through the hangar, before coming back to the desks to confirm everything was in order.

Roper checked his watch.

"Danny, go open the hangar doors. Brad and Russ, go back to the car and get the fossil. The woman can work on it until the guns get here."

"Guns?" she asked. "What guns?"

She had nothing left to lose by asking questions, and she had the faint hope that if he could see her as a real person instead of a hapless victim, he might treat her as such.

He smiled at her, as if pleased by her question. And then he told her. But something in his eyes told her the reason he was telling was because he didn't plan on her being alive long enough to tell anybody else.

"The big guns, baby." He glanced down and picked up a sheaf of papers, then tossed them aside and turned on the computer on the desk. "The Pentagon wanted something to fight the fucking terrorists with, so they commissioned a new assault rifle for U.S. forces. It's real good for getting up close and personal in a fight, so naturally, we figured every terrorist group from al-Qaeda to Hamas would like a few so they could fight back."

"You're giving away U.S. military secrets?" She was appalled.

"Not giving, selling." He punched a few keys, and after a couple of seconds, a soft glow of illumination reflected onto his face from the monitor. "There's a difference, and it's a time-honored transaction. Free trade, they call it. It's how the American weapons merchants have armed the world. I'm just getting my share, that's all." He tapped a few more keys, then looked up at her. "I get a few Siberian diamonds to take to Antwerp, and a whole new trade route opens up between Russia and the United States. It's the new world economy, the underworld economy, and I'm in. Business, that's all it is. Just business, with me in the middle to grease the wheels for all the world's fanatics."

"Like who?" she asked.

He let out a snort of disgust and gave his attention back to the computer, ignoring her.

She looked around the hangar again, desperately seeking a way out and not seeing a damn thing. Then she spied a miracle—or the world's most awful disaster—walking down the middle of the hangar.

Quinn. He was handcuffed and roughed up, being pushed rudely along by a very sullen Christian Hawkins. In a flash, she understood what was happening, and she was both intensely relieved and thoroughly horrified. They'd come to save her, with Hawkins dragging Quinn in like he was a hard-won prize.

How in the world, she wondered, had they found her so quickly?

Then she knew: Hawkins. He'd been heading back to Roper when he'd left the warehouse in Lafayette. He was working both sides toward the middle. But from the looks of Quinn, she suddenly doubted whose side he was really on.

Don't be crazy, she told herself. Hawkins and Quinn had been together forever—but Christian looked very cold, very hard, and like he didn't give a damn about the man he was shoving ahead of him.

"*Jefe*, boss man," Hawkins called out, giving Quinn a final, rough push forward. "Here he is, just like I promised. How about that money?"

Roper looked up at the sound of their approach, and a truly diabolical expression came over his face.

"Cristo," he answered, his teeth flashing white in a broad grin. "You found the son of a bitch."

Hawkins grinned, a predatory curve that caused Regan's heart to miss a beat.

"For fifty thousand dollars, I would find you the devil himself."

Roper laughed. "Yes, and bring him to me in chains. This is turning out to be my lucky night all the way around." He walked over to where Hawkins and Quinn had stopped in front of the desk. In an instant, his laughter stopped and his smile turned grim. "You fucking bastard," he said, grabbing Quinn around the back of his neck and squeezing hard. "Nobody steals from Roper Jones. Nobody. I'm going to turn you fucking inside out for even trying. What did you think you were going to do with my diamonds, huh? Keep them for yourself and the woman?"

Quinn gave him a long look, but no answer. Roper's face flushed, turning ruddy with anger. His eyes flashed an electric, dangerous blue, and for a second, Regan feared he might do something horribly violent, right then, right there.

"I'll take cash," Hawkins interjected coolly. "Small bills."

"Small bills?" Roper repeated, turning his attention to Hawkins and releasing Quinn. A short laugh escaped him. "You're fucking crazy, Cristo. No problems, eh?"

The rumbling entrance of a forklift drew everyone's attention to the hangar door. The *Tarbosaurus* nest was on a pallet, its uneven shape causing it to rock from side to side. Regan could hardly bear to watch, her breath was caught so tight in her throat.

"Small bills." Roper laughed again. "Wait until you see this." He waved the forklift over. "Put it here." He cleared a place on the desk without the computer.

This is awful, Regan thought, watching the two men named Danny and Brad manhandle the fossil of Wilson's dreams, dropping it on the metal desk with a thud. Plaster dust and shards flew off the fossil in a settling cloud, accompanied by a terrible cracking sound.

She bit back a curse. It sounded like they'd just broken the heart of the thing, fractured it right through the middle. What a nightmare. They hadn't been careful when they'd picked it up with the museum's portable hoist either. All they'd cared about was the plaster jacket and the small canvas sack Wilson had been using to put the diamonds in.

Roper had put the sack in the pocket of his suit coat, and now pulled it out.

"See what else you can get out of there, and put the rest of the diamonds in with these," he ordered her, dropping the canvas bag next to the fossil. "And hurry up, we're running out of time."

Time for what? Regan wondered. *More mayhem? Murder?*

She glanced at Quinn, hoping for a clue as to what she should do. The slight nod he gave her could have been her imagination. It was hardly a movement at all, but she followed his lead and turned her attention to the fossil and the hundreds of rough diamonds embedded in the plaster.

She'd hardly gotten started when some compelling force made her look back up. Her gaze collided with Hawkins's, and her heart caught in her throat.

Christian Hawkins was looking at her, looking long and hard, his eyes dark, intense, and filled with enough raw appreciation to make a shiver go down her spine.

His predatory smile returned, as if he knew exactly what had just happened to her inside the privacy of her skin, and with an insolence she wouldn't have thought possible, he let his gaze slide down the length of her body.

Suddenly she wasn't at all sure what was happening. She looked back to Quinn. He'd been hit, hard, more than once. She could see the swelling on his lip, the bruise starting under his eye.

What had Hawkins done? Beaten him? For the fifty thousand dollars?

Every doubt she'd ever had, every story she'd ever

read about Christian Hawkins, came back to her in that moment. What did she really know about Hawkins, besides the time he'd done in jail, and the fact that Quinn trusted him?

Yet Quinn had been hurt, and Hawkins was the one turning him in to the man who had threatened to remove his head and feed the remains to the dogs.

As if sensing a change in their luck, the two rottweilers roused themselves from the side of the desk and padded around to the front. At a signal from Roper, low growls began emanating from their throats.

Whatever composure Quinn had been holding on to up until that point was clearly shaken by the sound. He slanted a glance to Hawkins and got a disdainful shrug for his trouble.

"This is your fucking problem, Younger, not mine." He turned back to Roper, but first let his gaze slide over Regan again. "The money, if you don't mind."

"Sure, Cristo," Roper said slyly, following the path of Hawkins's eyes. "You can have your money, unless there's something else you want."

A true grin curved Hawkins's mouth, and he let out a short laugh. "She's for sale?"

"Everything in this building is for sale, except his life." Roper jerked his thumb in Quinn's direction. "I'm keeping that for myself."

Regan watched, horrified, as without so much as a twinge of emotion, Hawkins turned his back on Quinn and walked toward her.

"Everything, huh?" he asked, coming to a stop in front

of her and reaching up to slide his fingers up her cheek. "She's a bit of a mess."

"She's had a big day, but if you want time to clean her up a little, I can get one of the Jack O' Nine girls down here with some clothes and makeup."

Regan would have jerked away from him, but she was frozen to the spot by his callous betrayal. Quinn couldn't possibly have put his trust in someone who cared so little. Or could he have?

"No," Hawkins decided after a lengthy pause. "I'll take her just the way she is. How much for half an hour?"

"Half an hour?" Roper laughed. "Touch her again, Cristo. Trust me, you're going to want more than half an hour."

For the second time, Hawkins met her gaze, his eyes very dark, very intense, darker even than she had imagined. With his hand sliding back down her face, he moved closer to her and slowly ran his thumb over her lips, very gently from one side to the other, and against every rational thought in her head she felt the rest of the world begin to recede. Fear, she told herself, fear was making her feel so odd.

"Don't move, honey," he whispered, before bringing his mouth down to hers and whispering again against her lips. "Don't move, and everything will be okay."

His other hand came up to her waist and slid around to cup her bottom and pull her in closer to his body, until she could feel the long, hard length of his legs pressed against hers, feel the lean hardness of his torso and the steely strength of his arms.

She started to protest, and he pulled her even tighter, his mouth came down on hers even harder, and yet more sweetly, if a forced kiss could even begin to be sweet.

"Shhh," he whispered, relenting just a little, before kissing her again. Some of his heat washed into her then, the heat from his pelvis, the soft, wet heat of his tongue sliding along her lips, asking for entrance. She gasped, just the slightest gasp, and to her horror, he took full advantage of her lapse, pressing his tongue into her mouth.

She trembled in his arms, with anger and shame, and an undeniable awareness that Christian Hawkins was a world-class kisser—and a world-class heel.

It wasn't until he broke off the kiss that she realized his hand was cupping her breast. Then she realized it all too much. Damn him. Damn him. Damn him.

She couldn't even look at Quinn.

"You're right," he said to Roper without taking his gaze from hers. "I want her for an hour. Five hundred dollars."

"You're a rich man tonight, Cristo. Live a little," Roper cajoled. "Keep her until you've had enough. I'll have one of the girls figure the price."

Which Regan figured would turn out to be the full fifty thousand dollars, no matter what Hawkins did or did not do with her—and he wasn't going to do much. She was going to make damn sure of that.

"It's a sucker's bet," she said under her breath, so angry her voice shook.

In answer, he laughed, soft and low, and took her hand in his. "We'll see. Come on, sweetheart. There's a Motel Six just down the road."

He was too strong to resist, and rather than be dragged, she did her best to keep up with him. It was only near the door that she dared to look back at Quinn. What she saw startled and confused her. She didn't know what kind of expression she'd expected, but it sure as hell hadn't been satisfaction.

HAWKINS hurried her through the door as quickly as he could. He had a death grip on her hand, and more than a few errant thoughts running like crazy through his head.

She was sweet. Damn, she was sweet. No wonder Quinn had been all over her in the warehouse. Even unwilling, she'd warmed to his mouth just the slightest bit, and the softness of her mouth had done more than just warm him. Hell, one more minute of kissing a reluctant Regan McKinney, and he would have been as hard as the Rock of Gibraltar.

For friendship's sake, he was going to keep that information to himself. Quinn had been cool, but he'd probably strangle him in his sleep for getting an erection with his girlfriend.

"H-how, h-how could you?" she sputtered beside him, having to race to keep up with his long strides.

"It was easy, honey." Too damn easy, which didn't do a damn thing to improve his mood.

"You can't, I can't...we, w-we can't leave him," she insisted, starting to balk, trying to slow him down. Desperation rang in her voice. "They'll kill him."

"Not if I can help it," he gritted out between his teeth. "Come on." He hustled her along even more quickly, breaking into a run.

"Where are you taking me?" she demanded to know.

"To Jeanette. Just stay put when we get there. The FBI is on its way."

They rounded the corner of the last hangar in the row, and skidded to a stop in front of the '69 Camaro. He opened the door and started to put her in, but she resisted him.

"What are you doing? We can't leave him. I won't." She was adamant, her hands digging into his upper arms, keeping him from putting her into the car.

"Regan, Regan." He tried to calm her. "Quinn is the last person I would ever leave anywhere. I'm going back to him, right now, but you have got to stay here."

"Why?" She was looking up at him, the same desperation he heard in her voice making her face stark.

"Because that's what Quinn wants, just like he wanted me to get you out of there any way I could." He let his words sink in for a second.

"Quinn wanted you to do that?" Her voice went from desperation to a mix of hope and confusion.

"Yes, that was for Quinn," he told her, then lowered his mouth and gave her one last, soft, slow, sweet, wet kiss. It was a rotten thing to do, but he'd practically heard her come in the warehouse, and he was half hard just from pretending to kiss her, and she was ungodly sweet, and he was just a little bit scared for Quinn—so he kissed Quinn's woman. When she opened her eyes, he kissed her again, just on the tip of the nose. "And that was for me. Now stay put."

He crossed over to Roxanne and got his submachine gun out of the backseat. He still had the extra magazines in a pouch on his belt, but he no sooner turned to leave than he swore.

"Hell." Things were happening faster than he'd expected.

"What?" she asked, rising back out of the car.

"Don't." He gestured for her to get back in. "Stay with the car."

"What's going on?" she said, sliding back inside.

"I think Roper's guns have finally arrived." He pointed across the runway to a freight truck barreling toward the Avatrix hangar.

Chapter

Well, that had gone really fucking well, Quinn thought, watching Hawkins practically suck Regan's tongue down his throat while he had his hands all over her. Yessiree, now he could die a happy man.

Breasts. Hawkins had touched her breasts, which Quinn was sure he hadn't authorized. But then, a guy didn't think he had to tell a best friend to keep his hands off his woman's breasts while he was kissing her. He'd thought that was just one of those unwritten rules that all guys—except, obviously, Hawkins—knew about.

And now came the real fun part.

He caught Roper's eye, only because to put it off any longer couldn't possibly be to his advantage. He was going to get hurt tonight. He'd known that going in, but he was counting on Hawkins to keep him from getting too busted up or killed.

Despite the breast thing, which he was definitely going to bring up at a future date, there wasn't anyone he trusted more. With Regan out of the way, nobody's hands were tied—except his own, of course, but only until he needed them. Even a flex cuff could be rigged for a quick escape.

He knew Hawkins, knew he was already headed back inside the hangar with a full arsenal of goodies for creating mayhem. If the FBI showed up as well, that would just be great.

If they'd all do it before Roper got too excited about his knife or his dogs, that would be even better.

The guy *was* getting a bad look in his eye, like he wouldn't mind having some fun before the guns showed up.

Yessiree, now would be a damn good time for the cavalry to arrive.

The rumbling of a truck engine turned his attention to the open hangar door, and Quinn breathed a sigh of relief. The guns, no doubt. Not the cavalry, but close enough. Closing the deal should buy him at least a half an hour before Roper took his head off.

Or at least that's what he'd thought.

"Hey, pretty boy," Roper crooned, stalking him from around the desk. "You think you're pretty fucking smart, don't you? Well, let's just see how deep pretty is. You've been nothing but trouble for me from the beginning of this deal, and now we're gonna settle the score. Brad, Danny, hold him."

Strong hands came around him on either side and dragged him backward into a chair, where they held him with bone-crushing diligence.

The knife blade glinted in Roper's hand, and in the next moment, he struck.

Searing, white-hot pain streaked through Quinn's body. He gritted his teeth against crying out, and at the same time thanked his lucky stars Roper hadn't decided to gut him on the spot. The bastard had gone for his face instead, cutting him from his temple to his ear and making a bloody mess, but the injury wasn't mortal.

"We'll finish this later, Younger," Roper said, taking a handkerchief out of his pocket and using it to wipe blood off his knife. "You, me, and the dogs."

He dropped the bloody handkerchief on the desk and walked toward the truck pulling up inside the hangar. Good old Brad went with him, but Danny-boy kept his death grip on Quinn's arm and his 9mm leveled directly behind Quinn's ear. It was enough to keep anybody from making any sudden moves.

Looking around, he carefully noted the other two doors he could see, the two men besides Danny and Brad who had come with Roper, and the exact location of the small canvas bag full of diamonds.

REGAN couldn't take it. She couldn't sit still and hope for the best while Quinn was in Roper's clutches and his only hope was Hawkins.

Her glance strayed to Jeanette's ignition and the keys dangling from the steering column.

Did she dare?

Hawkins knew what he was doing, she was sure, but Hawkins was outnumbered, and though she kept looking, she hadn't seen sign one of the FBI.

And she couldn't just sit there. She just couldn't, not with Quinn's life on the line.

Quickly, before she changed her mind, she slid over the gear console and into the driver's seat. It felt different from the passenger side, distinctly, profoundly different. The driver's side had all the power. This was the side that made the decisions. This was the side that took the risks.

She reached for the keys—and hesitated. She knew what was going to happen when she turned the key. Jeanette was going to roar to life and eat her alive. The Camaro was going to shake and tremble with barely suppressed violence. She was going to want to eat, and what Jeanette ate was asphalt.

Regan looked out through the windshield at the old airport, at the runways and parking lots, and at all the pavement in between the hangars and the warehouses, all the pavement tying together the terminal and the old concourses.

There was more than enough asphalt, even for Jeanette.

"Okay, baby, be gentle. Don't hurt me, and I'll try real hard not to hurt you." Before she could change her mind, she turned the key—and lurched forward with a growl and a scream and an instantly dead engine.

"Clutch, clutch, clutch," she ground out between her teeth, mentally kicking herself for being so stupid. She knew about the clutch. She seldom used one herself, but she knew about them.

With the clutch in, she tried again and felt Jeanette come to life in all her growling glory, rising up around her like a phoenix from the ashes. Regan stepped on the gas, with the clutch still firmly in, and the Camaro shook like a wet dog, all over from her hood to her tail—and she roared.

Yes! Regan thought. She could do this. She could save Quinn.

Carefully, she let out the clutch while stepping on the gas, and went through another teeth-jarring lurch, complete with growl and scream and a dead engine.

She almost cried in frustration. Quinn needed her. She had to do this.

Twice more she got the car going, only to fail with the clutch, before she finally got Jeanette moving in first gear. She'd been told it only got easier after that.

HIDING behind a crate close to where Roper held Quinn, Hawkins knew exactly what he was hearing. He couldn't believe it, but he knew exactly what it was: Regan McKinney committing suicide the hard way. God forbid, if she accidentally got all the way to sixth gear, she was going to end up dying in Utah before she even knew she'd left the ground and gone airborne.

Why hadn't he taken the keys?

He was afraid that was going to be a question that haunted him for years to come. Right along with why in the hell hadn't he run faster to get back to the hangar?

Quinn had been cut. Roper had cut him with his fucking knife, which Hawkins was personally going to bury in his throat, and Quinn was bleeding from a long gash down the side of his face, bleeding like a stuck pig.

Son of a bitch. Where was the fucking FBI? The best Hawkins could do on his own was to take out three, maybe four guys before one of the remaining guys decided to take out Quinn.

The truck had rolled in carrying the guns, and Roper's men were busy unloading them. And what amazing guns they were, assault rifles for the new millennium, with Buck Rogers styling and the firepower to blow away terrorists or anybody else right through a brick wall. Roper himself had taken one of the guns out and was breaking it down. Hawkins was impressed. The OICW was a double-barreled weapon with the top barrel shooting 20mm high-explosive fragmentation rounds, and the second barrel shooting 5.56mm ammunition. It had a bayonet, a laser range-finder, and even a video camera mounted on top.

But what Hawkins needed now was another shooter, not another gun. And for God's sake, he did not need Regan behind Jeanette's wheel, hell-bent on turning this into the biggest cluster-fuck of the century.

He could hear her lurching closer outside the hangar. Hell, he could smell Jeanette's clutch burning. Down below him, he saw Roper gesture for Tommy Jenkins, one of his guys from the Jack O' Nines and Roper's whoring buddy, to go check it out. Everyone else grabbed an OICW, some ammo, and locked and loaded.

Perfect.

Running along the tops of the crates, he followed Tommy Jenkins to the hangar door. The minute Tommy stepped outside, out of sight of the others, Hawkins dropped him with a silent burst from the suppressed HK MP5.

Looking farther out, he could see Jeanette struggling to be set free, inching her way across the parking lot, heading for the hangar, straining to get into second gear.

And suddenly he thought, hell, this could actually work. As long as Regan didn't get herself killed. He raced back along the tops of the crates to cover Quinn.

Damn, Regan was a long, desperate minute away from him. If she could just find second, or God, please, third, she could have Quinn sitting in Jeanette's lap in under fifteen seconds. Less than ten, if she didn't choke. In five, if she'd had any idea of what in the hell she was doing. One, if she'd been Quinn.

But she wasn't Quinn, and she didn't know what in the hell she was doing. She was going to be too late.

Even the truck drivers had armed themselves and were ready for a shootout. There was no place for everything to go but downhill fast, and Hawkins quickly picked his best line of fire to cover both Quinn and Regan, thinking this would be a good time for Leeder to show up with his FBI buddies—and then the miracle happened.

He heard it coming straight at him. He heard it in the sudden surge of power. He heard it in the headers and the big block and the exhaust. Either Regan had found her way into second gear, or Jeanette had dragged her there. Third followed with a squeal of tires, and when she hit fourth, Hawkins was already screaming, *"Brakes!"*

By then, it was already too late for brakes, but that didn't stop her from hitting them—hard.

SWEET *Jesus, Mary, Joseph, and Jeanette.* Quinn had heard the Camaro coming, heard the low throaty growl he had fine-tuned to within a decibel of perfection, heard someone mangling her gears and her clutch—and he knew Regan had taken on the beast and was getting eaten alive.

Then she got lucky and started climbing her way through the gears. There wasn't a guy in the hangar who didn't stop what he was doing and turn to see what in the hell was heading his way in a rolling cloud of smoke and thunder.

But it was already too late.

Jeanette roared through the open hangar door, wheels spinning, smoke clinging to her tires, heading straight for disaster. Then Regan hit the brakes, and all hell broke loose—in slow motion.

Quinn watched the whole disaster unfold frame by frame, even as he dove for the desk. Jeanette went into a tail-spinning turn that plowed her rear end into a rack of barrels, breaking one open and spewing liquid fuel over a wide swath of the hangar, including the desk, which she'd barely missed.

The smell of gasoline filled the air, potent, breath-stealing. To Quinn's left, he heard a man scream. One of Roper's goons had been pinned in the wreckage. Roper had been knocked out cold and was lying facedown on the hangar floor, blood running from his head, gasoline pooling around his prone form. The dogs had disappeared in a flash of black tails and flying paws. Jeanette roared in fury, her tires smoking, but she didn't budge, not so much as a foot. Her tail end was buried under the twisted rack and the remaining barrels, the power of her engine making the whole thing rock, and shake, and grind together.

Quinn dragged himself to his feet, his mind racing, trying to catch his breath.

Geezus. He ran toward the Camaro, slipped on the slick floor, and fell in a heap. Swearing, he scrambled back to his feet. Shit. He could smell the heat coming off Jeanette, heat off her tires, heat off her screaming engine—and the whole fucking place was doused in gasoline.

Ripping his cuffs off, he slid up the side of the Camaro and tore open Jeanette's door. Regan stared at him wide-eyed, trembling, a cut across her forehead. Gas was pouring down on the Camaro from the punctured barrels above.

Pulling her free of the car, Quinn took her hand in his and ran like hell.

Hawkins joined them at the hangar door, covering them.

They'd cleared the hangar and were skidding around the corner of a freight office building when Avatrix blew. The three of them hit the ground in a pile, forced down by the concussion of the explosion.

Looking up, Quinn saw a ton of debris go flying into the air, and a ton of it come flying down.

Behind them, half a dozen cars came to a screeching halt. He heard people piling out of the vehicles, and in the next minute they were surrounded by the FBI.

It was a zoo after that.

Fire crews were on the scene within fifteen minutes of the explosion, and the police weren't far behind.

Leeder, the Special Agent in Charge, secured the place for the FBI. Leeder and Hawkins had a brief conversation while the medics cleaned up Quinn and Regan. Quinn hadn't let go of her hand, not once, since they'd run out of the hangar, but she hadn't said a word to him. He'd asked her a few questions—"Are you okay? Do you hurt anywhere? Do you need some water?" But all he'd gotten was either a nod or a shake of her head.

It worried him. Like him, she had to be exhausted. She smelled like gasoline; her clothes were torn. She had a small white bandage on her forehead where the EMT had cleaned her cut. Dirt smudged her face, her arms, her legs. He knew she still didn't have any underwear, and for the first time, he felt bad about it. Real bad. He wanted to protect her, make her feel secure, keep her from harm—and all he'd done was lose her underwear and practically get her blown up.

Hell. This had to be the absolute worst first date of her life.

He looked back to the hangar, or what was left of it. The fire crews had gotten the fire out, and the wind had picked up, blowing the smoke off to the south. Slowly, the blackened, shadowed remains inside the blown-out shell began to take on distinct shapes, the most distinct being the burned-out chassis sitting in the middle of the hangar: Jeanette. There was nothing left of her, nothing at all but a smoldering pile of iron and smoking tires.

Damn, Quinn thought. *Damn.*

FROM the safety of her perch, sitting on the hood of Christian Hawkins's car—he called the car Roxanne—Regan took in the sight and saw the whole wild night replay in her head, from the minute she'd strapped herself into the Camaro in Cisco, until Jeanette had given her all in the Avatrix hangar. Behind her, dawn stained the eastern horizon, signaling the break of day, and by default, the end of night.

It was over. She hurt in every cell of her body, from all her cuts and bruises to the awful ache in her heart. But she'd survived. The night was over.

The greatest paleontology find of the century had just

gone up in smoke and debris—but at least the night was over.

She was holding Quinn's hand tight, looking at poor Jeanette, watching the fire crews douse her in water and foam.

As she watched, nearly too tired to breathe, an inexplicable sadness came over her, and she wondered if she was really holding on to anything at all—or if she should even try.

CHAPTER 28

By THE TIME they drove up to the house in Boulder, Regan felt like she'd been gone a hundred years. Everything in her world had been tossed up for grabs, and she wasn't sure what was left.

Wilson was home, and that had been her goal when she'd set out yesterday morning. Nikki was safe, half in love and half heartbroken—which made Regan wonder what had happened between her and the boy wonder— but safe.

As for herself, she was overwhelmed on overload. She needed time to think, to sort, to organize and catalogue, and somehow put the last fifteen hours in perspective.

She needed to sleep, have a cup of tea, take a breath, and ask herself some serious questions about what had happened between her and Quinn.

Quinn pulled Betty to a stop in the driveway just as the paperboy lofted a paper up onto the porch. Light was barely breaking over the eastern horizon. Birds were waking up in the trees.

In the backseat, Nikki grumbled, and Wilson woke with a start. Neither had been too happy with Regan's insistence on them coming home at the crack of dawn. But she'd been adamant. She needed everything back to normal, if that was even possible after the night they'd all had.

Everyone piled out of the car and headed up to the house. A police car was already parked outside, a protection detail called in by Hawkins, and Quinn went over to talk with the officers for a couple of minutes.

Inside the house, Wilson went straight through the kitchen, up the stairs, and directly into his bedroom, grouching about darned fossil thieves, and the quality of Siberian diamonds or the lack thereof, and why in the hell had the darn thing gotten blown up? Didn't anybody have any sense anymore? And what in the heck had some guy in Denver thought he was going to get away with by stealing dinosaur bones and stuffing them with stolen diamonds?

Guns, Regan could have told him, if he'd stopped long enough to listen. A bunch of guns stolen from the American military that had gone up in a ball of smoke and flame along with Jeanette and a couple of rottweilers she feared would haunt her dreams for years to come. The dogs hadn't been anywhere to be found after the explosion, though Quinn had told the police he thought they'd gotten away.

Roper hadn't gotten away, but a few of the men working for him had escaped the explosion and been picked up by the FBI.

A wave of heat and nausea rolled through her, almost bringing her to her knees. It had all been awful, just too awful, and she didn't want to think about it anymore. She had her family back. That's what she'd wanted. The only thing she'd wanted.

Dylan Hart, whom Regan didn't think she would ever forgive for involving them in this mess, had been able to confirm the theft of the *Tarbosaurus* nest from Ulan Bator's State Central Museum in Mongolia with his overseas connections. He'd also worked a deal that granted Wilson sole access to all the data the Mongolian paleontology team had come up with on the Cretaceous carnivore nest. It was a stunning coup, and one Regan knew her grandfather would hold over Dr. Houska's head for years to come—if he ever got over the loss of the fossil itself.

Regan stopped halfway across the kitchen when she realized Nikki hadn't followed her inside. Retracing her steps, she stopped in the open doorway and saw her little sister talking to Quinn. Nikki's face was very somber, an anomaly in itself, but Regan couldn't hear what she was saying.

She heard Quinn's answer, though, and it hit her like a blow.

"I can't promise you anything, Nikki, other than that I'll tell you if something happens to him."

Nikki said something else, her beautiful face growing even more serious, and Regan's heart tightened in her chest.

There weren't going to be *any* easy answers with the guys from Steele Street. No promises, and probably no future. Every one of them had almost died tonight—her, Nikki, Wilson, Quinn, Kid, Hawkins. She'd finally heard the details about Kid and Nikki's ill-fated attempt to reach the Southern Cross Hotel, and they had made her blood run cold. They'd all been in mortal danger tonight, and it was more than Regan could bear.

More than she could bear, even for love.

Love. Was that what this was? This wonderful, awful, almost painful ache she felt inside? Or was it exhaustion? Sexual overload? Quinn overload? Everything overload?

"No, Nikki. I can't tell you where he went, or when he'll be back." Quinn's voice carried much farther than Nikki's, and every word hurt. It hurt her, and it hurt Nikki. Regan could see her sister's mouth softening with pain.

Love, she thought again, watching his face. How could she afford to let herself love him when he would go, too, just like Kid, disappear in the middle of some night, and it would be one of the other Steele Street guys saying the same words to her—unless she stopped it now. Before the pain of losing him cut too deeply. Before she let herself decide that loving him, no matter what, would be enough.

Nikki turned then and, without a backward glance, headed toward her studio, her refuge.

Regan wanted to cry for her, and she wanted to shake Kid Chaos and demand to know what had gone on between the two of them. She had a feeling it wasn't something Nikki was going to feel like talking about for quite a while.

So, great. Wilson and Nikki had both deserted her and left her to face Quinn alone.

"Hey," Quinn said, coming up the steps. He dropped a quick kiss on her cheek, then took her arm and guided her back inside the kitchen. "The cops will be here for as long as we think necessary, or as long as you want them—whichever comes last."

He closed the door behind them, and Regan felt so powerful and so keen a need to let him fold her in his arms that she knew she had to do this quickly, or not at all.

"I'm really tired, Quinn," she said, before he could even begin to get comfortable in the house. "I'd like to just go to bed now."

"Sure," he said, but the wary look in his eyes told her he was picking up on what she was trying so hard to say without coming straight out and asking him to leave.

"Alone." There, she'd said it.

His mouth tightened at the corners. He was quiet for a long moment. When he spoke, his voice was so soft she could hardly hear him. "Do you want me to stay in the house?"

Okay, he wasn't going to be casually polite. So neither was she.

"No . . . I, um, I don't think that would be such a good idea," she said, but she had to look away when she said it. She couldn't out-and-out tell him she didn't want him to stay. She couldn't lie like that and look him in the eye while she did it.

The room hummed with silence before he quietly asked, "Do you want to see me again?"

God, he wasn't going to make this easy, and she didn't quite have the courage to completely throw him away. Not yet.

"Maybe . . . maybe we could go on a date. Sometime. Later," she said desperately.

DATE?" Quinn repeated, feeling a tremor run through him, a very uneasy tremor. He wasn't precisely sure what she meant, but he didn't think dating could be good, especially if it was later.

Later than what? he wanted to ask, but didn't quite dare. He'd thought they'd kind of skipped the dating stage for something a lot more meaningful.

"Sure. Later. It's what people do. Maybe we could, uh, get to know each other better that way."

Or maybe not, was what it sounded like, and his uneasy tremor started to turn into a full-blown quake. Get to know each other? What the hell did that mean?

How could he possibly know her better? He knew he'd loved her since he was sixteen. Knew the sound of her voice filled him with a sense of joy and well-being he would never have dreamed possible. He knew what she tasted like in the middle of the night with her legs wrapped around his shoulders—incredibly, mind-blowingly good. Amazing. It was a physical sensation that registered in every cell of his body, all at once, every-where. He'd never known anybody like that before. He didn't want to know anybody else like that, ever—even if it was possible, which he very sincerely doubted. If what he felt with her had been easy to find, he would have found it long before this. God knew, he'd put in plenty of effort, all of it pretty damn good fun.

But Regan, she was beyond fun. Way beyond. And if she wanted to date, he could stop thinking like a guy long enough to take a few steps back and date—but not later. No way was he going to wait for an ominous-sounding "later."

"How about if I pick you up in, let's say, an hour?" Okay, that had been a little harder to say than he'd hoped it would be, because he'd *hoped* to be spending the next hour or eight sleeping with her, making love with her, not getting kicked out of her house.

But he could date instead.

Sure he could, if that's what it was going to take to get her past whatever it was that had put that look in her eye. The look that told him she was confused and ex-hausted and maybe a little afraid of everything that had happened between them.

"The sun won't even be up in an hour," she said.

"Good point," he conceded.

"And I really am tired," she added, taking a step back. "It's been a long night."

And that was a huge understatement.

"How about if I get opera tickets for tonight?" Hawkins had a great connection to the Denver Opera Guild. "Or we can have dinner." His first choice. He'd much rather look at her from across a candlelit table than to sit watching anything else, even if it was *La Traviata*.

"I have to work in the morning," she said, retreating another step.

He was losing ground, fast. He could feel it slipping out from under his feet like a California mud slide, and he got an awful feeling that if he let her get away from him now, he wouldn't get her back.

"Takeout," he offered. "I could bring Chinese takeout, for everybody, and we could all, uh, eat together, you, me, Wilson, and Nikki, and maybe we could play cards."

Strip poker on seven-card stud was a good game for him. He could have her down to her birthday suit in two hands. Of course, Wilson and Nikki would also be down to theirs, which wasn't at all what he had in mind.

The look she was giving him told him he'd sounded way too desperate with that last idea. He needed to get a grip. She'd had a wild night, probably the wildest night of her life, and he could understand that she might need a little downtime.

He just wished to hell she'd spend it with him.

But she wasn't going to—he could tell by looking at her. She needed some space. And he needed to be grown-up and give it to her.

Shit.

This didn't look good. This didn't look good at all.

CHAPTER 29

AFTER FOUR DAYS and twenty-eight unanswered phone calls, Quinn was pretty damn sure he'd figured out what she meant by "dating later." She meant never—but he'd be damned if he was going to accept that. He knew what she'd felt when she'd been with him. He was a smart guy and not given to self-delusion, and he was *not* a one-night stand, not for Regan McKinney.

Besides, he was dying without her. He had nothing left to lose.

Skeeter and Johnny still had his COPO Camaro broken down, and they'd made some adjustments to Roxanne, so Hawkins had asked him to give the Challenger a spin, and he'd spun himself and the big green machine all the way up to Boulder.

He missed Jeanette, but there was always another Jeanette out there somewhere, waiting to be rebuilt.

There was only one Regan.

He pulled up to the curb in front of the McKinney house, let out a short breath, and swung out of the car. He didn't allow himself to hesitate. He knew she was home. He'd radioed the cops on his way up the turn-pike.

Clearing the front porch steps in two long strides, he crossed to the door, gave the doorbell one intrigued glance, and pushed the button.

A bloodcurdling scream erupted from the house.

Holy shit. He jumped back, wondering who in the world was dying.

Then it hit him, and he grinned.

Christ, that was just what he needed, when he was already nervous as hell.

There was probably no need to ring the doorbell again, so he waited.

And waited.

Until he finally heard someone coming.

The door swung open, and his breath actually caught in his throat at the sight of her. It was Regan, and she was wearing a dress, a killer dress with tiny ruffled straps on a wraparound halter top guaranteed to knock him down dead. It was blue, with blue and white flowers swirled all over it, and it made her skin look cool and creamy. She did not tan, ever, and her shoulders were enough to break a grown man's heart.

"Hi," he managed, which was more than she seemed to be able to do.

She looked frozen in the doorway, despite the ninety-seven-degree day.

"Do you have a minute?" he asked.

"No," she whispered after an endless silence. "I . . . I have a luncheon. At the university. For the geology department."

She was lying. What he didn't know was why. So he pushed her. "Are you speaking?"

"No."

"Then you have a minute. Can I come in? Please?"

He could tell by the stricken look on her face that ingrained politeness was the only thing that got him through the door.

Okay, he told himself. *Don't panic.* He'd given this a lot of thought. Sure they'd had a crazy night together, maybe one of the craziest ever, but there had been more than craziness, and she had to know it. She was scared, was all. Scared of him, of what they'd done, of what she'd felt. He was going to make that all go away.

She led the way into the kitchen, and he followed, counting every step as a victory. She had her hair rolled up in kind of a French style, very elegant, and there was the faintest sheen of dampness on the nape of her neck. He wanted to start licking her there and work his way down to the really good stuff. But he wasn't going to do that. No. He was going to behave. He was not going to seduce her or push her into something she needed time to think about. He was playing for keeps, and that meant having patience.

She came to a sudden halt in the hallway, and to keep from running into her, he caught her with his hands, the biggest mistake he could have possibly made. Her skin was so soft, and so warm.

"Sorry, I—" Hell, he wasn't sorry. He was speechless with wanting to pull her into his arms and kiss her. He should let go of her. He knew it. He just couldn't do it. And so much for his good intentions. Hell.

"Quinn, I . . . I can't do this." Her voice sounded very weak, like she might start crying any second.

"Can't do what?" he asked, gently turning her in his arms.

"Be with you. See you." Her eyes were downcast. All he could see was the top of her head, until he lightly grasped her chin and tilted her face up toward his.

That's when he saw her eyes, and what he saw made his heart plummet into the pit of his stomach.

"You've been crying," he said. Her eyes were red-rimmed, the soft gray color washed out.

"Ever since you left." The admission came hard to her. He could tell by the way she shifted her gaze to the floor.

"Why, Regan? If that's how you feel, why haven't we been together?"

"Because I don't have the courage for it. That night . . . I can't live like that, Quinn. Never knowing if you're safe. Violence around every corner. People putting a price on your head." Her gaze came back up to his. "I love you, Quinn. More than I ever dreamed I could love someone, but it would kill me to live like that."

She loved him. Quinn felt the words ease the tension that had been building in him since she'd all but pushed him out her front door. He could handle the rest of it if she loved him.

"You stole my heart, Regan," he told her. "And I don't particularly want it back."

"Oh, Quinn," she said, and he didn't think he'd ever heard a sadder voice. It was more than he could take.

Still holding her chin in his hand, he lowered his head to give her a sweet kiss, just a kiss, just a moment of his mouth on hers without any of the crazy heat that had so consumed them Friday night.

But she undermined his innocent intentions with an unbidden sigh and the slightest touch of her tongue to his lips. It was a fleeting caress, just the briefest touch of dampness, but it was enough to challenge him to his core.

He held himself very still, knowing how easy it would be to give in to the sudden surge of heat she'd sent streaking through his body. How easy it would be to find himself with her legs around his waist, his body pressing her back against the wall, and her dress gathered up in his hands.

He couldn't do it. He couldn't afford to give in to all the lovely, earthly lust she inspired. They'd made love four incredible times that night, and it hadn't been enough to hold her to him. If he wanted her, he had to give her something more—and he definitely wanted her.

"Come with me, Regan," he said, lifting his head from hers. "Can you give me an hour? There's something I want to show you. Someone I want you to meet."

She held his gaze for a long time before she nodded her acceptance. "I ... um, okay," she said hesitantly, every doubt she had written on her face and echoing in her voice. "Just an hour."

He didn't give her a chance to change her mind. In minutes, he had her buckled in to Roxanne, and the Challenger fired up and ready to roll.

They didn't have far to go. Fifteen minutes of maneuvering crosstown traffic through Boulder got them to the east side and a new housing development of high-end homes.

Regan instantly knew where they were, and whom he wanted her to meet, and for the first time since he'd walked back in her door and back into her life, she felt the stirrings of hope.

Meeting a man's mother for the first time could do that to a girl.

"This is your mom's house," she said, and he nodded.

"She doesn't know we're coming," he said. "I didn't want to get her hopes up and then have you turn me down."

"Is it going to be okay? Us just showing up like this?"

In answer, he let out a short laugh. "Trust me, Regan.

She's my mother. I could show up at two o'clock in the morning with half the Barnum and Bailey circus in tow, and she'd be glad to see me—and then she'd feed everybody. I hope you're hungry."

She wasn't. Not at all. Especially now. But she was excited. He'd brought her to meet his mother.

"My mother died a long time ago," she told him. She didn't know why she told him, but suddenly it seemed like something he should know. "My dad, too."

"I remember," he said, surprising her. "Wilson used to talk about your parents a lot, when he'd have us out there on some godforsaken hillside, scratching in the dirt. Every time one of us whined—and there was plenty of whining—he'd tell us another story about your mom and dad and what great adventurers they both were, and sometimes he'd sort of wander into the story of how they died." He reached up and caressed her face, his thumb gliding smoothly across her cheek. "I'd kiss you," he said softly, "but I don't think you want to meet my mom looking like I just tumbled you in the backseat."

No, she guessed she didn't, but she was tempted. Darn tempted. She'd missed him so terribly, and he looked good enough to eat, in a white polo shirt, button-fly jeans—yes, she'd noticed—and his snakeskin cowboy boots.

At the front door, he rang the doorbell once before letting himself in with a key. "I've never actually lived here," he explained, "but Mom likes me to have a key and come and go at will. It's just her way, I think, of trying to make up to me for all those times we didn't have a place to go. Crazy, huh? Like I don't have a house in Evergreen and an apartment at Steele Street."

"You have a house in Evergreen?" she asked, naming a town up in the mountains but close to Denver. It was amazing what she didn't know about him.

"Yeah. I guess we never got to that part, did we?" The lock turned, and he opened the door wide, gesturing her inside.

"No. We didn't." She walked into a large foyer that flanked an even larger great room, and her eyes opened wide. The house was beautifully decorated with broad strokes of color and eclectic furniture, rich tapestries, wool rugs on wooden floors, and open beamed ceilings. Regan's first thought was that Nikki would love it. Nothing matched, but everything fit together perfectly.

"You want to know what's even crazier?" he asked, following her inside and shutting the door behind them. "I make a point of showing up unannounced at least once a month, just because she gets such a kick out of it."

Regan thought she'd been in love with him before, but he'd just won her heart forever.

"Hey, Mom!" he hollered, taking her hand and leading her through the great room toward an open set of French doors off the large kitchen. "She's probably in the garden. I don't know where the girls are, probably shopping. They're like an Olympic tag team at the mall."

"How old are they?"

"Fifteen and thirteen. Hellions both." He grinned.

"Oh," Regan said, catching sight of a woman pruning rosebushes in the backyard. "What's your mother's name?"

"Solange."

The woman rose to her feet, turning toward the house, and it was all Regan could do to keep her feet moving.

"She's French?" she asked, glancing up at him.

He came to a stop at the open door and met her gaze. "Half French from her mother's side."

"Quinn!" his mother called excitedly from the yard, and Regan returned her attention to one of the most beautiful women she'd ever seen in her life. Solange was Quinn Younger, female version, with long dark hair that fell in a stylishly silky cut to her shoulders. Features that were chiseled on him were exquisitely delicate on her. They had the same green eyes, the same dark brows, except hers were elegantly shaped. She was dressed in a sleeveless red knit top and black capris with ballet slippers on her feet. She wasn't wearing makeup, but she didn't need makeup. The warmth of her smile made her glow.

She automatically wrapped her arm around Quinn's waist when she came up, and when she took Regan's hand during the introductions, she didn't let go.

"I am so pleased to meet you," she practically crooned, tucking Regan's arm next to her own and leading her out to a shady portion of the patio next to a small fountain with a fishpond. "Quinn, honey, why don't you bring us some tea."

And thus began one of the most remarkable afternoons of Regan's life. She'd never been so fussed over and catered to, or interrogated with such gentle grace. After about half an hour, the girls returned home, and the party picked up in pace. Food and photographs from Quinn's and the girls' childhoods started showing up at the table, and a garden tour was given. By the time Solange's husband, Jerry, got home from work, Quinn had the grill fired up—and through it all, a slow realization began to dawn on Regan: Quinn was easy to love, not hard like she'd feared so desperately, and she wasn't alone in loving him. She didn't know how much his mother knew about what he did, but a few things the older woman said made Regan feel Solange knew more than she liked. That she, too, had her fears and concerns, but she loved him anyway, without reservation.

Anyone who loved had a lot to lose, but who was willing to lose the love to lessen the risk?

Not her, Regan realized, not if it meant giving him up.

After dessert and coffee, Quinn stood up and offered her his hand.

"Come on," he said, with an irresistible grin. "I'm going to give you the real garden tour."

She took his hand, and the girls giggled, and Solange beamed, and Jerry fussed with the grill. The yard was huge, almost half an acre in back, and by the time they'd strolled through his mother's rose garden, the lights on the patio were nothing more than a luminous backdrop against the darkness of the night.

"Have you had fun?" he asked.

"More than fun," she confessed. "Your mother, your family, they're all wonderful."

"You'll like my dad, too. Things are a bit more rambunctious at his house. The boys are younger than Jessie and Lynne. I thought, if you'd like to keep dating me, we could go over there next week. What do you think? I can get you a good deal on your next set of tires if you say yes."

"Bribery?" she teased, charmed that he would stoop so low.

"Whatever it takes," he said, unabashed.

"I haven't thanked you yet for getting my car back to me." Her Taurus had shown up, none the worse for wear, the day before. It had broken her heart at the time, the reminder of him, and she'd spent the rest of the day crying, just as she had the day before and the day before that, but she didn't feel like crying anymore. "I suppose someone will be coming to pick up Betty." He had left her the candy-apple-red Coronet to drive, just like he'd promised.

"No," he said. "Keep her for a while."

"A free ride?" she asked.

"Free ride?" he repeated, laughing softly. He slowed to a stop and gently pulled her into his arms. "Honey, you can have all the free rides on me you want." His voice was husky and sweet, his words a little bit dirty in a way she well understood, and when his mouth came down on hers, Regan knew this was what she'd wanted. This was why she'd cried, this aching need she had to be with him, to make love with him and be loved by him.

"Come home with me," he murmured against her throat.

"To Evergreen?"

"Yes. Tonight. I want to make love to you for days on end without having to stop, just like a honeymoon." He cupped her face with his hands and kissed her mouth.

She kissed him back, then laughed. "You have to get married to have a honeymoon." The minute the words left her lips, she felt a change in him. His kisses became more languorous. His tongue delved deeper in her mouth. His body came up more powerfully against hers.

"Yes," he finally murmured, lifting his head. "Great idea. Let's get married."

She was speechless, and before she could think of anything to say, he continued.

"Don't say we're moving too fast. We're not." He sounded so sure of himself. "I feel like we're ten years late with this and four days behind schedule. So don't say it's too sudden, and don't say no."

"That only leaves yes."

"Yes," he agreed, a smile breaking over his face. "Perfect."

"You're crazy," she said, but she was smiling, too.

"Not really," he countered, his hands sliding down to her hips, holding her against him. "I'm in love, just like I was the first time I ever saw you naked in that tent."

She felt his arousal, and a wash of color flooded into her cheeks. "We can't make love in your mother's backyard."

"Well, we could . . ." He laughed. "Okay, we can't, and we can't go back to the patio until you can get my mind off sex, sex, and more sex."

"How are we going to do that?" She loved teasing him, and loved that he wanted her so much, but he was right. They couldn't go back to the patio with him looking like he was ready to jump her.

"We can talk about dinosaur bones," he suggested. "That usually settles me right down."

"Would you like to discuss recent paleontological evidence for the existence of warm-blooded dinosaurs in the polar regions?"

"Yeah," he said, taking her hand and starting to walk slowly back into the rose garden. "That ought to do it."

"Or we could talk about the Air Force."

He slanted her a wary glance. "And that will definitely do it."

"Your mother and I were talking—"

"For about five hours, nonstop," he interrupted, but she ignored him.

"She said she didn't know why you quit when you did. She said you still fly, all the time, for Steele Street."

"I do. It wasn't the flying that made me quit. Hell, it

wasn't even getting shot down that made me quit, at least not directly."

"What do you mean?"

He stopped, looked over at the patio, where his mom and Jerry and the girls were starting to clear the table. "Did you ever see any of the magazines that covered the story after I was rescued?"

"Yes. Every single one, I think."

"Even *People*?" he asked curiously.

Confession time, Regan, she told herself. "Especially the *People* spread. I, uh, have had that one taped to my closet door for about five years now."

He thought about that for a few moments, his eyebrows arching, trying not to grin—and failing. "This might be something we'll need to discuss at greater length later this evening—*much* greater length."

"We have to get out of this rose garden first." She loved teasing him just a little, loved the luxury of talking with him, taking their time. Loved knowing they had a tonight—and a tomorrow.

"Right," he conceded, trying to get serious again. "This is kind of hard to explain, but I didn't mind the *People* photo."

"You had your hand halfway down your pants," she reminded him, and managed to do it without blushing.

He grinned again. "Did you like it?"

"Very sexy," she admitted.

"Five years, huh?"

Oh, God, now he *was* making her blush.

"I think you're trying to tell me something really important."

"No," he disagreed. "Not important, just true. I didn't like being a hero, not on a coast-to-coast scale, and after a few months, I started to realize the country and the military and the politicians were never going to let it go. I'd become a commodity, instead of a pilot. So I quit. But, trust me, my mother does not want to hear that. She still thinks I'm a hero, not just a guy who was doing his job and managed to pay enough attention during survival training to actually survive—and let's not tell her otherwise. Okay?"

"She'll never hear it from me," she promised him, but not because she believed what he'd said for even a minute. His mother was right. Regan had not only seen the pictures, she'd read the articles in all those magazines, and he'd done more than just survive. He'd been behind enemy lines for over a week, outsmarting two armies to reach a landing zone where the Marines could get in to save him.

"Good. Come on." He took her hand and started down the path again. "I think if we're quick, and you don't get within twenty feet of me, we can leave the garden and get out of the house."

"But you're holding my hand," she pointed out, trying to keep up with him and not to laugh, and more than ready to be alone with him.

"Then we better be real quick," he told her with a wink.

Hours later, lying naked under a pile of quilts they'd

dragged out onto his deck, looking up at the moon and the stars, Regan stirred herself enough to rise up on one arm.

"You lied to me." It was an out-and-out fact, and she wasn't going to take it back.

"Not really," he said around a long yawn, not sounding too concerned about her accusation. He stretched his arms out full-length above his head, then reached for her and pulled her back under the covers beside him. "I swear to God, I did not think I had it in me to do it again. So technically, that wasn't a lie."

"That's not what I was talking about." And it wasn't.

"Okay, you mean the part where I told you we'd run out of whipped cream. Okay, you've got me. There *are* two more cans in the fridge, but I thought we might want to save them for morning. So technically, again, it wasn't a lie, because by my figures, we *are* out of tonight's allotment of whipped cream. Though, honest to God, I don't know what happened to four cans of whipped cream. You aren't that big."

"You are," she said, leaning down to whisper in his ear.

"Oh, yeah. Right." He rolled onto his side, suddenly sounding a little more alert, a definite gleam coming into his eyes.

"But that's not it, either."

"Ohhh," he said after a long moment's thought, then let out a laugh. "You mean when I told you I'd pay you a million dollars if you'd let me—"

She gave him a quick kiss, then said, "Hush, or I'll let

you do it again, and you'll owe me two million, but that's not what I'm talking about."

"Okay, I give. Which lie was it?"

"The one where you told me you didn't like being a hero."

"No," he contradicted her. "No points for you. I *don't* like being a hero. Tried it once, didn't like it."

"You tried it twice," she contradicted him back. "Once when you got shot down, and once when you walked into Roper's warehouse and gave yourself up for me."

"Oh, that."

"Yes, that."

"Well," he began, levering himself over her until he had her fully under him again on the quilts. "Technically that wasn't heroics. It just so happened, lucky for you, that it was the precise moment when I saw you standing next to Roper, in his clutches so to speak, that I realized I couldn't live without you. So that was pure survival on my part."

"Lucky me," she said, a smile playing about her lips.

"Lucky you," he agreed, easing her leg up around his waist. "So what's it going to be, lucky girl? Another million dollars, or do you want to go for the whipped cream?"

"I'll take the million."

"*Damn,*" he swore softly. "You know that's going to wipe me out."

"God, I can only hope so," she said, laughing as she pulled him down on top of her.

A long, bliss-filled time later, Regan roused herself from a drowsy half sleep.

"Quinn?"

"Hmmm?" came his barely audible reply.

"What happened to the diamonds?"

"Hmmmm."

She leaned down and gently nibbled on his ear, which got her more of the reaction she was looking for as his arm came around her and he began slowly dragging himself up from the depths of sleep.

It took a while.

"Diamonds," she murmured, giving him another nibble.

Finally, he let out a long, slow breath. "You mean the diamonds that got blown up at the airport, in the warehouse?"

"Yes."

He yawned.

"Well, those diamonds are in the process of being recovered by the FBI. The last I heard, they'd gotten about a quarter of a million dollars' worth out of the wreckage."

"And the others?"

"Others?"

"Um hmmm. The ones Wilson and I had already taken out of the *Tarbosaurus* nest and put in the canvas bag, the ones I vaguely remember you grabbing just before you pulled me out of Jeanette."

Even in the dark, she saw the smile that curved

his mouth. "Ah, yes. Well, *those* diamonds are in a CHF."

"CHF?"

"Contraband Holding Facility," he was quick to offer.

"And what, exactly, is a Contraband Holding Facility?"

His grin broadened. "So far, it's a coffee can in my kitchen at Steele Street, but we've been thinking of moving them to a more secure area."

A small laugh escaped her. "You stole the diamonds?" Good Lord. Regan McKinney was sleeping with a thief. She should have known. What she didn't know was what to think about it. She loved him. She'd loved him for fifteen years—but a thief. Good Lord.

"*Confiscated* is the word we prefer, confiscating and holding in lieu of allocation. It's all very official." His grin wasn't official. It was pure larceny.

"And who does the allocating?" Her money was on Dylan Hart. He was still the brains behind all the chop shop boys' adventures.

"Well, there's a guy at this little place in Washington, D.C., known as the Pentagon, and he's the one who decides how much we confiscate and how much we allocate. Some people call him 'Buck' Grant, but not very many. We mostly call him General Grant, or just 'sir,' as in 'yes, sir.' "

She went very still at his side. "Steele Street is part of the Pentagon?"

"Twenty-four/seven as a Special Defense Force team called SDF, but, given the nature of our work, our unique skills, and our rather slippery status over there, General Grant has always encouraged us to do a little independent fund-raising on the side, which he oversees. When we're needed, he wants to know his guys can respond, no matter who's in office or what political agenda is guiding policy and making budgets—and that's more than I've ever told anyone outside of Steele Street."

She believed him. She also understood what he hadn't quite said. "So you sort of steal for the government, when the opportunity arises."

"Or when we're outright asked." He grinned again. "At least I used to."

He turned toward her, shifting onto his side, his expression growing serious—and her heart slowed down for the space of a breath.

"We're going to have to stop meeting like this," he said.

"We are?"

"Yeah." He nodded. "I'm getting married real soon, going to have to give up wild women and chasing bad guys. Going to have to settle down, learn how to stay out of trouble."

"You are?" Now he had her attention, but good.

"Yeah." He smoothed his hand up over her hip. "I've met this woman, and I'm crazy about her, and I think there's lots of things the two of us would rather do than sit around and worry about if I'm going to make it home every night or not."

A lump formed in her throat, and for a second she was afraid she might cry. Instead, she kissed him.

"Sounds like a lucky woman," she said after a sweet moment, lifting her mouth from his.

"A *very* lucky woman," he agreed, pulling her back into his arms for another long kiss.

ABOUT THE AUTHOR

Of the mind that love *truly* is what makes the world go 'round, Tara Janzen can be contacted at www.tarajanzen.com.

Happy reading!

Can't wait to join Tara Janzen
in the next outrageously
sexy "crazy" adventure?

Read on for a preview of
Christian Hawkins's story in

CRAZY COOL...

Available October 25, 2005

THE MISSION:

CRAZY COOL

TARA JANZEN

CRAZY COOL

on sale October 25, 2005

TWENTY BUCKS SAYS the guy in the Armani suit is hired muscle."

Hired muscle? Katya Dekker looked up from her auction catalogue.

"Where?" She glanced around the outdoor amphitheater, her brow furrowing. She knew what her secretary, Alex Zheng, meant. She knew exactly what he meant, and she could only think of one reason for there to be any "hired muscle" at an art auction: *her*.

The thought only deepened her scowl.

She followed Alex's gaze across the delicately lit nighttime grounds of the Denver Botanic Gardens, search-ing through the crowd and the two dozen canopied tropical huts that had been erected for the dining comfort of the evening's guests. She found the "hired muscle" on the edge of a group of people next to the caterer's tent.

He was good, discreet, but she could spot a security detail at a hundred yards—and he had "high-priced bodyguard" written all over him, very high priced.

"What do you think of the suit?" Alex said. "I almost bought that one myself."

"No way, babe. Too structured. Too conservative," she told him, her gaze going over the man in the distance. There was nothing particularly remarkable about him, other than his choirboy looks, his shock of silky brown hair, and the alertness of his every move—the dead giveaway. He was quartering the gardens with his gaze, looking for God only knew what. Fund-raising art auctions hosted by the Denver Botanic Gardens were not hotbeds of intrigue.

"Not with my blue silk shirt," Alex countered. "So you don't know him?"

"No," she said, trying to keep her jaw from clenching, trying to hold back the first faint teasing of the headache she felt coming on. Even for August, the day had been unconscionably hot, and for Denver unbelievably humid, and the night wasn't setting up to be much better—especially now.

A bodyguard. Damn it. She knew who was behind this, just like she knew this wasn't the sort of event that required a bodyguard. Bottles of French wine and magnums of French champagne were being opened by bartenders in tuxedos. White-boxed dinners tied with forest-green bows were being delivered to the tables by waiters in tails. Every female patron at the art auction had been given an orchid wrist corsage upon arrival, and each man sported a boutonniere of exotic rain forest leaves and a bit of liana—even the choirboy. Tonight's auction was for the Amazon River Basin Coalition and in honor of the Botanic Gardens' new orchid pavilion. Alex had designed the boutonnieres, his contribution, and they were nothing short of fabulous, very masculine, very primal. They would speak to the Rain Forest God in every man, and to his wallet, according to Alex, who had impeccable taste and instincts—two of the many reasons he was Katya's right-hand man.

His six years with the Los Angeles Police Department were another.

"What about the other man?" he asked. "Next to the Jaguar Gate."

Two bodyguards?

"My mother wouldn't dare," she muttered, biting back a curse and turning toward the Jaguar Gate, a multicolumned, elaborately constructed plywood and papier-mâché portico serving as a grand entryway into the party.

There was only one man standing beneath the fierce black cat bridging the last pair of palm tree posts, and he turned away just as she looked at him. All she saw was his back and the champagne flute in his hand as he disappeared into the trees, but that was enough to make the hair on her nape rise in sudden, unexpected awareness.

She hadn't known the first guy, but this one...

After a couple of seconds, she let out her breath in a soft rush and told herself to get a grip. Of course she didn't know him. Maybe it was the cut of the stranger's dark hair, longer than most of the men's at the exclusive and rather elegantly conservative soiree, that had sparked her fleeting instant of recognition. Maybe it was his height, or the way he carried himself, or maybe it had been nothing at all.

She'd been wrong before in her life, an inordinate number of times actually, especially about men.

"Your mother would dare anything she thought she could get away with." Alex belied her statement with a short laugh. "As a matter of fact, her latest pork-barreling in Congress was a consummate dare to every budget-watcher in Washington."

Katya cast her secretary an annoyed glance. He did not look like someone who read the *Los Angeles Times* and the *Wall Street Journal* every single morning of his life—but he did, religiously, usually while drinking a double espresso and wearing his autographed Lakers jersey, which he'd had his tailor integrate into a cinnabar-colored silk robe. His hair was short, jet black, expertly cut, bleached gold on the tips, and moussed to artistic perfection. He had beautiful Asian/American features, a black belt in tae kwon do, and a boyfriend he'd left in L.A. His suit *was* Armani, his shoes Chinese red, his shirt snowy white and worn open at the throat with a loosely knotted Prada tie.

She didn't know how she was going to keep him with her in Denver, Colorado, or what she was going to do without him when he'd had enough of the former cow town and hightailed it back to Los Angeles.

"That's going to cost you a mocha latte," she said. Growing up in Denver as Senator Marilyn Dekker's daughter, Katya had lived, breathed, and eaten politics every day of her life. As an adult, she didn't touch the stuff. She voted. End of story. That, however, did not dissuade Alex from keeping her informed of every maternal political detail he gleaned out of the newspapers or saw on CNN—and every bit of unwanted news cost him a latte.

"And I'm still up on you by seven for winning the point spread on the Lakers game. The last time you got a mocha latte out of me was before the last Ice Age."

True, but he didn't have to rub it in.

"Mr. Armani Suit and his friend probably don't have anything to do with me. Let's just ignore them, and maybe they'll go away," she suggested, glancing back at her catalogue. She did not want to deal with unwanted bodyguards. Not tonight or any other night. "Our painting is up first. Maybe we should go check and make sure it's still in one piece."

Katya's newest addition to her art dealership business, the Toussi Gallery of Denver, had donated a large, beautiful floral painting by Oleg Henri to the auction. The staff at the Botanic Gardens had picked it up two days ago. It only made sense to go check on the painting before it went up for bid.

But Alex was like a dog with a bone.

"Sorry, luv. You're the only one here worthy of high-caliber security. My guess is your mother sicced the two freelancers on you. Though God knows why, unless she knows something we don't," he said, his tone of voice suggesting she give him her undivided attention until they figured this out. "I guess we could ask her Sunday morning."

"No, we couldn't," Kat was quick to say. Her mother was kicking off her campaign with a brief stop in Denver on Sunday, but there had been no plans for them to get together. Marilyn was too busy—thank God.

Stifling a sigh, Katya looked up at him again. "My mother is paranoid."

"About everything," he agreed, tracking the choirboy bodyguard with his gaze. "But this . . . I think this is about your youthful transgressions."

He *would* bring that up, she thought, feeling the headache start to win.

"Who was it you said you ran into tonight?"

"Ted Garraty," she said flatly, hating the turn of the conversation. "But I didn't exactly run into him. As a matter of fact, I made a point of *not* running into him."

She'd gone to school with Ted at Wellon Academy

in Denver. They hadn't been friends, but Wellon was small, very exclusive, and she and her date had ended up in the same crowd with Ted and his friends on prom night thirteen years ago—a night that had changed her life forever.

"Well, your mother obviously got ahold of the guest list and didn't like it."

Katya rolled her eyes in his direction. "I don't need a bodyguard to protect me from Ted Garraty, let alone two bodyguards."

But on that long-ago prom night, she had needed someone to protect her from Ted and his group of drunken friends.

Her gaze slid to the Jaguar Gate, but just for an instant before she forced her attention back to the catalogue. Just about every gallery in Denver had donated something to the auction, but the Oleg Henri was a true signature piece, and she expected its sale to help launch her into the Denver art world—not that her name wasn't already about as high profile as it got in the Mile High City.

And with that unpleasant thought, she finally did give in to another sigh. God, what an odd night. Seeing Ted had been nothing short of a ten on her weird-o-meter, and the visceral reaction she'd had to the second bodyguard had red-lined the weird-o-meter and hit an easy number one on her Don't Go There, Girlfriend list.

Bodyguards, damn it.

She'd known that returning to her hometown, the

location of her "youthful transgressions," had held the inherent risk of zealous parental meddling, but she truly hadn't expected her mother to jump in with both feet at her first event. Marilyn had left her well enough alone in Los Angeles, barring a couple of embarrassing intrusions into her personal life over the last several years. Professionally, though, her mother had been strictly hands-off.

But then it was here in Denver, not Los Angeles, that she had been associated with a high-profile, high-society, front-page, scandal-ridden murder of another senator's son. That sort of thing was bound to stir up even the most latent parental instincts, and Marilyn's had been pretty darn latent while Katya had been growing up—at least until Jonathan Traynor III had shown up dead in a back alley in lower downtown, a neighborhood known as LoDo, with a bullet through his brain, heroin in his veins, her phone number written on the back of his hand, and a bloodstained piece of her prom dress stuffed in his pocket.

Of its own accord, her gaze shifted back toward the gate again, and this time she let it linger.

No, she assured herself. The man who'd disappeared beneath the trees couldn't possibly be who she'd thought. A teenage car thief who had been sentenced to life imprisonment for Jonathan Traynor's murder thirteen years ago couldn't possibly be wandering around the Botanic Gardens wearing a suit and drinking French champagne. He'd been pardoned after two years in prison, justice had finally been served, but this would still be the last place he would show up, right? The last place he would ever be invited.

But for a moment, just a moment, her heart had raced and she'd remembered how it had been on another hot summer night in Denver. She'd been eighteen, a little crazy, a lot in love, and scared senseless by the intensity of living so far out on the edge she wasn't sure she'd ever get back to familiar ground. The boy had been a year older, the wild boy, the bad boy, the street thief who had saved her. That boy, the boy she'd loved, would never have murdered Jonathan, but he'd been convicted of the crime, and she'd sat by helplessly and watched it happen.

The trial had been a travesty, her silence a betrayal she still hated herself for, and deep in her heart, she knew he had to hate her for it, too.

HAWKINS drained his glass of champagne, wished it were Scotch, and took a breath.

Kat Dekker.

Son of a bitch.

She hadn't changed. She still looked like trouble with a capital T—wild blond hair, sea-green eyes, clothes so expensive it used to make his teeth hurt, all of it wrapped around a small bombshell package set to explode. That was Kat Dekker, one big bang for the buck, big enough to blow a man's life to hell.

Maybe this was all one huge coincidence, the two of them showing up at the same place at the same time, but he doubted it. She certainly couldn't have been the one to get him and Dylan called back from South America. She didn't have that kind of power, and she sure as hell hadn't bothered herself anytime in the last thirteen years to look him up. She especially hadn't bothered herself when he'd been arrested and thrown in jail, when he'd needed her the most.

Swearing again, he started across the lawn, skirting a string of canopied platforms decked out like jungle huts and working his way closer to the caterer's tent and Dylan, who was also working this cakewalk.

Hell. If this was a coincidence, it was one of the worst badass mojo coincidences he'd ever heard about. She was obviously part of the art auction, helping some guys move a painting, hanging around down by the stage, which was all decked out with fake palm trees and twisted vines, like a rain forest. She belonged here.

He didn't.

Dylan looked over and caught his gaze as he neared the caterer's tent.

"You saw our problem?" Dylan asked, the coldness of his gaze telegraphing his mood—royally pissed off verging on ballistic.

"Yes." Problem was a good way to put it.

"Do you think she's the reason we're here?"

Hawkins hated to think so. He *really* hated to think so.

"She wasn't named in our orders," he said, trying to convince himself as much as Dylan, who knew the orders as well as he did.

"She's the highest-ranking civilian here," Dylan said, his glacial gray gaze going to the woman on the amphitheater stage and giving her a cool once-over. "She hasn't changed at all."

Without wanting to, Hawkins found himself looking at her again.

"No. She's changed." He'd been wrong earlier, real wrong, the way he'd always been about her. She'd changed. Plenty. She wasn't scared, alone, and eighteen anymore. She wasn't the prom queen or the poor little rich girl tonight—two acts she'd had down pat—and she wasn't naked in bed with him. She'd been most of those things, most of the time, that whole crazy month they'd spent together.

Then the earth had opened up and swallowed him whole. He'd spent two years in the state penitentiary, thanks to Katya Dekker and her crowd of too-rich, too-fast, too-frickin'-dumb-to-stay-out-of-trouble friends.

And thanks to her mother, the mighty Marilyn Dekker. What a piece of work that woman was. Christian had been steamrolled, hog-tied, and locked up before he'd even known what had hit him.

"None of these cops seem to appreciate who she is, so maybe we better keep an eye on her. I'm going to put in a call to General Grant, in case there's something else going on here and this isn't as simple as it was supposed to be," Dylan said.

Hawkins slanted him a dry look. "There is nothing simple about you and me being at a frickin' garden party."

Dylan conceded the point with a grim smile.

Geezus, what a mess. Hawkins looked back at Katya Dekker and felt something cold harden in his chest. She'd cost him. Loving her had cost him.

If it hadn't been for Dylan and his Seventeenth Street lawyer working their asses off to get the case reopened, Hawkins knew he might still be in prison. What had clinched his pardon was the deathbed confession of a downtown vagrant named Manny Waite. In and of itself, the confession might not have been enough. Manny had been a lush whose grip on reality had been tenuous at best, but with one helluva lawyer and Dylan pushing hard to get him a pardon on one end, and poor old Manny giving it up on the other, Hawkins had been set free.

He'd been tough when he'd gone in, but not as tough as he'd thought, and not tough enough, not at nineteen years old. By the time he got out at twenty-one, he *had* killed a man, and his whole world had changed—all thanks to Katya Dekker.

Down on the stage, the auctioneer stepped up to the podium as Katya finished directing the placement of the first painting. The piece was at least six by eight feet of bright, oversize flower petals in a thickly ornate gilt frame. He recognized it as an Oleg Henri, nothing he'd want in his own collection, but a beautiful piece and one sure to appreciate in value once the artist became better known.

The irony of the night wasn't lost on him. Thirteen years ago, he wouldn't have gotten within a hundred yards of a place selling an Oleg Henri or any piece of collectible art. Thirteen years ago, no one would have let him. Back then, he'd looked exactly like what he was, a street kid on the take and one of the most successful car thieves ever to give the Denver cops a run for their money. Dylan had always had a way of looking innocent no matter what crime he was committing, but Hawkins knew he and the rest of the guys at the chop shop on Steele Street had always looked like trouble.

Just the way this damn garden party looked like trouble. Either he needed another Scotch, or he needed to be back on a plane to Colombia. What he didn't need was to be hanging around an art auction with a bunch of socialites—like Katya Dekker.

His gaze followed her as she crossed the amphitheater stage and went down the steps. There had to be a bounty on the dress she was wearing: a little black nothing, slit to the hip. With her mane of blond hair, her golden tan, and a pair of spike heels, she should have looked cheap.

But she didn't. She looked sleek and expensive. A California wet dream come true. Barbie with an attitude.

She had a tattoo, which, oddly enough, unnerved him. She hadn't had a tattoo at eighteen. It wasn't discreetly hidden on a hip or an ankle, or twined around her navel, and it wasn't a butterfly, or a rose, or a unicorn. Nothing sweetly banal for Kat; she'd decorated herself with a shooting star at the top of her arm, just below the curve of her shoulder.

Kee-rist. He shook his head. Kat Dekker was back in town.